W9-BRG-944

One Man's Flag

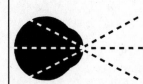

This Large Print Book carries the
Seal of Approval of N.A.V.H.

ONE MAN'S FLAG

DAVID DOWNING

THORNDIKE PRESS

A part of Gale, Cengage Learning

GALE
CENGAGE Learning·

Farmington Hills, Mich • San Francisco • New York • Waterville, Maine
Meriden, Conn • Mason, Ohio • Chicago

GALE
CENGAGE Learning®

Thorndike Press® Large Print Thriller.
The text of this Large Print edition is unabridged.
Other aspects of the book may vary from the original edition.
Set in 16 pt. Plantin.

LIBRARY OF CONGRESS CATALOGING-IN-PUBLICATION DATA

Names: Downing, David, 1946–
Title: One man's flag / by David Downing.
Description: Large print edition. | Waterville, Maine : Thorndike Press, 2016. |
  ©2015 | Series: Thorndike Press large print thriller
Identifiers: LCCN 2015040076| ISBN 9781410486752 (hardcover) | ISBN
  1410486753 (hardcover)
Subjects: LCSH: Intelligence officers—Great Britain—Fiction. | Women
  journalists—Great Britain—Fiction. | World War,
  1914-1918—Ireland—Fiction. | Ireland—History—1910-1921—Fiction. | Large
  type books. | GSAFD: Spy stories. | Historical fiction. | Romantic suspense
  fiction.
Classification: LCC PR6054.O868 O54 2016 | DDC 823/.914—dc23
LC record available at http://lccn.loc.gov/2015040076

Printed in Mexico
1 2 3 4 5 6 7 20 19 18 17 16

This book is dedicated to my grandfather,

Gerald Percy Constantine,

who served in India during the Great War
and many years later introduced me
to the joy of making up stories.

If you insist upon fighting to protect me, or "our" country, let it be understood, soberly and rationally between us, that . . . as a woman, I have no country. As a woman I want no country. As a woman my country is the whole world.

— VIRGINIA WOOLF

HISTORICAL NOTE

The Britain that went to war in 1914 was more than an island state on the edge of Europe. The British Empire also included largely self-governing dominions, colonies ruled by London's appointees, and, in the case of Ireland, another island nation long subsumed by its larger neighbor.

When war broke out, the white-settler-ruled dominions — Canada, Australia, New Zealand, and South Africa — took it for granted that Britain's fight was theirs and sent soldiers across the world to play their part in the motherland's struggle. But it was different for those living under direct British rule, who were given less choice in the matter and who had less stake in the outcome. In many such places — India and Ireland foremost among them — resentment of British rule was already growing at a rapid pace, and those demanding greater autonomy were bound to see the empire's moment of peril as their moment of opportunity.

In India the movement for self-rule was led by the Congress Party, most of whose leaders, including Mohandas Gandhi, were prepared to accepted the British argument that change would have to wait until after the war. But there were also powerful groups in both Punjab and Bengal that refused to wait and instead set about mounting campaigns of violence against British rule.

The situation in Ireland was similar. The long campaign for Home Rule — a roughly analogous status to that enjoyed by the white dominions — had finally been won in 1914, only to be postponed when war broke out. This was accepted by many but failed to satisfy those demanding full independence. And here, as in India, there were many who believed that the wait had already been too long.

As always, an enemy's enemy might prove a useful friend. Even before the war, both Irish and Indian groups had reached out to the Germans, and once the fighting was under way, these contacts were pursued with increasing vigor.

A German Who Could Pass for an Englishman

High on Darjeeling's Observatory Hill, Jack McColl stared out at the snow-draped Himalayas. The view was as magnificent as everyone in Calcutta had told him it would be, so he sat there on the British-manufactured wrought-iron bench and tried to take it in. And all he could see was the glow in Caitlin Hanley's eyes as their train snaked through the snow-clad Rockies.

A year had passed since then. Eight months since the day she'd stormed out of his London flat, leaving him feeling like the ultimate fool.

Eight months of war and worrying about his brother. Eight months of waiting for Caitlin's brother to meet his executioners. Eight months of wishing he hadn't betrayed her.

He sighed and looked at his watch. It was time he went to arrange his meeting with the German internee.

When war broke out the previous August, Jürgen Rehmer had been a high-ranking employee of the North German Lloyd shipping company, with a plush office on Calcutta's Dalhousie Square, a beautiful villa overlooking the Maidan, and many close friends among the British community. Then the news of hostilities had reached India and armed police had appeared at his door. Within a matter of hours, he and his wife were on their way to the hastily established internment camp at Katapahar, a few miles south of Darjeeling. They'd been there ever since.

McColl took the path back to Chaurasta Square, making sure to scan the bushes on either side. He wasn't expecting an attack, but such caution had become second nature in Calcutta after so many terrorist incidents. Darjeeling was probably safe, although these days you never knew, and he no longer went anywhere without his Webley revolver.

The police station was on Auckland Road, not far below the square. He was escorted through to the local commissioner's office, where a fellow Scot named Gilzean was already waiting for him. A strong whiff of whiskey accompanied the handshake.

McColl took the proffered seat and looked around. The office was almost as sparse as his hotel room. A map of the district adorned one wall, but the others were bare, and the highly polished desk boasted only a single pen, a wooden tray containing a small sheaf of papers, and a framed photograph of several men standing over a dead tiger.

"The camp's about five miles south of here," Gilzean told him. "I assume you'll be wanting to see your man tomorrow morning?"

"That sounds good. How do I get there?"

"I'll have one of our chaps take you down in a tonga. We try not to use our automobile unless we have to — the roads are a nightmare. He'll pick you up at nine, all right? And I'll telephone the camp and let them know you're coming."

"Have you met Rehmer?"

"Aye, once. A decent chap for a Hun, but then I suppose most of them are. It's a pity the ones that aren't seem to be in charge."

"Yes." Since there seemed nothing more to say, McColl got back to his feet.

Gilzean wasn't done. "So what do you want with the man?" he asked.

There was no obvious reason not to tell him. "Some information about someone else. Back in August, when he was questioned in Calcutta, he mentioned a name that has come up several times in connec-

13

tion with gunrunning. He was questioned again in January —"

"I know. He refused to say anything. What makes you think he'll change his mind?"

"His wife's ill."

"Ah." Gilzean's initial reaction was a look of disgust, but he managed to shrug it away. "We are at war," he said, as much to himself as McColl.

"We are indeed," McColl agreed. And where would they be without that comforting mantra? he wondered, walking back up the hill toward his hotel. To his ears at least, it sounded a tad more hollow with each passing Indian day.

When he woke up the following morning, the mountains had disappeared behind a curtain of mist. Over breakfast he went over what he knew about Rehmer, which wasn't very much. The German had been good at his job, an affable dinner guest, better than average on the polo field. Two British neighbors had spoken out against his arrest but had quickly withdrawn their protests when news of the German behavior in Belgium had reached Calcutta. With a British victory now clearly essential at any price, locking up a few relative innocents for a few months seemed a small one to pay. There

14

were those like McColl's recently acquired friend Cynthia Malone who argued that there seemed little point fighting the Hun if you sank to his level, but such dissenting voices were few and far between. McColl had had no pat answer for them, other than a vague but strong sense that a victory for German militarism would be worse for the world than would a victory for Germany's opponents. And there was always the highly salient fact that the Germans were actively seeking to kill his brother, Jed, his old friend "Mac" McAllister, and their several hundred thousand comrades manning the trenches in France.

Which was why he was doing unpleasant jobs like this one, McColl reminded himself. Sometimes that seemed reason enough. Sometimes it didn't.

Emerging from the hotel entrance at nine o'clock, he found his transport ready and waiting. The driver, a young Bengali policeman, introduced himself as Salil and the pony as Kipling.

"And how are you discovering Darjeeling?" the Indian asked in English once the tonga was moving.

"I like it," McColl answered, although as yet he'd seen precious little of the town. After leaving Gilzean the previous afternoon, he'd considered dining at the Darjeeling Club — the Calcutta Department of Criminal Intelligence chief had promised to get his name put down as a guest — but knowing the sort of people he'd encounter and what range of opinions would be slid, tipped, or shoved down his throat, he'd decided to eat at his hotel instead. After that he'd retired to his room and read a few more chapters of *The Ragged-Trousered Philanthropists,* the new novel that Cynthia had insisted on lending him.

"Were you born here?" he asked Salil.

"No, sahib. In Calcutta."

"You prefer it here."

Salil shook his head. "When the sun shines, Darjeeling is a fine town. But in the rain and the cold . . ." He shivered at the thought. "And my wife and son are in Calcutta," he added.

Road and railway ran south in tandem, crossing each other at regular intervals as they climbed toward Ghoom. Densely wooded hillsides receded into the mist, and, hearing chanting in the distance, McColl thought he could see the blurred outlines of a monastery hanging above the valley. In Ghoom they turned east down a gently winding road through tea plantations before arriving at their destination, a cluster of

16

wooden buildings on a partially cleared, east-facing slope. Although two sepoys guarded the gate, the fences on either side looked eminently scalable. But then where would an escapee run to? The remoteness of the camp's location was enough of a deterrent.

The internees were housed in two barracks, one for the men, one for the women and children. Many of the latter were playing outside, apparently enjoying themselves, but McColl found it hard to imagine how the adults filled their days in a place like this, particularly since none of them knew when if ever they would be released.

One of several wooden cabins housed the administration, and the man in charge — a Yorkshireman named Marshall — was waiting for him on the veranda. The man shook hands but seemed disinclined to conversation. "You can use my office inside," he told McColl, and without waiting for assent ordered a loitering subordinate to "bring Rehmer up here." Two minutes later McColl was alone with the German.

Jürgen Rehmer looked all of his fifty-four years, with a face badly worn by life in the tropics. He was about six feet tall, with cropped gray hair, blue eyes, and regular features. He was, as the saying went, one of those Germans who could pass for an Englishman. McColl found himself idly wondering whether the Germans had the contrary saying.

Speaking German, McColl asked Rehmer how he was.

As well as could be expected, was the gist of the answer.

"And your wife?"

"She is unwell."

"I heard that she was and am sorry to hear she still is. But perhaps I can help in that regard."

Rehmer's look was both hopeful and suspicious. "You will have to explain that."

McColl sighed. "I won't insult you with pretense. I'm here to offer you a deal — you tell me everything you know about Franz Kopping and you and your wife will go free. I will personally escort you both to Calcutta, and once she has received the medical treatment she needs, I'll put you both on a boat to some neutral port. Batavia, I expect. From there you can go where you want."

Rehmer shifted slightly in his chair and gave McColl a long, cold stare. "Let us be clear," he said eventually. "You are asking me to choose between my wife and my country."

"Yes," McColl agreed. If their positions had been reversed, he knew which he'd have chosen, but a man like Rehmer probably loved them both with a similar kind of passion.

"And you consider such a proposition honorable?"

"I've had jobs I enjoyed more," McColl admitted wryly.

"But you're just following orders?"

"Something like that."

Rehmer shook his head. "My inclination is to tell you to go to hell. But I'm not the only one involved. I shall have to discuss this with my wife."

McColl nodded his agreement. If he was going to play this sordid game, he might as well play it to win, and giving Rehmer a decent stretch of time to dwell on the future loss of his wife might possibly do the trick. "I'll be back in two days," he told the German.

Once Rehmer had been led away, McColl asked Marshall how ill the wife was.

"Hard to say," was the answer, "but I think she'll last long enough for your purposes."

McColl ignored the gibe. "What does she need in the way of medicines?" he asked.

"She doesn't, according to our doctor. She

just needs a drier climate."

On the ride back to Darjeeling, McColl was less than responsive to Salil's cheerful chatter, and the sepoy eventually retreated into a hurt silence. After reporting the gist of his conversation with Rehmer to Gilzean, McColl walked up Auckland Road to the club, received the promised guest membership, and ate a large though unimaginative lunch. Several members introduced themselves, but taciturnity bordering on rudeness won him the solitude he wanted. Doubtless they all knew why he was here — Darjeeling in winter was a small community by Raj standards — and he had no desire to discuss his business, or indeed anything else, with any of them.

After eating he sequestered himself in the library, where a fortnight-old copy of *The Times* painted a glowing account of the recent British offensive near Neuve-Chapelle. Actually, as McColl knew from friends in Calcutta, the attack had been a disaster, with a quarter of the forty thousand troops involved either killed or wounded. Since almost half of those casualties had come from the Indian Corps, London had lost no time in passing the bad news on to Delhi. There was quite enough disaffection already, and losses like this would only cause more. McColl thought it unlikely that the recent passage of a new Defence of India Act — one that gave the Raj authorities increasing powers of arrest and detention — was wholly coincidental.

Outside, it was still overcast, but he revisited Observatory Hill anyway, seating himself on the thoughtfully placed bench and staring out at the sea of mist that shrouded the valley and mountains. He didn't like this task he'd been given. He didn't much like being in India, so far away from the war's epicenter, but he was the only Urdu speaker the Secret Service Bureau possessed, and he did have experience dealing with Indian revolutionaries, albeit in San Francisco rather than India. The Ghadar organization he'd investigated in early 1914 had finally brought their revolt home to the Punjab a few weeks earlier, but it had swiftly fizzled out, largely thanks to the work of an Indian infiltrator. McColl had been mentally packing his bags when his boss, Mansfield Cumming, had decided that the escalating terrorist campaign on the other side of India required his attention.

Perhaps it did, but McColl was far from convinced. In Bengal a series of robberies and assassinations sponsored by the Jugantar terrorist group had brought the authorities close to panic, and by the time McColl reached Calcutta, the India Department of Criminal Intelligence, the local police, the India Office, and Vernon Kell's Military Intelligence Section Five had all been enlisted as part of London's response. There was, he soon found out, no shared agenda or accepted chain of command. As McColl had come to expect when intelligence agencies fished in the same stretch of river, each outfit was devoting as much time and effort to stealing its rivals' rods as it was to catching fish.

The newly assertive Jugantar was well organized and effective, its leader Jatin Mukherjee good at choosing and hitting his targets and adept at foiling British attempts to locate and arrest him. People were dying, the British *looking* increasingly helpless, but as far as McColl could see, there was no chance of Jugantar's actually *winning.* Robbing a store in Roddha the previous August had netted the group fifty Mauser pistols, but all the intelligence pointed to these as the only guns it possessed. No, Jugantar was certainly an annoyance, and rather more than that to those it killed, but it didn't have the weaponry to mount a serious challenge, not on its own.

German help would be necessary, and there had been rumors — even plausible ones — that some contact had been made. And with their support for Ghadar, the Germans had demonstrated a definite interest in helping any Indian group that might cause the British sufficient trouble in the subcontinent to make them think twice about sending more troops to Europe.

One of these rumors had involved a businessman named Franz Kopping, and a subsequent investigation by the Singapore authorities had uncovered a past association with Jürgen Rehmer. Questioned the previous September, Rehmer had denied more than a passing acquaintance and claimed he knew nothing about German intelligence in Asia or arms shipments to India. Since then he'd been left to enjoy his captivity in peace, until some bright spark in the DCI office in Calcutta had picked up the news that Rehmer's wife was seriously ill.

A lever, as one man put it. An inducement.

Now that he'd met Rehmer, McColl found himself almost hoping that the German would treat his offer with the contempt it probably deserved. Which wasn't very patriotic of McColl, but the older he got, the less patriotic he felt. Growing up among people who wouldn't trust an Englishman any further than they could throw him, having a front-row seat at the establishment cock-up popularly known as the Boer War, and actually experiencing a whole host of other cultures — all of which suffered the same delusion that theirs was the best — would have put a dent in anyone's ability to swallow the risible notion of one's country right or wrong. Meeting Caitlin Hanley had just been the cherry on the cake.

McColl didn't believe that people like the Rehmers should ever have been interned in the first place — deportation would have served the same purpose and been much less vindictive.

Some people claimed that war brought out the best in people. And maybe it did — it sure as hell brought out the worst.

McColl walked back down the hill and stopped off at the club to write a couple of letters. He filled the one to his brother with jokes, the one to his mother with vignettes of life in India. After dropping them off at the post office, he walked back to his hotel for another hour with *The Ragged-Trousered Philanthropists*. It wasn't a book to cheer one up, but it was certainly hard to put down.

■ ■ ■ ■

Next day the sky remained overcast, Kangchenjunga and the other peaks hidden from view. After breakfast McColl walked north up the ridge, passing St. Andrew's Church and a dead-looking Government House, eventually reaching a native village, where one of the inhabitants asked with some concern whether the sahib was lost. Back in Darjeeling he had drinks and lunch at the club, where a rumor was going the rounds that two Germans had escaped from the Katapahar camp. No one thought they'd get far, and McColl wasn't worried that Rehmer would be one of them — he didn't seem like the sort of man who would ever abandon his wife. He ordered another whiskey and listened to the old hands at the next table tell a recently appointed plantation manager that he'd arrived too late to experience the real India. How the Indian waiters kept a straight face was anyone's guess.

McColl had hoped the sky would clear so he could take in the famous view from Tiger Hill, but nature refused to cooperate, and he settled instead for a walk to a nearby Tibetan temple. The going was mostly downhill on the way, and soon after passing a white stupa with a low dome and golden spire he saw the temple in the distance, amid a forest of poles bearing brightly colored prayer flags. The forecourt contained several prayer wheels. After leaving some money, he gave one a spin and offered up a half-serious prayer that Caitlin Hanley would forgive him. Some hope.

The trek uphill was much more demanding, and by the time McColl reached Auckland Road, he was seriously out of breath. Remembering the rumored escape, he stopped in at Gilzean's office to find out if one had actually occurred. It had. Two young men — boys, really, as neither was yet sixteen — had left the camp early the previous night without telling their parents. According to friends, they intended to walk to China and then somehow find their way back home to Germany, where of course they planned to enlist. Gilzean was unsympathetic, but to McColl they were just another pair of victims, in thrall to the general madness. Later that evening, gazing out his hotel window at the rapidly darkening hills, he wondered whether the two boys had begun to regret their patriotic impulse.

If they had, it hadn't been for long. Mc-

Coll's arrival at the police bungalow on the following morning coincided with that of a cart containing two young bodies. One blond boy had two exit wounds in his chest; the other had half his head blown away. Both looked younger than their fifteen years.

The soldiers escorting the cart seemed in an ebullient mood; one or more of their Lee-Enfield MkIIIs had no doubt done the damage. Shot trying to escape, as the saying went.

Gilzean had the decency to look embarrassed, but no one was going to kick up a fuss about a couple of dead Germans, not after Belgium.

McColl had his own concern: "Do the other Germans in the camp know what's happened?"

"They soon will — the army sent someone down to warn the camp commander."

McColl sighed. "Well, there goes any chance of getting Rehmer to talk."

Gilzean shrugged. "Maybe he'll realize we mean business."

McColl gave him a look but didn't try to argue. He took the ride back up to Katapahar with Salil and faced Jürgen Rehmer across Marshall's desk for the second time. The German was coldly contemptuous. "The answer is no."

"And your wife is happy with that?" McColl asked, hiding his own self-disgust.

Rehmer's look was pitying. "I would have given you what you asked," he told McColl. "It is she who insists I say no."

After the guard had taken the German away, McColl sat there for several minutes staring out through the open doorway at the limply hanging Union Jack and fog-shrouded trees beyond. He told himself what Rehmer had told him at their previous meeting, that he was simply following orders. It didn't help.

The sky refused to clear, either that afternoon or overnight, and mist still clung to the rooftops when McColl left Darjeeling on the following morning. He could still visualize Kangchenjunga and the other peaks in all their awesome splendor, but he knew that the image that would truly stick in his mind was the one of the two slaughtered boys in the cart.

When they reached Tindharia, the train from Siliguri had already arrived, and several tables in the restaurant room were occupied by British families intent on escaping the imminent prospect of Calcutta's stifling spring and summer. It was allegedly well worth escaping. McColl's only previous experience of real heat had been his summer in South Africa, and according to those who had suffered through both, the Bengali version was several times worse.

Thinking about South Africa as his train continued its descent, he remembered that Gandhi had arrived back in India a few months earlier. The now-famous Indian had been one of the stretcher bearers who had carried McColl down from Spion Kop, and McColl had followed Gandhi's political career ever since. It would be good to see him again, he thought, if only to ask the Indian why he had pledged his support to the British war effort. After what Caitlin had told him about Gandhi's pacifist ideals, it had seemed a surprising position for the Indian to take, but one that McColl had found vaguely comforting. There was no shortage of knaves and fools who supported the war, and having someone of Gandhi's humanity and intelligence defending its necessity made McColl feel a little better about his own reluctant belief that it had to be fought and won. He would love the chance to discuss it with him. Gandhi was in Ahmedabad, on the other side of the country, but maybe their paths would cross again.

The wait at Siliguri seemed endless, but the Mail left on time at 8:00 P.M. His private berth in the first-class coach was spotless, and once the attendant had been convinced that all he needed was sleep, McColl was left alone with the rhythm of the wheels until they reached Santahar, where a change of gauge meant a change of train. He was awakened again by the drumming of the wheels on the new Hardinge Bridge across the Ganges. Opening his window to a warm, caressing breeze, he saw the almost-full moon hanging above the vast river, the smoke from their engine smudging the first light of morning.

By the time they reached the next stop, it was light enough to read by the window, and after buying a clay pot of tea from one of the platform sellers, he reached for Tressell's book. Before going to sleep, he had read the chapter called "The Great Money Trick," in which the hero, Owen, during a work break, explains the essence of the capitalist system to his fellow workers. It was cleverly written, and try as he did, McColl could find no flaw in Tressell's logic. The system did seem like a giant sleight of hand.

Why was he reading a socialist tract? To know the enemy, as he'd jokingly told his

Section Five counterpart Alex Cunningham? To prove how open-minded he was to friends like Cynthia? Neither, in truth. It wasn't the first such book he'd read over the last six months, and he knew the reason all too well — Caitlin Hanley. The woman he'd loved and deceived and whose rebel Irish brother he'd caught, imprisoned, and effectively sentenced to death. Colm Hanley was still in Brixton Prison as far as McColl knew, awaiting execution.

McColl's relationship with Caitlin had opened his eyes to a lot of inconvenient truths, particularly when it came to serving the British Empire. And eyes once opened were hard to close — he might not have seen her for over seven months, but he still saw the world, at least in part, through her ideals and explanations. Which both pleased and annoyed him. It was a way of keeping her in his life, but the continuing censure of someone who never wanted to see him again was sometimes hard to live with. Caitlin would find Tressell's critique self-evident and find fault only with the minor roles he gave to women.

McColl put the book down, wondering where she was now, what she was doing.

The train chugged on southward across flat delta country for the last hundred miles, stopping just twice before it slowed to a crawl for the final approach to Calcutta's Sealdah station. After arranging for the delivery of his luggage, McColl worked his way out through the teeming crowd to the tonga stand and climbed aboard the first in line. "Great Eastern," he told the driver, who wasted no time in whipping his pony into motion.

They cantered westward down Bow Bazaar. It was only nine in the morning, but noticeably hotter than it had been five days before, and by the time the tonga reached the corner of Dalhousie Square and turned down Old Court House Street, McColl could feel the sweat gathering on his forehead. The British bobby outside the hotel looked hotter still in his uniform, and the electric fans in the Great Eastern's lobby were already working overtime. Once ensconced in his room, McColl flicked the switch and stood for a while beneath his own whirring blades, reassessing his earlier thought that a cheaper hotel might be more discreet. He took a bath to wash off the journey and was drying himself when his luggage arrived from the station. The room boy who came with the porters had a cable from Cumming in London. Reading it, McColl learned that he had been formally seconded to the Calcutta DCI with instructions to uncover and thwart any German plans to arm the Bengali terrorists. Encrypted reports from Singapore, Batavia, and Bangkok would follow.

Almost as an afterthought, Cumming noted that Colm Hanley's execution had been fixed for March 30. Reaching for *The Statesman* he'd picked up the station, McColl discovered that today was the twenty-ninth.

It was a moment he'd dreaded. If there was no last-minute reprieve, if Colm Hanley died in the same shooting-range shed at the Tower of London as his erstwhile republican comrades, then Caitlin would never forgive him.

McColl grimaced. Who did he think he was kidding? A reprieve, a pardon, neither would make any difference to her. A change of heart from Caitlin was as likely as snow in Calcutta.

One of Ours

It was an early spring day in London, warm and sunny, with fluffy white clouds scudding across a pale blue sky. Such weather was supposed to lift the heart, but Caitlin Hanley felt only the faintest of cruel stirrings as she walked down Jebb Avenue toward the Brixton Prison gates. This was the last visit — by this time tomorrow the brother she had helped to raise would be in the ground.

Her step faltered at the thought, but she had to be strong. With the rest of the family three thousand miles away, she was all he had.

Spring hadn't reached inside the prison. The whitewashed walls, the cold faces, the mingled smells of disinfectant, smoke, and urine — all were familiar from seven months' worth of visits. The only change was in Colm's clothing — the prison uniform was gone, and for one mad moment she thought he was going to be released. But then she realized: Brixton had reclaimed its property prior to sending him off to the Tower.

The mesh screen precluded hugs, but once sat down they could grip each other's hands through the semicircular hatch. A stranger might have thought Colm in high spirits for someone with less than a day to live, but she could see the hint of panic in his eyes and hear the slight hysterical edge to his voice.

"So what's new in the world outside?" he asked, as if determined to keep things normal.

She told him. If he wanted the latest bulletins from Europe, the latest news from Ireland and home, then what was she to say — that their last thirty minutes together would be better spent in angry laments and floods of tears?

"I've had letters from everyone," he said after she'd passed on some family news.

"From Dad?"

"Even Dad. He tried, I can see that now. But he doesn't understand that times have changed."

"No," she agreed. "And the others . . ."

"Well, what can they say? 'We're thinking of you. We're sorry to lose you.' " He made a face. "Let's not talk about it. I knew I was leaving them behind when I got into this. One way or another."

She shook her head. You don't ever leave your family behind, she thought — you just close your ears to their voices inside your head.

"I don't expect them to understand," he was saying. "But you do, don't you?" It was almost a plea. "We've always been the fighters, you and me."

"I do," she said. It might be only partly true, but it was what he wanted to hear, and her not agreeing with how he had chosen to fight no longer seemed to matter.

"Remember that time we stole Mr. Peterson's dog?" he asked. "Everyone knew he beat the hell of the poor mutt, but we were the ones who did something about it."

She remembered, all right. The look on Aunt Orla's face when the police showed up at their door.

"Ten minutes," a voice intoned from the doorway behind him, shocking them both.

She couldn't believe that this was the last time she would see him. "I don't know what to say," she blurted out. "I've never felt so helpless in my life." She looked around the room as if it might provide an answer. "I know there's nothing I can do, but I can't seem to believe it."

He squeezed her hand. "But there is," he told her. "Two things."

"Tell me."

"First — this is hard to say, but they won't give my body back to you."

"I'm still trying to get the embassy to intercede."

"I know, but I don't want to go back to America. So let them have me for now. When the time comes, when we have our independence, then take me to Dublin. Will you promise to do that?"

"Of course," she said, as if discussing such an arrangement were the most natural thing in the world.

"The other thing . . . well, I've been thinking." He allowed himself a smile. "There's not much else to do in here — and what I want, what I really want, is for you to tell our story." He wriggled on the seat, and she knew he wanted to get up and pace. As a boy he'd never been able to sit still. "I admit it," he said. "I used to look down on journalists and writers — I thought you all spent too much time just watching and listening when the world needed taking by the throat. But seeing the way the English told our story, I realized how wrong I was. And how important people like you — people who tell the truth — really are."

"I've done my best," she told him, and she knew that she had. The British press hadn't been interested, but she had managed to place several pieces in the American newspapers.

"I know, I know. But I was thinking of a pamphlet — a book, even." Both fists were clenched, his eyes entreating her. "I thought you could go to Dublin and talk to the other men's families, to the leaders. Explain our motives and expose all the lies that the British press has told about us. Tell the world about our war of independence."

Listening and looking, she had a sudden mental picture of Colm in Prospect Park, riding his first bicycle. "I can do that," she said, her eyes beginning to brim with tears. She wanted to go back there, to the park, to Coney Island, to the stoop outside their brownstone, to a time when both of them still had a future. A sob escaped her. "I'm sorry," she said.

He gripped her hand harder. "Don't be. This was my choice."

"If I hadn't brought Jack McColl into our house, you wouldn't be here." The tears were rolling down her cheeks.

"Ah, don't cry." Colm squeezed her hand a little tighter. "You know, there's one thing

I've never told you. He tried to let me go that night."

She stared at him. "What do you mean? What happened?"

"He just told me to run. I didn't believe him at first — I thought he would shoot me in the back. But then he said that you'd asked him to help me, and I got angry. I thought you were treating me like a child. Not showing any respect. For me or the cause."

"Time," the warder said, hovering in the doorway.

She felt taken aback by this new information — why had he never told her this before? But now was hardly the time to ask, and there'd never be another. She wiped the tears from her eyes. "I will tell the story," she told him.

He smiled. "And you can say I died well," he said. "I'm not afraid, and I intend to do it right. If they say I didn't, they'll be lying."

"I know."

He grasped her hand again and brought it to his lips.

"Time," the warder said again, placing a hand on Colm's shoulder.

"One last thing," her brother said as he got to his feet.

"What?"

"Remember me."

"How could I not?"

A last wave, and the far door clanged shut behind him. She sat there sobbing for what seemed a long time, until an officer cajoled her onto her feet. The walk back to the gate was a gallery of unsympathetic faces.

Once out on Jebb Avenue, she just stood there for a while, not knowing what to do. The thought of sharing a crowded tram was unbearable, and eventually she just started walking westward, in the general direction of her lodgings.

How was she going to spend the next fourteen hours? What did one do with oneself in such a situation? Drink the hours away? Hide in the noisy darkness of a nickelodeon?

How could she wish away her brother's last hours on earth?

There'd been so many months of waiting, of pestering embassy officials and lawyers, of mourning a life that wasn't yet over. And at the beginning, through August and September, when no one else seemed interested in anything but the movement of armies, she'd been utterly alone with her anguish. Her father had refused to cross the Atlantic; her other brother was unwilling to leave his pregnant wife. Aunt Orla had announced she would come, and it had taken all Caitlin's strength to discourage her — the thought of losing her surrogate mother to a German U-boat was more than she could bear.

And then Michael Killen had appeared at the door of her room in Clapham, a tall, red-haired Dubliner with sad green eyes. He told her he was there on behalf of the Irish Citizen Army, the workers' defense force created by union leader Jim Larkin during the 1913 lockout. The ICA was now the military wing of Irish socialism. Colm's operation had not been sanctioned by the ICA leadership, but most of those involved had been members, and Killen was here to see that those who'd been caught and imprisoned did not feel abandoned. He couldn't visit Colm himself, but he wanted Caitlin to tell her brother that in Dublin his name was revered.

She'd been grateful for that, and for the talks they shared in the days that followed, which eventually ended in bed.

But then he'd gone back to Dublin, leaving her alone once more. With Colm to visit and his fate occluding all else, she'd been forced to relinquish the New York newspaper job that had so excited her six months before. Marooned in London, she had filled her days with long, exploratory walks and spent the evenings nursing drinks in her local pub, where the male regulars quickly learned to let her be. On one particular occasion, finding herself in Limehouse, she had remembered reading that Sylvia Pankhurst, after breaking with her famous suffragette mother and sister over their support for the war, had set up home in nearby Poplar.

Caitlin had found her at home and been welcomed like a long-lost sister. When, halfway through their first conversation, she had suddenly burst into tears, Sylvia had proved a sympathetic listener. Other visits had followed, in which her new friend advised Caitlin not to let her brother's fate determine her own. She had eventually responded by penning an admiring piece on Sylvia's work among East End women, which her former editor in New York was only too happy to print.

Michael Killen had also returned on those two occasions when Colm's comrades were about to be executed, carrying messages from their families that a sympathetic priest delivered to the condemned cells. Colm would be the last to die — the British, as far as Caitlin could judge, had been reluctant to execute an American, for fear of upsetting a potential ally. If her brother had agreed to a public show of remorse, one lawyer had told her, he would have been on a boat back home.

But he hadn't, and for Colm's sake she had swallowed her anger and resigned herself to the worst. Michael had arrived in London a few days earlier, for what would be the last time. He would probably try to see her that evening, might even be waiting at her lodging house now, but she knew she wanted to spend this night alone. And he wouldn't try to dissuade her. They weren't that close, and both of them knew they never would be. She wasn't at all sure why she was still sleeping with him — neither of them seemed to derive much joy from the process — and her original hope, that sleeping with someone new would help her forget Jack McColl, had so far proved in vain.

She thought about Colm's revelation, that Jack had actually offered to let him escape. So at least he had tried; he hadn't been deaf to her plea. She must have meant something to the man. Not enough to tell her who he worked for, or that he was spying on her family, but something.

As she carried on up Crescent Lane, waves of sadness rolled over her, each one coursing forth tears. And she wasn't sure who they were for anymore. For Colm, of course, for her and Jack perhaps, not to mention a world in which thousands were dying each day for nothing more real than a flag. And where that was concerned, she had to admit, her brother was just the same. His flag might be a rebel flag, his death less a matter of chance, but this mad attachment to nations and land was what united them all.

She crossed the road to the common and walked toward her lodging house on the northern side. Two women in black were sitting on a bench, watching their almost identical toddlers kicking around a bright red ball. Sons who would never play with their fathers again.

As she had half expected, Michael was waiting at her lodgings, sharing a mug of tea with her Irish landlady. Up in Caitlin's room, he confirmed that all hope of reprieve had passed and went through the motions of offering to stay the night. When she told him no, he said he would meet her outside the Tower entrance at eight o'clock next morning. On past occasions a notice that an execution had been carried out had always been posted on the gatehouse wall.

He was a kind man, she thought as he disappeared down the stairs. Just not one who touched her heart. She would need his help in fulfilling Colm's request.

She didn't feel hungry but knew she ought to eat, and she managed to consume a plate of pie and mash at the café a few doors down. The pub on the corner provided a bottle of scotch, which she carried home.

Her room looked out across street and common, and once an attempt to divert herself with work had failed, she took chair and glass to the window and sat watching the world go by. There were still a lot of automobiles on the street, but rather fewer horses. An occasional brightly lit tram slid past, striking sparks on the overhead wires as it took the curve toward Kennington. Every now and then, she detected motion in the darkened park beyond — lovers, perhaps, but more likely people walking their dogs.

Picturing Colm in his Tower cell, it all seemed too ridiculous. Her brother, like one of Richard III's princes, or Thomas More, or poor Anne Boleyn, or any of those famous people who, deliberately or not, had dared to cross the British Crown. Well, there was no doubting Colm's deliberation — as he'd said himself, the choice had been his.

How he had come to make it — that was something else again. Why had her younger brother been so ready to follow a rebel like Seán Tiernan to the gates of death and beyond? The absence of a loving mother, the presence of an unloving father? His own character, which she herself had often feared was weak?

What did it matter now?

She tore herself away from the window and lay down on the bed, certain that sleep wouldn't come. But the scotch must have done its work, because the sun was streaming between the undrawn curtains when she woke with a start.

It was gone seven.

The authorities had refused to reveal the time of execution, and she searched her heart for Colm's — was he still alive? Surely she would know if he wasn't?

Nothing felt different. She hurriedly changed into clean clothes and went out. She didn't have long to wait for a 30 tram, and the journey to Waterloo seemed quicker than usual. After walking across the bridge, she took the District Line train to Mark Lane. Emerging from the station, she realized what a beautiful day it was, the sun shining in another clear blue sky, the faintest of breezes ruffling the Union Jack that floated above the Tower. She had imagined chill mists rising up from the river, foghorns singing their melancholy song, not this brutal light.

"A good day to die," she murmured to herself, remembering the Sioux chief's famous line. What rubbish, she thought. For someone in terrible pain, perhaps. For anyone else there was no such thing.

As she walked down toward the gate, her ears were alert for the sound of gunfire beyond the wall to her left. Colm had been so pleased to learn that he would be shot rather than hanged. "A soldier's death," he had called it.

Michael was already there, and his expression told her all she needed to know. She buried her face in his shoulder and sobbed.

"I spoke to the man in the gatehouse," he told her eventually. "His personal effects are there for you."

She dried her eyes, took a deep breath, and went to collect the burlap sack that contained his books — Irish history, every one — his clothes, watch, pen, and journal. The thought of reading the latter was almost more than she could bear.

She signed her name, gave the official a contemptuous look, and went back to Michael.

"What do you want to do now?" he asked.

Just cry and cry, she thought. "A cup of

tea," she said. It seemed as appropriate as anything else.

In the café on Eastcheap, she told Michael what Colm had wanted her to do and asked if he could help her find the other families. He looked doubtful for a minute but said he would see what he could do. It occurred to Caitlin that the Citizen Army might have its own reasons for keeping an American journalist at bay. It had already occurred to her, with a sharp pang of guilt, that the story Colm wanted told might not prove as glorious as he imagined it to be. "When are you going back?" she asked Michael.

"On the evening train. I'll give you my address in Dublin. Have you a pen?"

She loaned him Colm's, which seemed fitting.

"And I'll write to you once I've fixed something up, all right?"

"All right. And thanks for being here, Michael."

He smiled wryly. "I know you wish he'd never laid eyes on a green flag, but he was one of ours in the end, and we care for our own."

She kissed him lightly on the cheek and wished him a safe journey home.

In her room that afternoon, between the bouts of helpless crying, she went through the press clippings relating to Colm and his operation that she'd collected over the months. The official story seemed full of contradictions and omissions, but for all she knew, the plotters' account might prove equally flawed. She would find out. For Colm, for herself. And she would try to discover whether what they had done had made any difference. She wanted to know, no matter how painful the answer might be, if his sacrifice had been worth it.

But Colm's wasn't the only story she wanted to tell. As night fell, she felt a sudden guilty realization that his death had freed her once more. He was gone, and she would honor his request, for her own sake as well as his. But not to the exclusion of everything else. Until that terrible night the previous August, when the police had come to tell her that Colm had been arrested, she'd spent five long years learning to be a journalist. All those days fighting off drunken editors and feeling the odd woman out in a boisterous male newsroom, all those raised eyebrows when she produced her press card, all those hours outblaséing the other crime reporters over city morgue cadavers, when all she wanted to do was throw up, preferably on her so-called colleagues. She wasn't about to waste all that, and Colm wouldn't want her to.

She'd gotten good at her job in those five years, good at encapsulating people and places, at writing snappy prose, at keeping her rage sufficiently under control so as not to antagonize those she sought to convince. And in the end she'd won the post she dreamed of. Well, that was gone, but there'd be another, and God only knew there were stories to spare. The eight-month-old war was crossing the world like a tornado, throwing them out in every direction. Soldiers' stories, workers' stories, women's stories. Before the war, people had complained that things were changing too fast, but now they were changing even faster.

She ought to be in her element, she thought. And by God she intended to be.

BHATTACHARYYA

The steam ferry worked its way down the crowded Hooghly in the wake of a jute ship bound for the Bay of Bengal. The ghats on either bank were crowded with bathers and washerwomen, the wharves and docks a hive of activity. Away to the left, the squat, rectangular blocks of the local Fort William dominated the eastern skyline.

It was a pleasant half-hour journey to the botanical gardens, where McColl had arranged a meeting with an informer named Narayan Gangapadhyay. The choice of location had, as ever, been difficult — the number of places in Calcutta where a European and an Indian could share a lengthy conversation without arousing curiosity or suspicion was limited. Caitlin would surely have claimed that this said all there was to be said about British rule in India, and while McColl would not have gone that far, he was willing to allow that it did say a lot.

He'd been told by several people that the botanical gardens were well worth a visit in their own right, if only to see the famous banyan, reputedly the largest tree on earth. And he was enjoying the trip downriver, the ferry chuffing its way through the heavy traffic in the early-morning sunshine. They were passing the main commercial docks now, as the river slowly curved to the right, past the once-fashionable suburb of Garden Reach.

After the captain had eased his boat alongside the jetty, McColl stepped ashore and studied the painted map of the gardens that adorned the ticket booth's wall. The Orchid House was not far away; the banyan, which looked some distance beyond it, would have to wait. Business before pleasure, he told himself as he walked up an avenue lined with soaring palms. To his left, beautifully kept lawns and flower beds stretched away toward a small lake. Most of the plants were native to the tropics, but the English signature was unmistakable.

The first sign that something had gone awry was the Indian constable standing sentry at the door to the Orchid House. He raised a warning hand and carefully checked McColl's police accreditation before letting him in. "Inspector Forsythe is senior rank," he added helpfully.

It wasn't much hotter inside, but moisture misted the air. Forsythe, a red-faced Englishman in tropical suit and topee, was crouched over the body, which was lying amid a bed of crushed yellow orchids. Two Indian subordinates and what looked like a gardens official hovered above him.

There was no mystery about the cause of death. A homemade dagger — just a sharpened length of steel — had been plunged with such force into the back of Gangapadhyay's neck that the point stuck out through his throat. A torrent of blood had been released, enriching the soil for those orchids not crushed.

McColl introduced himself to Forsythe and explained the situation.

"So the enemy got to him first," was the inspector's summation. "I was wondering why he still had money in his pocket."

"Did you find anything else?"

"Nothing."

McColl looked down at the young Bengali. He couldn't have been more than twenty. "I need to search his room before anyone else does," he told Forsythe. "You don't need me here, do you?"

53

"No. But I'll need a statement at some point."

"Fine, I'll be in touch."

McColl hurried back down the avenue of palms to the jetty, where the steam ferry was about to leave. The only two other passengers were Europeans, and neither was splattered in blood. Remembering the cross-river ferry that linked this jetty with Garden Reach, McColl asked the captain if it had recently departed.

"About fifteen minutes ago."

"Did you notice any of the men who took it?"

"No."

McColl took a seat near the bow and willed the boat on against the current. Garden Reach was a long way from Gangapadhyay's room in Black Town, but there was no knowing what form of transport the killer would be using. Jugantar had rich backers, and an automobile wasn't out of the question.

The heat was rising, and he could feel the sun grilling the top of his head through the thin felt hat. He had always thought he looked ridiculous wearing a topee, and the other popular option — wearing two felt hats, one inside the other — wasn't much of a sartorial improvement. But the only other option was not going out. It was barely April, and his single hat was clearly inadequate.

It took forty minutes to reach the Chandpal Ghat and the best part of another to convince the tonga wallah that he was serious about visiting Black Town. Once destination, route, and fare had been agreed upon, the Indian set the pony in motion. They trotted up Strand Road, crossed the busy approach to the Howrah Bridge, and, after rounding the mint, turned in to the maze of narrow streets that made up the largest native quarter. McColl had never been to Gangapadhyay's home but had learned the address when posting him money for services rendered, along with the fictional letter suggesting it came from a generous uncle. And if there was anything there to find, he wanted to be the one who found it.

Their journey through Black Town elicited many stares, but only a few seemed hostile. Gangapadhyay's rooming house was accessible only via a narrow alley and, along with its courtyard, seemed completely hemmed in by other buildings. McColl told the tonga-wallah to wait and walked down the alley, scattering giggling children. The front doors were open, but the chairs in the hallway were unoccupied, the table with its ledger untended. He was looking for Number 8, but none of the doors seemed to bear a number.

Hearing movement behind one, he rapped on it with his knuckles.

The door inched open to reveal a couple of big brown eyes and a riot of raven hair.

"Gangapadhyay?" he asked.

A finger emerged, pointed upward, and withdrew itself. The door closed.

McColl started up the wooden staircase, which creaked violently and showed alarming signs of rotting away. At the top of the second flight, he stopped to check the Webley in his pocket.

The doors were numbered on the upper floors, one with a metal plate, the others with chalk scrawls. He could hear nothing inside the rooms, but the men would all be at work, the women most likely down in the courtyard doing chores and watching the children.

Number 8 was on the second floor, at the rear of the building. There was a metal lock on the door, which looked likely to cause a problem — breaking in would be noisy. But a tentative turn of the new-looking knob proved successful, and he was quietly pushing the door open when someone or something crashed into the other side, throwing McColl back into the corridor.

Before he could get to his feet, an Indian man had leaped over him and raced away down the stairs.

McColl gave chase. Down the stairs he thundered, ignoring the sound of splintering wood that accompanied his descent. A head emerged from one doorway and just as quickly withdrew when its owner spotted McColl's white face. When he reached the ground floor, he saw that the Indian was halfway down the alley, about thirty yards ahead. He was clutching a piece of paper in his right hand.

McColl reached the street as his quarry turned in to an alley on the other side. The waiting tonga-wallah, mouth gaping, somehow managed a heartfelt wail as his fare ran past. He hadn't been paid.

The young man could run, and McColl was still twenty yards adrift when the Indian took the next turn. Rounding the corner, he was greeted by a vista of stalls and shoppers, which filled the street ahead. Only another fifty yards and the man would be lost in the crowd.

McColl could try to drop the Indian with his Webley, but chances were good he would hit someone else. If he did, he might easily get beaten to death by an angry mob. So he just kept running, without much hope.

The Indian ran into the throng, but as he was taller than most, his bobbing head remained in view. McColl had just waded into the crowd himself when another man suddenly stepped into his path, knocking him to the ground.

The assailant was full of apologies, but the glint in his eyes suggested a job well done. He then let out a cry of surprise and darted down a hand to retrieve the Webley from under the wheel of a cart. Gun in hand, finger on the trigger, he turned to McColl with a grin that could best be described as wicked.

A widening zone of silence fell across the market, until only faraway voices were audible. McColl's life didn't pass before his eyes, but his bowels came close to moving, and his fright must have been all too evident.

The Indian laughed out loud, baring several gold teeth, nimbly reversed the gun, and offered it butt-first to its owner. "This must be yours, sahib," he said, the golden smile cracking his face from ear to ear.

McColl took his leave with as much dignity as he could muster and, sweating profusely, walked slowly back to the rooming house, where the tonga-wallah greeted him like a long-lost brother.

He felt like stepping aboard, closing his eyes, and not opening them again until he was once more on safer ground, but instead he forced himself back up the stairs to Gangapadhyay's room.

He was hoping that the informer's killer had not had time to finish his search, but there was nothing there to suggest as much. The mattress had been pulled off the bed; the only drawer lay facedown on the bare floor. A single change of clothes had been tipped out of a relatively new suitcase, the toilet bag emptied of toothbrush and razor. An English edition of Trollope's *Barchester Towers* was wedged between the rusty springs of the bedstead, reminding McColl that these people — both the Jugantar rebels and informers like Gangapadhyay — were educated men. Almost all of them members of India's nascent middle class.

He told himself that most of their fellow countrymen were too busy trying to feed themselves to care who their rulers were. A few educated men, no matter how determined, were not going to compromise the British war effort.

Whatever was written on the piece of paper the killer had taken was unlikely to be that important. Which was fortunate, because McColl didn't suppose he would ever find out.

He descended the stairs and walked back to the tonga. He felt more than slightly weak in the knees and decided that hunger had to be part of the reason. "The Bristol Grill," he told the driver.

They drove back toward the river and eventually turned south toward the stock exchange. The heat was still rising, and the cool caress of the restaurant's electric fans was one reason McColl liked the grill. The food was another. As he looked round at the other diners — almost all of them businessmen — McColl reflected on one of the Raj's central paradoxes, that its ultimate rulers — the civil servants and soldiers — mostly eschewed such modernity, preferring the abysmal cuisine at their clubs, where the punkah wallahs who worked the mechanical fans fought a far less successful battle against the torpid heat.

He took his time over lunch, enjoying two iced whiskeys before working his way through the usual mulligatawny soup, chicken curry, and caramel custard. Through the window he could see the air on New China Bazaar shimmering in the heat, shifting his view in and out of focus.

None of his colleagues would be at their desks until the temperature started to fall, so he walked back down Old Court House Street to the Great Eastern, making the most of what shade was on offer. After stopping at the desk to pick up a letter from Jed, he was pulled up short by a copy of *The Statesman* that someone had left on a lobby chair. LAST OF THE AUGUST SABOTEURS EXECUTED was the headline halfway down.

There wasn't much more. Just Colm's name and a rehashing of the plot. It was prominently placed, though — someone in authority here in Calcutta had taken the opportunity to remind the Jugantar rebels of the fate that awaited them.

McColl remembered the first time he had met Colm, at the family home in Brooklyn — the adolescent anger that had spilled from his face. And he could still see the young man's expression when his friend Seán Tiernan was killed beside him — an almost joyful desperation.

Caitlin would be devastated.

And, if it was possible, even angrier with him.

Upstairs in his room, McColl read the letter from his own younger brother. Jed's friend Mac — whom McColl knew well

61

from his car-selling days — had been wounded in February, but "in the best way," slightly enough to cast no shadow over his future well-being, seriously enough to warrant a week's hospitalization and a fortnight's convalescence in the loving care of his fiancée, Ethel. And that was about it when it came to news — Jed had clearly written with the censors in mind. He couldn't tell McColl where they were, only that it was very noisy and that when the wind was blowing in the right direction, they could sometimes smell the sea. There hadn't been many casualties of late — "the Boche have realized that successful attacks need a lot of preparation." The British generals, by contrast, were proving themselves intelligent, courageous, and incredibly solicitous of their men's welfare. "Just like our old neighbor Jimmy Dalglish in Glasgow," Jed added. He was sure his brother would remember Jimmy.

He did indeed. Jimmy Dalglish had been a thug and a rumored killer, as thick as he was cowardly, and happily unaware that other lives might be as real as his own.

McColl laughed, but only briefly. This wasn't the first report he'd had from France that suggested failures of leadership reminiscent of those he'd experienced himself in

South Africa. The sort of men who had contrived to leave him and several hundred others at the mercy of better-placed Boer sharpshooters on Spion Kop were still running the British army.

He put down the letter and closed his eyes, hoping to God that Jed would come through it all. McColl had been absent for much of his brother's childhood, and over the past few years he had tried to make up for that and to look out for the boy. But he was powerless now.

As powerless as Caitlin had been.

He wanted to send her his condolences, to tell her how sorry he was, but of course that was out of the question. She would probably think he was twisting the knife.

Next morning a cable arrived from Cumming in London. McColl read it once in the cool telegraph office, then again in the shade of the palms outside. This, he thought, might change everything.

He found Alex Cunningham and Douglas Tindall sitting in a shaded section of the police headquarters' inner courtyard, drinking coffee fresh off the boat from Kenya and trying hard to "liaise." Tindall was the local Department of Criminal Intelligence chief, a tall, fair-haired Cumbrian. His placid temperament masked a quick mind, and McColl liked him a lot better than he liked Cunningham, who had somehow managed to elect himself local representative of both Kell's Section Five and the Indian Political Intelligence Office.

Cunningham, for his part, openly resented McColl's trespassing on what he considered his own organization's patch. Section Five's remit might be domestic security, but as far as Kell and his minions were concerned, "domestic" encompassed the whole British Empire.

McColl wasted no time in sharing his news. "Our people in America have intelligence of a German arms shipment."

"They've said so before," Cunningham replied dismissively. "The shipment always seems to vanish."

McColl extracted Cumming's cable from the jacket on the back of his chair. "According to this, in the months before Christmas the Kaiser's people on the West Coast amassed 8,080 Springfield rifles, 2,400 Springfield carbines, 410 Hotchkiss repeaters, 500 Colt revolvers, and 250 Mauser pistols, along with decent supplies of all the relevant ammunition, and they put the whole lot on a boat. That's definite. And though they don't know where it is at this moment, our people are in no doubt at all that it's headed this way. Remember that Ghadar member we arrested last month in Lahore who let slip that a boatload of guns was expected? Well, it seems he was telling the truth. It obviously didn't arrive in time for him and his friends, but it looks like it'll get here eventually. And once it does reach this side of the Pacific, we all know who the Germans will give it to. Ghadar are out for the count, so it has to be Jugantar. Sometime soon, on some Bengali beach, Mukherjee and his friends will be unloading all the guns they need."

"That does sound a bit worrying," Cunningham conceded reluctantly.

"It's more than bloody worrying," Tindall said coldly. "With eight thousand Springfields, Jugantar could turn this province upside bloody down. Instead of sending more troops to France, we'd have to start bringing them back!"

"Okay, it might be serious," Cunningham said, putting up a hand. "Assuming for a moment that this boat *is* on its way, how are we going to intercept it? Does the navy have enough ships to patrol the whole coastline?"

"No, they don't," McColl answered. "So we'll have to help them narrow the search.

The gunrunners can't just turn up on any old beach and hand their cargo over to the local peasants — someone from Jugantar will have to meet them. Someone who knows the time and place. It's him we have to find."

Cunningham's grunt was pessimistic, but Tindall had something to offer. "As it happens, I've got somewhere for us to start. Or rather some*one* — a young man named Abhijit Bhattacharyya, who arrived on the boat from Rangoon yesterday evening. He boarded at Batavia, which was enough to make the duty officer consult the suspect-persons list. And Bhattacharyya's name was on it. He used to be a member of the same so-called youth club that Jatin Mukherjee set up and which two of the Garden Reach robbers belonged to."

"Who haven't been seen since the court granted bail," Cunningham added disgustedly.

Tindall ignored him. "Bhattacharyya works for his father, who's one of Calcutta's wealthiest merchants, and he seems to travel a lot — he recently visited Bangkok as well. All of which may be perfectly innocent and the nationalist politics just a youthful phase, but if Bhattacharyya is a member of Jugantar, he has the perfect cover for liaising with the Germans."

Cunningham pulled himself up in his seat. "Let me have a go at him."

Tindall had other ideas. "I think we'll keep you in reserve. Bhattacharyya is an Urdu speaker, and McColl's is much better than yours."

"I bet the little bastard speaks English as well as I do," Cunningham protested, but Tindall was having none of it.

Their relative fluency was neither here nor there, McColl realized. Tindall might not be certain of him, but he sure as hell didn't like Cunningham. McColl asked where Bhattacharyya was being held.

"He's in a holding room down at the docks. It seemed more discreet than bringing him here, but the news is probably all over Black Town by now."

"I'll get down there," McColl said, rising to his feet. "What's the duty officer's name?"

"Byrne."

This could change the outcome of the war, McColl thought as he hailed a tonga a few minutes later. This was why he'd joined the Service.

The port administration's offices were on Napier Road, just north of the Hastings Bridge over Tolly's Nala canal. Byrne, a lean

Englishman with sideburns far bushier than the hair on his head, showed McColl the entry against Bhattacharyya in the current blacklist and then escorted him to the holding room, where the Indian detainee looked up from his book with the air of someone generously accepting an unwarranted interruption. The book, McColl noticed, was John Reed's *Insurgent Mexico.*

Abhijit Bhattacharyya was tall for a Bengali, with the lighter skin of the typical Brahmin. Slightly overlong hair was brushed back from a wide forehead, above large eyes and a mocking smile full of very white teeth. According to the record, he was twenty-six years old.

McColl took the seat of authority behind the tea-stained table. "Would you like to speak in Urdu or English?" he asked in the former.

"English will be fine," Bhattacharyya decided.

"Your full name?" McColl asked.

The Indian smiled. "Abhijit Anup Bhattacharyya," he articulated, syllable by syllable.

"Address in Calcutta?"

"Three Lansdowne Road."

It was an impressive address for an Indian. "Occupation?"

"I work for my father, Gautam Bhattacharyya. You've probably heard of him."

"I have. What exactly do you do for him?"

A shrug. "This and that. Anything that requires travel, though. My father is getting old."

"What was your business in the Dutch East Indies?"

"What business is that of yours?"

"Your past affiliations make it my business. I believe you once belonged to a youth club named after Swami Vivekananda?"

The young man nodded, as if granting McColl an unexpected point. "When I was a boy, yes."

"You know that the club was set up by Jatin Mukherjee?"

The Indian pushed out his chest and pulled back his arms, as if he were stiff from sitting too long. "The name rings a bell, as you English say, but nothing more than that."

Now he was tapping his foot, McColl noticed. "Mukherjee is the leader of the Jugantar terrorist group."

Bhattacharyya smiled. "Is he really? I have heard of these people, of course. But I never knew their leader's name. That is interesting."

"Your club used to meet in a building on

Cornwallis Street," McColl persisted, throwing in the last of his information. "Young men dedicated to building a new India."

"Yes."

"An India without need of the British."

"Of course. What nation can grow when another one rides on its back?"

It was a good answer, McColl thought. Caitlin, he thought with a pang, would certainly have approved. "You say you have never heard of Jatin Mukherjee — have you heard of Amarnath Dutta and Kaushik Dasgupta?"

"I don't believe so, but these are common names."

"These two men were arrested on suspicion of involvement in the Garden Reach dacoity."

Bhattacharyya grimaced. "Why do you not say robbery? Must you steal our language, too?"

The foot was tapping again, but try as he did, McColl couldn't convince himself that the Indian was even the slightest bit worried. "You have never met these two men?"

"Not that I'm aware of."

"So you would be surprised to discover that they both attended the same youth club on Cornwallis Street?"

70

"When?"

"Between 1909 and 1911."

"I had left by then. I started work for my father in 1908."

"So you've never met these men?" he asked again.

"If I have, they must have used false names," Bhattacharyya said, his face a study in innocence.

"Why would they do that?"

Another shrug. "They are criminals, you tell me. Who can say what a criminal will do?"

McColl tried not to show his annoyance. "They consider themselves patriots, just as you do. The dacoity was doubtless carried out to raise money for buying weapons."

"How should I know?"

"Don't you think such methods are justifiable?"

Bhattacharyya gave him a look. "If I say yes to that, you could put me in prison."

"So why not say no?"

"All right, no. I understand the temptation, but no."

"You would not condone violence in any circumstances?"

Bhattacharyya shook his head.

"No, or you refuse to say? I'm simply

interested. Consider this a philosophical debate."

Bhattacharyya laughed. "Philosophical debate! You're just trying to incriminate me."

"There's no one else here."

"And your word and mine would be treated alike in a British court? You are joking, I think."

There was more than a little truth in that, McColl knew. Which was not a comfortable thought.

"But I will answer your question," Bhattacharyya said unexpectedly. "I think that violence is sometimes necessary when it comes to expelling an invader. In Belgium today, for example — how else will the Belgians eject the Germans? You British say you took up arms because the Germans invaded Belgium. So how can you object — philosophically, of course — when Indians take up arms to eject you? The fact that the invasion took place a century and a half ago makes no difference — we are still invaded. No, the only real issue — from a philosophical point of view — is whom the violence should be directed against. The occupying forces, certainly; their Indian helpers, sometimes; innocent civilians, never. Although I have to add that political reality is, unfortunately, seldom so clear-cut."

McColl was reluctantly impressed. He doubted whether any of his colleagues could have mounted a defense of British rule that was even half as well thought through. He was, he realized, getting nowhere. "You still haven't told me what you were doing in the Dutch East Indies."

"It's confidential, but I don't suppose my father would mind your knowing. He is thinking of setting up an office in Batavia, and I was sent on a forward reconnaissance, as your soldiers would say. Premises, local workers, that sort of thing."

"Your father would confirm that?"

"Of course."

He probably would, McColl thought. Either out of loyalty to his son or because it was true. And there'd been nothing to stop young Abhijit here from working for both Daddy and Jugantar. McColl asked the obvious question: "Did you visit the German consulate while you were in Batavia?"

"No."

"Or meet any German official?"

"No. Why should I?"

"Because my enemy's enemy is my friend?"

Bhattacharyya looked exasperated. "We can win independence by our own efforts.

We certainly don't need another European master."

"I'm sure you don't," McColl agreed, "but would you refuse such help if it were offered?" Colm Hanley and his group hadn't planned on handing Ireland over to the Kaiser, but they'd been more than willing to swap anti-British favors.

Bhattacharyya just shrugged.

McColl gave him a long, hard look. He felt fairly sure that the young man in front of him was a fully paid-up member of Jugantar and might even be the group's principal go-between in its dealings with the Germans. But he had no proof. A British court would probably jail the young man anyway, but the prospect of a few months' patriotic detention wouldn't open Bhattacharyya up. McColl needed a likely conviction for treason, and the real prospect of a firing squad, if he were going to get the Indian talking.

He stood up. "Well, that's all for now."

"How long will I be kept here?" Bhattacharyya asked. "I have done nothing wrong."

"I can't tell you that, I'm afraid."

"You can't just keep me here."

"The Defence of India Act says we can. I expect you were on your travels when it was introduced. We can detain you until we are satisfied that you pose no threat to the rule of law."

"And whose law would that be?" Bhattacharyya asked sarcastically as McColl let himself out.

The Bengal Club, like many of the better-known British establishments, faced the Maidan across Chowringhee Road. McColl found Tindall in the shaded back garden, enjoying the slight breeze engendered by the punkah wallah's exertions and sipping at a very large whiskey and tonic. McColl ordered the same, and the two of them shared small talk while they waited for Cunningham. Tindall, it turned out, had been in Calcutta for more than ten years and was looking forward to that much again. "I know everyone says it's the most horrible city in India," he said, "and the hot season really is dreadful, but there's just something about the place." He gave a wry smile. "My wife, I'm afraid, feels different, and now that the children are at school back home . . . well, she misses them and she loathes this climate. She went up to the hills last week, so the next few months will be a bit lonely." He lifted his glass. "When she's gone, I have to be careful I don't drink too much."

Cunningham arrived just in time to share the next round. "Sorry I'm late," he said, sinking wearily into the rattan chair. "Crisis at home — a snake slithered out of a drainpipe and almost gave the ayah a heart attack. One of the old hands blew its head off with a twelve-bore." He turned to McColl. "So what did you get out of Bhattacharyya Minor?"

"Not a great deal," McColl admitted once Tindall had signed for their drinks. "He makes no secret of his nationalist beliefs, but having them isn't a crime. And there are thousands of Indians who think like he does yet wouldn't dream of turning such thoughts into action. It's entirely possible that he's as innocent as he says he is."

"But you don't think so?" Tindall suggested.

"No, I think he's the man we're looking for — Jugantar's link to the Germans. Or one of them at least."

"That's good enough for me," Cunningham said. "And locking him up should put a spoke in their wheels — finding a replacement won't be easy."

Tindall disagreed. "We can't just lock him up — his father's an important man in the

Bengali business community. We'll need *something* to put before a judge."

"There's one thing we could do," McColl said. "Take his picture and send it to our people in Batavia. They've been keeping an eye on the German consulate there, and since he denies ever going near it, proof to the contrary would be pretty damning."

"As long as we keep him locked up in the meantime," Cunningham conceded.

"How long would it take to get a reply?" McColl asked Tindall.

"Oh. There's a boat every two or three days, four days to get there, a couple to sort things out — we should get a cable in a fortnight or so."

"We can certainly hold him that long," Cunningham insisted.

McColl disagreed. "We should let him go but keep him under constant surveillance. We'll need some locals . . . That Indian in the Punjab who scotched the Ghadar plot — wasn't he a sepoy working undercover? The regiments here must have men who'd be willing to spend a couple of weeks watching Bhattacharyya for a decent bonus."

"After Neuve-Chapelle I should think not being shipped to France would be reward enough," Cunningham noted cynically.

"After what happened to Gangapadhyay,"

McColl retorted, "we may have to offer rather more than that."

"We certainly need men who are motivated enough to do a good job," Tindall said. "If Bhattacharyya realizes he's being followed, he won't lead us to anyone." He studied his freshly empty glass. "But it might work. I'll talk to the regimental commanders tomorrow. See what they've got to offer."

The police photographer — an enthusiastic young Bengali — accompanied McColl to the local prison, where Bhattacharyya was now in comfortable, albeit solitary, confinement. A second night in custody had not improved his mood, and McColl's refusal to speculate about the length of his incarceration only made him angrier. But he raised no objection to having his photograph taken. "One day a picture in British police files will be a badge of honor," the Indian said as his countryman set up the camera. A few minutes later he greeted the click of the shutter with an anticipatory smile.

The man in the resulting photograph looked anything but a threat to the empire, and McColl found himself having doubts as he took it down to the ship. Had he misread Bhattacharyya? Time would presumably tell.

If he had, Cunningham wouldn't let him forget it, but who the hell cared about Cunningham? He handed the envelope containing the picture to the steamship captain and gave him the name of the agent who would be waiting on the dockside in Batavia. As he left, two sailors were waiting to pull up the gangplank, which seemed like a good omen.

Four days later Bhattacharyya was released from custody and followed to the family home by two of the four Bengalis whom Tindall had hired on their British CO's recommendation. From then on, the two pairs worked twelve-hour shifts, reporting to McColl at the end of each. They all seemed like nice lads, and McColl hoped he'd never find one with a knife sticking out of his throat.

Days went by, and his watchers insisted that Abhijit Bhattacharyya was unaware of their surveillance. Which, if true, was somewhat depressing, because the man showed no sign of leading them anywhere useful. He spent most of the daylight hours at his father's godown, and when he did venture farther afield, for either business or social purposes, there was nothing obviously suspicious about the people he met. McColl spent his mornings checking them out and could find nothing to suggest that they were other than what they seemed — smart, successful businessmen, getting on with business. If these young men belonged to Jugantar, the Raj was really in trouble.

Afternoons nothing much moved. In April it had been hard to imagine more oppressive weather, but May was decidedly worse. Cumming had written "suggesting" that McColl move into permanent accommodation more befitting his status, but the glaring lack of electric fans in the flats he visited persuaded McColl to stay where he was. His expenditure seemed negligible — the Raj's chit system was unmatched when it came to generating a false sense of financial security — and if Cumming got shirty, he was willing to make up the difference from his largely untouched salary.

The evenings were marginally better, but his social life was hardly expansive. After finishing *The Ragged-Trousered Philanthropists,* he took a tonga out to Alipur and the bungalow that Cynthia Malone shared with her civil servant brother. After they'd debated Tressell's ideas with their usual friendly combativeness, McColl was saddened to hear that the brother had been called back to England and that she was going with him. "I'm tempted to stay," she said, "but I think I'm too old to live here on my own. And much as I love India, I do miss British culture. Not to mention spring and autumn."

He would miss her, he thought, as the tonga took him home. Partly because she was one of the few people he'd met in India who actually seemed to like the place and partly, he knew, because although she was twenty years older, Cynthia had reminded him of Caitlin.

An answer arrived from Batavia. "They recognized him," McColl told Tindall, "but not for the reasons I'd hoped. He was picked up the moment he arrived — an Indian traveling from India to a neutral country apparently sets off an alarm. He took care of his father's business just as he said he did, and then he started visiting brothels. Eleven of them before our men gave up."

"Hell," Tindall said quietly.

"We've been barking up the wrong tree," McColl decided. "I have, that is."

"Back to square one, then."

A sharp rap on the door swiftly gave way to a face. "You are needed, sahib," a constable told Tindall. "A shooting on Clive Street."

McColl went along for the ride. The road had been closed off about a hundred yards north of Dalhousie Square, leaving all the side streets crammed with travelers keen to express their frustration. In the middle of the cordoned-off area, a dead horse with a gaping head wound was still tethered to what looked like a large metal box on wheels. The latter had CHARTERED BANK OF BENGAL emblazoned on its side.

There was one uniformed man on the ground who wasn't moving and another sitting with his back to the fallen vehicle, receiving medical attention from a nurse.

There was a cow on the pavement beyond, watching with apparent interest.

Two British police detectives were already on the scene, along with a sizable number of Indian subordinates. "They got away with about ten thousand rupees," one told Tindall, a figure that McColl mentally reconfigured at around eight hundred pounds.

"Jugantar?" Tindall was asking.

"Most likely. They were educated men, according to the guard."

Men with more money to finance their revolution, McColl thought. Men who

could use the guns that were coming to set
the Raj ablaze.

THE NIGHT WATCHMAN

It was unusually sunny in Dublin, but not particularly warm. Caitlin Hanley was sitting at the only outside table of a pub on Wellington Quay, coat buttoned against the breeze that was blowing up the Liffey. A half-full glass of stout sat in front of her, alongside a sad-looking, partially eaten cheese sandwich. Through the open window behind, she could hear loud Irish voices discussing that afternoon's racing at Leopardstown.

Almost two months had passed since Colm's death, and although she was still prone to fits of weeping, the tide of grief seemed like it might at last be slowly beginning to ebb. When Michael Killen finally sent word to London that the relatives of those involved in the operation had agreed to meet her, it felt like an invitation to reengage with the world.

That morning she'd taken omnibuses

across the city to visit the parents of the two men captured at Eastleigh after a long and bloodless exchange of fire with the local police. The O'Farrells in Kilmainham — a works foreman and his wife — were as ashamed of their younger son as they were proud of his older brother, now serving with the British army. Patrick had always been difficult, his mother kept saying, as if that explained his republican beliefs.

The Giffords in Cabra were intensely proud of their only son, who had always been "a lovely boy" and would be now forevermore. He had taken the fight to the English oppressor, as every real Irishman should. They had killed him, of course, but others would follow in his footsteps, and sooner or later there'd be statues to all the brave boys outside an Irish parliament.

All that the two couples shared was their astonishment at meeting a woman reporter and their ignorance of the event that their sons had been involved in. They had little idea how their boys had become involved or what exactly they had hoped to achieve, and even less of what had happened on that August evening. Caitlin hoped that Maeve McCarron, the sister she was seeing that afternoon, might help with the first two questions — siblings usually knew more than parents — but the third seemed increasingly likely to remain a mystery, particularly where Maeve and her brother were concerned. He had been killed at Godalming, and his partner, Brady, had been missing ever since.

Caitlin took a sip of the stout and pushed the sandwich plate farther away. A phalanx of uniformed children was being marched down the opposite quay by two young schoolmistresses, one to the fore, one to the rear. Half an hour earlier, a troop of soldiers had marched by in the same direction, and Caitlin had the sudden heartsick feeling that she was watching their future replacements in what people already called "the mincing machine in France."

She shivered and went back to her notes. What did she actually know?

There was no dispute about Colm and his comrades' intentions. The press had called it a campaign of sabotage but had never, as far as she knew, spelled out the specific targets. These had been four railway bridges, whose simultaneous demolition would have drastically delayed the transport of British troops to their ports of embarkation for France. Had the would-be saboteurs been German, Caitlin felt pretty certain that no one would have questioned the soundness of their military logic or the genuineness of their patriotic motives.

But they hadn't been German — they'd been Irish or Irish-American — and there hadn't been any obvious benefit to their compatriots in slowing down an English army en route to the Continent. Had the Germans offered them something in return? If they had, no one seemed to know what. "We needed to show them we were serious," Colm had told her, which made some sort of sense. But had there been any more to it than that? Had guns been promised if the plot succeeded?

Who had these eight men been? Tiernan and at least three others had been members of the Irish Citizen Army, but Colm had not, and neither, she assumed, had his fellow American, Aidan Brady. The previous day Caitlin had talked to James Connolly, the current commander of the ICA, at his Liberty Hall headquarters, and he had assured her that the operation had not been officially sanctioned. She'd believed him, particularly when he added that he almost wished it had been. So the eight men had been acting on their own initiative, on behalf of Ireland. "Just volunteers," as Colm had claimed.

Which brought her to the last question —

what had actually happened that night? At the Arun bridge, Colm and Seán Tiernan had been ambushed by McColl and others. According to Colm, Tiernan had been shot without warning and had been forced to surrender. At Eastleigh the police had been waiting for the two whose parents she'd seen, and the ensuing gun battle had come to end only when the boys ran out of bullets. The pair at Romsey had actually brought down their bridge but shortly thereafter had both been caught. So far, so clear.

The events at Godalming were more a matter for dispute. According to the official report, Brady had murdered two police constables in cold blood, then managed to make his escape after police fire killed his partner, Donal McCarron. Colm had refused to believe this version of events, but as Brady had not been seen or heard from since, there was no one to offer another.

She would have to talk to the relatives of the dead policemen, Caitlin realized. They might know or guess that something was not quite right in the police story, might even blame their loved ones' superiors or colleagues for the deaths.

And then there was the other victim. At their last meeting in his flat, McColl had mentioned the murder of a night watchman several days earlier — he'd been killed, or so McColl had claimed, when the Irish invaded his quarry site to steal the explosives they needed. Colm had denied this, saying that Tiernan had told him the dynamite was part of a military shipment to Egypt, which Irish dockers in the Port of London had intercepted and smuggled out.

Caitlin had wanted to believe her brother but feared that just this once McColl might be telling the truth. And sure enough a search through the local papers of towns lying close to a working quarry had eventually turned up the story. She had gone to see the night watchman's widow and found the woman still struggling to accept what had happened. The police had told her that those responsible for her husband's death had been killed a few days later, while committing another crime, so there'd be no need of further proceedings.

Which didn't look good. Killing the oppressor's armed police was one thing, but murdering an unarmed civilian was something else again. She could imagine the justification — what was one man's life when millions were being slaughtered by the capitalist machine! — but it still left a sour taste. Colm's shining martyrs were looking somewhat tarnished.

It also reminded her of McColl's claim that he had witnessed Brady killing a policeman in Paterson, New Jersey, the previous spring. Here, too, she had only her ex-lover's word to go on, but that story also somehow rang true.

Was he an essentially honest man who had just told one big lie? Well, what if he was? Did a life of nonviolence excuse one murderous moment?

She stared out at the rippling river. What if she decided, after all this, that Colm's operation had been merely a sideshow, eventually killing ten people for no discernible gain? The Germans could hardly have been impressed, and none of the English and Irish she'd talked to had seemed persuaded to change their minds. On the contrary, as far as she could tell, the whole sorry business had only served to confirm existing prejudices.

What could she do with such a conclusion? She knew how the journalist should answer. But what about the sister? And the woman who thought Ireland should be free?

She told herself not to prejudge. She had more relatives to talk to, and she wanted to further sample wider Irish opinion.

It was time to go. Her appointment with

Maeve McCarron was at three, the address half a mile north of the river. As Caitlin crossed the Liffey and started up the street of that name, she found herself thinking about money. She could afford to stay another week in Ireland, and maybe a few more in London, but that was about it. She could always ask Aunt Orla to send her some, but she didn't really want to. No, once she had learned all she could on Colm's behalf, she would go home. But not across the Atlantic — the sinking of the *Lusitania* a few weeks earlier by a German submarine had gotten her thinking about other routes and the possibilities they offered. There seemed no problem with the North Sea routes to Scandinavia, and while Denmark offered a chance to witness the imminent introduction of women's suffrage, Norway was currently home to the Russian writer Alexandra Kollontai, who'd been writing and fighting for a socialist feminism for almost a decade. According to Sylvia, who had met the Russian in London before the war, she was not only brilliant but also a really nice person. "And, like all European revolutionaries, she speaks several languages. It's only we English who can't be bothered."

There were so many important stories being eclipsed by the war. If Colm's allowed her the time, she planned to research a piece on the republican women's auxiliary organization, Cumann na mBan, while she was in Dublin. And it had occurred to Caitlin that she was ideally placed to investigate what one of Sylvia's friends called the "great tragedy" — the decision by German socialists, after decades of preaching workers' solidarity, to support the Kaiser's war. As an American she could travel to Berlin and actually ask them why they'd done it. Kollontai knew most of them and would be able to give her introductions.

These were stories that any decent journalist would love to research and write. And what a chance to prove that a woman could do the job as well as a man, and perhaps even better. Afterward she could travel to Russia via Finland, take the train across Siberia, and a ship home from Japan. The only dangers of a voyage across the Pacific were emotional ones. But maybe by then her memories of the wretched man would finally have let her be.

Reaching the house on Mary Street, she paused for a moment to compose herself, then let the heavy knocker drop.

When Maeve McCarron answered the door, Caitlin recognized her. She had passed the slim, raven-haired woman on the stairs at Liberty Hall, on her way up to see James Connolly. Maeve had been wearing a silver Cumann na mBan badge, the letters *CnAmB,* in flowing Gaelic script, set against a miniature rifle.

Caitlin introduced herself and was led through to the parlor, where a formal family photograph had pride of place on the mantelpiece. The adolescent girl was obviously Maeve, the young boy in short trousers her brother, Donal. There were several shelves of books and a pile of magazines on a corner table. The one on top was the latest issue of *The Irish Volunteer.*

They both sat down. As a woman journalist, Caitlin was used to people chafing at her gender, but Maeve was more suspicious of the scribe. "I agreed to meet you," the Irishwoman said, "because you lost a brother, too. But I want to know what your intentions are."

"My intentions?"

"There are many ways to tell a story. Some more useful than others."

As Caitlin explained about Colm's request, she could hear her own doubts seeping through. Maeve heard them as well. "So what if the story proves less than glorious?"

It was a relief to acknowledge the problem.

"There are three things I could do," Caitlin said. "I could print the truth. I could print an edited version, which leaves out the less comfortable bits. Or I could decide to keep silent."

"And which will you do?"

"I don't know. First I need to know the truth."

Maeve thought about that for a moment. "I doubt I can help you much," she said eventually.

"Did you know about the operation before it happened?"

"Yes. Donal told me about it the night before they left." She paused. "I was his sister, but I was ten years older, and both our parents died when he was only eleven, so I sometimes felt more like his mother."

"I was seven years older than Colm," Caitlin said, "and our mother died when he was small."

"It seems we have a lot in common," Maeve conceded, her expression softening.

"Mmm. Tell me about Donal."

"That's easy — and hard. He was an ordinary boy, with the usual share of virtues and flaws. He was always brave, physically at least. And loyal to a fault. He wouldn't have let the others down."

No, Caitlin thought. She wondered if

Aidan Brady had let Maeve's brother down.

"Did you know he went to St. Enda's?"

"No, I didn't. I've heard a lot about it." St. Enda's was the school that the well-known nationalist Patrick Pearse had set up before the war, as a font of truly Irish education. "Is that where Donal became a republican?"

"Oh, no. We both got that from our parents. But you should talk to Pádraig Pearse. He's an extraordinary man."

It wasn't the first time Caitlin had heard Pearse's praises sung, but she was interested in why a woman would do so. "In what way?" she asked.

Maeve smiled. "Oh, that's hard to put into words. There's a passion there that's hard to ignore. And an honesty. If you meet him, you'll see what I mean. Donal admired him, despite their political differences."

"Donal was a socialist, like you?"

"What makes you think that I am?"

"I saw you in Liberty Hall the other day."

"Ah. But I don't want to give you the wrong impression — Donal would have *said* he was a socialist, but he was no theoretician. He wanted action and adventure, and he wanted to hit the English and their Irish puppets where it hurt them."

95

"Is that what he told you they were going to do?"

"More or less. He didn't give me any details — they'd all been warned not to do that — but he made it clear they were carrying the fight to England."

Caitlin didn't want to upset Maeve, but she felt she had to ask: "Did you try to stop him?"

Maeve thought twice before answering. "I didn't encourage him, but no, I didn't try to stop him either. Donal was a grown man. I would have preferred that my brother stay safe in Dublin, but that wasn't an argument likely to appeal to him. And I had no political or moral objection to what they were planning."

"You're aware of what happened that night?"

"Most of it, I think. Connolly sent a man over to London . . ."

"Michael Killen."

"You know about him?"

"I know Michael quite well."

Maeve must have read something in her tone. "Well, he's a good man."

"No, no, nothing like that," Caitlin insisted. *We just sleep with each other, we're not in love,* was what she felt like saying, but she didn't know how the other woman

96

would take such a frank admission. She had no idea how feminist Cumann na mBan was — were its members equals in name but followers in fact, as the label "auxiliary" suggested? That was something she wanted to find out, but this wasn't the moment. "Did you meet Donal's partner on that night — Aidan Brady?"

"No. Did you?"

"I did, in the States. Seán Tiernan introduced him to Colm. But I don't how Brady met Tiernan — Colm never said."

"What was Brady like?"

"Powerful," was the first word that came to mind. "Intelligent. Committed."

"But?" Maeve asked, picking up on Caitlin's ambivalence.

"I don't think there's any love in his heart."

"Ah."

"I don't know him well," Caitlin said. But well enough, she thought.

Maeve gave her a wry smile. "I've met men like that," she said. "We're all socialists at Liberty Hall, and most of the men are fond of telling you how and when they came to realize that the world needed turning upside down. And among all those men who learned it at their father's knee or experienced it firsthand at work, there's a group that gives me the shivers. They're every bit as passionate, every bit as brave, but there's something missing. And then you find out why they hate injustice so much — it all goes back to their childhood and the injustice they suffered then. Not from the state or the owners, but from mother or father or both. Their socialism is rooted in resentment and hatred, not love."

Caitlin knew exactly what the other woman meant but had never heard it expressed so clearly. She told Maeve that after finishing this assignment she was hoping to write a piece on Cumann na mBan for the American press. Would the Irishwoman suggest some people Caitlin could talk to, in addition to herself?

Maeve looked delighted by the prospect. "Of course. When do you think that might be?"

"I'm not sure. I still have to see relatives in Limerick and Belfast. And I need to get an idea of what ordinary people think — the ones who don't have a political agenda."

"They'll think what their situation tells them to think. People with sons or husbands in the British army are not going to fancy the idea of their boy being blown up in England. Most of those who'd like to see the back of the English think that Home

Rule is just a matter of time, so why fight for something that's coming anyway? And yet there'll always be some who'll cheer any Irish resistance to English rule, no matter how badly conceived it is. You can probably count the number of people who've really thought things through in the hundreds, and even they'll disagree with one another."

It was the first time she had sounded bitter, Caitlin thought. "I'm sorry about Donal," she said.

"And I about your Colm. But better they died fighting their own war than someone else's."

There was no disputing that, Caitlin thought as she walked back to her hotel. The sky had clouded over during their talk, and rain had just began spattering the pavement when she reached the doorway. She was standing in the lobby, wondering whether to write letters home in the bar or up in her room, when a bespectacled man in a tight-fitting suit approached her. "Caitlin Hanley?" he asked, with a perfunctoriness that suggested he already knew the answer.

"Yes."

"My name is Finian Mulryan, and I'd like a short word if that's possible. I'm speaking on Mr. Connolly's behalf, you understand."

"Oh. All right. Shall we go into the bar?"

"If you like," Mulryan said, looking more flustered than an ICA man should by her forwardness. He bought them both half a pint, though, mild for her and bitter for him, and almost succeeded in suppressing his surprise when she offered him a cigarette.

Her talk with Maeve had reawakened something, Caitlin realized.

"First off, my condolences on the loss of your brother," Mulryan said, with what seemed like genuine feeling.

"Thank you."

He paused, as if embarrassed by what he had to say. "We — Mr. Connolly, that is, but not just him — as armies go, we're very democratic, so I'll stick with 'we' — we are a tad worried about what you might be planning to write on the matter of you-know-what. One of the relatives you talked to . . . well, they came to us, and said you were asking questions about an English night watchman who was killed around that time."

"That is true."

"But as far as we can tell, no newspaper ever mentioned such a man, and he never came up at the trial."

"Also true."

Mulryan still looked embarrassed, but she

no longer thought he was — it was just his natural affect. "You see, the way it is," he said, "we arranged these conversations for you, and we were expecting a commemoration of those who've been lost."

"I do see," Caitlin said. She took a sip of the mild and sized him up — what was the best way to fob him off? And as she asked herself this, she knew what she hadn't known in many months, what her own priorities were. A journalist first, a supporter of Irish independence second.

"You see we're fighting a war," he was saying. "And no army can afford to dwell on the other side's casualties. It's bad for morale."

"Of course it is," she agreed, "and you have no need to worry. I feel no obligation to print everything people tell me. I lost a brother, so I need to know the full story for my own peace of mind, but I have no intention of besmirching his memory or handing his executioners a propaganda victory." All of which was true, she thought, albeit far from the whole truth. But she didn't want to upset Connolly and risk losing his co-operation.

Mulryan looked relieved. "That's good to hear," he said with a smile. "Your brother will never be forgotten in Ireland."

101

"I hope not," she said, restraining a sudden unexpected impulse to reach out and slap the man.

When he was gone, she sat back with the rest of her drink and lit another cigarette. Michael had raised the same subject with her the other night, dismissing her doubts at first, then backing off when she refused to do the same. Was he under orders to shadow her journalistic endeavors? And when he had passed on his doubts at the direction she was taking, had Connolly decided that rather than risk her confidence in Michael, he would send someone else to confront her?

Was she suffering from paranoia? Or was she just attracted to duplicitous men?

At least she hadn't fallen in love with this one.

The following morning she took the train to Limerick. After a night of rain, the countryside was green as a rebel flag, but the small clusters of Irish boys on almost every platform were off to fight for the Union Jack.

She ate a quick lunch in the Limerick Station buffet, then took a hansom into the center. There were a few fine buildings, but her first impression was of narrow streets and widespread poverty, and the romance of the name, which she'd carried with her since childhood, seemed sadly inappropriate. After taking a room on Rutland Street, she asked directions from the desk clerk and walked down a succession of increasingly shabby streets to the home in question.

The two young Kierans — Breslin had grown up in Limerick, Coakley in Belfast — had suffered mixed fortunes on that August night. After blowing up their bridge, they had lost themselves in the Hampshire lanes and run into an off-duty constable roused by the general alarm. Under the pretext of showing them the way, this bright young spark had successfully lured them into a local army depot, where they'd quickly been overpowered.

This twosome had waited six months for their execution, because the British had been reluctant to execute boys who were only seventeen. Eighteen was fine, and once they'd had their birthdays in Brixton, both Kierans had been taken to the Tower and shot.

The Breslin family was a large one, and Caitlin found mother, father, two of the sisters, and one of four brothers at home when she arrived. The sprawling, sparsely furnished house was off an alley close by the Shannon, a framed photograph of young

Kieran hanging in the narrow hallway.

Finding out who Caitlin was, they swiftly ushered her inside their cloak of collective grief. Over tea in the parlor, they didn't so much discuss the events that had killed their son and brother as unpack the historical context like a worn and much-loved map.

They knew for an absolute fact that an Irishman's killing of an Englishman could never be classed as murder. A thousand years of English occupation had made that so. Their Kieran and her Colm had not faced justice; they had just been struck down by a greater power. One day things would change, and then both boys would be remembered for the sacrifice they'd made.

They grieved for their loss but were proud of it, too, and assumed that Caitlin must feel the same.

After leaving the house, Caitlin walked out to the middle of the long stone bridge and stood there staring at the river and the rising hills beyond. Was that how she felt? Was that how she wanted to feel?

No, was the answer that came to mind.

Why was that? She felt Ireland's oppression as keenly as anyone; she wanted the English out. And the brother she loved had tried to speed them on their way.

So why did she feel no pride?

She was back in Dublin by lunchtime next day and spent the afternoon moving from café to café on both sides of the Liffey, asking people what they knew of the August events and what, if anything, they thought the perpetrators had achieved. Her Irish-American accent cushioned her against hostility, but many of the people she approached were clearly suspicious, and several politely refused to express an opinion. The views she did succeed in eliciting proved as diverse as Maeve had said they would be. Colm and his partners were "the best of the best," "traitors pure and simple," "a hapless bunch of idjits." All of which offered confirmation of the one thing Caitlin knew she had learned — that the loyalties of Irishmen and -women were a lot less straightforward than she'd been led to believe.

She and Michael had agreed to meet that evening, and it was only the prospect of spending time alone that persuaded her not to cancel. At dinner he asked her how the story was going and quickly changed the subject when she insisted on talking of something else. "Tell me more about America," he said, and she did her best to oblige.

He would be better off there, she thought at one point — what was there for him here but either years of frustration or the sort of exploit that had killed her brother?

Upstairs in her room, it was easier to pretend than refuse, but she knew it was the last time. Once he'd gone to sleep, she lay there thinking about the other men she'd "known," as their old family priest would have put it. There hadn't been that many, despite what others had sometimes seemed to think. After the first experience with poor Danny Cryer, she'd always enjoyed the sex, which she knew from talks with other women was far from usually the case. But until Jack McColl came along, the physical pleasure was all she'd felt, because nothing else had been shared. He'd been different — or at least she thought so at the time. He had given every sign of enjoying who she was.

Ironic, she thought, that the one man who seemed to truly like her was the one who had betrayed her.

Let it go, she told herself, or you'll never get to sleep. Work was what mattered now; a love life would have to wait.

She was not done with Dublin — Maeve and Cumann na mBan were definitely unfinished business — but she needed a rest from Ireland and its problems. Tomorrow she would take the train to Belfast and visit the other Kieran's family. And then she would have a long think about how she intended fulfilling Colm's request. There was no hurry with this story, and there were others more urgent to tell. From Belfast she would take a boat to Glasgow, where working-class women had initiated and then organized the rent strikes now sweeping the city.

Michael was gone when Caitlin woke up next morning, so she left a letter at the desk, saying she hoped to be in touch sometime in the next few weeks. It was raining outside on Grafton Street and still raining four hours later when she stepped off the train in Belfast. The Coakleys' neighborhood seemed even more down-at-heel than the Breslins' had done, and it did nothing to brighten her mood. Neither did the ensuing encounter with Kieran Coakley's parents. She was invited into their neat little parlor, but that was the extent of the welcome. Maureen and William Coakley were angry about their only child's death, angry with him and just about everyone else, including Caitlin herself.

"So your brother was one of them?" Maureen Coakley asked aggressively.

At first Caitlin thought they were doubting her bona fides. "Yes, his name was Colm. He was executed in April."

"Did he ever realize what a mistake he had made?"

"No, he —" She stopped herself. "Is that what your son thought?" she asked.

"He was seventeen!" Maureen almost shouted.

"Like that idiot Kieran Breslin," her husband added. "How old was your brother?" he asked.

"Twenty," she said.

"Old enough to know better," William Coakley said. "But it's the leaders I blame. They find these young men, fill their heads with romantic nonsense, and they send them off to die. More martyrs to sing their stupid songs about. And for what this time? Home Rule's been promised once the war ends — after all the centuries of oppression they never stop talking about, couldn't they wait another couple of years?"

"And what are you going to write?" his wife asked Caitlin. "Something to glorify them? Something to fool their families into thinking that their loss was actually worthwhile? How can you live with yourself?"

Caitlin took a deep breath. "I was hoping

to write the truth," she said, more mildly than she felt.

William grunted his disdain. "The only truth is that they threw their lives away. Or worse, someone else threw their lives away for them. But no one wants to read that. That's not considered patriotic these days. You can't write songs about that."

Caitlin got to her feet. "I'm sorry you feel that way," she said. "I didn't know your son. He may have thought he was doing something brave and selfless —"

"Oh, he did," the boy's father said bitterly.

"He was seventeen," Maureen Coakley repeated, this time more in sadness than anger.

On the bus back into the city center, Caitlin stared dully out the window at the passing Falls Road. The Coakleys had shaken and angered her, but she also felt strangely grateful to them for showing her so clearly the other side of the Breslins' coin.

She might not be proud of Colm, but she was not the least bit ashamed of him either.

She didn't linger in Belfast, boarding that night's boat to Greenock. Taking a turn on deck before retiring to her cabin, she watched a clearing sky unveil the stars as the lights of Carrickfergus fell away to port.

The words of the song came unbidden to mind, heavy with the sorrow of an Irish exile, all his memories of childhood happiness passed on "like the melting snow." And as she leaned against the deck rail, she pictured Colm as an eight-year-old, earnestly naming each bird in the Prospect Park aviary and turning to her for approbation. And then she finally gave herself over to weeping, for her brother and Ireland and all the tragic absurdity of their fatal collision.

Arriving in Glasgow, Caitlin set out to find Sylvia's friend Helen Stephens. As a Scottish suffragette, Helen had endured several prison sentences and force-feedings in both London and Glasgow. When the movement had split over support for the war, Stephens, like Sylvia, had joined the peace camp, but in recent months a citywide battle over housing and rents had come to dominate the political landscape and her work at the headquarters of the Women's Housing Association currently took up most of her time. This was the address that Sylvia had given Caitlin, and she arrived on the doorstep just as Helen was on her way out.

"You've come at the perfect moment," the Scottish woman told her. She was slim, probably in her mid-thirties, with big blue eyes and red hair constrained in a bun. Her clothes, in various shades of blue and gray, were what Aunt Orla would have called "sensible." She was on her way over to Govan to see Mary Barbour — "You must have heard of her?"

"I know the name, but not much else." The Scottish accent reminded Caitlin of Jack, something she supposed she would have to get used to.

Helen nodded. "Like I said — the perfect moment. Leave your suitcase behind my desk — it'll be quite safe there — and come with me."

As the tram took them across the Clyde, Stephens filled her in on the situation. "Times have been tough here. Food prices have been shooting up, and with men away in France there's so many homes with less coming in. The moment the war started, they moved all the construction workers who hadn't joined up into the munitions factories. You wouldn't believe how quickly that created a housing shortage, though I expect you could guess how quick the landlords were to seize their chance. When people like that start squawking 'We're all in it together,' you know you're in trouble. With all those prospective tenants to spare, they could raise the rents, evict all who couldn't pay, and have no trouble finding replacements.

"And then along came Mrs. McHugh," Helen said with a smile. "The straw that broke the camel's back. She had a wounded husband at home, two sons still in France, and five other children to feed. But she couldn't pay the new rent — she was a pound short! — so the landlord told her she was being evicted.

"She refused to accept it, and her neighbors backed her up. When the landlord's agent arrived, there were three hundred women waiting for him, and they chased him all the way back to his office and broke most of his windows. Even the London papers carried the story, and the landlords have been lying low ever since. They must be hoping the protests will blow themselves out, but there's no sign of that happening yet. Mary Barbour's the leader down here in Govan."

They got off the tram in a busy shopping thoroughfare but were soon in a maze of tenement streets. Many buildings had a strip of paper affixed to the lower sash window, proclaiming a simple message — WE ARE NOT REMOVING.

"We printed thousands," Helen told Caitlin.

As they turned the next corner, Caitlin saw a woman sitting in a straight-backed chair. She was busy knitting, but a shiny brass trumpet leaned up against the wall beside her.

"She's standing sentry," Helen explained. "If a factor or a bailiff appears, she'll sound the alarm."

Caitlin noticed that the chair was placed to offer a view of three streets.

Mary Barbour's house was halfway down this one. It was cramped and sparsely furnished, but inviting just the same, reminding Caitlin of her poorer school friends' homes in Brooklyn. Mary was a woman of around forty, with short dark hair; her face, stern and slightly masculine in repose, became almost beautiful when she smiled. Once Helen had introduced them and tea had been made, Mary readily agreed to answer questions. She was pleased by the attention, Caitlin thought, but not for egotistical reasons. This was a woman with a mission. Or several of them.

Mary quickly passed over her country childhood and early adult life in Govan and seemed more interested in the future than the rent strikes she had helped to start.

"There's one thing we have to thank the war for," she said. "Women are finding their power at last. We've taken on the men's jobs and done them every bit as well. It took us a while to get organized, but now that we have, we're winning. At least for the moment."

Caitlin asked her how she felt about the war.

"I think it's an abomination. The women who say that opponents of the war are letting down their boys at the front . . . well, I understand their feelings, but I can't agree with them. The war is the real betrayal. If the —"

She was interrupted by a sudden trumpet blast outside. Helen and Mary were through the door in seconds, Caitlin close behind them. Up and down the street, women were pouring out of the tenements. One held a bag of flour and a spoon, while two others were wielding wet towels.

The objects of their wrath appeared around the corner — a man in an ill-fitting suit and a blue-uniformed constable. The former was clutching a paper in one hand; seeing the women rushing toward him, he pushed out the palm of the other, as if to ward them off.

It didn't work. A phalanx wall of women

advanced upon him, their chant of "We are not removing" growing ever louder.

A missile of some sort flew over the intruders' heads. The policeman raised his hand, opened his mouth, and then had second thoughts. The two men edged backward and finally turned to run, pursued by two young girls throwing pieces of coal. Caitlin noticed that once the men had outrun them, the girls took care to gather up the fuel. "Won't they be back with more men?" she asked Helen.

It was one of Mary's neighbors who answered. "There's many more women in Glasgow than there are shites in blue."

Later that night, on the train heading south, Caitlin felt better than she had in months. The women she'd met in Glasgow — and her conversation with Maeve in Dublin — had reminded her of her own purpose, of who she'd been a year ago, of who she could be again.

Back in London there was more good news. Caitlin already knew that the *New York Chronicle*'s European correspondent had gone down with the *Lusitania;* now she discovered that the paper wanted her to replace him. An accompanying letter from Mary Keaton, her successor as woman's correspondent at the *Times* and a friend of the *Chronicle*'s editor, explained the offer. On the one hand, it seemed that neither of the latter paper's first choices had been eager to brave the Atlantic; on the other, Mary had recommended her to the *Chronicle*, offering Caitlin's past work on the city desk, along with her recent freelance submissions and private letters, as proof of her zeal and intelligence.

After reading through both letters twice, Caitlin stared out the hotel window at the mews below, where an old man was lovingly polishing an automobile, occasionally pausing to admire his work. Now she could go to see Kollontai, she thought. Now she could go to Berlin and ask the German socialists what the hell they thought they were doing. Now she could go to the trenches — preferably those of both sides — and find out what the soldiers were really thinking.

In her last letter, Aunt Orla had worried that Colm's fate might consume his sister, too.

It won't, Caitlin silently reassured her aunt and herself. I won't let it.

HARRY & SONS

The bungalow was halfway down a pleasant, tree-lined avenue in Ballygunge. The tip-off — badly spelled on a fragment of yesterday evening's paper — had been shoved through the local police station's letter box at some point in the night, and the constable sent to check it out was lying in a pool of his own blood a few feet short of the bungalow's door. The men wanted for the Chartered Bank van robbery were presumably still inside.

It was getting dark, McColl noticed. If a breakout was contemplated, it would have to be at night. Not that darkness would help whoever was inside — there were almost a hundred armed police in the cordon that surrounded them.

He wondered how many of them there were. Five men had taken part in the robbery, but there was no way of knowing how many were holed up in the building opposite. They'd ignored Tindall's megaphone appeal to surrender and offered no reply to one unauthorized shot through a window. McColl might have doubted they were there at all if it weren't for the occasional twitch of a curtain. That and the lifeless body in front of the door, which was rapidly merging into the shadows.

He and Tindall were in sole possession of the bungalow across the street, having sent its Indian owners to a place of greater safety. Everything in the large front room looked English — the furniture, the books, even the decorator's choice of color — but it still felt foreign. Was it the faint smell of Indian spices or something less tangible he didn't recognize? Looking around the darkening room, McColl knew that most Englishmen would see such cultural mimicry as a sign of the Raj's strength. So why did he feel the opposite?

A whistle screeched outside, followed first by the crack of a single shot, then a full-blooded fusillade. As McColl stepped toward the window, it exploded in front of him, showering him and Tindall with fragments of glass. Feeling as if he'd been stung by a hundred wasps, with blood coursing down one cheek, he took a second to realize that his eyes were still working and that three Indians were racing toward him, Mausers in hand.

The rifle fire was almost constant now, and two of the Indians were hit almost simultaneously, blood and brain erupting from their shattered skulls. The third man was only ten feet from the gaping window, eyes wide and straining every sinew, when McColl squeezed the Webley's trigger and put a bullet through his chest. The man stumbled to his knees, offered McColl a last triumphant sneer, and plunged face first into the bone-dry earth.

As their myriad cuts slowly healed over the next few weeks, McColl and Tindall watched the Jugantar campaign expand. There were several more dacoities in broad daylight, a judge and a senior policeman shot down by lone assassins at either end of Chowringhee Road and strong rumors that a number of prominent local businessmen had given Jugantar large sums of money rather than suffer a similar fate. The few men arrested proved as loquacious as the dead van robbers, and the search for an actual German connection in Calcutta seemed elusive as ever.

In mid-June the monsoon arrived. At first it felt like liberation, but soon McColl was remembering what old hands had told him in May, with that peculiar English delight in sharing bad news — that the rains would actually be worse. And they were right. The heat, which showed no sign of abating, was now accompanied by frequent downpours and levels of humidity that literally took the breath away. Half the people McColl met seemed sick in one way or another, and two-thirds were scratching some part of their anatomies. Eczema, impetigo, prickly heat — Calcutta seemed to be hosting an itching contest in which participation was compulsory. Insects loved such weather. First there were weeks of ubiquitous greenflies, then a plague of little black beetles that emitted a dreadful smell when crushed.

As their frustration grew, and rather to his own consternation, McColl found himself liking the locals less and less. On one hand, the general Indian disinclination to support the authorities' campaign against the terrorists made it hard to trust those he didn't already know, while on the other he found himself increasingly irritated by the syco-phancy of those supposedly on his side. After losing his temper with one perfectly amiable Indian constable, he realized he was in danger of becoming one of those Anglo-Indians whom he most despised, an irascible, arrogant bigot who thought India owed him a living and who these days expected every Indian to be as gung ho about beating the distant Hun as he was. For only the second time in his life — the first had been in South Africa — he found himself longing for home.

He was also beginning to doubt whether his own presence in Calcutta was doing anything useful for the war effort. Having set himself the task of finding the boatload of arms, he was now far from certain it still existed. Or indeed ever had. If such a shipment really was en route to Bengal, surely by now they'd have unearthed some proof that it was expected? Some days McColl found it hard to remember why he'd been so keen to join the Service and hard to credit his idiocy in putting that before her.

He transmitted his professional doubts to Cumming, who was predictably unsympathetic, responding to McColl's insistence that he wasn't really needed in Calcutta with claims that Tindall had reported the opposite. "This German arms shipment could threaten our whole position in Asia," his chief wrote from London, as if McColl needed reminding. It seemed he was stuck there until the wretched boat turned up.

And then, a week or so later, new intelligence arrived to bolster his chief's case. It now seemed that the shipment had left the Americas only a few days earlier and would probably take six weeks or more to reach the Bay of Bengal. Meeting to discuss their next step, McColl and Tindall agreed that six weeks would have seemed a decent stretch of time to find the recipients if they hadn't already been vainly searching for that many months. But they smiled as they said it — both men felt happier now that they were certain they weren't chasing shadows, imbued with fresh purpose now that they knew the clock was ticking against them.

With every known enemy under more or less constant surveillance, it was a friend who provided the lead they needed. McColl had met Partha Chaudhuri almost two years earlier, in a showroom on Bombay's Apollo Street. At that time McColl had still been one of Cumming's businessmen-spies, seeking out nuggets of intelligence while ostensibly hawking a luxury automobile around the globe. The Indian had admired the car, but not with a straightforward purchase in mind. He was a merchant from Calcutta and interested in starting an agency there for British and American manufacturers.

Their conversation had no commercial

consequences, but the two men had enjoyed each other's company, and Chaudhuri had insisted that McColl look him up if he were ever in Calcutta. Soon after his arrival in January, McColl had followed up on the invitation, partly for the pleasure of seeing the Indian again and partly because he felt an instinctive dislike of the social barrier dividing the British from their often reluctant hosts.

At two subsequent dinners, they had shared their enthusiasm for automobiles and cautiously sounded each other out on the war and its likely consequences. McColl had also been invited to Chaudhuri's home, an impressive two-story house on the country side of Ballygunge, where he had met the businessman's wife and two sons. After dinner, sharing a smoke on the moonlit veranda, he and Chaudhuri had felt sufficiently at ease with each other to risk the subject of politics. The Indian, it turned out, was an ardent nationalist but not a fan of Jugantar. A pacifist, he wanted nothing to do with violence or terror. He wanted the English to leave, but with the smiles of people who'd enjoyed their visit and perhaps even learned from their hosts.

Chaudhuri had been smiling himself that evening, yet there was only anxiety in the

Indian's eyes when McColl ran into him crossing the Great Eastern lobby one morning in mid-July. "Can you dine with me tonight?" the Indian asked.

"I'd be happy to. Where —"

"At Peliti's. I'll reserve a table for seven o'clock."

"All right."

"I must dash now," the Indian insisted.

As he watched him walk out through the hotel doors, McColl noticed Chaudhuri pause to scan the street before venturing onto the pavement. Something wasn't right.

That evening Chaudhuri was late, the first time McColl had ever known him be so. And when he did eventually arrive, he looked unusually flustered but declined McColl's invitation to explain. "Let's eat first," he said, looking round at their fellow patrons. "We can talk in the garden."

Over dinner — a particularly scrawny chicken — they settled for small talk, if discussing a global war could be so described. Both were eager to believe that things were going well but far from convinced by the official optimism that filled the newspapers. The Second Battle of Ypres, which had ended a month or so earlier, had confirmed a rather depressing pattern to engagements on the Western Front, in which one side attacked and gained a few miles and was then forced all the way back again. At the cost, what's more, of thousands of casualties.

Chaudhuri was pleased that an Indian soldier had been awarded the Victoria Cross after the initial Ypres battle, the first of his countrymen to be so honored, but he was appalled by the German use of poison gas. So was McColl, particularly since his brother had been on the receiving end. Jed had made light of it in his letter, preferring to emphasize the week's leave granted in consequence, but McColl had heard from other sufferers at second hand and guessed that his brother had been badly frightened. Both sides insisted that the other had been the first to use gas, and McColl's instinctive reaction was to hope that his side was telling the truth. But really it made no difference. Both would certainly use it now.

There was a constant drip of good news from the Gallipoli Peninsula near Constantinople, where the British had landed earlier that year, but try as they had, neither McColl nor Chaudhuri had found any supportive evidence for this optimism in the occasionally published maps of the fighting. Mesopotamia was the only place where any obvious progress was being made, and Chaudhuri was highly gratified that Indian troops formed the bulk of the army advancing up the Euphrates.

The most interesting event of the early summer, as far as McColl was concerned, was a zeppelin raid on London on the final day of May. The cost in lives had been infinitesimal when compared to the losses sustained on French battlefields, but it seemed to McColl — and Chaudhuri was quick to follow his thinking — that this was the future of war. The zeppelins could carry only a few small bombs and incendiary devices; like airplanes, they were used mainly for reconnaissance. But there was no reason that the latter in particular should not increase in size and carry a commensurate weight of bombs. Sooner or later man's conquest of the sky would transform the way he fought his wars.

Their discussion of these matters absorbed both men through dinner and might have been further pursued on the garden veranda had the matter on Chaudhuri's mind not been so pressing. "A young man came to see me yesterday," the Indian began. "At my office on Clive Street. He was well spoken, well dressed, and I would guess well educated. He told my secretary that his name was Maitra and that a firm in Jamshedpur with whom we do business had sent him to see me. But once he was in my office, he changed his story. He told me he represented an organization of patriots that needed funds for its struggle against the British."

"Which organization?" McColl asked.

"He was coy about that. 'One whose name you would instantly recognize,' he said to me. When I told him I'd only heard of Jugantar, that made him smile, so I presume that's whom he represents. Anyway, I said he was probably wasting his time with me, that I gave money only to causes I supported and that I was opposed to the use of violence that groups like Jugantar espouse."

He broke off as the waiter brought their glasses of port. Every other occupant of the long and crowded veranda was white, McColl noticed. Not to mention male. The smell of cigar smoke mingled with the usual outdoor whiff of shit.

"Anyway," Chaudhuri continued, "this young man smiled again and said that he and his people weren't asking for money — they were demanding it as their right. If the British could raise taxes to pay for their armies, so could Indian nationalists — if one were more legal than the other, that

127

was only because the British wrote the law. Those Indians who had grown rich enough to buy villas in Ballygunge had a moral duty to support those impoverished by British rule." Chaudhuri smiled wryly at that, as if recognizing the grain of truth contained within. "And of course he was telling me they knew where I lived."

"Did he name a sum?" McColl asked.

"Twenty thousand rupees."

McColl grunted his surprise.

"It is not so much. I could afford it. The money is not the problem."

"What is?"

"I am torn, as you say. Between my family's safety and my dislike of these people. I do not want my money to pay for murders."

"Of course not. So how did you answer him?"

"I said I would pay but that it would take me a few days to raise the cash. He seemed quite happy with that — I have a feeling I'm not the first rich man they've approached. We agreed that he'd come back on Friday." Chaudhuri took a sip of his tonic water and looked inquiringly at McColl, as if he'd just asked McColl a question.

"It doesn't sound like you need my advice," McColl said. "It sounds like you've made up your mind."

"I've come to you because I believe you work for the police. If you don't, then tell me now and we can go back to talking about airplanes."

McColl was surprised. "What makes you think so?" he asked somewhat stupidly. A simple yes or no would have done much better.

Chaudhuri looked apologetic. "I have told no one," he said quickly. "But in answer to your question . . . well, when you came to Bombay as a car salesman two years ago, you also met with a friend of mine named Vikram Khare — do you remember?"

"I do." Khare had been a friend of the Bombay-based Englishman whom Cumming suspected of selling Indian and Ceylonese harbor plans to a local German agent.

"Well, when Vikram and I realized that the Scotsman we both met in Bombay were one and the same man, we knew that you must be working for your government while you traveled with your automobile. A neat arrangement, we both thought, at least in peacetime. When war broke out and you turned up here without a car, I naturally assumed that your other job was taking up all your time. Was I wrong?"

McColl had to laugh. "No," he admitted. "But if you simply want this man arrested, you'd be better off going to the local police. I can give you —"

"No, you misunderstand," Chaudhuri interrupted him. "I intend to give these people what they want — I value my family too much to refuse. And I don't care if I never see the money again. But I would like to help end their campaign of terror. So I'm proposing that you and your people — whoever they are — arrange to follow this man when he leaves my office on Friday, and hopefully he will lead you to his partners in crime. All I ask — all I beg — is that you don't let yourselves be seen anywhere near the office and that you never let these people know that I had anything to do with their capture."

"I can promise you that," McColl said, with all the confidence he could feasibly muster. "Did you agree to a time on Friday?"

"No. He refused to."

"Not to worry. I can have watchers outside from when you open," McColl assured the Indian.

Chaudhuri shook his head. "I took a look from my window this afternoon, and anyone hanging around outside will be too obvious.

I think it would be better if you waited in our post room downstairs. Once this man leaves my office — which is on the second floor — I can tell you on the speaking tube that he's on his way out."

"That sounds like it would work," McColl agreed.

"And after that I think I shall take my family away for a while. Just in case. I promised my sons that one day I would take them to see America, and this sounds like a good time to do it."

By six in the morning on Friday, McColl was ensconced in the Chaudhuri & Sons office post room, feeling the day's first sweat on his forehead. He had noticed the absence of a fan straightaway on arrival, and his only hope of not drowning in perspiration was an early call from the extortioner. Even the mango tree he could see through the window seemed to be dripping with sweat, but this was of course an illusion — it was still engaged in shedding a night of copious rain.

The post room's staff had been given the day off, but McColl was not alone. He had considered keeping the business to himself — of late the suspicion had been growing that Jugantar had sources of information inside police headquarters — but following even a well-dressed Indian through Calcutta's streets was work for more than one, especially if the one was white. So the two brightest sepoys used in the Bhattacharyya surveillance were sitting there with him, both staring placidly into space and not mustering a drop of sweat between them. Their names were Sanjay and Mridul.

The other reasons for McColl's discomfort were the grease-paint covering his face and lower arms and the turban wound around his head. It wasn't a disguise that would fool a searching glance, but it was better than nothing, and the dhoti was actually a damn sight cooler than his usual shirt and trousers. Every now and then, he would catch one of the two Indians smiling at him and know exactly how strange he must look.

He tried to fill his mind with something other than impatience. He had had a letter from his mother the previous day, expressing her horror at Jed's getting gassed. It had been lovely to see him, she said, but he'd been keen to get back, "though heaven knows why." Jed was still coughing fit to burst and said "the brass could use him to keep the Germans awake at night."

She also wrote of rent strikes convulsing Glasgow, news that hadn't made the Indian papers. The strikes were all being run by

132

women, his mother said, "which somehow feels both wrong and right."

Those last words took McColl back to the first time he and Caitlin had made love. She had seduced him and been, in almost every way, more forward than he'd ever imagined a respectable woman could be, but the wrongness had felt so right.

He moved his chair out of the shifting sunlight's path. He had thought the pain of losing her would gradually diminish, but the opposite seemed to be happening. He had thought he would think of her less, but lately there was rarely an hour of the day from which she was absent. He sometimes felt that her near-constant presence in his waking mind was all that kept her out of his dreams.

He needed to draw a line under the affair, but how? He could write to her, he supposed — a letter to the Brooklyn address should find her eventually. She'd probably tear up the letter without reading it, but curiosity might give her pause, and she might reply. He felt in desperate need of a kinder good-bye; he couldn't bear the one he had, the picture of her face that morning, so angry and betrayed, so disappointed in how he'd behaved, in who he was.

What had he expected — a cheery fare-well?

The morning dragged by without any sign of the fund-raiser. In the office it grew hotter and hotter, and the air seemed palpably thinner, as if he were climbing a mountain. McColl worried that his makeup was running, but his companions assured him it wasn't.

When someone did rap on the door, it was only to herald the arrival of lunch — three enamel mugs brimming with chicken curry and a greasy Indian flatbread. McColl was happily spooning curry into his mouth with the right hand when pained looks from his companions reminded him that he was holding his bread with the forbidden left.

Soon after that, the rain descended, a few large drops turning in seconds to sheets of the stuff, removing the tree from view and drumming up a storm on someone's tin roof. It didn't last long, abating as swiftly as it had begun, as if one of the local gods had suddenly turned off a heavenly tap. The tree swam blearily back into view through the steam rising up from the ground.

McColl was noting his own nostalgia for freezing drizzle when the door swung open and Chaudhuri's secretary appeared. "The man is here!" he whispered excitedly before swinging it shut again.

It wouldn't take their quarry long to pick up his money. As one sepoy slipped out the back door — according to their plan, he would make his way round to the street — McColl opened the inner door by a quarter inch and applied an eye to the crack. He assumed he would hear the man's feet on the stairs, and only a few seconds later he did. The young Indian came into view, wearing a light-colored suit and a topee and carrying a furled umbrella. What better disguise, McColl thought, than that of an Indian aping his rulers?

He and Mridul hurried down the corridor, and McColl put his eye round the jamb. The young Indian was walking south toward Dalhousie Square on the near side of Clive Street; Sanjay was crossing the crowded street to shadow him from the far pavement. McColl set Mridul in motion down the near side, then hung slightly back himself, trying to keep his men and Chaudhuri's visitor in view. The two sepoys seemed bright lads, but if it came to a choice between losing their quarry and risking revealing themselves, they'd been told to opt for the former. This made their job a lot harder, but McColl was determined not to put Chaudhuri at risk.

A middle-aged European with a very red face was walking toward McColl, who remembered too late that a local would make every effort not to get in the white man's way. A heavy clash of shoulders sent the other man reeling, and as he hurried onward, McColl heard an outraged voice rising shrilly behind him. He cursed himself for not staying in character — there he was worrying about the sepoys giving the game away and he might well have done so himself. For several seconds he half expected the shrilling of a police whistle, which seemed bound to spook their quarry. But none sounded above the usual bedlam — if the insulted party had sought official assistance, he had apparently done so in vain.

Reaching Dalhousie Square, the object of their attentions walked down to the tram stop in front of the post office and climbed aboard a stationary car. The first sepoy followed him on, and so, a few seconds later, did the third. With his makeup unlikely to survive such close scrutiny, McColl decided not to follow suit. After watching the tram squeal round the curve and pass in front of the Bengal Secretariat building, he hailed a passing tonga and told the driver to follow. "Yes, sahib," the driver said, after only a quick look back.

They moved up Bow Bazaar Street, the tonga recovering lost ground each time the tram stopped. After alighting in the Sealdah station forecourt, their Indian strolled north up the little Municipal Railway line, looking somewhat incongruous in his smart clothes. The young man was almost bouncing along, McColl noticed — he was clearly pleased with himself.

The tracks ran alongside the Upper Circular Road, and the sepoys, now walking together, kept to the shadows of the shops lining the western side. McColl paid off his driver and followed, but as the crowds on the pavement thinned, he reasoned that three pursuers might be one too many and allowed the distance between himself and the others to slowly widen. They were almost out of the city, so there couldn't be far to go.

Fifteen minutes later one of the sepoys appeared in the distance, walking back toward him.

"Where is he?" McColl asked when they met.

"He went into a shop," the sepoy told him. "Harry & Sons — it sells bicycles and gramophone records."

A few minutes later, the two of them strolled past the premises in question. After sending Sanjay back, McColl lingered as long as he dared in the near vicinity, calculating angles of sight. Narrow alleys separated the two-story building that housed the shop from its neighbors, but the street in front was reasonably wide and the yard at back was spacious and almost empty. As far as he could tell, both front and back entrances would be visible from the roof of the government waterworks, which stood behind a high brick wall around a hundred yards away.

Risking one quick glance up at the shop's upper story, he saw a line of shuttered windows and smoke belching out of a makeshift chimney — someone was cooking something. It had the air of a fortress, he thought, perhaps a tad fancifully. Or perhaps not. But one thing was certain — this wasn't the sort of place that a young man like Chaudhuri's visitor would normally call home.

Early next morning McColl and Tindall arrived at the waterworks manager's home, a sprawling white villa in Alipur surrounded by towering palms. Alan Huckerby was already up, as the sounds of shouting made abundantly clear. A friend had seen the manager's wife flirting outrageously with her tennis partner, and he absolutely insisted that she end their association — he didn't give a damn that they were only one game away from the trophy.

His wife screamed back that he could drown himself in the Hooghly for all she cared.

As McColl and Tindall approached the open doorway, the servants standing on either side suddenly became aware of them. The glee vanished from their faces, leaving only the usual mask.

"Please tell the sahib that he has visitors," Tindall told the one who looked like the bearer.

The two of them waited on the veranda, staring out at the rain-soaked lawn and enjoying the lack of heat, until Huckerby joined them. Tindall knew the man slightly and introduced McColl. "We have a favor to ask you," he told the manager before explaining their need to use his works as an observation platform. Huckerby didn't even ask who or what it was they planned to observe — he was, McColl noticed, still trembling with anger. "As long as your chaps don't get in our way," was the manager's only comment. He offered one resentful glance back at the house, then ushered them over to the bougainvillea-draped garage, where a gleaming Fiat Brevetti was lurking.

Automobiles were Huckerby's not-so-secret passion, and McColl's ability to more than hold his own when it came to discussing them proved useful that morning, in both raising the manager's spirits and ingratiating himself. After picking up Sanjay and Mridul at their barracks, they all drove to the waterworks, where Huckerby helped them find a perfect spot for surveillance, on a platform behind a louvered opening high up inside the main building. No one could enter or exit Harry & Sons by either door without being visible to the naked eye, let alone to men with field glasses. The latter, McColl knew, should not be used after a certain point in the afternoon, when those under surveillance might notice a reflected glint from the setting sun.

As he watched, two Indians emerged from the shop's back door, chatting away and carrying tin cups. They walked across to the outside well, raised a bucket and filled the cups, then picked their spots, lifted their dhotis, and squatted down for their morning crap. One was the man they'd followed from Chaudhuri's offices.

Was one of these two men Jatin Mukherjee? The only photograph in the authorities' possession had been taken almost ten years earlier, when the future Jugantar leader hadn't been more than sixteen. Scanning the two faces through the field glasses, McColl decided that either or neither might belong to the man they most wanted. Which wasn't much of a help.

As the two men washed themselves, McColl caught the distant strains of "Ave Maria" on the morning breeze. It was Caruso's record from the year before, playing, presumably, on one of Harry & Sons' gramophones.

After making sure that Huckerby realized how important it was that word of the surveillance didn't leak out — Tindall suggested he tell his employees that the government was counting the traffic on the Upper Circular Road — the two of them left Sanjay with the glasses and hailed a tonga to take them back to police headquarters. A meeting of the liaison group was scheduled for that morning.

"I know Huckerby," was Cunningham's first response to McColl's account of the day's events. "He once told me he preferred automobiles to horses. But I can't see the point of waiting around. Why not just bag the bastards? We don't want another Bhattacharyya fiasco."

McColl shook his head. "We were only guessing about Bhattacharyya. We *know* that this man belongs to one of the movements — he told Chaudhuri so."

"He wouldn't be the first to wrap up simple theft in a rebel flag."

"He wouldn't, but Chaudhuri was convinced by this one, and so am I." Though *why* he was so sure was hard to put into words. How could he explain to Cunningham that the young man's walk and his double-sided wardrobe reeked of rebellion rather than crime? He didn't try. "If we take them in, they'll just clam up. We agreed that unless they get their hands on a lot more guns, these people can't really hurt us. It's their German contact we need to find, and he won't visit them in prison."

"A week," Cunningham offered grudgingly. "But a joint operation. Your two men and two of mine on six-hour shifts. Reporting to us each day."

"Fair enough," McColl said — when the week was up, he could always ask for more. Cunningham didn't have the temperament for this sort of work, he thought. They both knew that conspiracies were a maze of connections and that the only sure way of finding the people who mattered most was to track every last lead down, but the Section Five man lacked the requisite patience.

The rest of the day was spent in finding and briefing a posse of sepoys and creating a roster of duties. The operation was officially scheduled to start the next morning, but the waterworks observation post would be manned overnight. McColl went back for another look after dark, joining Sanjay's partner, Mridul, at the louvered opening. An invisible moon behind them flooded their vista with pale light, and the four men in the backyard were further lit by the fire they had started. Every now and then a murmur of voices carried on the breeze, and McColl was tempted to see if he could get himself within earshot. One thing that dissuaded him was the near certainty that some local would see him skulking by and raise the alarm. The other was the glint of a gun he thought he saw in one of the talkers' hands.

Caitlin spent the early summer in London, settling into her new job as the *New York Chronicle*'s European correspondent. The paper's only other employee on this side of the Atlantic was its military correspondent in France, a retired soldier from Virginia whose dispatches suggested — to Caitlin at least — a pronounced preference for Parisian delights over those of the front. His articles were long on strategy and short on the actual fighting, great for armchair generals back home but somewhat inadequate when it came to informing America what this particular war was really like. This, Caitlin rapidly discovered, could be better researched in the pubs and cafés close to the London termini where recovered soldiers gathered for a final fry-up before returning to France.

Her first piece on the subject drew predictable objections from "the man on the spot" that she was poaching his territory, but their editor back home was sufficiently shocked and impressed by what she had written to ignore his protests. Although no one spelled it out, she felt she'd been given a green light to write about anything she considered relevant. Which was wonderful. She had every intention of being a real European correspondent, unlike some of her peers in London who seemed to think their remit ended at Dover and most of whom relied on the same agency reports for anything that happened on the dangerous side of the Channel.

Caitlin hadn't yet broached the matter of a visit to the fighting front with the authorities or with her editor, neither of whom were likely to view such a prospect with favor. But it seemed to her that she was ideally suited for such a task — as a woman and as an American. Any fool could pass on official statistics, whether of the dead or the meager yards their sacrifice had won, but someone neutral was more likely to see through patriotic delusions and a woman more likely to uncover the real experience behind all the male posturing.

In the meantime there was no shortage of worthwhile stories in London. One of the first pieces she sent home was on Sylvia

Pankhurst's work in the East End, which war conditions had rendered even more vital. Caitlin's new friend was still campaigning for the woman's vote, but that was the least of her efforts. Sylvia was spearheading the opposition to the new National Register, which everyone knew was the first step on the road to conscription, and the new Defence of the Realm Act, which seriously curtailed civil liberties. Besides banning a wide variety of activities, from building bonfires to feeding birds with bread crumbs, the latter dealt a crushing blow to freedom of speech. According to the new act, no person was allowed "by word of mouth or in writing" to "spread reports likely to cause disaffection or alarm among any of His Majesty's forces or among the civilian population."

Sylvia was also looking to the future, imagining an East End with centrally heated homes and nursery schools for all children, while starting up a "cost price" restaurant for those struggling to pay wartime's rising food prices. She always had new stories of families in trouble, some feeding themselves on boiled bread, others starving for days at a stretch.

It was in the restaurant that Caitlin occasionally managed to get her friend alone for a few minutes. With the war a year old, women were doing so much more, Sylvia told her one day. They were driving buses, running libraries, even joining the police force. And even if they were all sent back home once the fighting was over, the experience would stay with them.

She said this matter-of-factly, without her usual bubbling enthusiasm, and within a few minutes seemed close to tears. Later, talking to Sylvia's American friend and colleague Zelie Emerson, Caitlin asked when Sylvia had last taken a holiday — or even had a few hours' rest.

"I've no idea," Zelie said, adding that it wasn't just work that was wearing her down. "Keir Hardie is probably dying."

"Oh," Caitlin said. She knew that Sylvia had been in a relationship with Britain's most famous socialist but thought it had long been over. She said as much.

"It is and it isn't," Zelie said. "No one really knows what they mean to each other. Not even Sylvia, I sometimes think. But he's still important to her. She'll be devastated when he dies."

But when Caitlin next saw her friend, she seemed in better spirits and full of hope for the future. When Caitlin said she was probably going to Norway and Germany, Sylvia seemed truly excited for her and wistfully lamented that she was too busy to come along, too. Arranging the trip took much longer than Caitlin expected. The war had made travel between countries more difficult, even for neutrals. Suspicion was rife, and all the countries she planned to visit insisted on knowing her reasons for doing so before they would even consider letting her across their thresholds. In July she spent an inordinate number of hours in embassy reception rooms waiting to present her credentials and make her explanations, only, in many cases, to be told that these had to be assessed in the home country.

But finally, in the first week of August, she had all the permits she needed, at least to reach Berlin. Early on the eighth, a taxi carried her and a bulging suitcase across a sunlit but still-sleeping London and disgorged them both outside King's Cross. With an hour to wait for her Newcastle train, she ate breakfast in the buffet and watched a stream of Indian soldiers march past on the platform outside. In their puttees and turbans, they looked a strange amalgam of East and West, exotic and somehow sad.

She bought newspapers for the train and a copy of the popular *Woman's Weekly*. She was done with the former by the time they reached Hitchin. The battle news might be important, but the way they wrote it both angered and bored her. It was full of names — of towns, villages, hamlets — that she hadn't heard before and never would again. After reading the reports, the only thing she knew about these places was that space in their graveyards was now at a premium.

She had heard of Warsaw, which the Germans had just taken from the Russians, but no one seemed interested in whether the Poles felt liberated or conquered anew. And the report of more landings in the Dardanelles just filled her with rage — even her landlady in Clapham knew that that campaign was dead in the water.

The *Woman's Weekly* was more informative, though not always by design. There were several recipes for gooseberries, which would allow their adoptees to hold apples in reserve for the winter months, and an advertisement from Nestlé urging people to send tins of the firm's milk to the soldiers at the front. "I'm doing my bit, save me from milkless tea," the tagline read. The idea of sending the milk themselves had apparently not occurred to Nestlé, but such profiteering was becoming common. While many were dying, some were raking it in.

Mrs. Marryat's advice page was highly entertaining. There was a long discussion as to whether a woman should insist on marrying her betrothed when the latter had lost a limb and offered to set her free. It was the man's decision to make, Mrs. Marryat decided. She was inclined to allow a hostess to pass the vegetables if no maid was at hand, reluctantly revealed that there was no treatment by which thick ankles could be quickly reduced, and offered a detailed prescription for whitening one's neck. All of which seemed much more interesting than the news that the Battle of Biskupice had ended, wherever Biskupice might be.

The train reached Newcastle soon after four that afternoon, and, much to Caitlin's surprise, her ship left on time a few hours later. It was flying the Norwegian flag, but most of the passengers seemed anxious — no one had forgotten the *Lusitania*. She slept better than she expected and emerged on deck the following morning to a reassuringly empty sea. A couple of British destroyers were sighted later that day, but that was all, and after another peaceful night they docked in a still-sleeping Bergen.

The journey to Christiania was beautiful. The train climbed slowly away from the coast, up onto a broken plateau, where isolated farms sat deep in the valleys and huge forested slopes reared up toward the summer snow line. Apart from a short break for lunch in the busy restaurant car, Caitlin spent the whole day soaking up the views and felt almost cheated when darkness finally fell.

It was almost midnight when the train arrived, and the search for a vacant hotel room took another exhausting hour. When she woke the following morning, breakfast was already over, and she had to search out a meal on Christiania's strange-feeling streets. It was only later, sitting with her coffee and staring out the café window, that she realized what made them seem so different — the absence of uniforms.

The address for Alexandra Kollontai that Sylvia had given her was a hotel in Holmenkollen, a village in the wooded hills that overlooked the city. She took a horse-drawn cab, not knowing what to expect. The Russian might be away, or she might be busy and less than enthralled at having to deal with a stranger. In the event, she couldn't have hoped for a warmer welcome.

"This is wonderful," Kollontai said after reading the letter from Sylvia. "I've just been invited to speak in America. You can tell me what to expect!"

She spoken English well, albeit with a heavy Russian accent. According to Sylvia, she was over forty, but she certainly didn't look it. The long, dark hair framed a beautiful face, and the sprightly way she moved suggested someone half that age.

She insisted on making tea. "And you must stay here with me while you're in Christiania."

While Kollontai was in the kitchen, Caitlin cast her eyes around the room, taking in ramshackle towers of books and a desk wildly strewn with papers. After she'd answered the Russian's questions about Sylvia and the situation in England, Caitlin asked what her host was working on.

"Oh, several things. I've been working on a book on society and motherhood for years now, but it should be finished soon. And there's a pamphlet called *Who Needs War?* which I sent to a comrade in Switzerland, who sent it back covered in critical comments and exclamation marks, just the way my old headmaster used to do with my essays."

"You must have regretted sending it."

Kollontai laughed. "Oh, no, most of the comments were sensible enough, and Lenin's a kind enough headmaster. Have you heard of him?"

"I've heard the name, but that's about all."

"He's the leader of the Bolsheviks. They're the rougher half of the old Social Democrat Party — most of the leaders are in exile."

"And they're against the war?"

"Oh, yes. Though not all war, as Lenin was at pains to point out. Civil wars and wars of liberation are another matter."

"And you agree with that?" Caitlin asked. Talking to Kollontai, she was becoming increasingly aware of how little she knew about European politics.

"His arguments are convincing. The fact that so many socialists supported the war turned me into a pacifist for a while, but I think I'm over it now."

"Ah, I wanted to ask you about that. Not for publication," Caitlin added quickly. "For myself. Why do *you* think so many abandoned their principles when the time came?"

Kollontai smiled. "I'm writing a piece for *Communist* magazine on exactly that."

"Communist?"

"It's the Bolshevik magazine. I have become a Bolshevik," Kollontai added simply. "They're the only Russian party that truly opposes this war."

"So why?" Caitlin asked.

"I was actually there in the Reichstag

when they voted the war credits," Kollontai said. She shook her head, as if still unable to believe what had happened. "I was horrified. It felt like everything was lost. My German friends — Klara Zetkin, Rosa Luxemburg — they were as shocked as I was, but, having said that, I should add that it wasn't really a surprise to them. The German Party has been moving to the right for years, and when the moment came, I don't think most of the leaders had any doubts which way they should jump. If they opposed the war, that wouldn't have stopped it — not in Germany at least — so why put twenty years of social advance at risk with a mere gesture? It was easier to point out that fighting czarist Russia was a progressive thing to do. And let's not forget personal ambition. All of a sudden, the establishment was treating the party leaders as equals, asking for their opinions, offering them important jobs. A lot of heads were turned."

"I think it was the same in England," Caitlin said, remembering Sylvia's sad account of her mother's and sister's embrace of the war.

"How about America?" Kollontai asked. "Will I find support for an antiwar position, or are people just taking sides?"

Caitlin shrugged. "I don't think there's

any appetite for joining the war," she said carefully, "but I haven't been home since it started, so I'm not best qualified to say. I can put you in touch with people in New York and San Francisco whom you might find interesting. Women mostly." She named several and described their areas of concern. "They're all feminists of some sort, and some would call themselves socialists."

Kollontai looked doubtful. "They sound — forgive me for being blunt, but I get the impression that these are bourgeois . . . middle-class women, idealists of one kind or another."

"I suppose they are. Most American socialists are men, and most of them think that women's issues can be safely left on the back burner until after the revolution."

Kollontai smiled. "It is the same in Russia. The feminists think they can win equality in a capitalist society, but socialist women know that capitalism makes equality impossible, because all relationships under capitalism are property relations. Including those between men and women."

Caitlin looked at her. "I can see that in theory, but in practice? Are you saying that all relationships between men and women are doomed from the start?"

The Russian woman shook her head. "It

is not as simple as that. More working-class women are going to work, becoming economically independent, taking more control over their own lives. And some middle-class women are beginning to understand the psychology of their dependence on men and the ways in which they themselves have connived at their submission. Some women from both classes have said, 'Enough, I'd rather spend long stretches of my life alone than imprison myself in a relationship which can never be equal.'

"But all that said, most women have no desire to live like nuns. Here, let me read you something . . ." She walked over to her desk and searched through a pile of paper for the appropriate sheet. "I hate quoting myself, but I was pleased with this section — it says exactly what I meant it to say, and a friend translated it into English." She cleared her throat. " 'But when the wave of passion sweeps over her, she does not renounce the brilliant smile of life, she does not hypocritically wrap herself up in a faded cloak of female virtue. No, she holds out her hand to her chosen one and goes away for several weeks to drink from the cup of love's joy, however deep it is, and to satisfy herself. When the cup is empty, she throws it away without regret and bitterness. And

156

goes back to work.' "

"That is good," Caitlin agreed, wondering whether she was capable of living and loving like that.

"The future will be better, but we have to live in the present," Kollontai said. "I have had a husband and several lovers — I have one now. He's in Sweden at the moment, and I'm looking forward to his return. He's a kind man, and we think a lot alike, but if we're still together two years from now, I shall be surprised. Because no matter how enlightened the man is, he's been brought up to see men and women differently, and the progressive man's desire for an equal partner will always be at war with his need for her to be feminine and all that he thinks being feminine entails — the modesty and the spirituality and the submissiveness, whether in love or sex or argument or anything else. We are both trapped in his preconceptions, and he cannot accept our independence. Or, more often than not, satisfy us physically. I think most women feel this, but they tell themselves they've chosen the wrong man and try another. They don't realize that every relationship is corrupted, to a greater or lesser degree, by the kind of world they're living in."

"I'm not entirely convinced," Caitlin said.

McColl might have deceived and betrayed her, but he had certainly satisfied her physically and shown no obvious inclination to subvert her independence. Or at least that was what she'd thought before the betrayal came to light. "It seems too mechanical to me. I mean, I accept the fact that economics determines a lot, including the way men and women have come to see each other. I'm just not sure that it determines everything. The world seems much richer than that, somehow. Its possibilities, I mean."

"Ah," Kollontai said, a gleam in her eye. "Let's talk about that."

And they did, exploring their differences and agreements for several hours, until even the Norwegian daylight had begun to fade and the chances of finding a cab had just about disappeared. "There's a spare room and bed," Kollontai announced, "and we can send for your luggage in the morning."

They sealed the deal with a schnapps, giggled their way through the production of an omelet, and had another glass for luck. McColl had been hovering in the back of Caitlin's mind throughout their conversation, and now she found herself spilling out the story of their relationship.

Kollontai's response was brutally clear: "You're still in love with him!"

Caitlin was quick — too quick, she realized — to deny it. "No I'm not. How could I be?"

Kollontai smiled and shook her head. "These things have a natural span. Yours got interrupted in the middle. Your mind's said good-bye, but your heart has unfinished business."

"How the hell could it ever get finished?" Caitlin exclaimed.

"I don't know," Kollontai answered placidly. "Maybe you just need to talk it through with him."

Caitlin threw up her arms. "Even if that seemed a good idea, I have no idea where he is." She wasn't sure which she found more upsetting — not knowing where he was or caring that she didn't.

"That does make things difficult," Kollontai admitted. "What is the British Okhrana called?"

"God only knows. In cheap novels it's usually the Secret Service."

"Do you know where their headquarters is?"

"I haven't a clue," Caitlin said, though of course she knew where he lived. Or *had* lived a year ago. He might have moved since then, might be dead. For all she knew, he had volunteered that August and died in

159

France that fall. She thought she would have felt something if he had, but that was probably just sentimental nonsense. There'd been no sudden constriction of her heart at the moment her brother died.

Caitlin was Kollontai's guest for the next four days. The two women walked each morning in the sun-dappled woods above the hotel and usually ate a large bowl of *sodd* — a mutton, potato, and carrot soup — in the nearby village before returning for an afternoon's work. While Kollontai put the final touches to her magnum opus, Caitlin read through those sections that had already been roughly translated. She found much to agree with in the Russian's writing and much to discuss in the evenings that followed. She hadn't felt so stimulated, so engaged, since her days in New York City as a young journalist. Kollontai was trying — successfully, it seemed to Caitlin — to weave a coherent political program out of those three issues that felt most important to them both: the exploitation of the poor, the oppression of women, the slaughter now under way on so many battlefields. It seemed so simple, yet it encompassed the world. Lying awake one night, Caitlin found herself feeling sorry for her dead brother and for all the others who allowed their political dreams to be circumscribed by borders.

Kollontai had several contacts in Berlin she thought Caitlin should talk to, and as the German frontier guards were likely to go through any written material she was carrying, Caitlin spent an hour memorizing the names and addresses. The Russian also urged her to attend an antiwar conference due to take place in Switzerland early in September and promised to send a letter of introduction to the organizing committee before she herself took ship for America. When the two of them finally parted company at the Christiania railway station, Caitlin felt that she'd found a new friend. One she might never see again, given the state of the world, but no less important for that. As the train carried her south into Sweden, she started work on an article she hoped would encourage her fellow Americans to attend one of the meetings on Kollontai's upcoming tour.

It was late evening by the time the train reached Halsingborg, and as her ferry chugged across the Skagerrak, the summer sun was sinking behind what a male passenger insisted was Hamlet's castle. "To be or not to be?" he asked Caitlin, with a smile he no doubt considered seductive.

"Not to be," she told him coldly.

Another train took her down the coast to Copenhagen and a dingy hotel almost next to the station. She was hoping to interview the suffragette leaders who had won Denmark's women the right to vote earlier that year — Sylvia had given her two names and addresses — but all of the next day and most of the one that followed were eaten up by long waits at the American legation and the German consulate. By the time her transit passes and visa were finally issued, there were only hours to spare before her departure, and a frantic ride in a highly expensive taxi failed to find either woman at home. Arriving at the station, she had barely set foot on the train when the guard blew his whistle. When it reached the small port of Gedser just before midnight, she found the one small hotel already full and was forced to spend the night on a very hard bench in the departure lounge, surrounded by her luggage.

The twice-weekly sailing left at seven, the sun already high in the sky, the Baltic almost flat in the warm, windless air.

In Copenhagen she'd been offered a choice of two routes. One was overland, took twelve hours longer, and involved a transit of the Kiel Canal crossing in which passengers were held at gunpoint to prevent them from raising the lowered window shutters and spying on the German Navy. So Caitlin had chosen the sea crossing, which she only now discovered involved a passage liberally strewn with mines. Several male passengers mounted a permanent watch in the bow, and their cries of alarm whenever a piece of driftwood bobbed into view kept everyone's nerves on edge. When the houses of Warnemünde finally loomed into view and the two-hour crossing drew to its end, Caitlin breathed a heartfelt sigh of relief.

It had turned into a beautiful summer day. Standing in the queue outside the long wooden shed that housed those supervising the entry formalities, she went over the questions she wanted to ask in Germany. Why had the German socialists signed on to the war? Kollontai's explanation had been convincing, but Caitlin wanted to hear it firsthand from those most closely involved. Did they still think they'd done the right thing, and were the German people still behind their government and army? Were the ordinary soldiers still behind their leaders, or had the reality of war turned their initial enthusiasm into something else — quiet determination perhaps, or something much less positive? And lastly, on a more personal note, what reward had the Germans promised Colm and his friends in return for their sabotage mission? She knew the name of the Deutsches Heer major who had overseen their explosives training on the farm outside Dublin, and if the man hadn't died in the last seven months, she meant to seek him out.

It was a fine list of questions, she thought, one any journalist would love to sink her teeth into.

Two sentries in Landwehr red and blue flanked the entrance to the shed, and the queuers shuffled in between them, clutching their luggage and papers. Inside, a row of uniformed officials sat behind two long tables, examining the visas and passing the suitcases on for searching. Caitlin had been waiting only a few moments when she noticed another, less obvious group of officials. These men, all in plainclothes, were stationed all around the hall, lurking and staring and accosting any traveler they deemed suspicious.

She didn't feel worried. The names and addresses that could give her away were all in her head, and there was nothing in her suitcase to suggest she was anything other than what she claimed to be — a journalist from a neutral country seeking a German perspective on the war.

Her official was courteous enough, if short on smiles. He was handing back her papers when another voice asked in perfect English for her intended address in Germany.

It was one of the plainclothes officials, a short, sharp-nosed man with a serious five-o'clock shadow.

She resisted the temptation to question his credentials and told him she was going to Berlin.

"Where in Berlin?" he persisted.

"At the best hotel I can find," she said. "Can you recommend one?"

Ignoring her question, he barked out a few words in German, causing the official behind the table to hastily scrawl something across her entry form. "You will report to the central police station by tomorrow evening," he told her, reverting to English. "With the address at which you are staying."

"Where is the central police station?" she asked, but his attention had moved to the piece of paper that the soldier searching her suitcase had just brought back. It was Sylvia's letter of introduction to the two Danish suffragette leaders, which Caitlin had neglected to jettison. How could she have been so careless?

He read it through, folded it up, and placed it in his pocket. "No documents in English are allowed into Germany," he said brusquely, and turned away.

Caitlin felt relieved, though on reflection she could think of no good reason to be so. The letter was hardly incriminating, unless being a friend of Sylvia Pankhurst had become a crime. The connection could encourage the German authorities to watch her more closely than they might have done otherwise, but protesting now was pointless and might make matters worse. She would just have to learn to be more careful.

She picked up the returned suitcase, gave the official her brightest smile, and walked on through to the outside world, where the Berlin train was waiting.

The scheduled journey time was just over four hours, but one of these was spent in the Rostock station, where connecting services were awaited and passengers invited to take lunch in a capacious platform buffet. Caitlin wasn't that hungry but took care to see what remained on offer after a year of blockade. There was certainly a lack of variety but no sign of an overall shortage — starving Germany into submission would clearly take a while yet.

As she left the buffet a train pulled in on the adjoining platform and began to disgorge its passengers. Those in the rear coaches were all soldiers, in varying states of health. While some almost ran for the exits and others strode along nonchalantly behind them, the final third hobbled slowly past, supporting themselves with sticks and canes. Curiosity aroused, Caitlin followed in their wake, out through the booking hall and onto the forecourt, where a large crowd had gathered. Women were embracing their husbands, boyfriends, sons, and brothers, wide-eyed children regarding their returning fathers. Her eyes were drawn to one couple — a limping soldier with a blood-stained bandage around his head and a young blond woman in a cornflower blue dress, both with tears streaming down their cheeks as they clung to each other.

Watching them, Caitlin found herself stricken by an overwhelming sense of loss and for several moments couldn't think why. But then she realized — it was envy. Were Kollontai's few weeks of joy the most she could ever hope for?

The thought rolled around in her mind as the train steamed south across the North German plain and was only banished by the scene awaiting her in Berlin's Stettin Station. This time around, the next train over was preparing to leave, the soldiers leaning out the windows talking to relatives and friends on the platform below. They all seemed to be shouting to make themselves heard; there were many brave smiles and a brittleness in the air that seemed not too far from hysteria. How many would come back minus a limb? How many would come back at all?

A whistle sounded, the engine billowed steam, and everyone seemed to be shrieking at once. As the train pulled clear of the platform and the waving arms disappeared in the dusk, those left behind walked back up the platform, heads bowed and silent, all animation drained from their faces.

Except for one woman who simply stood there gazing after the vanished train, quietly sobbing her heart out.

The Abominable Huns, as the British had taken to calling them. Hold the presses, Caitlin thought — Germans are human, too!

WAITING FOR BAGCHI

The ten days of surveillance that followed proved less productive than McColl had hoped. Four different men were spotted in the backyard at one time or another, but never all at once. In the first three days, two went out for food, one to visit a backstreet printer, one, ever so smartly dressed, to sit with a young woman and her chaperone on a Ballygunge veranda. In the next three, one man visited a house in Black Town, another a photographer's studio across the river in Howrah, a third Thacker, Spink and Co.'s bookshop on Government Place, where he purchased Jack London's *Iron Heel.*

A stream of customers visited Harry & Sons. Some went in with bicycles clearly in need of repair, some came out with gramophone records, but none stayed long and none, as far as their subsequent shadows discovered, were anything other than honest customers.

Meanwhile the printer and the photographer, the houses in Ballygunge and Black Town, were all being watched around the clock, causing Cunningham to sarcastically wonder whether additional sepoys should be brought back from France. As the week progressed, McColl's pleas for patience fell on increasingly deaf ears, particularly once Sanjay and Mridul had reported that their cover story was no longer cutting much ice among the Indian staff at the waterworks. Sooner or later someone would talk.

It was on the Friday afternoon that things began coming to a head. Tindall, McColl, and Cunningham were going through the latest reports when one of the former's Indian officers arrived with news: the young men at Harry & Sons were feeding a pile of papers onto a bonfire in the shop's backyard.

"That does it!" Cunningham said triumphantly. "They must know they're being watched. We'll have to go in now."

"If they thought they were being watched, they'd be burning them inside," McColl insisted. He felt far from certain that this was the right course to take.

"True," Tindall agreed, "but there has to be a reason they're burning them. Whether or not they're aware of our interest, it looks

170

like they're preparing to leave. I think Alex is right on this one — we have to arrest them."

McColl reluctantly gave way. "But it'll take some arranging — I don't think this lot will give up without a fight. And it'll be dark in a couple of hours."

Tindall considered. "There are four, right?"

"Including the store owner. Who does seem to be involved."

"And how many guns have been seen?"

"Just the one, and I wasn't sure it was a gun. But my guess is that all of them are armed."

"With Mausers from Rodda & Company," Cunningham muttered.

"Most likely," Tindall agreed. "But whatever the truth of it, we have to assume they all have guns and act accordingly. I don't want any of my men killed."

"Or any of the enemy, if we can help it," McColl said emphatically. "Dead men won't tell us where the German guns are coming ashore."

"I realize that," Tindall said, wiping his brow with his handkerchief.

"Well, it's your show," McColl assured him, looking to Cunningham for support. Tindall had more experience than either of them at this sort of thing.

Cunningham grunted his agreement.

"All right," Tindall said after a few moments' thought. "We'll surround the place and invite them to surrender. He went off to drum up the necessary troops, leaving McColl and Cunningham to snatch a quick meal at the Great Eastern before darkness arrived with the necessary cloak and they could take a tonga to the back entrance of the waterworks, close by the smelly canal. Sanjay and Mridul were both on the observation platform, the former peering out, the latter fast asleep. McColl and Cunningham had a turn at the louvered opening, taking in the now-familiar sight of four young men sitting round a fire.

There was something almost touching about them, McColl thought. Their youthful eagerness, their obvious camaraderie. They could have been students discussing a forthcoming game or debating the way to a better world. And tomorrow they would all be in prison. All those still alive.

The evening passed, the sounds of the city subsiding and splitting, until the occasional shout in the distance felt like an invader. In the surrounding streets, the yellow glimmers of candles and kerosene lamps winked out one by one, until the glow of the still-burning bonfire felt like the center of the world. The sky was cloudless, a near-full moon rising above the fields to the east.

Tindall arrived soon after eleven, having done the rounds of the various units now lurking nearby. He had fifty men in position, he told McColl and Cunningham. Most had modern rifles, and the unit leaders knew what was expected of them. Once the ring was tightened in the morning, the terrorists would quickly realize that they had no hope and throw in the towel.

The three of them bunked down in Huckerby's spacious office, leaving Mridul on watch upstairs. But after a fruitless half hour spent trying to get to sleep, McColl abandoned the effort and joined the Indian at the observation post. It was past midnight, but there were still two men sitting by the fire, watching the flames and occasionally exchanging a remark. They didn't look like men set on leaving, and McColl found himself wondering whether he should have fought harder against this operation. Perhaps it wasn't too late. Should he wake Tindall and try to convince him? There was plenty of time to move the police and soldiers back out.

He had almost decided to do so when an Indian appeared in the street below. The man was neither walking nor running, looked, indeed, as if he were trying to run without drawing attention to the fact. His head was turning from side to side, as if he didn't know which way an expected attack would come from.

It was too dark to make out the face, but there was something familiar about the figure. Something in the way he moved, perhaps.

It was Bhattacharyya.

McColl's first reaction was to curse his own stupidity. The second was a feeling of admiration, the third a quiet sense of triumph. They had him.

As McColl expected, he halted outside the shop, glanced up and down the street, then turned to the door. He rapped on it quietly, clearly intent on not waking the neighborhood, and then again, much louder, as if he no longer cared. The men by the fire heard the second rap, and one went through the shop to let the visitor in. A few seconds later, both reappeared in the yard. Words were exchanged, and three sets of eyes turned toward McColl in the waterworks tower. The brightest of the three reached for the water jug and doused the fire.

"They'll be leaving now," McColl said. "Send up the white flare," he told Mridul.

As he half tumbled down the stairs to Huckerby's office, the huge waterworks windows suddenly filled with dazzling light. Tindall was already on his feet, Cunningham rubbing his eyes. McColl quickly explained what had happened and left them to put on their boots.

The constables camped out in the waterworks yard were already jogging through the gate, on their way to line the street that ran from east to west a few blocks south of Harry & Sons. A second group stationed in the gasworks would be doing the same a similar distance to the north; a third would be leaving its derelict warehouse base and blocking the way to the west; a fourth was already covering the canal to the east. With the moon now high in a still-cloudless sky, the escapers couldn't hope for much help from the night.

He could hardly have hoped for better circumstances, but McColl couldn't shake a gnawing pessimism. These people had eluded the best efforts of the DCI for years — why should tonight be any different?

Since Tindall had not seen fit to give him a specific task, McColl felt free to do whatever seemed appropriate. He was following the last of the constables across the Upper Circular Road, intent on joining their cordon, when he saw two figures traversing the street in the other direction. As they disappeared between two of the shops that lined the eastern side, another flare exploded above him — red this time, Tindall's prearranged signal that men were leaving from both front and rear.

The escapees should be picked up by the troops behind the canal, but there was no point in leaving matters to chance. McColl started running down the side of the waterworks' northern wall, thinking to intercept them before they reached the water, and had a fleeting glimpse of the two men down another long alley as they ran a parallel course. A few people were ducking their heads out of doorways, awakened by the fireworks display overhead, but they pulled them inside again when guns opened up somewhere behind McColl. Those escaping out the back must have run into the cordon.

A few seconds later, he reached the canal, a stretch of stagnant water some twenty feet wide between sloping banks about six feet high. On the far side, where McColl had expected men with rifles, a moonlit scrubland dotted with palms stretched emptily into the distance.

A hundred yards to his left, one man was

already waist-deep in the water, the other scrambling down the bank to join him.

More shots echoed in the distance.

A worn path ran along the top of the bank, and McColl hurried along it, shouting at the two men to stop. They responded by opening fire with their pistols, the bullets whining harmlessly past. This lack of accuracy was comforting, but McColl's return fire was no more precise, both men ducking their heads long after the bullets had passed. Then, while one continued wading toward the eastern bank, the other dropped further into the water to make himself less of a target and fired twice more.

His partner was now scrambling up the far bank. McColl took careful aim but missed again, and after one poignant look at his half-submerged friend, his target headed off across the scrubland.

There was shouting in the distance and signs of movement farther up the canal, but the man was getting away. Conscious that he had only three bullets left, McColl steadied his arm and fired once more, but the man seemed to stumble at the worst possible moment. Running on, he was soon no more than a fading shape.

The man in the canal had let off another two shots in the meantime, with a similar lack of accuracy. He was now clambering out of the water on McColl's side and raising his arms in surrender as soon as he physically could. It was Bhattacharyya.

The two of them walked toward each other. McColl knew he should shoot this Indian — if not to kill him at least to restrict his mobility — and leave himself free to pursue the partner. He couldn't do it.

"I ran out of ammunition," Bhattacharyya volunteered as he drew nearer.

A minute later a group of Tindall's constables appeared on the far side of the canal, and McColl, without much hope, sent them off in pursuit. The reason for their earlier absence, he later discovered, was alarmingly simple. Ordered to line the canal, they had simply guarded the bridges. What kind of man, one appalled constable asked McColl, would deliberately place his body in a channel full of shit?

Over breakfast at the Great Eastern, McColl heard the unmistakable sound of distant cannons and assumed that some dignitary was visiting the city. Arriving at Tindall's office for a postmortem of the previous night's events, he found that he'd been misled. According to Cunningham, some idiot army officer, noticing that it was August 4, had decided to mark a full year of war with a twenty-one-gun salute across the Hooghly. Using live shells. Two houseboats had been sunk, and two children were missing, presumed drowned.

The governor, worried that the police might make a bad situation worse, had insisted that Tindall take charge, leaving McColl and Cunningham to review events without him.

The picture, still fuzzy at 2:00 A.M., was now clear enough. Of the five men known to have been staying at Harry & Sons, two were dead, two still at large, and one — Bhattacharyya — in custody. Two of the three men who had clambered over the back wall had been shot dead in the alleys beyond, but the other had vanished from view and was probably hiding somewhere in Black Town. The man who had escaped from McColl had eluded the subsequent search of the surrounding countryside; two constables, seeing movement in the distance, had shot and badly wounded one of their own.

Harry & Sons had been searched in the immediate aftermath and again a few hours later with the help of natural light. The shop had yielded little, just three tags attached to the handlebars of bicycles left for repair, each bearing a single name with no accompanying address. The four terrorists had been sleeping on camp beds in two of the upstairs rooms, their clothes — both traditional and Western — were as neatly hung as their mothers would have wished. McColl went through every pocket in search of a telltale laundry, train, or library ticket but found none. The only other personal effects were books, and these yielded no helpful markings; the opening pages of one volume, which might have held the owner's name in ink and imprint, had been assiduously ripped out and probably thrown on the fire. The enemy was proving himself a worthy adversary.

All they had was Bhattacharyya, and he, having offered his life to ensure a comrade's escape, seemed unlikely to spill any beans.

There were still the printer and the photographer, who now could be questioned without fear of raising an alarm, and Harry's neighbors, one or more of whom might have seen something revealing over the last few weeks. Whether they would share such information with the police was a moot point. McColl was not hopeful.

Neither was Cunningham, but the Five man's disappointment was mitigated by self-vindication. "If we'd arrested them straightaway as I suggested, we'd have four in the bag now rather than one."

"You don't know that," Tindall objected, but only halfheartedly.

He was right, McColl thought, but then everyone was on occasion. "Why don't you bring the printer and the photographer in?" he suggested. "I'll get back to the shop and make sure Tindall's men are asking the right questions."

As his tonga rattled down Bow Bazaar Street, McColl thought the looks turned his way seemed more than usually hostile. The news of the cannon-fire deaths had presumably spread by now. The fool who'd ordered it should be court-martialed but would probably receive nothing more than a few words of admonition. Perhaps Jugantar would send him a letter of thanks for boosting their recruitment.

There wasn't much sign of the Raj's popularity on Upper Circular Road that morning. Four officers had spent the last few hours knocking on doors, a pair working either side of the dusty street, and though they seemed proficient enough to McColl, none of the residents had told them anything useful.

McColl went back to Clive Street for lunch, then checked out Cunningham's progress with the printer and the photographer. The latter was a dead end — the terrorist had been booking the man to take pictures at a friend's upcoming wedding. The printer was still refusing to talk but was almost certainly guilty of churning out pamphlets and posters for proscribed political groups. Cunningham guessed he would eventually admit to the dubious customers but then deny all knowledge of names or addresses.

McColl made his way back to Harry & Sons, where he and Tindall's men had agreed to meet before paying their evening calls. The four policemen were out in the yard when he arrived, sitting on the same chairs that the Jugantar boys had occupied. It crossed McColl's mind that these four were about the same age as the terrorists; the only difference, he thought with a sinking heart, was that his lads, though nice enough, were probably less intelligent.

There was no point starting much before seven, and while they were waiting in the gathering darkness, there was a hammering on the front door. Hoping against hope that it might be another terrorist who didn't know that his comrades had been arrested — a German courier would really make his day — McColl stationed men on either side of the building and went to answer the door.

Opening it, he found himself face-to-face with a Bengali boy of about fifteen. The boy jumped when he saw a white man and jumped again when armed Indian police appeared around both corners of the shop. "Who are you?" he blurted out. "Where is the bicycle repairman?"

At McColl's gesture the police hustled the boy into the shop and closed the door.

"What's your name?" McColl asked.

"Subrala, sahib. But it's my father's name on the bicycle." He was looking around as he spoke. "That's it over there. My father's name is Narayan."

McColl remembered that name on a tag.

"But it hasn't been mended," the boy said disappointedly. "The chain is still loose."

McColl sighed. He could think of no reason not to let the boy take his father's bicycle. Subrala was still looking round, eyes full of surprise. "Where is everything?" he asked. "Have they gone away?"

"Why would you think that?" McColl asked him.

The boy shrugged. "It was so full in here — you could hardly move for all the gramophones and boxes of records. And there must have been twenty bicycles."

After the boy had gone, McColl gathered

the police officers together and told them what he'd learned. "Shifting that much stuff would have taken several carts," he said. "Someone must have seen them."

And several people had. But the three carts they remembered, which had stood outside the shop for a whole day and night the week before, had not borne any identification. Which ruled out the state railway and the more prestigious moving firms, but not much else. It was only toward the end of the evening that a Bengali from two houses down told them something useful. Arriving home for lunch one day, he had seen the movers loading their carts, and, leaving an hour later, he had noticed the same two men chatting to the owner of the next-door *chaikhana.*

McColl and one of the officers revisited the closed and boarded teahouse and eventually persuaded the frightened woman inside to open the door. Her husband was whom they wanted, she almost wailed. And he had gone away, leaving her to cope with everything. He had spoken to the movers, but he hadn't said anything to her. He never did.

McColl asked when he'd be back.

"Three weeks," was the depressing reply. He'd gone to visit his brother in Bombay.

Their names were Asok and Amarnath Bagchi, and no, she didn't have the brother's address.

McColl apologized for frightening her and said they would return to interview her husband.

It was something, he thought as they walked back across the street. There seemed a fair chance that the man would have asked where his talking companions were from, and finding the movers might set them on the terrorists' trail once again. Something, but not much. By the time he came back, the trail would be cold, if anything in Calcutta could be so described.

BERLIN CORRESPONDENTS

Berlin felt much like London, the streets crowded with automobiles, the pavements and cafés with men in uniform. The main difference was that German soldiers seemed incapable of marching in silence — they were always bellowing out a song, even at six in the morning.

As Caitlin ate breakfast the following day, a smiling young American approached her table and introduced himself as "Jack Slaney, a third — now a quarter — of our great American press in Berlin. The other half is over there," he added, pointing out two middle-aged men in suits who were sharing a table on the far side of the room.

Over coffee he answered her practical questions.

Was there any scrutiny of outgoing copy, and if so, was it censored?

Yes and not yet, he told her, the latter because neither he nor his colleagues had pushed any criticisms to an unacceptable level, and the Germans were still intent on bending over backward to keep them and their country sweet.

Was there more than one way of dispatching copy if extra speed or discretion were required?

Yes to speed, but it was expensive; no to any hope of secrecy, unless she planned on setting up her own wireless station.

"Do they supply interpreters? I suppose you speak German." Her own lack of languages had worried Caitlin since she'd first left the States several years ago, but so far her only attempts at remedying the situation had been a few halfhearted hours with a French grammar during Colm's time in Brixton.

"I just about get along," Slaney told her, running a hand through his thick brown hair. "But yes, they'll give you an interpreter. When you see Gerhard Singer at the foreign ministry, he'll assign one to you. But don't make the mistake of thinking that he's only an interpreter. He'll also be reporting back on everything you say and do."

"Ah."

"Oh, they'll make an effort to start with, make sure you see their better side. As far as we're concerned, they're desperate for

187

good publicity, and if you write what they want you to write, you'll be the toast of Berlin. That said, they have no illusions that we'll ever join the war on their side, so they'll settle for what they consider an evenhanded approach, because that encourages American neutrality."

"What about our colleagues over there?" she asked, tipping her head toward the two older Americans.

Slaney rolled his eyes. "They're only interested in generals — Berlin's like heaven to them. They were so pro-German in the first few months of the war that their own editors took them to task. Now they just stick to reporting the battles."

"And you?" Caitlin asked him sweetly.

He grinned. "Oh, I'm a pragmatist. Truth if you can, a pregnant silence if you can't. And I give the Germans their due. They're not the fiends the English say they are, but they're not exactly victims either. The things they did in Belgium were pretty bad, but then think how the Belgians behaved in the Congo."

Caitlin smiled. "Well, I'm Irish, so I've no great love for the English."

"You should be sure to tell the Germans that," Slaney said, waving his empty cup at a passing waiter. "They'll cut you more slack."

"Mmm." She looked around the crowded room. Her first regrettable task after spending one exceedingly comfortable night upstairs was to find cheaper long-term accommodation. "Are you staying here?" she asked Slaney.

"God, no. I do a lot of my business in the bar — it's a good place to meet people, and it's convenient for most of the government offices — but it's way beyond my paper's means. I've got a room on Uhlandstrasse, close to the Ku'damm, on the other side of the park."

"How did you find them? How can I find one?"

"It's easy. Depressingly so — every dead soldier frees up a bed. I think there's one going free in my building. I'll ask the *Portierfrau* if you like."

That afternoon she had her first meeting with the government official responsible for liaisons with the foreign press. Gerhard Singer was about forty, with hair graying at the temples and a vaguely harassed expression — in his smart gray suit he could have passed for a Wall Street broker. His spacious second-floor office in one of the larger stone buildings on Wilhelmstrasse boasted a deep red Oriental carpet and vast expanses of highly polished wood.

Singer spoke near-perfect English and, as Slaney had intimated, seemed relieved that she spoke no German. An interpreter would be provided for officially arranged visits and for any she chose to arrange herself. A trip to see a prisoner-of-war camp had been scheduled for the very next day, and Singer was sure that she, like the other neutral correspondents, would be eager to see how enemy prisoners were being treated.

She would indeed, Caitlin said. She would also like to talk to as wide a cross section of German women as she could — particularly those who she presumed were now working in jobs previously done by men and those with husbands or sons at the front. She was eager to get a picture of how the nation as a whole was responding to the challenges of war.

Singer thought this a very worthwhile project. Misunderstandings arising out of ignorance could benefit neither country. "I have relations in the United States," he added. "In Des Moines, Iowa. Do you know it?"

"I'm afraid not," she told him, fighting off a vague memory that the train carrying her and McColl to Chicago had passed through the city.

"Well, America is big and has many people of German descent. We in the fatherland have a great affection for your country, and it pains us when disputes arise. The business of selling ammunition to Russia, for example — it has disappointed many Germans."

"I'm sure it has," Caitlin agreed diplomatically. It was the first she'd heard of it, which didn't say much for her preparatory research.

"We understand that the United States has close ties with the other English-speaking countries — all we ask is that Americans view this war dispassionately, objectively, that they don't mistake English propaganda for the truth."

"I'm an Irish-American," she told him. "I grew up distrusting English propaganda." His smile was almost ecstatic, so she decided to push her luck. "And of course I would like to visit the fighting front," she added matter-of-factly.

The smile vanished. "I doubt that would be possible for . . ." His voice dried up.

"A woman," she suggested.

"Well, yes. It is a dangerous place."

"There are female nurses working at the

front, are there not?"

"Some way behind the front, yes. But . . . I doubt that my superiors would be prepared to sanction such a visit. Imagine you were wounded or killed by a stray bullet or shell?"

"I wouldn't like that, of course. But neither would a male reporter."

"Yes, but . . . it's not the same, is it?"

"It should be."

"Of course, my dear. But the world we live in . . . Imagine the headlines!"

She could see his point but was disinclined to admit it. "It's hard to write about a war you haven't witnessed."

"I can see that. But . . . Leave it with me," he said abruptly.

"Of course."

"Singer's a smooth bastard," Slaney acknowledged the next morning as the two of them waited for a tram on the Ku'damm.

"Isn't he, though?" Caitlin agreed. She had taken the room above Slaney's in the house on Uhlandstrasse, and the two of them had just had breakfast together, sitting outside a sidewalk café. The large second-floor room had proved cheap and perfectly adequate, with a window overlooking the street and a distant view of the

Kaiser Wilhelm Memorial Church. The bed was harder than she liked but would probably do her good. There was a small table for the typewriter she had hired the previous afternoon from an office shop on the Ku'damm.

They were on their way to the Hotel Adlon, where Singer or one of his minions would be collecting the entire neutral press corps for the promised visit to the camp. It was another fine August day, the temperature in the seventies, and Caitlin was already regretting her agreement to Singer's request that she wear "modest clothes." He was clearly worried that a hint of bare female flesh might provoke a riot among the sex-starved prisoners.

The other correspondents — the two Americans, a Swede, a Spaniard, and an Argentinean — were already gathered on the pavement outside the Adlon, and while they all waited for the promised transport, her fellow countrymen introduced themselves with a mixture of courtesy and condescension that left her wanting to punch them both in the nose. They also announced that they were leaving next day for the East Prussian front and a possible audience with the mighty Hindenburg.

"Don't worry," Slaney muttered. "If they

do get to meet the great man, they'll ask him all the wrong questions."

Singer arrived with two automobiles, and the eight of them crammed themselves in with the drivers. The camp was just outside the city and clearly a work in progress. Rows of newly built wooden sheds stretched away to a distant line of trees; Caitlin counted thirty-three, and more were under construction. The one they entered was crowded but clean, and the prisoners — English, French, and Russian — seemed healthy enough under the circumstances. Allowed to sample one section's upcoming lunch, a beef-and-cabbage stew simmering in three giant cauldrons, the journalists had their expectations confounded. It didn't taste at all bad and certainly seemed nutritious.

Caitlin was pleasantly surprised, Slaney less so. "They wouldn't be bringing us out here if the prisoners were going to drop dead at our feet," he said flatly as they strolled down the hard-packed path between the sheds.

They passed a group of French prisoners, all of whom stared at her. More wistfully than lecherously, she thought. Perhaps they were thinking it might be years before they made love to a woman again.

She turned back to Slaney. "But have you

any evidence that other camps are worse?"

"No," he admitted.

"They are good at organizing things," she thought out loud. "They're so thorough."

"Tell that to the Belgians."

She gave him a look. "That's a low blow, isn't it?"

"Maybe. But think about it — when things go wrong for organized people, they tend to take it as a personal slight and react more violently than someone with lower expectations."

"Perhaps," she conceded as they strolled back toward the entrance gates. "And speaking of thorough, yesterday I had the distinct feeling I was being followed."

"You probably were, but I shouldn't take it personally. I think they follow everyone at some point or other. Most of the time, they accept that we're who we say we are, but every now and then some bright spark in an office decides that one of us might be a spy and needs investigating. So they follow him — or in your case her — for a few hours or days, get reassured, and turn their attention to someone else. It's part of the game. Annoying but harmless."

And good to know, she thought. She would be well advised to "reassure" them before she tried to contact any of Kollontai's socialist friends. Give it a week at least. But there seemed no harm in talking to those socialists now supporting the war or in seeking out Colm's instructor.

Back at the Adlon, she took Singer aside. "My younger brother believed in a free Ireland," she began. "A year ago he was part of a sabotage operation in England that ended in failure. He was caught and executed."

"I'm sorry to hear that," Singer responded automatically. He was clearly surprised.

"Thank you. But the reason I'm telling you this is that he and his comrades were trained by a German major. Not a mercenary, an agent of your government. I have no wish to write about this," she hastened to add, "but I was very close to my brother, and if it is at all possible, I would like to meet this man. My brother admired him greatly, and talking to someone Colm worked with during his final months would mean a lot to me."

"What was the major's name?"

"Manfred Suhr."

"I will make inquiries," Singer promised. He had the air of someone who had just received a rather nice present.

She thanked him profusely and thought she might as well keep up the pressure. "I was hoping there'd be news of my trip to the front."

He shook his head. "No, no. Nothing as yet."

The following morning Caitlin visited the redbrick building on Dorotheenstrasse, just around the corner from the Adlon, which housed the War Academy. Slaney had suggested she might find it interesting, and she soon realized why. There were no students these days — the academy had been turned into an inquiry center for those whose relatives had gone to war. In the main hall, a circle of desks was manned by those too old to go; they took down the names and sent younger men from the local garrison scurrying off to consult the files within. It was, unsurprisingly, a place of polarized emotions, from the barely containable elation of those who received good news to the heart-rending grief of those whose world had just collapsed.

Caitlin stayed only a few minutes, the journalist in her glad she had come, the woman feeling like a voyeur.

She was only a few feet from the Adlon entrance when a man intercepted her. He had his back to the sun, and for a moment she didn't recognize him, but when he spoke, she knew who it was.

She had met Rainer von Schön on the *Manchuria,* the liner that had carried her and Jack McColl from Shanghai to San Francisco in February 1914. The German, a water engineer, had boarded the ship in Tokyo, but Jack had met him earlier in China. And despite spending most of the voyage in her cabin with Jack, she had gotten to know the German quite well. A decent man, who missed his wife and children, was proud of his country and its achievements, and yet regretted the growing militarism that the Kaiser and his generals seemed determined to promote.

Seeing him there, remembering those weeks, a flood of memories rose up inside her.

He was just as surprised to see her, but clearly pleased. He insisted on taking her for coffee and cake — "Berlin has the best in the world." As they walked down Unter den Linden, he plied her with questions. How long had she been in Berlin? Was she here as a journalist? Was she here on her own?

"If you're asking if I'm here with Jack McColl, the answer is no," she told him. "We parted company more than a year ago."

"Oh, I'm sorry to hear that. You

seemed . . . Sorry, I . . ."

"Don't worry about it. But I'd rather not talk about him."

He nodded. "Of course."

"How are your wife and children?"

"Oh, fine. Fine. They're in the country. With my wife's parents in Saxony. Berlin's no place for them at the moment."

"It seems remarkably normal to me."

They reached the junction with Friedrichstrasse, where von Schön decided that the Café Kranzler was too crowded and took her across to the facing Café Bauer. As he ordered for them both, she studied the vast room and its clientele. Both were getting on, but the former at least was still full of splendors, from the huge mural depicting Roman life to the largest newspaper display cases she had ever seen.

Von Schön saw what she was looking at. "Before the war they used to import eight hundred newspapers from all over Europe," he told her with obvious pride.

"Impressive," she murmured.

"And what about your family?" he asked, echoing her concern for his. "They lived in New York, I believe."

"I think they're all right. I haven't been back for a long time." She paused. "I lost my younger brother," she said. "He got involved in Irish politics, went to the home country, and fell in with a group of . . . well, I guess you'd call them revolutionaries. They contacted your government, which sent explosives and someone to instruct them in their use. Just after war broke out, they tried to blow up some railway bridges in England, and Colm was caught. He was shot in March," she added, and felt surprised by how calmly she could say it.

Von Schön looked shocked. "But that's terrible. For him and you, for your whole family. And you say my government was involved?"

"Oh, yes. One of your officials is trying to track down the instructor for me." She told him what she had told Singer.

"Well, I know some people in that line of work — it was impossible to avoid them working outside Germany. I shall also make inquiries."

"Thank you."

The coffees arrived, along with two pastries bursting with cream, and conversation ceased for the next few minutes.

"I assume you were not involved in any way yourself?" von Schön said after using a napkin to clear the cream from his mustache.

"I knew nothing of their plans until it was

200

too late."

"You must feel very bitter toward the English. Was that why you and Jack — I am sorry, you said you didn't . . ."

"That was part of it. But it's all over now." And no, she thought, she didn't feel any animosity toward the English people. How could she with a friend like Sylvia?

He smiled. "I am sorry. For you and for Ireland."

"Yes, well. Are you still working as a water engineer?"

"In a way. I can't really tell you, I'm afraid." He smiled. "Military secrets, you know. Let's just say that soldiers like to drink and wash."

"You must have been to the front."

"Several times."

"And how do you think the war is going? For Germany."

He shrugged. "We are fighting on enemy soil, which has to be better than fighting on our own."

"You see no possibility of a quick end to it all?"

"No. But then what do I know?"

There was something different about him, she thought. Something sadder. Perhaps he had lost a close friend.

He was calling for the check. "I regret I

must go — I have a meeting to attend. But I will inquire after your Major Suhr, and if you will give me your address, I will be in touch. Perhaps we could have dinner one evening?"

"I would like that." She gave him the address on Uhlandstrasse, and said he could also leave messages at the Adlon. "It was good to see you," she said as they parted. He gave a slight bow, gently clicked his heels, and walked off down Friedrichstrasse.

The weather remained seasonably hot and humid for the next week. Caitlin saw a lot of Jack Slaney and entertained herself for several days with the thought of seducing him — after all, the men in the prison camp were not the only ones who missed sex. But she soon found out that Slaney had a childhood sweetheart back in the States, whom he meant to marry and to whom he was touchingly faithful. She liked him too much to put him in the way of temptation.

So work it was. Fortunately, Gerhard Singer proved an efficient provider of copy material. There were trips to General Staff headquarters, to a munitions factory, and to schools for both infants and adolescents; meetings were arranged with representatives of predominantly female organizations rang-ing from a sewing club to a nurses' trade union. And she was also allowed to take her interpreter out onto the streets and into the cafés, where she could sample opinions about the war and the peace that hopefully lay beyond it.

Few of those she talked to had any doubts that their country would emerge victorious — when had Germany ever been defeated? War was terrible, of course, but there was almost universal agreement that the government had had no choice. People were resigned to a long period of hardship, and many naturally feared for the lives of their fathers and sons at the front. In all this they were much like the English and the French, and no doubt the Russians and Turks. They all shared the same self-righteous resolve — they were right, and they would damn well see it through, no matter what it cost them. Which, as far as Caitlin was concerned, showed up the absurdity of the whole wretched business. If she could get that across to American readers, she might help build resistance to her country's involvement and save a few thousand lives.

As Slaney drunkenly remarked one evening, it seemed to him that the people of Alsace and Lorraine should decide who governed them, not those in faraway Berlin or Paris. And as for settling international disputes by holding vast shooting contests, you might as well just have a ball game, which would certainly be a lot less bloody and waste less time and money.

This was not a theory she shared with the two socialist members of the Reichstag whom Singer arranged for her to interview. Both men seemed thoroughly middle-class to her — their dress and affect seemed miles away from anything Caitlin associated with people intent on changing the world — but she tried her hardest not to prejudge them. Unfortunately, Kollontai's predictions of what they would argue proved all too accurate — that the German people would never have forgiven them, that they couldn't risk all the social advances, that fighting reactionary Russia could only be progressive. The phrases rolled out, phrases, Caitlin thought, that these men had used to convince themselves. She had come armed with a sheaf of quotes from earlier years and watched with interest as each man was irritated, annoyed, and finally angered by her refusal to offer absolution.

There was no mystery here. Germany's Social Democrats had welshed on their own beliefs for the most basic of reasons — fear and self-interest. In the lonelier hours of darkness, they probably knew as much themselves, but in daylight and company they just about managed to sustain the pretense.

Slaney's reaction, when she told him about the interviews, was predictable. Why would she expect *any* politician to sacrifice a career for principles?

But some had, she pointed out. Several of the people that Kollontai knew had refused to follow the general line and had set up an antiwar party of their own. Two — Rosa Luxemburg and Klara Zetkin — were now in prison, while Karl Liebknecht had been forcibly enlisted and was now serving on the Russian front.

Slaney had an answer to that: "Ah, but they've all written 'revolutionary' in the career box. They can't afford to abandon their principles."

This had infuriated her for some time, although she wasn't quite sure why. She supposed it was the glibness of his cynicism and the implied corollary that any journalist worth his or her salt needed to take a jaundiced view of anyone promoting a political line. She didn't want to go that far. Suspicious yes, but there had to be some room for hope.

■ ■ ■ ■

Singer had news when she saw him next. Major Suhr was in Turkey, he told her, doing much the same job as he'd done with her brother, and there was little prospect of his returning to Germany before the year was out. His wife, however, was willing to talk to Caitlin. "She was in Ireland with her husband," Singer said, as if anticipating a refusal. "And she did meet your brother."

Caitlin's interest was piqued. "I'd like to meet her."

The Suhrs lived in Wilmersdorf, in a rather grand-looking house that backed onto a park. According to Singer, Freya Suhr spoke English quite well, so Caitlin could afford to dispense with her usual interpreter. A maid opened the door and showed her through the house and out into the rear garden, where a pretty blonde not much older than Caitlin was sitting beneath a canopy umbrella.

She rose languidly to her feet and greeted Caitlin with a smile. "Please, have a seat. Emmi, coffee and cake."

"It's good of you to see me," Caitlin said, sitting down. With a vista of sunlit grass and trees and a happy chorus of birdsong, she needed only a whiff of hot dogs to conjure up a Prospect Park picnic. Which was enough to make anyone homesick. She took a deep breath. "I hear your husband's in Turkey."

Freya sighed. "But at least he will be safe, I think. Better teaching the Turks how to blow things up than doing it himself at the front." She raised a hand. "I'm sorry. You have lost a brother already. My . . . what is the word? Condolences?"

"That is the word."

"They were brave boys."

"You met them?"

"Only once. I complain about so many days in the city, and Manfred let me come with him one day, out to the farm where they stay. I remember two men with American accents, the big man named Brady and your brother, Colm. He liked to joke, I think, and Manfred tells me he is quick to learn."

That sounded too good to be true, Caitlin thought. Colm had always been all thumbs when it came to anything mechanical.

The maid arrived with the coffee and cakes, which would have tasted good in peacetime, let alone a year into England's blockade. In between mouthfuls Caitlin asked Freya Suhr how she saw women's role in the German war effort and received a predictable answer.

"To support our men, I suppose. My friends and I are all knitting gloves and socks for the soldiers." She smiled. "I'm afraid mine are not very good, but I will get better if the war continues. My little brother thinks the Russians will surrender before Christmas and that the English and French will not fight on without them."

"Is your brother in the army, too?"

"Yes, in East Prussia. So he knows how things are going there."

Caitlin paused. "I'm glad you have a younger brother," she began, "because you will know why I must ask this question. I want — I need — to know what my younger brother died for. The operation that he and his friends mounted was clearly intended to assist the German war effort, so I'm guessing that the German government had offered them some material support in return. Did your husband ever tell you what that was?"

Freya shook her head. "If there was anything like that, Manfred never told me. I think it is more a matter of a common enemy and friends doing what they can for each other. I am sure they are not forgotten here in Berlin, and that our government is doing what it can. There may be difficulties — the English rule the seas for now — but I am sure we are trying to help. We would be foolish not to, don't you think?"

"Yes," Caitlin agreed. Why did she have the feeling that that Freya Suhr had been thoroughly coached in what to say?

Walking back up the long Uhlandstrasse she asked herself what the German government might be trying to tell her. That they were actively helping the Irish republicans? Then why not make up some concrete quid pro quo for the original operation and give her the satisfaction of knowing that her brother had died for something real? There was only one reason she could think of — either that there had been something on offer or that something similar was happening now. Something they might have told a grieving sister but not a foreign journalist.

Which wasn't much help to her when it came to vindicating Colm's self-sacrifice, but she could hardly blame the Germans for that. If they had new plans to arm the Irish rebels, they wouldn't want the enemy forewarned.

A Hill by the
Burhabulang River

There was no letup in the enervating weather. If ever so slightly cooler, it was just as wet and twice as humid. As one old hand told McColl in the Bengal Club bar, the only thing to do in August was look forward to September, when the store catalogs arrived from England and people could start picking out the gifts they wanted for Christmas. The man was so enthused by the prospect that McColl refrained from pointing out that this year things were bound to be different.

In the days following the Harry & Sons fiasco, Tindall came down with a serious stomach bug, leaving no one to narrow a widening rift between his colleagues. Having already blamed McColl for leaving the raid too late, Cunningham now insisted that one of McColl's team must be leaking information to the terrorists. How else could he explain the arrival of the alarm raiser on the night in question? His own team, of course, was above suspicion.

They fell out further over Bhattacharyya. Before becoming ill, Tindall had given McColl first crack at the Bengali, who proved as obdurate as ever. After apologizing for lying at their earlier interviews, he announced that this time he would simply remain silent. And nothing McColl said over the next half hour succeeded in shifting the young Indian's resolve. Reduced to reading facial expressions, McColl thought he detected the glimmer of a smile when he asked whether Jatin Mukherjee had been among those living at Harry & Sons, but he had no way of knowing whether that meant yes or no. After two such sessions, he reluctantly passed the baton to Five, and the next time he saw Bhattacharyya's face, it was covered with bruises. Cunningham deflected McColl's anger with infuriating smugness, having apparently extracted information where his opponent had failed. When the information in question turned out to be false — the wealthy Indian whom Bhattacharyya had shopped turned out to be a friend of the governor — McColl felt a little smug himself, but the Bengali was the only victim. An enraged Cunningham had him placed in solitary confinement, ostensibly to wear him down, actually to punish his native impudence.

There were more spot checks at the stations. Two ships from Batavia were searched from keel to funnel after tip-offs that proved malicious. Several random raids in Black Town angered the locals to no useful end.

The search for the movers continued, but without a name or a destination it was like looking for a needle in an Indian dung pile. The firm in question had to be local, but there were hundreds to choose from, and most were unregistered. So where had the carts transported Harry's effects? The city, the suburbs, a nearby town? Had they taken them to a train or to one of the myriad wharves on the river? The gramophones might be in Burma by now, or halfway up the Khyber Pass.

There was no other choice but to wait. McColl was cheered by a letter from Jed, announcing a full recovery from the gas poisoning. It was "quite quiet" on the British section of the Western Front, his brother reported almost ruefully — Jed had always chafed at inactivity.

It wasn't so quiet on the various battlefields. Indeed, one of the local papers had recently estimated that five thousand soldiers were dying every day. If correct, that meant almost two million had perished already.

Toward the end of the week, McColl endured a long, hot train ride to Chittagong, where the local police had arrested a possible German spy. The man claimed he was a Swedish naturalist and had papers so cleverly forged that they couldn't be distinguished from the genuine article.

There was a reason for that, as McColl informed the preening captors — they *were* the genuine article. The Swede was released with many apologies and sent back to the wild to continue his cataloging of Burmese mountain butterflies. McColl took the train back to Calcutta, this time overnight, and spent some of his sleepless minutes wondering whether counting pretty insects while half the world bled was something to admire or detest.

He'd been back only two days when the officer responsible for the twice-daily check on the *chaikhana* reported the return of its owner. McColl took the Bengali-speaking Sanjay along for the interview but needn't have bothered — Asok Bagchi spoke perfect Urdu.

Had he spoken to the removal people hired by Harry & Sons?

He had, the Indian said. But that was all

213

he had done. He knew nothing about the people in Harry & Sons. He had spoken once to the proprietor, maybe twice. But definitely no more than that.

"You're not in any trouble," McColl reassured him. "I'm only interested in the removal people. Do you know where they came from?"

Bagchi shook his head. "They didn't say."

"Do you know where they were taking the shipment?"

"Howrah station."

McColl saw a glimmer of hope. "Are you sure?"

"Oh, yes. The morning they left, the man in charge told me they were in a hurry, because loading ended at eight."

That was even better. "I don't suppose he told you where the train was going?"

"No, sahib."

It didn't matter, McColl thought as he and Sanjay rode back down Harrison Road. The Howrah Bridge, when they reached it, was the usual bedlam, but their driver refused to let anything slow their progress and seemed to take an inordinate delight in cutting across stranded automobile taxis with their profusely sweating white passengers.

The station and freight yards backed onto

214

the river south of the bridge, with the offices occupying an area larger than Dalhousie Square. It took McColl a quarter of an hour to find the relevant one, but that was the difficult bit. The shipment ledgers were arranged by destination, date, and time and included an inventory of goods being shipped along with names and addresses of both shipper and recipient. The only general-merchandise train scheduled to leave at the time in question was the morning Madras, and the relevant ledger was duly fetched.

Five minutes later McColl had his answer. A shipment containing, among other things, "twenty-three gramophones" had been sent to Balasore, a small town about 120 miles south of Calcutta. Looking at the map that an eager railway official supplied, McColl noticed how close the town was to the sea.

In the ledger the space for the recipient's name and address contained only the former — a Mr. Banerjee. He would collect — had already collected — the shipment at Balasore station.

They were in the hunt again, McColl thought as the tonga took them back across the teeming bridge. From Tindall's office he cabled the police in Balasore, asking whether the town had a gramophone shop, particularly one that had just been opened. No reply arrived that morning, but when he and Tindall returned from a long and pleasant lunch at Firpo's, there was one on the DCI man's desk. "Yes," an Inspector Naysmith had reported. "The Universal Emporium opened for business three weeks ago. Are you looking for a particular model?"

The police train set out for Balasore just before midnight. Once a small army of officers had been rounded up — no minor undertaking — Tindall had spent the better part of two hours convincing the governor that Calcutta would not be swept by lawlessness in their absence. The relief on his face as their train rattled clear of the Howrah terminus was plain to see.

The other good news was that Cunningham had called in sick that morning — he hadn't gone into details — and was back in his bed in Ballygunge.

Tindall was soon snoring in the compartment they shared, but McColl was wide awake. There was something magical about a journey through the Indian night, even one not punctuated by frequent stops. As the train chugged westward through the flat and often flooded fields, its engine trailing smoke across the heavens, he stood by the open window feeling as close to contentment as he ever did. Each copse of swaying palms, each moonlit platform lined with sleeping bodies — at moments like this, India felt like a gift. Maybe one not given freely, maybe one that wasn't deserved, but accepted with gratitude just the same.

After passing Kharagpur Junction, where the line from Madras diverged from the route to Bombay, he reluctantly took to his berth, and it seemed like only minutes before one of Tindall's men was shaking him awake. "We're there."

It was three-thirty in the morning, and clouds now blanketed the night sky. Half a dozen tracks away, the Balasore station platform was mostly shrouded in darkness, its two hanging lamps imparting only the faintest of yellow sheens to the multitude sleeping beneath them.

He heard voices through the window on the other side. On the cinders below, Tindall was talking to two men in uniform, one English, one Indian. These would be the local police, who'd been asked to meet the train but not, under any circumstances, to go anywhere near the Universal Emporium.

Half an hour later, all the men from Calcutta were lined up ready to go. Rather to McColl's surprise, this had been accomplished with only an odd whispered curse to break the silence — Tindall was determined that this time the terrorists would not see their nemesis coming. The march from the darkened yard was managed in an almost ghostly hush and raised only a handful of heads among those sleeping on the platform.

Balasore was a small town that had seen better days — according to Tindall, the English, the Danish, and the Dutch had all established trading stations here before the former took full control of the subcontinent. Now there was little to recommend it and little to distinguish one darkened street from another. It was almost four-thirty, the first hints of light showing in the eastern sky, when the local police chief, whose name was Jenkinson, brought the column to a halt. The Universal Emporium was round the next corner.

Jenkinson and Tindall went forward to check the approaches and returned ten minutes later. Then the whole force wheeled round the corner, onto a much wider street lined with shops. A hundred yards down, one group peeled off into an alley, and McColl noticed the Universal Emporium sign that someone had painted above the entrance of a one-story building. As other groups moved to cover the far side and the rear, a large constable eyed the front door and waited for the word. When it came, he put his head down and charged, the doors splintering open with a crack that seemed likely to wake the whole town.

Other constables poured through the breach. Tindall and McColl waited, aware of doors opening farther up the street, silently praying that they wouldn't hear shots within.

"We have them, sahib!" an officer called from the doorway.

They went in, passing through a shop room full of gramophones to reach the living quarters at the back, where two naked Indians were lying facedown on the floor.

Tindall grimaced. "Give them their clothes, for God's sake."

The two were brought dhotis, which they pulled on in silence. When asked their names, they shook their heads and smiled.

Another constable entered the room. "There are people outside, sahib," he told Tindall. "What shall we do with them?"

"Tell them to go away," Tindall said brusquely. "And you two," he went on, addressing the other two officers present, "take these men back to the train. Use the rear door. I'm assuming you'd rather we didn't use the town jail," he added, turning to Jenkinson.

The police chief shrugged. "I doubt these men will have many supporters in Balasore, but better safe than sorry."

The two men were led away.

McColl looked round the room, which was much more cluttered with personal effects than those they'd searched at Harry & Sons. "Maybe this time we'll find something useful," he murmured.

"Let's find a cup of tea," Tindall told him. "By the time we've drunk it, the sun will be up."

The small crowd outside seemed curious rather than hostile, and several offers of tea were forthcoming once Tindall explained that the men inside had been dacoits in the pay of the Germans. This seemed to satisfy all those present, although McColl did hear one man ask a neighbor what part of the country these Germans were from.

"Tea for the sahibs" came in souvenir mugs from the 1911 Delhi Durbar, and the two of them sipped the scalding brew on the shop's veranda, surrounded by staring locals. It would have made a good picture for all the empire lovers at home, McColl decided. He tried to think of a suitable title. Breakfast on the Job? Another Day in

Charge?

The sun came up with its usual swiftness, and they got to work. Two hours later they had three things to show for their search, all of which seemed significant. Among these were a pair of maps, one hand drawn on a page torn from a school exercise book, the other an official printing. The former offered annotated directions to a village named Kaptipada, which the local police chief informed them was about thirty miles to the west. The same village was on the printed map, and right alongside it someone had scrawled three sets of initials. Two more had been scribbled beside Sharata, a village five miles farther west.

One explanation — and McColl couldn't think of another — was that the initials represented terrorists hiding out in the relevant locations. If so, the JM at Kaptipada might well be Jatin Mukherjee. Which would be a coup.

The second map had been produced by the Bengal Railways and bore four crosses at what looked like significant choke points. McColl was immediately reminded of the maps he'd studied at Victoria Station a year earlier and the British official's description of which bridges the Irish group would need to bring down if they wanted to slow the army's embarkation for France. This map, McColl reckoned, showed where Jugantar would cut the lines connecting Bengal to the rest of the country, the lines the British army would have to use to reinforce their garrison in the event of a major rebellion.

The third clue was harder to read. There was a Crescent Bicycles calendar on the shop room's wall, the month of August showing, unmarked by the proprietors. Idly turning the page, McColl noticed that someone had drawn a line round the week beginning September 5. All the following months were blank.

It could mean almost anything, but something told him it was important.

He took what was left of his tea out onto the veranda and stood there scanning the dusty street. What lasted a week? Not birthdays or weddings, and Ramadan lasted a month. Some Hindu festivals could drag on for quite a while, but none of Tindall's men knew of any around that time.

And then it occurred to him. Back home a train or a boat usually arrived at a particular hour, but here in Asia the distances were so much greater, the timetables more indicative than precise. Trains or boats were often hours, sometimes days, late in reaching their destination. What if someone or something was supposed to arrive during that week? The ship they were seeking would be crossing a fair bit of ocean and would have difficulty in timing its arrival more precisely. And the same would be true of a German messenger, whether traveling overland through Burma or by sea from Batavia or Bangkok.

He might be completely wrong, but as a theory it fit the facts. If, as seemed likely, the terrorists were hiding out some distance from the coast, they were probably waiting to learn exactly where and when they should meet the boat. The message would probably come to the emporium and then be taken to wherever it was they were staying.

McColl went back in and explained his thinking to Tindall. "If we leave a couple of our men to staff the shop," he added, "any messenger would fall right into our hands."

Tindall scratched his head. "That sounds like a good idea, but how would they carry it off? "I don't suppose any of them know anything about gramophones."

"The damn things must come with instructions. And they'd only have to sell them."

"And the bicycles? How will they repair them?"

"Badly, I expect. But seriously, it can't be that difficult, and it'll give them something to do."

"The whole street knows we arrested the two who were there."

"So? Spread the word that the owners in Calcutta were shocked to find out these men were criminals and are sending two more to take their places. Then bring two new men down from Calcutta. You might even find some with a knowledge of bicycles."

Tindall raised both hands in surrender. "All right. We'll staff the place until the end of that week. If we still need to. If those sketch maps are what we think they are and we catch these buggers in Kaptipada, then that may be an end of it." Discovering that there were local maps at the police station, he sent off a constable to fetch them and drummed his fingers for the fifteen minutes it took for the man to get back. After examining them the DCI chief announced himself satisfied. "A quick march up the river and they won't know what hit them. I think we might have them this time."

By midafternoon they were halfway to the small town of Udala. That was the nearest they could get to Kaptipada on a half-decent track, and Tindall had "borrowed" Balasore's only automobile — a 1906 Oldsmobile L — from its reluctant Indian owner to take them that far. Accepting the owner's chauffeur had been part of the deal, and the Indian in question took his duties extremely seriously, laboriously working his way round any obstacle — McColl was sure he took pains to avoid a large leaf on one occasion — and keeping their overall speed at not much more than walking pace. He also insisted on frequent stops to "let the engine breathe."

Not that hurrying would have helped. Four horses had been found to mount an advance party, but the rest of the constables were having to walk the twenty miles and even at this pace would be some way behind.

It was almost dark by the time they drove into Udala, where the advance party had requisitioned the village school for the marchers and arranged elephants for their bosses to ride the next morning. This both excited and alarmed McColl, who'd never been up on one.

The marchers had another, albeit shorter, walk awaiting them. They arrived around ten, somewhat the worse for wear, and examined their new surroundings with evident dismay. They were used to the streets of Calcutta, not this other India.

A sentry post was established on the path to Kaptipada — Tindall didn't want any local villager taking news of their presence to the terrorists five miles upstream. He, McColl, and Jenkinson had been given beds in the government bungalow, under mosquito nets hung from the wooden beams, but first the stifling heat and then the deafening clatter of rain on the roof made sleep a patchy affair.

Their driver had also been offered a bed but had opted to sleep in his charge, perhaps afraid that a passing local might climb aboard and drive it away. When McColl ventured out in the predawn light, the Indian was stretched across the backseat, legs hanging over the door, and snoring loudly enough to annoy the monkeys, who were chattering wildly in the branches above and hurling down pieces of bark.

They left soon after sunrise. Getting aboard the elephant was a challenge, but once McColl was up, he soon got used to the peculiar motion of the giant beast beneath him, and the early-morning ride through the dripping forest was most enjoyable. This was Kipling's India. At one point McColl thought he heard the roar of a distant tiger and felt vaguely let down when a local handler told him it was only a leopard.

After a couple of hours, someone brought the column to a halt and an officer walked back to tell Tindall that the village was just a short distance ahead. A small reconnaissance party was dispatched, and the three of them were helped down off their elephants. It was already quite hot, and a layer of steam seemed to cling to the jungle floor. In the branches above, a host of brightly colored birds were singing up a storm.

An hour or so later, two soldiers returned with the news that three young men from the city were staying with the richest man in Kaptipada, one Kumar Bandopadhyay. His bungalow was at the other end of the village. Their two colleagues had it under observation.

There was no point in delaying. After handing out a few basic instructions, Tindall led his men on up the path and through the gauntlet of stares aimed their way by the local villagers. As they neared the bungalow, the party split off into two columns to encircle it from both sides, but McColl's first sight of the building told him they needn't have bothered. An Indian, presumably Bandopadhyay, was sitting placidly on the veranda, fanning himself with a palm frond and clearly expecting visitors.

"They've gone," McColl muttered.

"Looks like it," Tindall said stoically.

Ignoring their obvious hostility, Bandopadhyay ordered a servant to bring them all drinks — "It is hot this morning, is it not?" — and answered the leading question only once everyone's thirst was slaked. Yes, it was true that three young men had been staying with him — they had left the previous day. Until this moment he had assumed they were foresters — they had told him as much and left for the forest each morning, returning after sundown.

When Tindall said equably that he didn't believe a word of the man's story, Bandopadhyay just shrugged and smiled. He made no objection to their searching his home, having doubtless already removed anything that might incriminate himself or give any clue to his recent guests' next port of call. They searched it anyway and found only a few discarded garments. McColl was working his way through these when Tindall noticed a still-smoldering fire behind the house.

The two men went outside, and Tindall stirred the ashes with a stick.

"They didn't leave yesterday," McColl

decided, his eyes on the wall of jungle that almost encircled the open space at the rear. For all they knew, Mukherjee was out there now, watching them from hiding. But it didn't seem likely.

Tindall pulled a map from his pocket. "The road we took to Udala is the only obvious way out of here. I suppose they could have made a detour around us, but it would have been risky."

"They probably went across country," McColl said. He should be feeling down-hearted, he thought, but for some strange reason he didn't. "In their position I'd have done some exploring over the past few weeks and had my escape route planned in advance."

Tindall sighed. "You're probably right. So which way did they go?"

"Oh, east. They'll be heading for the coast."

They went back inside, and Tindall told Bandopadhyay that he was under arrest.

"On what charge?" the Indian asked indignantly.

"Ah, that's the wonder of the new act," Tindall told him with uncharacteristic acidity. "We don't need to worry about that until *after* we've locked you away."

Ten constables were sent off to visit the

other village on the captured map, but without any real hope of finding terrorists. If the ones in Kaptipada had received advance warning of the police expedition, they'd have made sure that their comrades did, too. Tindall's one hope was that the latter had not been so careful about what they left behind.

The rest of the party made its way back to Udala, where the chauffeur was fighting a rearguard action against village youths keen to leave their fingerprints all over his gleaming car. His escape was further delayed, moreover. Tindall had decided to make things more difficult for the fugitive terrorists by spreading word of substantial rewards for any confirmed sightings. Some of his officers would carry the news, but they needed guides to find the many villages, and recruiting them took most of the day. It was long after dark when the Oldsmobile crawled back into Balasore, the driver celebrating their first flat stretch of surfaced road with a giddy speed of twelve miles an hour.

The rest of Tindall's available men, who had arrived back an hour or so earlier, were sent to patrol the railway line that the terrorists would need to cross if they wanted to reach the sea. Most looked tired enough to miss a herd of stampeding elephants, but McColl understood Tindall's urgency, even as he welcomed the prospect of sleep for himself.

The DCI chief was certainly determined not to let the opportunity slip, ordering up more reinforcements from both Calcutta and the local garrison before McColl had finished his morning ablutions. The two men then trudged through teeming rain to the local jailhouse for more unproductive chats with Bandopadhyay and the men from the Universal Emporium. The latter were keen to share their knowledge of gramophones, and the former stuck to his original story, that whoever his guests had really been, he had thought them simple foresters.

The light was beginning to fade when the train bringing extra police and soldiers arrived at Balasore station. Two Calcutta officers were chosen, briefed, and sent to man the shop; the rest were divided between the railway cordon and those units advancing cross-country from Kaptipada. But by sundown there was still no reported sighting of Mukherjee and his comrades. Had they slipped across the line during the previous night, when the watchers were widely spaced and probably half asleep? Or had they gone to ground in some dense stretch of forest? If the marks on the calendar meant what McColl suspected, they still had plenty of time to meet the boat.

It was unbearably hot and humid that night, and McColl, who these days had trouble getting to sleep even in a fan-cooled room, found himself wide awake and almost swimming in sweat inside the small compartment he shared with Tindall. There was a reason, he thought, that Indians slept in the open.

It wasn't much cooler outside, but at least a faint breeze was blowing toward the Bay of Bengal. McColl walked down the side of the train toward the yard throat, where one of the two sentries that Tindall had posted was amusing himself by walking a rail like a high-wire artist, using his rifle for balance. McColl gave him a wave and turned back, picking his way across the weed-choked sidings that lay between the station and their train. The low platforms to his right were, as usual, liberally scattered with sleeping bodies — given that most Indians spent a lifetime within five miles of their villages, it always amazed McColl that the stations and trains were so crowded.

He was nearly level with the last carriage when he realized that the other sentry was conspicuous by his absence. Glancing round, he noticed movement behind the train. The sentry, most likely, but he decided to make sure. McColl rounded the rear of the stabled train just in time to see whoever it was duck out of sight beneath a carriage. Which was strange behavior for a sentry.

He reversed his steps round the back of the last car, but there was no one crossing the sidings. The figure he had seen was still beneath the train.

It might be a railwayman or some errant youth who couldn't sleep, but something more sinister seemed likely. As McColl walked swiftly toward the carriage in question, a sudden flare of light condensed into a blazing pinprick, confirming his worst suspicions. The man had lit a fuse.

McColl's first impulse was to rush forward, his second to halt some ten yards short of the man, whom he could just about see, crouched beneath the carriage with what looked a bomb in his hand.

What should he do?

"Cut off the fuse!" he yelled. "Or pull it out! If you don't, I'll have to shoot you and do it myself!"

The figure didn't move; the fuse kept burning. Maybe the man hadn't understood him, but McColl didn't know the Bengali for fuse. Maybe there was no way to stop it now. The thought of moving any closer to the bomb terrified him.

Heads were appearing in windows, voices asking what all the shouting was about, and he realized he should have fired a warning shot, if only to alert those men still sleeping in the carriage above. He fired two shots into the air. "It's a bomb!" he screamed. "Get out of the carriage!"

A rifle cracked, and the figure beneath the train slumped forward, the bomb slipping out of his grasp, the burning fuse apparently extinguished. Or had he just fallen on top of it?

The explosion was answer enough. A jagged flash, a thunderous crack, and a forceful shower of flesh that sent McColl reeling backward and dumped him onto his rear.

He lay there for several seconds, watching smoke give way to stars. He could still see, still hear. His body, though splattered with blood and God knew what else, was still in one piece.

The carriage in front of him seemed undamaged. At either end its lucky inhabitants were clambering down the vestibule steps to see what had happened.

Tindall helped McColl to his feet, offered him a handkerchief to wipe the gore from his face, and stared thoughtfully down the train. "I suppose we should make sure he only had the one."

No vaudeville comic could have bettered the timing. The words were barely out of Tindall's mouth when another flash lit the whole station area and half the last carriage exploded into the air.

A frenzied search found no more devices, but the damage had been done. Four men were dead, and four more seemed certain to lose limbs. The missing sentry was found with a length of wire embedded in his neck.

It seemed probable that the man was one of Jatin's, sent to disrupt and discourage the police pursuit, but, if so, he wouldn't be telling them.

The morning passed without news, either from those out searching for the missing terrorists or from the stand-ins at Universal Emporium, whose only visitors had been penniless locals eager to hear the strange noises one could make by dropping a tiny needle on something round and black. The whole expedition could end up with nothing, McColl thought, as he watched the hastily constructed coffins lifted aboard a Calcutta-bound train. Eight months of chasing Jugantar, eight months of frustration, failure, and too many deaths.

Their luck turned. The peasant escorted into the carriage by a local policeman was from a village a few miles to the east, one close to the Burhabulang River, between Balasore and the coast. As he spoke no English or Bengali, the policeman had to interpret.

That morning, soon after sunrise, five strangers had walked into the peasant's village and tried to buy food at the shop. They had obviously been hungry, and their clothes were ragged and wet, but their accents were those of rich men, and they had tried to pay with the first ten-rupee note that most of the locals had ever seen. Questions had been asked, a scuffle had broken out, and one of the strangers had pulled a pistol and shot two villagers. One was only slightly wounded, but the other man was dead.

The other strangers had quickly drawn their weapons, and the five of them had retreated down the street, with the angry but unarmed villagers in cautious pursuit. Soon the gunmen had reached a river, a tributary of the Burhabulang, which barred their way, and they had taken turns to cover one another as they swam across. The villagers had pretended to let them go, but

236

once the strangers had passed from sight, two men had picked up their trail.

"Can you show me where this all happened?" Tindall asked, unfolding the best map they had.

The peasant stared for a several seconds at the mass of lines, squiggles and words placed before him, then shook his head. McColl doubted he'd ever seen a map before.

"He'll have to take us there," Tindall realized. "How did he get here?" he asked the local officer.

"On a donkey."

"Well, tell him we'll be leaving in an hour or so. Give him something to eat in the meantime."

The peasant listened and offered what seemed a pithy reply.

"He wants to know about the reward," the officer reported.

"All in good time," Tindall said with a reassuring smile.

Though obviously less than satisfied, the peasant followed his keeper out.

An hour later they were ready to go. Tindall's force of seventy-odd men would converge on what seemed the likeliest village and be brought on from there if that proved the wrong one. Tindall, McColl, and a few other officers would follow the donkey on horseback.

The horse caused McColl almost as much trepidation as the elephant had done — apart from two short rides in the Punjab that January, he'd not been astride one since South Africa — but the animal proved remarkably docile. With the sky clearing and the temperature soaring, he was perhaps as cowed by the heat as his rider.

It took them two hours to reach the village, which straggled along a single street leading down to the wide Burhabulang. Half of Tindall's force was already there, and another quarter arrived in the next thirty minutes, which was more than enough to continue the pursuit. Their helpful informant led them west to the tributary, where another man was waiting to take them on. The men they wanted, he reported through the interpreter, were only a mile or so ahead, encamped on a hill not far from the river.

Getting everyone across the tributary looked likely to delay matters, until a helpful villager disclosed the existence of a ford not far upstream. Less than half an hour later, McColl was staring up at the hill and the copse of trees on its summit, where the wanted men were hunkered down.

There were several mounds of earth in front of the trees, which offered a modicum of cover, but there were only five of the terrorists. As Tindall began deploying his much larger force, sending groups round each flank of the hill with orders to link up beyond it, a lone shot was fired from inside the copse, causing several men to hit the ground but otherwise causing no harm.

A statement of intent, McColl thought. These five would not surrender lightly.

There was no real contest, though, between five men with pistols and sixty or more toting rifles. Soon a rain of bullets had ripped the leaves from the trees that sheltered the rebels, and Tindall's main force was crawling forward across the marshy ground without suffering any apparent casualties. It was slow but remorseless, and around an hour had passed when McColl noticed a sudden diminution of the enemy's returning fire. A few minutes more and it stopped altogether. Either the terrorists had run out of bullets or they were saving the few that remained for themselves or for a last hurrah.

The officers kept firing for a few minutes and, after receiving no further response, mounted a headlong charge. Tindall had given orders, more in hope than in expectation, that the rebels should be taken alive, and to his and McColl's relief no more shots rang out. There was only the one triumphant shout — "We have them, sahib!"

He and Tindall walked up to the cluster of shredded trees and surveyed the human damage. One of the Jugantar men had been killed by a bullet to the head, and two had been injured, one only slightly, the other shot in the neck, belly, and thigh.

The latter's face matched their picture of the young Jatin Mukherjee, and the man himself admitted in a whisper that that was who he was. As his captors looked down at him, he offered them a smile that was part defiance, part amusement. It was the look, McColl thought, of a man who had lost a battle but knew his side would win the war.

The wounded men and the corpse were taken to the village, where a cart was commandeered to carry them on to Balasore. The other two were marched to the town jail, where Tindall and McColl questioned them that afternoon. Neither they nor their slightly injured comrade in the hospital had anything to say on the subject of German arms. Their leader needed an emergency operation, and McColl and Tindall had to wait several hours before they could interview the man they'd been seeking for most of the year. Jatin regained consciousness early that evening, but speech was clearly difficult, and only one whispered sentence emerged from the heavily bandaged throat: "I alone am responsible."

When Tindall asked him for what, Jatin simply smiled.

They left him under guard, intent on starting again the following morning, but during the night Jatin surreptitiously tore the stitches from his wounds and bled himself to death.

Cunningham arrived in Balasore the following morning, having shaken off whatever bug had laid him low. Responding to the news of Mukherjee's suicide, he was his usual compassionate self. "If only the rest of the scum would follow his example," was the Five man's idea of an epitaph.

Tindall gave him a contemptuous look. "The man had courage," he retorted. "If he'd been English, he'd be up for a medal."

Cunningham was taken aback, but not for long. "Well, at least we've put a bloody great spoke in Jugantar's wheel!"

And in that McColl supposed he was right. As a leader, Mukherjee would be hard to replace, and there seemed little chance of their getting their hands on the soon-to-be arriving guns. The divisions that might have been needed in India could now — God help them — be sent to France. Where they might make a crucial difference to how things went on the Western Front. Which might even save his brother's life.

Tindall and Cunningham returned to Calcutta that evening, taking their train and most of the officers with them, but McColl elected to stay on in Balasore. Mukherjee's Jugantar cell might be broken, but McColl was convinced that the guns were on their way; if the weapons were landed and dispersed, there'd be other Indians more than willing to use them. He had less faith than Tindall in the competence of the local police, and he still had vivid memories of that day the year before when the Dublin authorities had allowed 90 percent of a similar arms shipment to slip through their fingers.

He took a room in the town's only half-acceptable hotel, resigned himself to nights without a cooling fan, and settled down to wait. Assuming that the news of Jatin's death had somehow filtered out, there seemed a fair chance that someone might turn up in Balasore with more recent news of the shipment.

Saving his only book for the long hours of

darkness, he spent the days familiarizing himself with the nearby coastline, a picture-perfect sandy beach that stretched both north and south for almost twenty miles. If and when the ship arrived, there was nowhere it could dock. A smaller boat would be needed to bring the guns ashore.

Each day, between nightfall and dinner, he checked in at the emporium, where Tindall's two men were learning the gramophone and bicycle trades. They didn't seem like the brightest sparks in the bazaar, and it was only the fear of being spotted that stopped McColl adding a lunchtime visit to his schedule.

His fears turned out be well founded. Six days into their vigil, one of the men turned up at McColl's hotel. His demeanor was apologetic, which didn't augur well.

A man had come to the shop, a Bengali, around thirty years old, well dressed.

"What did he want?" McColl demanded to know. "What did he say?"

"He said, 'I need a bicycle for my nephew Prabir.' "

"And?"

"It's hard to explain, sahib. I said, 'How old is he?' and he just looked at me, as if he was waiting for me to say something else. And when I didn't, he just repeated what

243

he had said: 'I need a bicycle for my nephew Prabir.' I said, 'Yes, I heard that, but we have different sizes for different ages.' He looked upset and shook his head and said, 'Thank you,' and then he walked out through the door. My colleague and I, we looked at each other and laughed, but after a short time I began to think perhaps this man is suspicious, yes?"

"How long ago was this?" McColl asked.

"One hour, I think. Perhaps a little more."

"Come with me," McColl said, grabbing his jacket. The station was a ten-minute walk away, the next train for the north standing in the platform. After ordering the guard to delay its departure, McColl and the officer began working their way through the coaches. They found their quarry in second class, sharing a compartment with two Indian businessmen and rather obviously trying to conceal himself behind a copy of *The Statesman*.

The man looked older than thirty to McColl, and less sure of himself than the other Jugantar people he had met. He blustered briefly in perfect English before abruptly changing tack and meekly submitting to ejection from the train. A search of his clothes and body failed to produce a weapon or any incriminating papers, but

244

McColl had no doubt that this was the man he'd been waiting for. It was only a short walk to the town police station, where he could interrogate the man in private.

Fifteen minutes later McColl was facing him across a table. "Name?" he asked.

The look on the young man's face was that of a rebellious child.

"It doesn't matter," McColl said, putting down his pen. "You can just be a number to the hangman."

"Hangman?" the Indian blurted. "What have I done to deserve hanging? I'm just a . . . I have done nothing."

McColl smiled at him. "Just a messenger, you were going to say. Well, in law a man who carries messages for terrorists is as guilty as they are." He wasn't at all sure whether this was true, but it sounded believable.

"I delivered no message," the man said stubbornly.

"No, you didn't, but you intended to, which amounts to the same thing. Let me bring you up to date on your conspiracy. Jatin Mukherjee is dead; he will lead no rebellion in Bengal this —"

"I don't believe you."

McColl took out the picture of Mukherjee's corpse and silently passed it across,

245

thankful that Tindall had insisted on having it taken. Some Indians, the DCI man had said, would need more than an English say-so to believe that their hero was dead.

This one believed it now. There were tears in his eyes, McColl noticed. "He was a brave man. He fought a good fight. And he lost, just as you have. And you will pay the final price, just as he did. Do you have a family?"

"What? Yes."

"Children?"

"Two. Boys. What —"

"If you want to see them again, you will tell me the message you were sent to deliver."

"If I do that, I shall be a traitor."

"Yes. But no one will ever know. I promise you that."

"*I* shall know."

"True. And if you keep silent, you will die, and in the days spent waiting for your execution you'll know that you've abandoned your sons," McColl went on remorselessly. He wasn't enjoying himself, but he could see that the man was weakening.

"And if I do tell you — what will happen to me?"

"I will let you go. I won't even ask who gave you the message."

"You won't?" the Indian asked disbelievingly.

"As long as you take an oath not to engage in any subversive activity for the duration of the war."

The Indian regarded him, wanting to save himself, wanting to be loyal.

"Look," McColl said. "You came here to give them a place and a time and probably a coded signal for when the ship arrives." The Indian's expression told him he'd guessed right. "But those guns will never reach Jugantar now, whether you tell me the message or not. You have nothing to betray anymore."

"There is my comrade on the boat."

So there was only one Indian aboard, McColl thought. The rest would be hired hands. "What can I say?" he went on. "The affair is over. We shall probably catch your comrade anyway, but as of this moment you have a chance to walk away. To live."

"To live as a traitor."

"To live," McColl repeated. "Your boys will have a father," he pressed on, knowing that it was necessary and feeling the shame of it anyway.

The Indian closed his eyes. "My name is Barun Ray."

"And the message?"

"The early hours of the tenth off Chandipur Beach. The ship is the *Celebes*."

"And the signal?"

"The ship will flash a light four times. Those on shore must do the same."

"Thank you."

Ray gave him a weary look. "What happens to me now? Can I go back to my family?"

"No. You will write to them, tell them that your friends have asked you to stay in Balasore for a few days."

"But you promised."

"I said I would let you go, and I will. When we have the boat."

MEN'S MESS

With ten days having passed since her arrival and her relationship with the German authorities showing no visible sign of strain, Caitlin decided it was time she talked to the opposition. Among the list of contacts she had memorized in Christiania, there was one that Kollontai had deemed safer than the others — a woman named Erna Drahn. "She's over eighty," Kollontai had said, "and she doesn't go out much, so the police will probably not be watching her. But there was nothing wrong with her mind when I last saw her, and she'll know what's going on. She's been a party member for more than forty years."

Drahn lived in Friedrichshain, and Caitlin took a tram out to see her on the Tuesday evening, after, she hoped, losing any official shadow in the Wertheim department store on Leipziger Platz. She was wearing her least conspicuous clothes and, as far as she could see, attracting no unusual interest from her German fellow passengers.

After she'd found the flat and knocked on the door, a shout invited her in. Erna Drahn's health had clearly deteriorated since Kollontai's last visit, and she was now effectively chair-ridden. But there was nothing wrong with the old woman's spirit, and she knew enough English to make a stilted conversation possible. Once Caitlin had set the watchful blue eyes at ease with the anecdote that Kollontai had given her to recount, there was no holding back.

Most of those party members who had rejected the leadership's shameful line were now in prison, Erna told Caitlin. But not all. Though she herself was out of touch with the latest developments, she was confident that the opposition was making itself heard in one way or another. Caitlin should speak to Rolf Wehler, who as far as she knew was in hiding in Niederbarnim. She would make inquiries and find Caitlin a trustworthy interpreter, because Rolf didn't speak English. "He will tell you what is going on, and you can tell your American readers that despite the traitors of August, socialism is alive and well in Germany."

They talked for almost an hour, until it became clear that Erna had exhausted herself. Caitlin helped her into the other room, but an offer of further assistance was given short shrift — "Most evenings I can still manage to undress myself. Let yourself out, my dear, and come again in a couple of days."

On Thursday evening Caitlin caught another tram out to Friedrichshain, and this time a good-looking boy answered Erna's door.

"This is Friedrich," Erna told her. "He will take you to Rolf."

"Wonderful. When?"

"This evening, of course," Friedrich replied, as if surprised that she didn't know.

He couldn't be more than sixteen, Caitlin thought, which would explain why he wasn't in uniform. She wondered whether the lack of advanced warning was deliberate, a sign that they didn't completely trust her.

"We will leave now," the boy added, gazing out at the gathering dusk. "By the time we get there, it will be dark."

It was a long walk to the tram stop and a long wait once they reached it, which time Friedrich filled with questions about America. He seemed impressed by the fact that she'd had first-hand experience of the famous prewar strikes at Lawrence and Paterson and even more struck by the fact that she'd actually seen the American West, albeit from a train. "Are there still shoot-outs in the street?" he wanted to know, and he seemed disappointed when she told him there probably weren't.

As predicted, night had fallen by the time they reached Niederbarnim. After turning off the wide Frankfurter Allee, they entered an area that reminded Caitlin of the Man-hattan tenement districts she had visited as a cub reporter. Few of the closely packed buildings had electricity, and their court-yards were often piled high with rubbish, much of it reeking in the summer heat. Despite the lateness of the hour, there were still many children out on the street, some of them literally clothed in rags. Every last one stared at Caitlin as if she'd just come from the moon.

When they reached the corner of Rolf We-hler's street, Friedrich called over one of the watching boys and sent him ahead, doubtless with instructions to check that the coast was clear. Once he'd returned a few minutes later with a grin and an up-raised thumb, Friedrich led her along the street to one of the five-story blocks. Rolf Wehler lived on the fourth floor, and need-less to say there wasn't an elevator.

The flat was lit by candles. As far as she could see, it comprised two rooms, a kitchen and a living room, both of which doubled as bedrooms. They had passed the communal bathroom on the landing outside.

Wehler, who she guessed was in his forties, was a thin man with eyes that never seemed to settle. He introduced his blond wife, Anna, a tired-looking woman who had obviously once been a beauty, and her father, Grigor, who looked Caitlin over with an interest that didn't seem purely platonic. Glancing round the meager flat, she realized that books were the only thing not in short supply. Piles rose up from the wooden floor like a three-dimensional map of Manhattan.

Clearly anxious to start, Friedrich asked for her first question.

She had it ready: What were those German socialists who rejected the war doing now?

Wehler's answer made the others laugh. "Prison sentences, mostly," Friedrich translated.

"And those who aren't in prison?"

"We are spreading the word. This" — he handed her a roughly bound sheaf of paper with the words "Die Internationale" emblazoned on the top sheet — "was written in the spring and has been distributed throughout the country. Illegally, of course. The authorities have seized all the copies they could."

"What's in it?" she asked.

"Our explanation of what happened in August and our program for the future." He smiled. "It's very simple, really. Either the bourgeoisie and the proletariat have common interests or they don't. The idea that they have none in peacetime yet suddenly acquire them when a war breaks out . . . well, that's completely absurd, is it not?"

"It certainly sounds it."

"And we are not alone," Wehler continued. "The Independent Labour Party in England, comrades in neutral countries like Italy and Switzerland — they are saying the same thing. And others will join — the more prices rise to pay for the war, the more workers will see it for what it is, a struggle between rival imperialisms that serves no other interests. It is we who are fighting the real war, not Europe's bourgeois governments."

She couldn't let that pass. "A war? Are you prepared to take your protest that far? To argue for civil war?"

He listened to Friedrich's translation, then paused. "I am," he said eventually. "Others are reluctant, I know. Some think we should fight their war with pacifism. Some still believe that socialism must win through the ballot box, if we are to avoid a new tyranny."

"But you don't?"

"Each government is rounding up its own working class and sending it out to be killed — I don't think we can wait for democracy."

"But what can you actually do? Would you consider sabotage, for example?"

"I would not rule it out. But you must understand — we are still recovering from the shock of August. Our best leaders are in prison, and those like me who are still at large are hunted by the police. So there is little we can actually do at the moment. But it will get easier — I am sure of that."

Was he whistling in the dark? she wondered as she rode the tram back across Berlin. How many shared his vision? Only time would tell.

His phrase "the real war" had lodged in her brain. The war in the trenches was real enough for the men being maimed and killed each day. But was it real in the sense that a victory for either side would make a difference to the lives of ordinary people? She recalled the case that McColl had once made for the world's needing an English victory and decided that even if he'd been right and the English *were* more civilized than the Germans, the difference could only be marginal. Whichever nation proved victorious, the world wouldn't change that much.

And what about Ireland? Wehler would probably agree that Colm had been fighting a real war, but only because his comrades were republican socialists rather than mere nationalists. A victory for the latter would lead to a shuffling of faces and flags, but would it change much else?

On the other hand, if the poor won their "war" against their exploiters or if women won their "war" against men, wouldn't every last thing be turned upside down?

Was that what she wanted? It probably was.

She also knew that the majority of her American readers, warier of radical change, most certainly did not. Those fearful of eventual American involvement would be better served by a simple antiwar message, one that highlighted the existence of antiwar groups within the warring countries and the moral equivalence between the two sides that this suggested. She had to take her readers with her, she thought. If America was ready for more, then Kollontai was on the way.

She wanted to bounce ideas off Slaney, but there were no lights in his window — he was either out or already asleep. As she let herself into her room, she saw that an envelope had been pushed under her door; it contained a note from Rainer von Schön asking her to dinner that day or the next. He was leaving Berlin the coming weekend, so this would be their last chance to meet. A telephone number was appended. She could, he suggested, ring him from the Adlon.

Next morning she did so, and an evening rendezvous was arranged. The restaurant he had chosen was only a short distance from Uhlandstrasse, the evening clear but chilly for August. It had been a fine summer, she thought, approaching the entrance. She found herself wondering what sort of weather the men in the trenches preferred. Being sopping wet doubtless made them miserable, but sunny days were perfect for snipers. It was bad news either way.

Von Schön was already seated at their table. He was evasive when it came to explaining his imminent departure — "even water engineers have secrets" — but did admit that he wouldn't be seeing his wife and children.

The restaurant was small and surprisingly empty. Von Schön ordered a bottle of Alsatian wine and plied her with questions about Ireland as they waited for the fish — "We still have the Baltic at least!" For a German he was extremely well informed about Irish politics, a fact he put down to the trip that he and his wife had made there just before the war. "Such a beautiful country," he said. "Such a sad history. When did your ancestors leave?"

She told him and found herself sharing stories of her Irish childhood in Brooklyn, all the ceilidhs and wakes she'd attended as a child, listening to tales of the Famine with a fiddle playing gaily in the background. All the villains from Cromwell to Asquith, the heroes and martyrs from Wolfe Tone to now, the collection tin making its rounds for the endless struggle "back home."

And there, lurking in a corner of her mind, were the other Irish faces of her childhood, the violent, tyrannical men, as often drunk as sober, who thought themselves God's gift to the women whose lives they blighted. "Did you know that Sir Roger Casement is here in Berlin?" von Schön was asking her.

"I didn't," she said, very surprised. Casement was an Irishman who had spent much of his career in the British diplomatic service and was famous for his prewar efforts on behalf of exploited natives in the Congo and Peru. He had recently become an outspoken advocate of Irish independence, and Caitlin knew from Michael Killen that he had traveled to America when war broke out to seek help for the republican cause. But she hadn't heard of his visiting Germany.

"He is here," von Schön confirmed, as if she might have doubted the fact.

She didn't, but she was beginning to doubt von Schön. How would a water engineer know that Casement was in Berlin? Surely it hadn't been publicized.

"I have friends in strange places," von Schön told her, as if reading her mind. "I thought you might be interested. As a journalist, of course."

"Of course." If her suspicions were well founded and her dinner companion was now working for his government in some capacity or other, how could she turn the situation to her advantage? As a journalist she *was* interested in Casement, but if the Germans didn't know that, they might offer a quid pro quo. "He might be worth meeting," she conceded, "but what I really want is a trip to the front."

"Have you asked?"

"Several times, but the answer is always 'Wait and see.' "

They spent the rest of the evening discussing safer topics — their impressions of China, favorite foods, American suffragettes. Von Schön had news of the latter that Caitlin hadn't heard and which brought a real surge of joy to her heart — back in the States a women's Liberty Bell was being forged to further the suffragette cause. Its clapper didn't ring, symbolizing the political silence their votelessness imposed on women.

The two of them parted amicably, with Caitlin fairly confident that she hadn't revealed her suspicions. And thirty-six hours later, at her very next meeting with Gerhard Singer, his welcome news would more or less confirm them. She began by asking if she could interview Casement.

"Of course," he said, as if surprised she should bother to ask. "He is a private citizen. You don't need my permission," he added, beaming at her with barely concealed satisfaction.

"I don't know his address."

"Oh, I can help you with that. Or better still, supply a driver to take you there. Will tomorrow do?"

"Why not? I don't suppose a decision has been reached about my trip to the front?" she asked innocently.

"Ah, yes. I almost forgot. There is good news there. The army has agreed to let you visit a hospital just behind the fighting line. You'll be able to talk to the staff and patients."

So von Schön had arranged that her price would be paid. "How far behind the fighting line?"

"Oh, a few kilometers. Quite close enough."

She would get to it somehow, she thought.

"You will leave on Friday — an overnight train to Trier, I think."

"That's marvelous," she said, and meant it — the prospect really excited her.

"But first Herr Casement. He lives in Dahlem, so it would be easier for the driver to pick you up at your lodgings. Shall we say ten o'clock?"

"Fine." One thing seemed certain: for reasons that weren't yet clear, the Germans wanted her to meet Casement and to go along with whatever it was the Irishman wanted. Where the first was concerned, she was happy to oblige. Meeting him would cost her nothing, and German gratitude might open doors that would otherwise stay closed.

Sir Roger Casement's Berlin lodgings were considerably more luxurious than Caitlin's. The tree-lined street close to the Grunewald was clearly a preserve of the rich, and Casement's villa was no smaller than any of the others. He had it all to himself, moreover, if one excluded the servants and the fresh-faced young man who answered the door. One of Michael Killen's asides suddenly made sense, not that Casement's sexual proclivities were any of her business.

The ex-diplomat appeared, a man of around fifty with dark hair and beard. His smile seemed forced to Caitlin, and he didn't look particularly well. "My condolences for the loss of your brother," he said, taking her outstretched hand in both his own. "To come all the way from America and serve in the way he did — that showed great courage and determination."

"Thank you," she said.

"I hope you will accompany me to Zossen this morning. Herr Singer has already sanctioned the use of your automobile."

"What's in Zossen?"

"Let me surprise you. It's not a long ride, and I don't think you'll be disappointed. And we can talk on the journey."

"Very well."

Zossen was apparently less than an hour's drive away. They were soon out of the city and motoring through a mixed landscape of woods and farms. Those harvesting the summer crops, she noticed, were mostly women and children.

She asked Casement how long he had been in Berlin.

"Ten months," he told her.

"And what are you doing here?"

"Seeking help, of course."

"Do the English know you're here?"

"Oh, yes. They tried to have me arrested in Norway."

She had a vague memory of this, but at the time her attention had been mostly on Colm. "So have you been successful?"

"You'll be able to judge that for yourself when we reach Zossen." He turned his eyes to the window. "It's a beautiful day, is it not?"

She took the cue and sat in silence, enjoying her escape from the city, wondering what his secret was. A warehouse full of rifles seemed the best bet, but how would he get them to Ireland?

They eventually arrived at a gateway manned by soldiers. Behind this, surrounded by a high barbed-wire fence, was a field containing four identical barracks, which bore all the signs of a small prisoner-of-war camp.

It was and wasn't, Casement explained. The occupants, many of whom were currently engaged in some energetic game with a ball, were all Irishmen who had volunteered for the British army and subsequently been captured by the Germans. "And now," he concluded triumphantly, "they have agreed to fight for Ireland."

They weren't very many, was Caitlin's first thought. She asked Casement for a figure.

"Fifty-six," he said proudly. "My Irish Brigade. You have to remember," he went on, seeing her expression, "these men *volunteered* for the British army. They're not natural republicans."

It still seemed a poor return on ten months' effort, Caitlin thought, but deemed it churlish to say so. "Can I talk to some of them?"

"Of course. We'll use the office" — he gestured toward what looked like an administration block — "as an interview room."

Five minutes later she was talking to two young boys from Limerick. They seemed willing enough to fight the English, though Casement's presence, there at her shoulder, might have had something to do with that.

And so, she thought, might the prospect of years twiddling their thumbs in a camp like this one. Both these boys and those who followed offered lip service to the cause of Irish independence, but she saw no sign that any were truly committed. They had joined this group for much the same reasons they had joined the British army: because it offered comradeship, a living, and a way out of their present circumstances.

Casement, she knew, would not want to hear this.

As they began their ride back, he tried to enlist her dead brother in support of his venture. "I only knew about his operation after the event," he said, "and at the time . . . well, I must admit I had my doubts about the usefulness of such action. But time has cured me of such timidity. Brave men should always be saluted, and if this is not an appropriate time to take the battle to the English, then I don't know what would be."

"What exactly are we talking about?" she asked, looking out at a row of elegant houses. On the front steps of one, a little girl was watching them pass, a doll clutched tight to her chest.

Casement didn't notice her. "In the medium term, a rising in Ireland, supported by German troops. Which will not only cost the English Ireland but most likely lose them the war. An outcome I'm sure you would welcome."

"I don't know." The English had killed her brother, but did she long for their defeat? She had found many Germans good company but saw little to admire in their leaders. In truth, she wanted both sides to lose.

He noticed her hesitation and probably misread it as a woman's aversion to violence. "This is Ireland's opportunity," he reminded her.

"I know. But do you really think an uprising could succeed?"

"With German help — yes."

"And they've agreed to provide it?"

"Not yet," he said, turning his eyes to the passing fields. "They are interested, they see the possibilities that such a move would open up, but they are not yet convinced that we are serious enough or strong enough. They are pleased with my Irish Brigade, but they want to see more volunteers. And that is where you come in."

"I don't understand."

His eyes lit up — he was one of those men who loved to explain. "These volunteers can only come from America. The Germans say to me the Irish-Americans have been talking a good fight against the English for over a hundred years, but what have they ever actually done? And, you know, the Germans are right. It is time they took up arms and joined us. And no one is better placed to put that case than you! As the correspondent of a big newspaper, you have a ready-made platform, and who could put the case for volunteering better than the sister of a young man who has already given his life for Ireland? Tell Irish-Americans about my brigade, tell them to join us!"

She knew that Colm would have lapped this up, and she felt more than a little depressed by the knowledge. Had he been that naïve? Was Casement? "How would they get here?" she asked. "Who would pay their passage?"

He waved that aside. "One man has come already, all the way from Chicago — I should have introduced you to him. I'm sure those interested will have the sense to contact Clan na Gael or the German embassy. But first they must want to come, must feel it is their duty. You see that, don't you?"

"I do."

"So you will do all you can? Write articles that have men queuing up to come?"

"I will," she said, with as much enthusiasm as she could muster, mostly just to shut him up. He seemed more than a little deranged, and she wondered whether living alone in a foreign capital for so many months hadn't proved just a bit too much. There was some sense in what he had said and in what he hoped she would do, but nowhere near enough. Did he really believe that a couple of articles in the American press would unleash a flood of willing recruits for his company-size brigade?

And even if it did, what would these men be fighting for? Nothing Casement had said suggested any advance on simple national-ism, and even Colm had gone further than that. There was no mention of class, let alone gender — he seemed as much in thrall to a flag as was any Englishman or German. The difference between him and them was that he had no seat of power on which to hoist his.

And yet, she told herself. She had met Irish rebels — Connolly for one — who would give even Kollontai a run for her money where awareness of class and gender issues were concerned. Whom exactly did Casement think he represented?

She asked him.

"The Volunteers, of course."

Which told her nothing.

"Do you agree with Jim Larkin that an

independent Ireland can only be a socialist Ireland?"

He was taken aback for only a moment. "An independent Ireland can be anything it damn well pleases."

Half an hour later, after they'd dropped Casement off at his villa, she sat there staring at the passing streets, wondering whether to write what he'd asked for. Her dead brother would certainly want her to. Her father, too, most likely. Michael Killen would approve. It might help the cause, and how could it hurt?

Why did she feel so reluctant? If Kollontai had asked her to write something comparable — a feminist appeal of some sort — would she have felt the same? Was it writing for a cause she objected to or the cause itself?

She rehearsed what she might say. That an Irish Brigade had been formed in Germany to fight for Irish independence, that it needed recruits, that it was time for Irish-Americans to put their bodies where their mouths were. All true. That it was pathetically small, that its leader seemed more than slightly unstable, that people who answered his call would, at best, be wasting their time and, at worst, throwing their lives away. The way Colm had done, she thought. For the first time, she admitted to herself how angry she was with him.

That aside, the second version was equally true. If the first was calculated to win recruits for Casement, the second was guaranteed to discourage them. A nuanced version, which offered both sides of the story, would favor the status quo.

It was the same with the task that Colm had given her, the task she'd been putting off. Anything other than a whitewash was useless to the cause, a cause, moreover, that she had once taken for granted. *Their* Ireland needed supporters, not truth sayers. Propagandists rather than journalists.

It was midafternoon by the time the late-evening train from Berlin reached Trier, where a new interpreter was waiting to shepherd her aboard the much less imposing rake of cars that would take them both on to Metz. Franz was a good-looking young man with classic clean-cut German features, blond hair and mustache; his uniform looked like it had just been pressed. His English, he said, had been learned at Oxford, where he had studied philosophy before the war.

The railway followed the Moselle River, and the scenery was mostly gorgeous, if one could ignore the symptoms of war that covered it like a rash. Waiting trains seemed to be stabled in every available refuge, some full of bored-looking troops, others of weapons or other supplies. Sometimes their train was held to allow another to pass, and on one occasion a line of windowless vans rumbling by in the opposite direction caused two nearby passengers to hurriedly cross themselves. A funeral train was her guess, one that Franz reluctantly confirmed. It felt like forever before it was past.

She had done her best to research the current military situation before leaving Berlin, and as far as she could tell, there were no major battles under way on the Western Front. Was this the usual casualty rate when things were quiet? Suddenly the figure she and her fellow journalists had casually come to accept — that of five thousand dead each day — seemed appallingly real.

Night was falling by the time they reached Metz, and, stepping down from the train, she heard a rumbling in the distance. At first she thought it was thunder, but this kept rolling on and on. "How far are we are from the front?" she asked Franz.

"About thirty kilometers."

The capital of Lothringen — or Lorraine, as the French had called it — seemed largely undamaged by the war, though Franz said that several months earlier the enemy had tried to bomb the steelworks. After losing several airplanes, he added smugly, they hadn't tried again.

Their hotel for the night had probably been the town's finest in peacetime but now seemed like a home away from home for officers on a break from the front. Several looked her over with the air of connoisseurs inspecting the new whore, and after dinner she made sure to place a chair under the handle of her door. Franz had told her to be ready at six for their morning departure, so she tried to get an early night, but it was only when the distant guns fell silent that she finally managed to sleep.

Next morning Franz was waiting in the lobby, having persuaded the kitchen to pack them both breakfast. The automobile outside looked modern enough underneath its coat of dust, and the driver — a corporal — gave her a welcoming smile. Soon they were out in the country and driving up through wooded hills onto what seemed a wide plateau. The sun was rising in a clear blue sky, promising another hot day.

After about half an hour, they crossed the prewar border. "We are now in France," he said, pointing out the wreckage of an old frontier post. She noticed the first graves a few seconds later, and after that there was rarely a moment when there weren't several crosses in view. They came in ones and twos and dozens; they came upright and leaning and facedown in the dirt. Few looked new, but none were really old.

"There was a lot of fighting here in the first few months," Franz told her.

They passed through several abandoned villages, with many houses ruined. One had a small cemetery that clearly predated the war; this was now a garden of chipped and broken gravestones, bordered by shredded trees.

The guns grew louder with each passing mile, and when they finally reached Martigny and the driver switched off his engine, it felt for a moment as if they were surrounded by drummers.

The hospital, a red-cross-emblazoned building that had probably been the *hôtel de ville,* filled one side of the square. A bizarre selection of ambulances, both motorized and horse drawn, were lined up outside.

"And now how far are we from the front?" she asked Franz, looking to the south. Was she imagining it, or was the skyline wreathed in smoke?

"Maybe five kilometers."

There was a German unit drilling on the far side of the square, and several French children watched them. Martigny had not been abandoned — perhaps the Germans had caught it unawares — and the looks that Caitlin was getting from its native residents were anything but friendly. Noticing a German flyer pinned to a nearby lamppost, she asked Franz what it said.

He walked across to read it. "It's the rules," he told her.

"And what are they?" she asked.

He hesitated. "The curfew times, some other things."

"Like what?" There was a familiar whiff in the air, but for a moment she couldn't place it.

He shook his head. "We're here to visit the hospital. Let's go in."

That was it, she thought. Blood.

"We have two hours in Martigny," he said over his shoulder. "And if you want to eat, we should leave an hour for that."

"We'll eat back in Metz."

He sighed his acceptance; he'd obviously been told to humor this woman as much as he could. As they passed into the lobby, the whiff became an acrid odor, overpowering but not quite masking the sweeter smell of disinfectant.

"Wait here while I find the man in charge," Franz said. He returned a few minutes later. "He's not here, but they say he'll be back soon."

"Well, let's look around, then," Caitlin said, heading for the nearest pair of doors.

"I don't think . . ." he began, but she was already pushing through them.

A big room — a council chamber, perhaps — was crammed with beds of all shapes and sizes, from iron bedsteads to simple wooden pallets. There had to be around forty of them, and none were empty. Most of the occupants seemed to be asleep, but a few turned curious eyes in her direction. The older of two nurses was striding toward her, asking questions.

"Wer sind sie?" — Who are you? — was a phrase Caitlin recognized. The rest was probably a variation on "What the hell are you doing here?"

She let Franz answer and watched the woman's expression turn from hostility to interest. *"Ein Amerikaner,"* she marveled, as if that were something weird and wonderful.

"Can she talk to me for a few minutes?" Caitlin asked Franz.

She could. The other nurse was shooed

away, ostensibly to check a patient, and Caitlin was ushered into one of the rare empty spaces, by a window overlooking what had once been a formal garden. The nurse's name was Dagmar; she was from Hamburg, where she'd worked in a large city hospital. Her husband had volunteered on the day that war broke out, and she had done the same. She'd been looking after brave boys ever since.

In answer to Caitlin's questions, she insisted that they had all the medicines they needed and that the soldiers were given excellent treatment — so much so that many men had later sent letters expressing their gratitude. Would Caitlin like to see these? Without waiting for an answer, Dagmar scurried across to her desk.

On the other side of the room, the younger nurse was wearing a look of disdain, and Caitlin made a mental note to see her later.

The letters were presented, and Franz translated a couple.

"Wonderful," Caitlin agreed. She asked if there were any woman doctors working at the front.

Dagmar looked scandalized. *"Nein."*

"Do you ever go up to the front with the ambulances?"

She did not. "Now," she said, ushering

Caitlin and her guide toward the door, "you must leave us to do our work."

Outside, the drilling soldiers had gone, but the dust they'd kicked up still hung in the air. A horse-drawn ambulance was pulling up and soon disgorged a man laid out on a stretcher. His clothes were soaked in blood, and each step of the bearers seemed to bring forth a cry of pain.

Caitlin turned to find that Dagmar had followed them out.

"There is an American doctor waiting here," Franz translated for her. "A Dr. Hoffman. She suggests you talk to him."

"Wonderful. Where can I find him?"

"In the operating theater. In the next building."

"Do you know how far we are from the fighting?" Caitlin asked Franz as they walked across.

"Maybe six kilometers."

In the building next door, another nurse informed them that the doctor was removing shrapnel from a soldier's head and neck but would be finished in a few minutes. He emerged in two, a fresh-faced young man from Chicago who rather ruefully told her that he'd been one of the first German-Americans to heed the fatherland's call. Over the next few minutes, he asked as many questions as Caitlin did and was disappointed to find that she hadn't been home for a couple of years. He was particularly keen to know whether Americans in general had grown more sympathetic to the German cause and how the Cubs were doing.

When other casualties were brought in for surgery, he commandeered a nurse to take Caitlin through to the wards, where, with Franz's help, she questioned a dozen or more patients. She asked them about letters and leave, about the food in the trenches and the enemy they fought.

Did they hate the French and the English as much as their songs suggested?

Not really.

Did they think the war would last into 1916?

More than likely.

There was no overt disaffection, no obvious bitterness, not even from those who'd been crippled or blinded. Franz might be censoring their replies or inducing self-censorship just by his presence, but she didn't think so — the facial expression tallied too well with the words. There was, she decided, a quite astonishing level of acceptance. These boys had been taken from home — or had taken themselves in a fit of patriotic zeal — and put in a narrow trench for months on end, at the mercy of the elements, to live with the ever-present threat of death by bullet or shell or bomb. And here they were, wincing with each painful movement yet joking among themselves and smiling up at her as if she were doing them a favor just by being there. She found this both awe-inspiring and crazy, but everyone else seemed to find it normal.

Once they'd been through the last ward, Franz, still fretting at their failure to secure the hospital director's permission to interview his staff and patients, disappeared in search of the missing man. "Please wait here," he told Caitlin as a motorized ambulance pulled up in a cloud of dust and another two casualties were hurriedly carried inside.

Curious, Caitlin walked across to the untended vehicle and peered in through the open rear doors. There was no medical equipment inside, just a polished metal floor for sliding the stretchers in and out. Would the orderlies notice if the doors were closed when they came back out?

What did she have to lose?

She crawled inside and pulled them almost shut behind her.

Several minutes went by, during which it

occurred to her that they'd probably be taking the empty stretchers back to the front. In which case they would find her.

But they weren't, and they didn't. Someone fastened the rear doors, two men climbed into the front seats, and away they went, rattling noisily down what had to be a dry mud track. Yes! Caitlin thought. I'm going to get there. I really am.

They drove on, the two Germans chatting away in the front, the guns growing noticeably louder with each passing minute, and soon her sense of triumph was fraying at the edges. Had she been brave or merely reckless?

They'd been traveling about fifteen minutes when something — an enemy shell, presumably — exploded so close that the ambulance rocked wildly to and fro, like a boat caught up in a bigger boat's wake. In the seats up front, one of the Germans said something that caused his companion to laugh out loud.

The noise outside now seemed more like a dull roar, but there were no more near misses. After another couple of minutes, the ambulance came to a stop, and a few seconds later the doors were flung open. She had a brief view of tents and a smoke-shrouded sky before one man started shouting and others appeared at his shoulders to see what he was shouting at.

She scrambled her way out of the vehicle with as much dignity as a feetfirst extrication would allow. "I'm a journalist," she said in English.

The first man continued shouting at her in German. This was some sort of clearing station, she thought. She was still some way from the front.

There was a sudden ear-piercing shriek, and a shell exploded beyond the tents, sending up a plume of earth. No one else seemed to notice.

That was twice this morning she could have been killed.

Another man had arrived in front of her, a doctor by the look of his gore-spattered gown. There were four men bearing a couple of stretchers behind him, and he waved her angrily aside to allow them access to the rear of the ambulance. One man had a leg that was almost severed just below the knee; his eyes were open, but he made no sound. The other had a blood-soaked groin and was moaning almost constantly. Once the stretchers were aboard, Caitlin was grabbed by the arms and marched around to the front of the vehicle, where, amid much ribald hilarity, she was planted in the lap of a blushing young orderly. As the driver turned the ambulance, she caught one last glimpse of the doctor's furious face.

The trip back seemed longer than the journey out. The boy whose lap she occupied kept his hands to himself, but the strength of the erection straining against her was hard to ignore. As was the constant wailing of the man in the back, who might never have another.

Back at the hospital, Franz looked ready to kill her. The middle-aged man at his side, face almost purple with rage, was presumably the director.

"You will leave now," the latter said in English before spinning on his heel and striding away.

The younger nurse whom Caitlin had wanted to interview was standing in the doorway, an expectant look on her face.

"I must use the bathroom before we go," Caitlin insisted.

Franz rolled his eyes, but, as Caitlin had hoped, he gestured the nurse over and passed along the request.

The nurse smiled and led her inside. When Caitlin came out of the bathroom, the girl gave her a crooked smile, handed across a piece of paper that bore two lines of German writing, and hurried away.

Caitlin stood there for a moment, wondering why the written message. Why not just tell her though Franz? Probably because the nurse didn't want to rely on one countryman's honesty. With the words on paper, Caitlin could elicit as many translations as she wanted.

She showed it to Franz in the hotel dining room that evening.

"Where did you get this?" he asked.

"What does it say?"

He shook his head. "It says, 'Women have always cleared up men's mess, and now the mess is other men.' "

Caitlin smiled.

"Is it poetry?" Franz asked.

OUTSIDE CUTHBERTSON & HARPER

As darkness fell on September 9, McColl, Tindall, Cunningham, and a mixed force of thirty policemen and soldiers were deployed just inside the line of trees that bordered the beach north of Chandipur. They hardly needed the cover — the sky, overcast and moonless, offered no illumination; they could hear the waves and smell the salt, but all they could see was a murky curtain. A blinking light might pierce the gloom if the boat drew close enough to shore, but its captain would not want to ground himself. A sensible man might give it up as a lost cause. Or risk another day out in the Bay of Bengal and try again tomorrow night. Or simply wait for dawn.

In the event, it was almost three in the morning when a fuzzy yellow light glowed through the darkness ahead. Four times.

The man Tindall had selected made the appropriate reply.

"I can't see a damn thing," the DCI man said, peering through his binoculars. "But they must be lowering a boat."

"It'll suit our boys," Cunningham added. He was referring to the occupants of the two Royal Navy dinghies, which should now be steering a course for the far side of the probable tramp steamer.

"I'll go down and say hello, shall I?" McColl said. He'd been given the honor by Tindall, a reward for suggesting they keep the emporium open. He was expecting the dinghy to contain the Indian and a couple of rowers at most, but three Indian officers had been chosen to accompany him just in case.

Reaching the water's edge, he could make out the dim silhouette of the newly arrived ship — it was smaller than he'd expected, with one funnel set toward the stern and lying around three hundred yards offshore. The dinghy was easier to see, more than halfway to the beach, riding in on the incoming tide. As it grew nearer, McColl could make out only two men, their backs toward him as they pulled on the oars.

His own Indians, all in plainclothes, stepped forward to help drag the dinghy up onto the sand. One man jumped out to greet them, and McColl could see the excitement in his eyes. "Jatin?" he shouted.

"I'm afraid not," McColl said, stepping forward and raising his gun. "Jatin is dead."

The man looked wildly round at his fellow Indians, as if he expected them to rush to his aid, then dramatically dropped to his knees in the surf.

His companion, who appeared to be Malayan, was still in the dinghy. He made no attempt to escape, simply shook his head and sat back down on his rowing seat.

It was as easy as that.

The two gunrunners were led away, and two of the Indian officers assumed their places in the dinghy, with orders to take their time rejoining the mother ship. The sight of their craft returning should reassure any watchers and focus their attention away from the navy dinghies closing in behind them.

McColl was joined at the water's edge by Tindall and Cunningham, and not long after that a single indecipherable shout came from the ship in question. McColl half expected gunshots to follow, but the ensuing minutes of silence were broken only by the thin blast of a whistle — the prearranged signal that the ship had been secured.

A captain and four more crewmen had been added to their bag. All were Javanese, and none even tried to complain at the seizure of their ship, let alone put up a fight. McColl assumed they would be sent back to the Dutch authorities in Batavia — there seemed no point in feeding and housing them at the Raj's expense. The ship would probably be confiscated.

As dawn soon revealed, the rusty old coaster wasn't much of a prize, but its cargo lived up to expectations. It took them most of the daylight hours to inventory the arsenal stacked in the hold, which consisted of more than seven thousand Springfield rifles, almost two thousand pistols, ten Gatling guns, and around three million cartridges. It was more than enough to mount a sizable rebellion, McColl thought, surveying the lines of open crates that covered the coaster's deck. Standing there, he found himself imagining the immediate future that Jatin and the Germans had conceived — the dispersal of guns to the waiting followers, the railway lines cut, the rising in Bengal that would, at the very least, keep half the Indian army at home and might even require a fresh infusion of troops from elsewhere in the empire.

A bold plan, now happily stillborn.

Next morning, with Tindall and Cunningham already returned to Calcutta and the emporium finally closed for business, Mc-Coll saw to Barun Ray's release and escorted him down to the station. En route the Indian repeated his promise to abstain from political activity until after the war was over and insisted on shaking McColl's hand when they parted. McColl hoped he was lying, but initially at least Ray proved true to his word. Sanjay and Mridul, who followed him home from Howrah station, spent several days waiting in vain for the man to even venture out.

A fortnight passed, and the bosses in London made clear their annoyance at Calcutta's failure to find any white-skinned enemies. McColl waved Cumming's latest cable at Tindall. "If there ever was a German agent in Calcutta — and I really am beginning to doubt it — he'd be far gone by now. But no, as long as there's trouble, he has to be here. They just can't imagine Indians causing all this mayhem on their own — there has to be a German lurking in the background, giving them instructions. Some evil mastermind with a sinister deformity like that ridiculous character in the serial that *Blackwood's* is running."

"*The Thirty-Nine Steps?* I think it's rather good."

"It's *fiction,*" McColl said bitterly.

Tindall grunted. "Speaking of Indians doing it on their own, your friend Bhattacharyya has escaped from Cuttack Fort."

"Has he really?" McColl felt rather pleased for the Indian. "When?"

"A week ago. No one's seen hide nor hair of him since. I only heard about it this morning."

"Well, good luck to him."

"I shouldn't be so pleased if I were you. He's one of the few Jugantar people who know how big a part you played in getting their leader killed. And they'll be out for revenge."

"True," McColl agreed, though he couldn't help thinking the threat was exaggerated. He did try to be more careful than usual over the next few days, but there was no way of avoiding the young man outside the Cuthbertson & Harper shoe shop, who calmly drew a gun from his pocket, aimed straight at McColl's heart, and pulled the trigger. When nothing happened, they stood there face-to-face for what seemed several seconds, mirroring each other's shock.

The Indian took flight, and McColl was again agonizing over whether or not he should try a shot on a crowded street when his would-be assassin ran headlong into the constable who was always on duty outside the Great Eastern.

"It was a Webley & Scott automatic," Tindall told the still-shaken McColl an hour or so later. "God knows where the little blighter got hold of one — they're only about two years old. And prone to jamming, I'm informed, which was lucky for you. If he'd been carrying something less fancy, we'd have been loading you onto a ship in a box."

That night, unable to sleep, McColl sat at his hotel window staring down at the quiet street below and wondering how many of Cumming's agents would survive the war. If they were faring as well as he was, probably not very many. In the last six months, he'd been shredded with glass, almost blown up, and been fired on by any number of people. On the two occasions that still brought him out in a sweat, he had literally stared down the barrel of his own mortality.

Down to his left was the stretch of pavement where his latest would-be nemesis had materialized. By all accounts he should be dead.

But he wasn't. Look on the bright side, he told himself, raising his head to watch the moon slip out from behind a cloud. All the near misses could mean somebody up there liked him. And when it came down to it, he'd been no closer to death than had his brother, or others fighting the war.

And he could choose to walk away.

As things turned out, the failed assassination attempt became his ticket home. McColl was no longer safe in Calcutta, and Cumming had realized as much. Either that or a new job had come up somewhere else. In the first week of October, as the local weather finally took a turn for the better, he received the cable he'd been hoping for, ordering him back to England on "the fastest available ship."

The journey home began at Howrah station late the following evening. According to the man at Thomas Cook, taking a train cross-country and a ship from Bombay was not only quicker than sailing straight from Calcutta but would also provide McColl with two spare days to indulge a whim and visit Mohandas Gandhi in his ashram outside Ahmedabad. If his old stretcher-bearer was away from home, then at least he'd have seen some more of India.

He wouldn't miss Calcutta, he thought, standing by an open window as the train rumbled out, the torpid night air clinging to his skin. He would miss Tindall and the billiards room at Spence's Hotel, but precious little else. His near encounter with death outside the shoe emporium seemed almost dreamlike in retrospect. Perhaps he'd been close to death so many times that his psyche had learned to absorb such shocks. Would that be good or bad? He couldn't tell.

The journey was long — thirty-six hours according to the ever-optimistic timetable — but he slept well enough through the nights and enjoyed the twelve hours at his window. His first impression of Ahmedabad, as the train slowed to enter the station, was of minarets and mill chimneys competing for sky and a dry heat so welcome after Calcutta's steam bath. His tonga from the station passed through an impressive gateway in the city wall and on down a long street lined with all the usual tradesmen. According to his Baedeker, the city had no resident Europeans, which no doubt explained the curious stares.

He had chosen the Empire Hotel for its central position, just outside the walled citadel that rose above the Sabarmati River. His room seemed clean enough for a one-night stay, and the desk clerk was happy to recommend a restaurant for lunch, if "much less dirty than the others, sahib" counted as a recommendation. The vegetarian curry was tasty and hopefully benign.

Once fed, he set out for Gandhi's new home on the western bank of the Sabarmati. The iron bridge across the quarter-mile-wide river offered picture-postcard views of the town behind him, but the sights below were rather more interesting. The riverbed was mostly dry, but people washed, swam, and bathed in — and cows contentedly drank from — the channels that carried the last of the summer rains. On the far side, the huge bats known as "flying foxes" were hanging asleep in the trees, apparently oblivious to the chattering monkeys all around them.

Gandhi's Satyagraha Ashram was about half a mile to the south, a beautiful house set back from the river. The young acolyte who greeted McColl was reluctant to disturb the boss, but McColl's description of their previous meeting on Spion Kop was dramatic enough to persuade him otherwise. Gandhi, who was reading in the shade of a colonnaded terrace on the other side of the house, recognized him immediately and almost leaped from his chair to shake hands.

The last time McColl had seen him, the Indian had been wearing a Red Cross uniform, and the minimal loincloth came as something of a shock. Fifteen years later Gandhi had to be into his forties, but there was no sign of added weight — if anything, he was wirier than he'd been before. Neither hair nor mustache showed any sign of graying.

Tea was brought and the two men left alone to reminisce about their meeting in South Africa. Gandhi was easy to talk to and even seemed interested in McColl's later life as an automobile salesman. McColl had heard that the Indian hated machines, but he now discovered there were exceptions — according to Gandhi, the Singer Sewing Machine was "one of the few useful things ever invented." It took a while for the conversation to reach politics and the war, and when it did, McColl felt obliged to admit that he worked for the government, quickly adding, "But not today."

An hour or so into the conversation, he felt sufficiently at home to ask Gandhi a personal question. "In South Africa you insisted on using nonviolent tactics against the authorities, but when the war began, you offered the British government your support. How could you do that if you believed in nonviolence?"

Gandhi raised his eyebrows. "How could I not? In the years of peace, I paid my taxes, knowing that they would be used to buy weapons; I accepted the benefits and protection they offered. I was a law-abiding citizen of the British Empire before war was declared, so how, in all conscience, could I abandon that empire in its hour of need?"

"But do you actually believe that a British victory will be better for the world than a German one?"

"I do not know. I know little of Germany, though it has to be said that some Germans have behaved very badly in Africa. But the British Empire has certain ideals with which I have fallen in love, and one of those is that every subject of the empire has the freest scope possible for his energy and honor and whatever he thinks is due to his conscience. I believe that is true of the British government as it is true of no other government, and I am convinced that one day, with a little encouragement, the British will set us Indians free to be the people we truly are. But first we must convince them that we are fit to be their partners, in the same way that their brethren in Australia and Canada have. And part of that is being prepared to lay down our lives for the empire we are all a part of."

McColl must have looked unconvinced.

"What is the alternative?" Gandhi continued. "Should we refuse to support the war, say it is not ours? That is what a people condemned to perpetual servitude would do, because they would leave their defense to their masters. How could such a people ever hope to deserve their freedom?"

McColl sighed. What Gandhi was saying made some sort of sense, but surely nonviolence was a sacred principle, not a tactic to be discarded when it ran counter to other principles. He suggested as much.

Gandhi laughed. "You are saying I contradict myself? I plead guilty. Some people say that consistency grows with age and wisdom, but my experience thus far has not supported this view."

After their conversation McColl walked back across the river with another ashram resident, an English-speaking young man from Bombay who seemed like a refugee from rich parents. Still wondering whether he lacked the imagination to understand Gandhi's ideas, McColl asked his companion whether he found them easy to follow.

"Not always," the young man admitted.

"I accused him of inconsistency, and he just laughed," McColl told him.

"Many have told him the same. We had a terrible row here last week. Gandhi insisted on taking an Untouchable family into the ashram, and several others left in protest. Supporters have told him they will not give any more money, but he won't change his mind."

"That sounds admirable to me."

"Yes, yes, it is. But this man who insists on sharing his home with Untouchables won't even share a meal with his wife. He insists that eating and shitting are equally disgusting and that both should be done alone. Now, doesn't that sound inconsistent to you?"

"I suppose it is."

"But it doesn't matter. He is a great soul. He will save India."

Which should have sounded ridiculous, McColl thought, but somehow it didn't.

Two days later he was standing in the stern of the steamship *Marmora* watching Bombay recede beneath a rapidly darkening evening sky. He was glad to be going home, back to the real war and enemies that had chosen to be so. If he'd been an Indian, he'd probably have seen things much the way his friend Chaudhuri did, but he could understand what made young men like Bhattacharyya and Mukherjee choose the paths they had. And thwarting them, while necessary, had brought him no real pleasure. Defending the empire against the Germans was one thing, defending it against its own subjects quite another, and the latter, in McColl's mind, was acceptable only if the subjects had willingly taken the Kaiser's shilling.

Which, he realized, raised any number of questions about how he would see his job once the war was over.

First they had to win it. And whatever it was Cumming had in store for him, he hoped it involved fighting Germans, not other rebels bent on using the war to sever their ties with the empire.

BAGS MADE OF SKIN

Leaving Germany was less straightforward than arriving had been. Caitlin was not required to take off her clothes at the Swiss border, but a female official was brought forth to check likely hiding places with vigorously probing fingers, and the male counterpart who spread the contents of her bags across two tables seemed overly interested in her underwear. It was an unfortunate end to her three weeks in the Kaiser's realm, three weeks in which she had garnered a better-than-expected impression of "the dreaded Hun," one she honed into a couple of articles over the next thirty-six hours as she waited in Berne for the conference that Kollontai had advised her to attend.

It was actually in Zimmerwald, a village eight miles to the south. Arriving there by horse cab on what she thought was the opening day, Caitlin learned from locals that the only group holding a meeting was an ornithological society, which had hired half the rooms at the Beau Séjour Rest Home. She took directions and sought out the building in question. As she'd anticipated, the topics under discussion on the colonnaded terrace were police informers and print runs, not the Lesser-Spotted Whatever.

It took her the best part of an hour to gain admittance to the conference. Journalists were not welcome, and Kollontai's promised letter had not arrived. It was only when one of the female delegates — a kindly Russian named Angelica Balabanova — took her to see Kollontai's "Uncle Lenin" that things turned in her favor. This short, bald, bearded man seemed, at first sight, a lot more ordinary than Kollontai had led Caitlin to believe, but he was good at arguing a case and, once convinced of her sympathies, managed to win her a watching brief and one of the no-shows' rooms. He was, she thought, excited by the prospect of American publicity.

Over the next few days, she sometimes wondered why she'd bothered. Discussions and formal meetings took place in a bewildering variety of languages, and it was only the help of another woman, an English-speaking Dutch socialist named Henriette

300

Roland-Holst, that kept her more or less in touch with what was going on. They all seemed to accept the old Second International line that class loyalties had precedence over national allegiances, but they definitely differed over how much abuse should be heaped on those who had decided otherwise during that fateful August. Lenin and his friends wanted no truck with the moderate socialists, now or ever, but a majority of those present were still hoping to induce a change of mind and insisted on a manifesto that simply put the case for peace.

Caitlin had her doubts about it all. They seemed like a very exclusive group, there didn't seem much evidence for the widespread support they claimed, and the picture-postcard village outside lent the whole proceeding an unreal air. And then there were the delegates. Sometimes she wondered whether these men and women, who were all so concerned about the world and its problems, weren't just a tad unworldly; they seemed to believe that anything obvious to them must be obvious to everyone else.

But they were trying to deal with the big issues and the terrible mess that the world was in. No one else seemed to be. She could see why Kollontai had thrown in her lot with this bunch, and when they all rose to sing "The Internationale" at the end of the conference, she felt almost like a believer. On the way back to Berne, she remembered something her father had once said, that a stirring tune could make a sucker out of anyone.

On her last evening in Switzerland, she wrote a long letter to Kollontai giving her impressions of the Zimmerwald gathering and a short piece for her American employers describing the secret conference and its rationale. As she'd promised Lenin, no names, dates, or places were included in the latter lest the Swiss authorities decide that their hospitality was being abused. Then, with one on the wire and the other in the post, she took yet another train, this one to the French frontier, where an equally rigorous inspection was conducted with rather more soothing shrugs and smiles.

She reached Paris on September 12, booked into a cheap hotel in Montmartre, and spent the next few days exploring the city and finding her professional feet. This was what her fellow journalists considered "the real world," the one in which most people thought that the war was worth fighting and that winning was what really mattered. Over the next few weeks, as the so-called Autumn Offensives got under way, the cafés were full of men poring over their papers and maps of the relevant parts of the front. The headlines dubbed them the Second Battle of Champagne and the Third Battle of Loos, which gave the impression that "try and try again" had become the French army's official motto. Both rumbled on with little apparent success, leaving all the café strategists frowning at their unchanged maps. At Loos the British had the decency to lose all the ground they had gained in three short days and then call the whole thing off.

But as far as Caitlin could tell, there was still no significant opposition to the war among the general public, and the only sign of it among the so-called intelligentsia was a new satirical magazine named *Le Canard Enchaîné* — "The Fettered Duck" — which was due to publish its first edition in a few weeks' time.

Paris itself seemed little changed from her only previous visit, several years before the war. There was rationing, but you could still get an excellent meal, and most of the theaters and cinema houses were open for business. After a brief pause to check the public mood, the fashion houses had reasserted themselves, and pale rose was in vogue that autumn, along with slightly lifted waistlines and sleeves that flared at the wrist. The couturiers gave no sign of having noticed that more and more women were wearing black.

Caitlin wrote a couple of pieces in this vein — her German ones had been well received by all but rabid Anglophiles — and wondered how she could get permission to visit the Allied front line. She wasn't optimistic but felt she had to try.

The British sector seemed a better bet — there would be no language problem, for one thing — but she soon learned from other journalists that the British authorities in France were unlikely to be sympathetic. She would have to pull strings in London and hope that those her friends and contacts approached would not know that her brother had recently died in the Tower. This was not unlikely — the sentences and executions had been much more widely publicized than had the names of those involved.

She contacted anyone who might be able to help — friends she made in the London embassy during Colm's incarceration, more recent acquaintances in Fleet Street, others she had met through Sylvia — and worked on their needs and prejudices — the Allies' desire to keep the American public on their side, the journalists' dislike of forbidden access, progressive women's hatred of unequal treatment.

All she wanted was what the Germans had already given her, a visit to a hospital just behind the front. A comparison piece should be good, and as far as she knew, no one else had done one. And if she got that close, then a visit to one of the towns where off-duty soldiers went to indulge their vices could also prove productive. She might even find one willing to smuggle her farther forward. The authorities' blanket refusal to allow women anywhere near the trenches irked her enormously, and their claim that it was for the women's own protection angered her even more.

As she lay awake in bed one night, two things occurred to her. One was that someone she already knew would find it harder to spin her a line. The other was that Jack's brother, Jed, and their mutual friend Mac were the only young men she knew who might be serving at the front. Jack had mentioned more than once how much he feared another war, because he guessed that the others would join the rush to enlist.

Had they? If so, were they still alive? How

could she find out?

It took a week of messages pinging to and fro between London and Paris before she finally reached someone with a sympathetic ear and access to the current service records. As of September 1, Jed McColl had been with the Royal Scots Fusiliers, and that regiment, she discovered without much difficulty, had recently been involved in the fighting around Loos, in which several thousand men had perished. Had he been one of them?

The news of his survival reached her three days later, on the same day as permission was granted to visit a field hospital just outside Arras. Hoping the British army's mail service was as quick and efficient as everyone said it was, she wrote to Jed, suggesting a meeting. She knew that the troops were rotated on a more-or-less weekly basis, a week in the forward trenches, a week in the support trenches, then a week behind the lines resting up, so she told him she would be in Arras for the first three weeks of October and hoped that he could manage to get there during that time. She told him she'd be staying at the Hôtel du Lac, hoping it would still be there. Two of the Paris-based British war correspondents had assured her it was the town's only decent hotel, but neither had been there for several months.

The Hôtel du Lac was still standing, unlike much of the town, which had clearly taken quite a battering in recent weeks. It was still subject to the occasional attentions of the German air force, but there always seemed plenty of warning, and the hotel had a large cellar. The off-duty troops who thronged the streets and bars seemed oblivious to any threat, but after what they'd all been through, a place like this was bound to feel like a haven of safety.

Caitlin visited the nearby British hospital on her second day there. It was messier than the German one, but in every other respect — the wounds and the smell, the cries and moans, the opinions of the doctors, nurses, and patients — there was little to tell them apart. Which would have been almost comical if it hadn't been so tragic. Over the next few days, she wrote half a dozen drafts of the resulting piece, each one a little less angry than its predecessor, until she was satisfied that she wouldn't just put people's backs up.

And then she waited, without much optimism, for Jed to turn up. Part of her almost hoped he wouldn't, and she had plenty of

time to assess her own motives for reestab-
lishing contact with Jack's brother. Was she
being professional and going after a story in
the way that seemed best? Or was she using
professionalism as an excuse to reopen the
past? A bit of both, perhaps. Kollontai's
"unfinished business" still seemed annoy-
ingly close to the mark.

She'd been in Arras for over a week when
Jed walked in through the hotel entrance.
She was sitting in the lobby and recognized
only the familiar walk — the short hair,
mustache, and uniform were all new.

He sat down beside her, shaking his head.
"I didn't really believe you'd be here," was
the first thing he said. "How are you?"

The smile was the same, the eyes more
watchful. "I'm fine," she said, trying to
ignore the sudden quickening of her heart.
Seeing him sitting there, she was back in
the dining room on board the *Manchuria,*
swapping jokes with her lover's brother.
"Look," she said, "why don't I get us a cup
of tea?"

"A beer would be better." As she walked
across to reception to request a couple of
glasses, she found herself taking deep
breaths. She had told herself this might be
difficult, and boy, had she been right.

She asked the clerk at reception for two

glasses of beer. At least Jed didn't look like Jack, she thought as she walked back toward him.

"What are you doing here?" he asked once she was seated again.

"I'm here as a journalist. I've just visited a hospital near here, and I did the same on the other side."

"The German side?!"

"We Americans are still officially neutral. I spent most of August in Berlin."

He shook his head again. "How are they doing over there?" he asked wryly.

"Much the same as you are over here."

He smiled. "Poor buggers."

"Is that how you feel about the Germans, that they're fellow victims?"

"No, not really. We try not to feel anything about them."

The beer arrived. "Cheers," he said, and took a swig. "Mmm, not bad."

"Didn't you and the Germans play football together last Christmas?"

His eyes lit up. "We did."

"In a friendly spirit?"

"More or less. The odd tackle over the top, but pretty friendly."

"What's a tackle over the top?"

"Going for the leg rather than the ball."

"Do you think there'll be another match

this Christmas?"

"I doubt it. The top brass weren't too pleased about the last one."

"Why not?"

He gave her a pitying look. "It's harder to kill people you know."

A group of British soldiers walked into the lobby, and while the corporal talked to the desk clerk, the privates happily stared at her. When one seemed set on introducing himself, his friends called him back. "Let them be," she thought she heard one boy say.

They all looked dreadfully young, but Jed seemed quite a bit older than she remembered. When they'd met on the *Manchuria,* he had still seemed a boy, albeit a nice one. He'd done a lot of growing up in the last eighteen months. So, she supposed, had most of Europe's young men. "Is Mac with you?" she asked.

He smiled. "Yes, we're still together. He's a sergeant now."

And Jed was a corporal, she noticed. "I've talked to a lot of soldiers," she said. "I used to hang around the cafés near Victoria and meet them coming and going. A few refuse to talk, but most are willing. It's probably the American accent."

"I can think of another reason."

She felt herself blushing, something she hadn't done in years. "Well, maybe that, too. Anyway, I don't get the feeling they tell me the truth. I don't mean they lie — they just don't tell me how they really feel about what you're all going through. Do they think they'll upset me, or do they just not want to think about it themselves?"

"Neither," Jed said. "They think it's a waste of breath. That anyone who hasn't been through it can never understand it, so what's the point? And they're right. It's like . . . oh, I don't know — I had a friend who said it was like trying to tell someone who's never had children what it was like to lose a child. They just wouldn't get it."

"But people have imaginations," she argued. "And I think it's only when people at home can imagine what it's really like that they'll do something to stop it."

This time the look was disbelieving. "You think ordinary people could stop this? How could they?"

"Okay, but humor me. Let me tell you what I think it's like, and you can laugh at my naïveté."

"I wouldn't do that."

"Well. First, the conditions are terrible, especially in winter. You're cold, you're wet, you've got lice —"

311

"I've just been deloused. But I wouldn't sit too close — they never seem to get them all."

"Just that would drive me mad," she admitted.

"You almost get used to it."

She shivered. "Anyway . . . the conditions are dreadful. And I presume you're frightened most of the time. With good reason. You never know when a shell might land right next to you, and you never know when the generals are going to order you over the top. Generals who've shown over and over again that they haven't a clue what they're doing. How am I doing so far?"

"It's all true."

"But?"

"You can't ignore the smells. Bodies out in no-man's-land that can't be carried because they fall apart in your hands. Dead horses and rats. Shit, of course — it's like living with a really bad fart for months on end. You can smell the front trenches from a mile away."

"What else?"

He took a sip of the beer and put the glass down with what seemed exaggerated care. There was a look in his eyes she'd never seen before. "Cruel" was the word that came to mind.

"I used to take the human body for granted," he began conversationally. "What you saw was what you saw. Just another person. And sometimes I still see them that way. But mostly they're bags, bags made of skin, crammed full of blood and flesh. And the bags get punctured so easily, and all that stuff falls out. Slithers out, usually. Brains, intestines. You see men who've suddenly realized that their bag has split, and they're desperately trying to hold it together, but they can't. You see someone you know well, someone you've seen talk and laugh and eat and smoke, and suddenly the mouth that did these things is gone and there's nothing there under the nose but blood pumping out, and the eyes are still open, full of horror. And you think, Thank God that isn't me." He fell silent, eyes turned inward, as if remembering something.

Caitlin said nothing for several moments, letting the waves of pity and anger slowly subside. "Shall I get us another beer?" she asked eventually.

"Why not? But first I must visit the gents'."

Back at the table before him, she took in the surroundings. The threadbare carpet wouldn't last many more weeks, and cobwebs were multiplying above the brocade

313

curtains. A harassed-looking officer walked in from the street and scanned the chairs, his young face crumpling in disappointment when he saw that no one was there to meet him.

Grinning, Jed sank back into his seat. "Hard to believe we thought this fighting business would all be a bit of a lark."

"One of the Germans boys I met said much the same," she told him. Where would governments be without a ready supply of young men craving adventure? "I've tried to get to the front," she told Jed, "but the authorities won't hear of it, and no one'll risk taking me without permission."

"It's not worth it," he said. "You'd never get there unobserved, and even if you could — what for? You wouldn't learn anything. It would be like visiting a prison — you'd see the cell, but that wouldn't tell you how it felt to be locked up for years on end."

"You're probably right, but I'd still like to go."

"Not with my help." He smiled to take the sting out of the refusal and then changed the subject. "It's probably none of my business, but what happened between you and Jack?"

There was that heartbeat again. "Didn't he tell you?" she asked, though she wasn't surprised. How could she tell Jed she didn't want to talk about his brother? Especially when she did.

"No, he didn't. I asked him a couple of times in my letters, but he never gave me a real answer. Was it something to do with your brother?"

"That was part of it." His failure to offer condolences was, she supposed, fair enough — he and Mac might have been on the train that Colm had tried to blow up. "You knew who Jack was working for? When we were all on the *Manchuria,* I mean."

"We had a vague idea he was doing work for the government, but he only actually told us in New York. I take it he didn't tell you."

"No," she said. And that was what had truly done for them, before Colm even entered the picture. The man who'd said he loved her hadn't even dared to tell her what his work was. How could she ever trust him after that?

"And he had a hand in arresting your brother?" Jed half asked, half guessed.

"Yes." She managed a wry smile. "Though he did try to let him go."

Jed smiled back. "Well, I can't say I'm surprised about that."

"I was."

"You shouldn't have been. He was crazy about you."

And I about him, she thought. But maybe crazy was exactly the word for what they'd had. Crazy never worked for long. "It seems a lifetime ago," she said, hoping to close the subject.

"Doesn't it," Jed said. "Well, at least Mac and I saw the world before we ended up here."

She couldn't help asking. "Where is Jack? Do you know?"

"In India, last I heard."

"Keeping the empire safe," she murmured. Her political influence over men was obviously less than she'd hoped. She didn't know whether to feel relieved or disappointed that he was so far away.

"Aren't we all," Jed said wryly. "I don't suppose you're going back to England in the near future?"

"Yes. I was only waiting to see you."

"I hope it was worth it."

"It was. And give my regards to Mac."

"I will. But the reason I asked — could you take a letter for my mother and post it once you get to London? It would be nice not to worry about the censors for once and write something natural. I could write it here if you don't mind waiting."

"Of course not."

He borrowed her pen, begged some paper from the hotel, and sat there scribbling for fifteen minutes. Watching him write to his mother, she could see the boy she remembered from eighteen months before, sharing a joke with Mac or out on the promenade deck with the missionary's golden-haired daughter.

Feeling tears well up in her eyes, she wondered whom they were for. For Jed? For all the soldiers out there with such an uncertain future? For the loss of all she thought she had known and felt on that ship?

It was in Dieppe that Caitlin noticed she was being followed once more. The young Englishman sitting on the other side of the half-empty restaurant kept giving her sidelong glances and then looking away when she stared at him. He might just be sex-starved, she supposed, but he made no attempt to engage her, and the fact that he wasn't wearing a uniform made her suspicious. Her hotel was only a hundred yards away, and a quick look back on reaching the entrance found him thirty yards behind her. There was no prospective suitor's knock on her door that evening, but he was there in the lobby next morning when she left for the boat.

She had grown accustomed to the presence of an official shadow in the days following Colm's arrest, when the British authorities were presumably still wondering whether she'd been involved, and again a month or so later when Michael Killen had first made contact on behalf of the Irish Citizen Army. The latter surveillance had lasted quite a while and ended for no apparent reason just after Christmas. Had the British finally realized she posed no threat, or had they, as Michael believed, simply run out of man power?

She didn't see her new shadow in the boarding hall at Dieppe, but the place was so busy that that wasn't surprising. She wondered what she'd done to warrant him. Had the British somehow gotten wind of her meeting with Roger Casement?

It had been an interesting two months, she thought as she stood on deck watching the French coastline recede. Kollontai, Berlin with all its contradictions, Casement and his sad bunch of soldiers, Zimmerwald's club of revolutionaries. The staffs and patients of the two field hospitals, who really differed only in the languages they spoke. All of them fighting their different wars.

She hadn't written the article that Casement had asked for. Such a piece would probably fall on deaf ears, but if by some miracle it didn't and numerous young Irish-Americans *did* hasten across the ocean to die for the cause, she didn't want to feel responsible. Knowing how bitterly Colm would have argued the point was upsetting, but not enough to change her mind. Hadn't the two of them always argued?

As for what she had promised her brother . . . well, what had she learned from Frau Suhr? Nothing, really. Colm and his comrades had not cut a deal with the Germans; they had hoped to prove that they would make an effective ally and had, in the end, shown little more than a willingness to die. An honest account would spread the blame widely. His father for never loving him, his acting stepmother for favoring his sisters, the British for mistreating Ireland, the Irish for romanticizing the struggle to evict them. Herself for not even noticing how far her brother had ventured down a path of no return. And, of course, Colm himself. He had sacrificed his life for a possible footnote in a history of glorious Irish failures. An honest account would leave nothing out, and one day she might try to write one. What she couldn't do was provide what Colm had asked for — a tale of righteous heroism, written in hope of inspiring more of the same. "I'm sorry," she told him and the rolling sea. "I think you were wrong."

She thought about Jed McColl, who a year ago had seemed so much younger than Colm, just a boy in thrall to the world he was slowly discovering, and who now seemed so much older than Colm would ever be. Which brought her back to Jack. He'd been crazy about her, according to Jed. She'd thought so, too, until that day — that moment that still made her blood run cold — when she'd realized the full extent of his treachery. And maybe he had been — Jed hadn't any reason to lie. It made no difference — there was no doubting the fact he'd betrayed her. And he was half a world away.

It was beginning to rain, and she reluctantly went back inside for the final half hour of the crossing. At Newhaven there seemed little in the way of inspection until her turn arrived and the official who'd blithely waved everyone else through insisted on searching her suitcase and demanded to see her passport. Removing the latter from the cardboard tube in which she carried it, he spread the document out on his table and subjected it to the minutest examination, fingering the seal to make sure it was the right kind of wax and requesting her signature for the sake of comparison. As she offered an apologetic glance to those queuing behind her, she noticed her shadow from the previous evening.

He was there again at Victoria, already out on the platform as she stepped down from the ladies-only compartment. Looking back from her cab as it drove across Chelsea Bridge, she could see several others behind them, but all had disappeared by the time they reached her Clapham lodgings. Of course the British police already knew where she lived.

The only obvious change to her room was a blanket coating of dust — if anyone had searched it, they had done so a long time ago. She shook off the coverlet, lay down on the bed, and asked herself whether a permanent shadow would get in the way of her doing her job. She couldn't see how. It was slightly unnerving — and probably intended as such — but since she was doing nothing illegal, she really had nothing to fear. Let them wear out their boots!

She felt a little less sanguine next morning. How would Sylvia Pankhurst and the London branch of Cumann na mBan, both of whom she planned to visit that day, feel about her bringing the police to their respective doors? In the event, she didn't have to find out. The Germans had finally executed Edith Cavell, the British nurse in Belgium whom they'd held for over two months, and given every journalist in Europe his or her story for the rest of the week.

Cavell, as Caitlin learned that morning at a Whitehall briefing for the neutral press, had died a martyr's death. This woman of forty-nine, who had nursed countless wounded men — English, French, and German — back to health, had been condemned for helping to hide just a few Allied soldiers, and the global campaign to save her had been coldly rebuffed. More proof, her hosts proclaimed, that the Hun was beyond redemption.

Her death was a godsend to the Allies, and Caitlin could hardly believe that the Germans had been so stupid.

It wasn't as if the Allies had much of a case. The American ambassador in London had been in frequent contact with his counterpart in Brussels, and the tale the latter told, which Caitlin heard from an embassy friend, was much less clear-cut than the British version. As far as she could tell, Edith Cavell had let her patriotic impulses take her way beyond the realm of nursing, to the point where she had actually helped to smuggle Allied soldiers across the Dutch frontier. This was in breach of occupation law and of the Geneva Convention. The Germans had every right to execute the woman but would have been so much wiser not to.

This wasn't a popular angle in Britain, and probably not in America either. She wrote a piece that largely ignored the Germans and painted Edith Cavell in simple colors, as someone who had chosen to die for her country, like the thousands of men who were perishing out on the battlefield. Like Colm, she thought, and found herself sourly wondering whether Cavell's vision of England had been any more real than her brother's of Ireland.

It took over a week for the furor to subside, and during those days her shadow mysteriously disappeared. Had his bosses decided that she was harmless? She could only hope.

Feeling liberated, she took the bus out to Poplar. Keir Hardie had finally died a month ago, and Caitlin was prepared to find her friend in mourning, but Sylvia, though red-eyed from tears or lack of sleep, was as busy as ever. With the war now into its second year, she was receiving hundreds of letters from soldiers bemoaning conditions at the front and almost as many visits from the families of those already disabled or killed. Sylvia gave what practical help she could and published the most heartrending accounts in *The Women's Dreadnought.* Reading through a recent copy of the magazine, Caitlin came across the obituary that Sylvia had written for her former lover, a man with the "heart of a child near to God."

The famous playwright George Bernard Shaw, in a short, bitter valediction, said he could "not see what Hardie could do but die." How could anyone expect him to "sit there among the poor slaves who imagined themselves Socialists until the touchstone of war found them out and exposed them for what they are?"

Seven-Inch Hems

The *Marmora* was not one of Peninsular &
Oriental's more modern vessels. It was
comfortable enough in an old-worldly sort
of way, but as the ship sailed westward
across the Arabian Sea, the captain seemed
disinclined to push its speed much beyond
ten knots, and even this caused the engine
to clank alarmingly. After complaints from
high-ranking passengers that their beauty
sleep was being interrupted, an even slower
pace was set at night.

McColl's fellow passengers were a mixed
bunch — Indian Civil Service retirees
returning to their homeland, businessmen
and government employees, young men
who had finally decided, for who knew what
reason, that it was time to join the colors.
There were a few wives, but the only single
women McColl noticed were a couple of
nurses intent on pursuing their vocation
much closer to the front. The company as a

whole seemed almost equally divided between those determined to uphold prewar standards of dress, decorum, and social precedence and those who saw the war as the perfect excuse to leave all that nonsense behind. When a crew member dared to dance with a passenger, some threw their hands up in disgust, others in jubilation.

McColl found himself angry with all of them, angrier than seemed sensible. He was also having trouble getting to sleep, though not on account of the engines — his mind was either racing or seething, and the cabin seemed claustrophobically small. After a week's worth of nights spent pacing the deck, he found that even the moon was making him angry, and he consulted the ship's doctor. "Something that'll put me to sleep," he urged the young Anglo-Indian.

The doctor was not so biddable. Before dispensing pills, he was keen to learn some personal history and, after listening to an edited account of McColl's recent experiences, asked him if he'd had a major shock.

"No . . . well, yes, I suppose so," McColl admitted. "Someone aimed a gun at me and pulled the trigger, but it didn't go off. I suppose that was a shock." Sitting there, he could feel a coldness spreading through his chest.

"Two, perhaps," the doctor said. "The first that you were about to die, the second that you weren't. This is delayed shock that you're suffering from. You're probably in a constant rage."

"Well . . ."

"I've seen it before," the doctor told him. "My sister was attacked in the street. Quite badly, but it looked for all the world as if she'd put the whole business behind her. Except she hadn't — she'd just buried it. These things have to be dealt with. And if your conscious brain doesn't do it, then your unconscious will find some way to punish you."

Which made some sort of sense. McColl decided not to complicate matters by telling the doctor how angry he'd often felt before the incident outside Cuthbertson & Harper's. "So what do I do?"

"Think about what happened. Feel it, relive it. There won't be a blinding flash, but if you stop repressing the feelings, they'll lose their power over you. In the meantime I'll give you some valerian to help you sleep."

"Thank you."

The doctor handed over a small bottle, with instructions already printed on the label. "Imagine how many men are experiencing this sort of shock in the trenches," he remarked. "Imagine how much anger they'll be left with."

McColl didn't find that a comforting thought. Would several million men be busily reliving the horrors of war for years to come? Over the next couple of days, he did make a conscious effort to reexperience those moments outside Cuthbertson & Harper's, and he found that immersion did indeed bring him out in a cold sweat. Whether it was that or the valerian, he began to sleep a little better and dislike his fellow passengers a little less fiercely. Score one for Freud.

After two weeks at sea, they reached Aden, and with the whole day needed for coaling, he took himself off for some sightseeing, first walking round Steamer Point and then hiring a covered horse-drawn carriage to carry him round the crater-set town. The loincloth-clad young boy who did the driving rarely stopped conversing with his horse, but as Arabic wasn't one of McColl's languages, the subjects under discussion remained a mystery. The town itself seemed sunk in torpor, with only a few graceful minarets to alleviate the overall impression of squalor and neglect.

After taking almost a week to traverse the

Red Sea, the *Marmora* reached the southern end of the Suez Canal. Earlier that year Turkish forces had reached the western bank — some had spent a few heady days on the African side — and though a general retreat into Sinai had followed, occasional raiding parties still emerged from the desert and fired a few shots at passing ships. The possibility of witnessing such excitement proved too much for the *Marmora*'s bored passengers, who crowded the starboard rail for the passage of the canal, staring hopefully out at the sandy wastes. Judging by scraps of overheard conversation, McColl gathered that the general expectation was of men in baggy silk trousers, scimitars glinting in the sun. He forbore from pointing out that the modern Turks had much the same dress and weaponry as everyone else and that the sighting of a Turkish field gun might not bode well for their ship.

He was more than happy to reach Port Said, where the coaling took place by night, hundreds of Arab boys carrying it aboard in baskets filled from adjacent barges. Several of his fellow passengers seemed entranced by the performance — "like ants building a nest," as one man put it. Several stood beside the rail long into the evening, handkerchiefs shielding their nostrils and mouths from the irritating dust.

Next morning they entered the Mediterranean. It was late October by this time, and for several days the skies were overcast. No warships were sighted, but that was hardly surprising, since the Allied ships in the neighborhood were all engaged in blocking their enemies' egress from the Adriatic and the Dardanelles. The only threat to the *Marmora*'s safety was the clutch of German U-boats based at the Austrian port of Pola, which had so far shown no inclination to attack civilian ships. Still, it paid to take precautions, and several lifeboat drills were held.

During these gray days in the eastern Mediterranean, McColl was surprised to find himself daydreaming of India — the awful climate and predatory insects were consigned to harmless anecdote, the vibrancy of light and color so conspicuous by their absence. And then, as the ship drew closer to its destination, he began wondering where Cumming might send him next. Out on a limb these past twelve months, McColl had little idea what the Service had been doing since he left England. Back then a turf war had been brewing with the War Office over who should take the leading role in neutral Holland and occupied Belgium, and the Service itself had been putting down roots in Sweden, Switzerland, and the United States. By this time Cumming had probably planted agents all across the Middle East, and maybe even in South America. Anyplace the Germans might meddle.

For all McColl knew, the Service had undercover agents in Germany itself. Several German spies had been captured in Britain, but not, as far as he knew, his old adversary Rainer von Schön. Where in the world was he at work?

Thinking of von Schön reminded him of Caitlin. He presumed she was still a working journalist, but he couldn't be certain — he hadn't seen an American newspaper since arriving in India. She was probably back in America — after Colm's execution what would there have been to keep her in England?

Toward the end of October, Caitlin took an early train from Euston and the afternoon ferry from Holyhead to Dublin. It was dark when she arrived, and rain was steadily falling as the taxi took her from the docks to the Imperial Hotel, where she'd stayed on her previous visit. Offered the same room overlooking Sackville Street, she instinctively refused and only later decided that this was her heart's way of saying good-bye to Michael Killen.

Next morning she walked up to Parnell Square, where Cumann na mBan's annual convention was being held, and sought out Maeve McCarron. Maeve was both surprised and pleased to see her — "I thought we'd seen the last of you!" — and quickly arranged her accreditation before racing off on some urgent errand. Caitlin sat through what sometimes seemed an interminable morning of procedural wrangles but found some compensation in the obvious commitment of the delegates. The afternoon brought more substantive debates on the role of the organization — was an auxiliary role a necessarily subservient one? — and the unveiling of the new Cumann na mBan uniform, which featured a military-style tweed jacket with four pockets worn over a long skirt. It was further decreed that the hem, "to be of really practical use," must be seven inches off the ground.

Practical use for what? Caitlin wondered. Running, presumably, which raised the question of why a member might need to run.

At the end of the day's proceedings, Maeve caught her at the door and insisted on putting Caitlin up for the duration of her stay. When working in a strange city, Caitlin usually liked the convenience of a hotel room, but Maeve's enthusiasm, and the help she might provide when it came to writing something about Cumann na mBan, persuaded her to accept the offer. After collecting her luggage from the Imperial Hotel, the two of them walked to Maeve's house on nearby Mary Street and talked until way past midnight. Maeve had heard of Alexandra Kollontai but knew nothing much about her, and she was fascinated by Caitlin's account of their conversations and the common ground they revealed between women on opposite sides of Europe. Caitlin was both amused and somewhat alarmed by Maeve's tale of a mock attack on Dublin Castle that the Citizen Army had conducted a few weeks earlier, no mention of which had appeared in the English papers. "You're not planning a real attack, are you?" she asked, only half in jest.

"Who knows?" was Maeve's response. "We've all heard Connolly say that this generation will shame itself if it doesn't take advantage of England's bother. I'm not saying it will happen, mind, although I wouldn't be shocked to find that someone is drawing up plans."

"But you couldn't take on the British army and hope to win, not alone." She told Maeve about her meeting with Casement in Berlin and the failure of his efforts to raise a significant Irish Brigade from the POWs. "And the last time I was here, I got the impression that most people were happy to wait for Home Rule."

"And they still are," Maeve admitted. "But the longer the war goes on, the more come over to us."

During the next few days, Caitlin saw the truth of this. Attaching herself to Maeve, she observed Cumann na mBan in action. At meetings of two new Dublin branches, she saw women flocking to join and heard how militant most of them were. At Liberty Hall, whose elegant frontage still bore the banner WE SERVE NEITHER KING NOR KAISER, she saw the office where the women produced their leaflets and papers and the printing press in the basement room they shared with the transport union and its Citizen Army militia. She attended first-aid classes that ended in drilling, Morse-code lessons, and rifle practice.

Maeve's own Cumann na mBan branch was organized into six squads, each attached to a unit of the Irish Volunteers. Their primary job was to tend the wounded and get them to the nearest field hospital, but unlike traditional nurses they also carried revolvers. No wonder these women needed their hems so far off the ground, Caitlin thought. They were training for war.

The realization unleashed a flurry of contradictory emotions. Excitement and admiration. Disquiet. Trepidation.

In prewar days those returnees from India who wished to avoid the Bay of Biscay's notorious waters had left the ship at Marseilles, caught the Blue Train to Calais and a suitable boat to Dover. The war, McColl found, had put an end to such speed and luxury. Reaching the French capital took two depressing days, and a rain-swept Paris seemed full of women in black. The war news was predictably bad: Bulgaria had joined the Central Powers, and the French offensives in Champagne and Artois had followed the familiar pattern — high hopes, ground gained, ground lost. The casualties were still being counted.

Since boarding the *Marmora* in Bombay, McColl had feared arriving home to news of his brother's death, and with each report he read, his sense of dread rose up another notch. When he reached Dover, the first thing he did was wire his mother, telling her he'd returned and asking for news of Jed. It was dark by the time he reached Fitzrovia, and her reply was on top of the pile inside the door. LETTER YESTERDAY, the telegram read. EVERYONE ALL RIGHT. WELCOME HOME.

McColl exhaled like a man who'd been holding his breath for days, then opened some windows to freshen the air before gathering up the rest of his mail. According to an older letter from his mother, his father had been ill and, though recovered, had now fully retired. His pension was "good enough, provided we spend it on things we need" — his dad, McColl suspected, would spend his retirement down at the pub. She named two neighbors who had lost sons, but try as he did, McColl couldn't dredge up their faces. The rent strikes were still going on; Glasgow's women, his mother said, had "better generals than the boys in France."

It was the last paragraph of a later missive from his mother that stunned McColl. "You won't believe it," she said, "but Jed ran into your old American girlfriend in France. She'd been visiting a hospital behind the front, and the two of them had a nice cup of tea together."

McColl was dumbfounded. He just stood there for a moment, staring into space. And the more he mulled it over, the more amazed he was. The idea of them "running into each other" seemed ludicrous, but how else could Caitlin have found Jed? And why would she have wanted to?

A faint hope stirred his heart, only to fade. If she wanted to contact him, she would have surely have done so directly — there was nothing devious about Caitlin.

She had found Jed amiable enough back in 1914, but as far as McColl knew, they'd never shared more than a few moments together, let alone become friends. Caitlin was a journalist first and foremost, but a "nice of cup of tea together" didn't sound like work. Jed might have omitted that bit on account of the censors — McColl doubted whether ordinary soldiers were allowed to talk to the press — but what journalistic reasons could she have had for seeking Jed out? McColl felt bewildered, felt like rushing over to France and asking his brother what the hell was going on.

It did mean that Caitlin was still in Europe, or had been in early October. If she hadn't returned home since, then where would she be? Paris or London, most likely. Once he had found out, he could make up his mind whether or not to contrive a meeting.

After sleeping badly, he went out in search of breakfast. A café on Tottenham Court Road provided eggs on toast, and over succeeding mugs of tea he read through an abandoned paper — England, he found, was still England. As he walked south toward the river, he realized that he'd finally left his sea legs behind and was taking the earth for granted again.

He had assumed that the Service was still run from the top floor of 2 Whitehall Court, and indeed it was. Cumming had always been early to work, and today proved no exception. Last time they'd met, the Service chief had been on crutches, having lost a leg in the motor accident that had killed his son, but there was no sign of them now — the artificial leg he'd been awaiting had clearly arrived. The office looked even fuller than McColl remembered, with papers, maps, and models spread in wild profusion. The painting of Prussian soldiers executing French villagers was still on the wall, in case he forgot who the enemy was.

Cumming was brusquer than usual — there was none of the usual chat about automobiles, sailing boats, and airplanes — but pronounced himself pleased by McColl's work in India. There'd been several more killings in Bengal since McColl's departure, and the situation was far from stable, but it did seem as if the Germans had shot that particular bolt. The new sources of trouble were elsewhere: in Persia a German named Wassmuss had won himself local disciples, and in Afghanistan a Berlin-funded group of Indian extremists was trying to interest the King in an invasion of the Punjab. "Without much success," Cumming noted. "And we're sending a few airplanes over the Khyber to show them how effective bombing can be. Not the real thing," he added, seeing McColl's face. "A demonstration. They should get the message."

The Service was putting its main effort into Belgium, where various train-watching networks had been set up behind the German lines. These were run from Rotterdam in Holland and were supplying copious and highly valuable intelligence of troop and supply movements. The one serious problem had been the failure to agree upon a simplified command structure, but it looked as if that were about to be solved — a meeting had been arranged to demarcate the territories for which the different organizations involved would be responsible. "In the meantime we've just lost one of our better agents. I presume you've heard about Miss Cavell."

McColl was surprised but supposed he shouldn't be. "I didn't know she was working for the Service."

"Oh, yes. A brave woman," Cumming added, as if slightly surprised by the possibility that such a creature might exist.

"No doubt," McColl agreed. If not quite the innocent the papers were weeping over. "Is that where you're sending me?" he asked. He couldn't imagine anywhere better.

"No," Cumming said, crushing that hope. "I'm afraid I'm loaning you out again." The Service chief looked uncharacteristically hesitant. "There are rumors — more than rumors — of a possible rising in Ireland," he said eventually.

McColl stifled a groan. For a second or two, he was back in the chilly Dublin waters, shivering with pain and fear as Brady and Tiernan peered hopefully down from the dockside above. Ireland held no happy memories, and once again he would be pitted against people whose cause was hard to deny, left defending the indefensible because the needs of the war trumped everything else. He would rather be in the trenches, he suddenly thought. And the way the war was going, they might even take him.

The sudden urge to resign lasted only an instant, unwittingly deflated by the man across the desk. "Forgive me for asking a personal question," Cumming was saying. "Am I right in assuming that Caitlin Hanley broke off your love affair when she discovered you were after her brother?"

It wasn't how McColl would have put it, but he couldn't dispute the gist. "More or less, but what —"

"Did you know that she met up with your brother in Arras a few weeks ago?"

"Yes, though I only found out last night. There was a letter from my mother waiting for me, and she mentioned it. She said that according to Jed, they just ran into each other."

Cumming smiled and passed a newspaper over the desk. It was a fortnight-old edition of the *New York Chronicle,* folded open at page four. HELL IS A SIX-FOOT TRENCH was the headline above Caitlin's name.

McColl skipped through the piece, thinking that she'd lost none of her way with words. He also thought he recognized Jed's voice in the quotes attributed to "one disillusioned British soldier," quotes that seemed calculated to cure the American public of any lingering thought that war might be romantic.

"We don't know that Jed is the disillusioned soldier," Cumming said. "She talked to others at a nearby hospital. And she could have made it all up, come to that. The point is, with half a million men to choose from, why did she seek out your brother?"

"Because she already knew him," McColl thought out loud. Why hadn't that occurred to him before?

"Perhaps. Or because she still feels a connection to you?"

This was the hope that McColl had dismissed the previous evening, but he didn't say so. "Perhaps," he said instead, allowing the possibility.

Cumming took back the newspaper. "So you haven't been following her journalistic career?"

"I've been in India, sir."

"Yes, of course. Well, she's made quite a splash according to our people across the pond. The pieces I've read seem pretty radical, even for Americans. She's become friendly with the Pankhurst daughter — the red one — and she even turned up in Glasgow and wrote a piece on the rent strikes there."

"She was always a progressive," McColl said, feeling absurdly loyal.

"Call it that if you like. And anyway, what she writes for Americans is neither here nor there. It's her European activities that worry me. She spent most of August in Germany, and one of the people she met was Sir Roger Casement. He's there to get help for the Irish rebels, guns for the rising we think they're planning."

"He does seem like the sort of person an American journalist would want to interview," McColl remarked.

"Ah, but she didn't. She's written about meetings with Russian exiles and German socialists, but there hasn't been a word about her meeting with him. Which leads me to think that their meeting had nothing to do with her job as a journalist and everything to do with her late brother's friends."

"I find that hard to believe," McColl said. But did he really? He had always thought Caitlin's hatred of violence would keep her on the sidelines, but maybe Colm's death had changed all that.

"And there's something else you should know," Cumming went on relentlessly. "Last autumn, while her brother was in Brixton, she took up with the man the Irish sent over to support him and the other prisoners. A man named Michael Killen, who we know is close to James Connolly, the union boss who's also the leader of the Irish Citizen Army. She spent more time with him in Dublin this spring, but as far as we know, they haven't met since — she spent most of the summer on the Continent."

Michael Killen, McColl thought, hiding his feelings as best he could. He hadn't expected her to take a vow of celibacy, but abstract knowledge was one thing, a name quite another. For a few shameful moments, he hoped Cumming would ask him to kill the man. Hoped in vain. "What do you want me to do?" he asked Cumming.

"Regain her confidence, if that's at all possible, and find out all you can."

McColl shook his head. "But she knows I work for the government that executed her brother. Why would she tell me anything?"

"Two reasons," Cumming replied. "Everything she's written in the last few months suggests that she's joined the antiwar camp. Whether that means she's now opposed to any form of violence is impossible to say — these people seem to juggle their beliefs to fit whatever they're feeling at any given moment. But if she really has become a raging pacifist, then she would be opposed to a violent rising in Dublin and might even help us nip one in the bud. Not likely, I know, but maybe worth a shot."

"And the other reason?"

"Oh, that she's still in love with you but won't admit it to herself. Hence the visit to your brother. Next time she's in Glasgow, she'll probably visit your parents."

McColl swallowed the sudden upsurge of hope and tried to see things clearly. He didn't like what he saw. Cumming's Caitlin didn't sound much like the woman he'd known, and the notion of her still being in love with him seemed depressingly far-fetched. He ought to say so, ought to tell Cumming that he would be wasting his time and talents in the vain pursuit of a woman who wanted nothing more to do with him. He ought to, but he didn't. "I'll give it a try," was what he said. When it came down to it, all that mattered was seeing her again.

Cumming nodded. "All the rebels who came to London are dead. Except for Aidan Brady, and the last we heard, he was back in America. Who else could recognize you from your time there last summer?"

McColl had spent his month in Dublin masquerading as a returned Irish-Australian; the only people who had seen him unmasked were the other patrons of

Killoran's Tavern, on the night that Brady had recognized and almost killed him. Those men had been sympathizers, not activists. He couldn't remember their faces, had never known their names. "Just Kell's people," he said, referring to the Dublin representatives of the Service's sister outfit, who handled home and empire intelligence. "Have any of them been turned in the last year?"

"Not that I know of," Cumming said, reaching for a pencil. "But I'll make inquiries."

"Do you know where Caitlin Hanley is now?" McColl asked.

"Oh, yes. She's in Dublin. Staying at the Imperial Hotel."

"She's being watched, then."

"Only a light touch. We had her followed back from France, but she soon realized what was happening, so there wasn't much point. Since then we've just kept track of where she's staying."

"Is she with Killen?"

"He hasn't been seen." Cumming rummaged in a file, brought out a photograph, and passed it across.

He was a good-looking man, McColl thought. Ignoring the surge of jealousy as best he could, he turned back to Cumming and chose his words carefully. "I loved that woman once. If it turns out she's part of a plot, I want you to promise me that she'll be sent back to America, not thrown in the Tower."

Cumming looked slightly taken aback, though whether by the outward display of emotion or the sheer cheek of the request was hard to say. He stared at McColl for several seconds before gruffly nodding his acquiescence.

Looking into the clear gray eyes, McColl knew that Cumming would keep the promise if he possibly could and be duly apologetic if the national interest demanded otherwise. It wasn't enough, but it was the best he could hope for.

Lovers Tell Each Other Secrets

This was the second time in sixteen months that McColl had been ordered to Dublin after a long spell abroad, and, as on the previous occasion, Cumming gave him permission to travel via Glasgow and the family home. He reached the house on Oakley Street early on the Friday evening and was astonished to find his mother out — "at one of her meetings," his father informed McColl, as if his housekeeper wife had been attending such things all her life.

Her eyes were shining when she arrived home just before ten and lit up still further on seeing her elder son. There had been an emergency meeting of the local rent-strike committee, she told him — the landlords had gone to law, and a mass rally was being organized for the day the business came to court. The women were in charge, she told him as she made them both tea, but the men from the workshops and yards had promised their support.

Over the next hour, as she recounted the events of the last year and explained how she herself had become involved, McColl was forced to the realization that his mother had been almost reborn. His father, by contrast, seemed diminished, by both age and the strangely altered balance of power between him and the wife he had bullied for so long. Which should be cause for celebration, McColl told himself, no matter how disturbing he might find it to see their roles reversed. When he gave his mother the silver brooch he had found in a Bombay bazaar, his father remarked how nice it was and how well it would go with a particular blouse.

She showed him Jed's recent letters, which were much more cheerful than the ones he wrote to his brother. Jed was protecting his mother from the sordid realities of his life in the trenches and the frightening thought that it might all be for nothing. She knew it, too. "I expect he tells you more," she said, both proud and sad.

In the old familiar bed that night, McColl thought about the change in his mother. Caitlin would see it as a sign that the world was changing for the better, and in this at least he knew she was right.

The following evening McColl took the overnight boat to Belfast; it arrived soon after dawn. Sixteen months earlier, waiting in the ticket queue at the city's Central Station, he had read about the shooting of Archduke Franz Ferdinand and his wife in Sarajevo; reading the newspaper now, it felt as if those two bullets had spawned a million more. There were battles everywhere — several in France, in Poland and the Carpathians, in Serbia and Macedonia, the Dardanelles and Mesopotamia. There was even fighting in the Cameroons. Across the world, men who had never met were busily trying to kill one another, with no apparent end in sight.

The train journey south seemed longer than last time, but he was still in Dublin by lunchtime. He called Five's HQ at Dublin Castle from a booth on the station concourse and asked for Jimmy Dunwood, Kell's top man in Ireland. When they'd met in 1914, McColl had found Dunwood rather too "army" but had come to respect his competence and, during the hospital visits that followed his own near-fatal encounter with Brady and Tiernan, had grown to like the man.

They arranged to meet at the bar of a nearby hotel, and McColl walked slowly there, wondering what he'd do if he suddenly ran into Caitlin. He realized he hadn't a clue.

Dunwood was there ahead of him, already sipping a pint. He looked heavier than he had the year before, the face a little redder, the eyes just as blue. "So you're here for the colleen," he said with some amusement after they'd taken seats in a quiet corner.

"Something like that. Do you know where she is?"

"Oh, yes. She spent her first night at the Imperial, but ever since then she's been staying with Maeve McCarron, who's quite a big wheel in Cumann na mBan. Her brother, Donal, was one of the bridge bombers."

McColl remembered the name. Donal McCarron had been Aidan Brady's partner.

"Am I understanding this right," Dunwood asked him, "that you and the Hanley woman were a romantic item at one time?"

"You are," McColl conceded.

Dunwood gave him a look.

"I met her in China," McColl explained. He could picture her emerging from the house on Bubbling Well Road, eyes alight with anticipation. "And she wasn't advertising her family's republican connections," he added in excuse before moving on to safer ground. "Tell me what sort of contacts she has here now. For a start, who or what are Cumann na mBan?"

"They're female Volunteers, in essence. Their relationship to their male colleagues isn't clear — one minute they're styling themselves as auxiliaries who do all the first aid and cooking, the next they're claiming equality and out taking rifle practice. Last year, after John Redmond announced his support for the war, the original Volunteers split — the majority went with him and became the National Volunteers." Dunwood paused to take a sip, then carefully lowered his glass to the table. "They're mostly in France now. The minority, who would rather fight the English than the Germans, still call themselves the Volunteers. They've committed themselves to a rising 'at the first possible moment,' which of course means bugger-all — because they'll never agree on when that moment has arrived."

"And Cumann support which faction?" McColl asked. A group of men had just come in, and one had given Dunwood a friendly nod.

"Cumann split as well, but with a majority opposing the war."

"And the Irish Citizen Army? Didn't that start as a union militia during the lockout?"

"It did. They were Jim Larkin's shock force, but Larkin went to America last year, and Connolly took over. Officially at least, the ICA is still subordinate to the Transport and General Workers' Union — you have be a union member to join it — but these days it's more than a workers' militia. Connolly calls himself a socialist *and* a nationalist, and he's made it very clear that he sees both the bosses and the English as his enemies. Your Miss Hanley's old boyfriend Michael Killen is one of his lieutenants."

McColl didn't want to think about Michael Killen. "How do the ICA people get on with the Volunteers?" he asked. "If they both favor action, you'd think they'd get together."

Dunwood shrugged. "If they have, they're keeping it quiet. And they spend a lot of energy taunting each other for being too timid."

"Okay," McColl said. "But I'm still confused. You said this McCarron woman is Cumann and Citizen Army, but Cumann are with the Volunteers."

"Not only. To be honest, it's hard to keep track. There are so many groups, and all with a different angle. Some are pure politics, others more cultural — promoting the Gaelic language, that sort of thing — and a lot of these people belong to several of them. Quite a few of the Cumann women are attracted to the Citizen Army because, on paper at least, it's much more committed to their women's-equality nonsense. Some are members of other women's groups who have offices at Liberty Hall. And they all know one another. Dublin is a small town, and we're really only talking about a couple of hundred people."

"So this McCarron woman will probably belong to several different groups?"

"More than likely. What exactly does Cumming hope the Hanley woman will tell us?"

"Whether a rising is actually planned. Is someone like McCarron — or Michael Killen — likely to know if one is?"

Dunwood shrugged. "Who knows? If the Volunteers or the Citizen Army — or both of them — are doing more than just mouthing off, then not many people will know. There were rumors a few weeks back that the Volunteers had set up a military committee, so we asked our informers to ferret around, but none of them found any evidence to confirm it."

"What's your instinct?" McColl asked, surveying his empty glass and telling himself it wouldn't be wise to have another.

"I can't believe they'd be so stupid as to launch an insurrection. They wouldn't get much public support — in fact, now that so many people have relatives in France, they'd probably lose what support they have. And there'd be no chance of success. They could mount some sort of demonstration — occupy Dublin Castle for a few hours, something like that — but how would that help them? A few days of headlines for a few years in jail doesn't seem much of a bargain."

"I hope you're right," McColl said. He didn't want Caitlin caught up in some bloody insurrection and ending up either dead or in prison.

Dunwood drained the last of his pint. "I still don't know why Cumming thinks Hanley will tell you anything."

"He expects me to worm myself back into her affections," McColl said dryly. Not for the first time, he wondered if the idea was as ridiculous as it sounded.

"I'd say you had your work cut out," Dunwood said. "Do you want us to call off the watchers?"

"No, not yet. Just let them know I'm here

and that I may be watching her, too. I haven't decided how to approach her yet. If I simply ask her to meet me, she'll probably say no."

"We can always arrest her and let the two of you chat in a cell."

McColl smiled. "I don't think she'd find that beguiling."

"So where are you staying?" Dunwood asked.

"The Royal, if they've got any rooms."

"In November with a war on? You'll be able to take your pick. Look, why don't you settle in today, and I'll have whoever's on surveillance pick you up in the morning. He can show you where she's living."

It sounded like a plan. After they parted company, McColl took a cab across the river. The Royal was as he remembered it, and empty as Dunwood had said it would be; McColl took a room high up at the back, after checking that the fire escape offered an alternative exit. A small restaurant on Dawson Street provided dinner, but none of the noisy pubs he passed on his way back to the hotel tempted him to make a night of it. Dublin seemed, superficially at least, undimmed by the war, but he was tired from all the traveling and eager to reach his bed.

Sleep proved elusive nevertheless. The rain started up again, and an overflowing gutter was soon beating a noisy tattoo on the iron steps outside. He lay there wondering how seeing her again was going to feel. Would it be the same or like a bubble bursting? He didn't know which would be harder to deal with. He told himself he was here to work, to do a job, to serve his country, and knew it was a lie. If he could, he would, but that was not why he was here.

It was still raining when he woke up. Dunwood's man — a thin Irishman of around forty with dark hair and anxious green eyes — found McColl finishing his breakfast in the hotel's dining room soon after eight. His name was Ardal Waldron, and his car, an anonymous black Ford, was parked out front.

They drove up past Trinity College, across the Liffey, and along Sackville Street, turning left onto Henry Street at the colonnaded post office. After a couple of blocks, this became Mary Street. "That's the house," Waldron said, nodding his head toward a small detached two-story dwelling with a dark green door and a large brass knocker. There were lace curtains behind the windows.

Waldron turned the automobile at the

next intersection and brought it to a halt behind another Ford, some hundred yards short of the house. A wave of an arm and the other car drove off. "The changing of the guard," Waldron murmured, and switched off the engine. "They usually go out between nine and half past," he said, taking out a cigarette case and offering it to McColl.

They had each smoked three by the time the door opened. Caitlin was first out. At this distance she looked unchanged, the slim figure encased in a long dark coat, unruly hair tied back in a bun. The way she moved and held herself was achingly familiar, and all the old thoughts and feelings welled up inside him — that he'd been so stupid to lose her, that he would never in his life find another like her, that if by some miracle she ever gave him a second chance, he wouldn't hesitate to seize it, even if that meant leaving the empire to look after its own salvation.

"That's the American," Waldron was saying. "And this is McCarron."

The other woman was shorter, with what looked from a distance like a lovely face and black hair pinned in a similar fashion. She was wearing a military-style jacket over a long black skirt.

The two of them walked off in the direction of Sackville Street, deep in conversation, but Waldron made no move to pull the car out. "Let's give them a good start," he said.

The women were not much more than specks when he deigned to turn the key and had long since rounded the distant corner when the men reached it in the Ford. But there they were, crossing Sackville Street a couple of hundred yards down. "Liberty Hall, I expect," Waldron said. "Most days they start off there."

And Liberty Hall it was. The two women were walking through the entrance doors as Waldron and McColl slowly drove past the imposing building. After parking out of sight around the next corner, Waldron led McColl down two alleys and in through the back door of what looked like a disused warehouse. Up some stairs, down a corridor, and they reached a room with a perfect view of the hall. A man was sitting with a telescope across his thighs. "McCarron and Hanley?" Waldron asked him.

The man shook his head.

"They're probably in the basement," Waldron guessed.

McColl stared out at the banner rejecting both King and Kaiser. A year ago it would have angered him, but not any longer. He felt an obligation to serve his country, but not because he thought it was best or always behaved correctly. It was the country and the people he knew, the one his brother and friend were risking their lives for. He supposed many Germans supported their country's war for much the same reasons.

And then there those whose countries were occupied, whose national feelings were denied, repressed, forbidden. McColl had not agreed with Jatin Mukherjee's terrorist tactics, but the man had been a patriot. He had died for his country. Many Bengalis would see him as a martyr, as someone to emulate. And no doubt many Irish people felt the same way about Colm Hanley and his friends, regardless of how reckless or murderous their operation had been.

For McColl the choice of tactics was what really mattered — he drew the line at certain methods. And this, he knew from their conversations, was where he and Caitlin were — or had been — in total agreement. It was okay to protest, march, or strike, to pursue any form of peaceful noncooperation, but they had both believed that the deliberate use of violence, for anything other than self-defense, was immoral and counterproductive. His only hope of bringing Cumming the intelligence he craved — always assuming he could persuade Caitlin to share the same space for long enough to listen — was to trade on her sense of the practical and her hatred of men's willingness to wreck the lives around them for no real lasting gain. An insurrection in Dublin was doomed from the start and would bring nothing but grief to the city and its people. It was in everyone's interest — Irish and English alike — to nip one in the bud.

If he got the chance, he would have to be very persuasive. He was under no illusions — she was probably cleverer than he was and had no reason to trust him. While his instincts told him to wait, another inner voice accused him of simply putting off the inevitable moment when she slammed another door in his face. He wasn't ready for that.

It was the evening of Friday the fifth of November, and the small explosions outside were fireworks lit by the local English in honor of their ancestor Guy Fawkes, the only man, as the old joke went, to enter Parliament with honest intentions. Maeve had a committee meeting in north Dublin, and Caitlin had walked to Sackville Street and the Imperial Hotel bar for a couple of drinks and the chance of professional company. But the English journalists who usually haunted the place were conspicuous by their absence, most likely out watching the fireworks.

She hadn't noticed the usual car that evening, which seemed to settle her and Maeve's dispute over which of them was being followed. "I'm not dangerous enough," Maeve had argued, to which Caitlin had retorted, "Neither am I." Perhaps it was nothing to do with politics, Maeve had mused, just some rich young man who'd taken a fancy to one of them. "Or both," Caitlin had suggested with a giggle.

If they did have an admirer, he was clearly too shy to approach them, and it did seem more likely that the G-men, for God only knew what reason, had decided to put the two of them under surveillance. It was almost flattering and not really inhibiting — all their work was done indoors, and no one ever followed them into Liberty Hall or any other building where Maeve had a meeting, although Caitlin had glimpsed a face in the window when one first-aid class dissolved into Irish dancing.

The English must be worried, she thought, taking a sip from her pint of Guinness in the sparsely populated bar. And there seemed a good chance they had reason to be. Maeve had no inside knowledge of anything definite in prospect, but both she and Caitlin had picked up on hints that *something* was brewing.

Which would be a hell of a story, and one she was well placed to scoop. This, and enjoying Maeve's company, had kept her in Dublin for longer than she'd intended, but over the last few days she'd come to the realization that a rising was still some way off. It was time she got back to London. There were only so many Americans interested in Irish matters, and the others deserved her attention.

She was draining her glass when a man appeared at her shoulder and settled himself onto the adjoining stool. "Miss Hanley," he said. It was Finian Mulryan, the republican who had come to see her in May, when she was visiting all the families for her piece on Colm's operation.

Another man took the seat on her other side, and for a moment she felt threatened. But both were smiling, and the place could hardly be more public.

"This is John McEvoy," Mulryan told her. McEvoy was a large man, with a pugilistic face and hair that almost leaped to attention when he took off his cloth cap. "Can we buy you another?" Mulryan asked.

She declined the drink but agreed to stay for "a little chat between friends."

The two men ordered beer with whiskey chasers. "The last time we met," Mulryan began after taking exploratory sips from both glasses, "you were planning a paean to your brother and the other brave lads who took the fight across to England."

"I don't think I used the word 'paean.' "

"Ah, perhaps not. But something worthy of their memory. As I remember, we arranged for you to meet all the relatives."

"And I did."

Mulryan nodded. "But unless we've missed something, nothing has been printed."

"I haven't finished it," Caitlin said waspishly. Mulryan was as outwardly friendly as he had been the last time, but there was something about him she didn't like.

He gave her a hurt look. "Might I guess that some were less happy than others about the choice their boys had made?"

"You could say that. But I just haven't gotten round to writing it yet. I've been too busy."

He looked unconvinced. "So it's not that you'd rather say nothing than — how shall I put it — gild the lily?"

"No."

Mulryan nodded again, as if he quite understood. He let his eyes roam round the bar, pausing to stare at the large painting of the Delhi Durbar that hung on one of the walls. "We hear that you met Roger Casement in Berlin," he said, turning back to Caitlin.

"You *are* well informed."

"He asked you to write a piece about the brigade he's putting together, one that would encourage American volunteers."

"Yes."

"But you haven't written that either."

He sounded like a disappointed uncle, Caitlin thought. He sounded, in fact, the way her father often had with Colm. Which made her angry. "Casement didn't impress me," she said.

"And rather than say so, you said nothing."

Mulryan was beginning to annoy her. "For which you should be grateful," she snapped back. "Look, I believe Ireland should have its independence, and I want to support those who are campaigning for it. But I'm not your Lord Kitchener. If you want someone to shout, 'Your country needs you!' then find an old man with a big mustache."

"Of course," Mulryan said. "But we did think, in view of your brother's sacrifice, that you might be more energetic in publicizing a cause we know you believe in. It seems we were mistaken."

Caitlin felt the emotional tug, but it wasn't as strong as it had been. She sighed. "I've spent the last two weeks researching a piece on Cumann na mBan, which I assure you I will write. And I shall say that Cumann na mBan is at the forefront of the struggles against both the war and the English occupation of Ireland, not to mention the struggle for women's equality. That they are an inspiration to the world. I shall be restating the Irish case against England while praising those who fight for it in the strongest terms I can. Won't that help your cause? Or don't you think the women's struggle is important? I think the level of women's involvement makes your struggle special, and something my fellow Americans will appreciate."

That shut Mulryan up for all of fifteen seconds. "You make a grand case," he admitted eventually.

"Perhaps it's time we got to the point," his companion said, reminding Caitlin of his presence.

"Which is?" she asked Mulryan.

"Well, Caitlin — can I call you that? — we're not here to talk to you about your writings — after our last meeting I was just satisfying my curiosity. You see, there's one thing you *can* do for us — and your brother's memory — something that only you can do." He took a sip of whiskey. "I believe you know a man named Jack McColl."

She tried to hide her surprise. "I *knew* a man named Jack McColl," she corrected him. Was that brittle voice her own?

"And no doubt you *knew* he was an English agent."

"Eventually." There was no need to fake the hurt in her voice.

"He's here in Dublin."

This time she didn't even try to conceal her . . . what? Shock? Alarm? What did she have to be alarmed about?

"We think there's people in London who're worried we might spoil their war, and he's been sent to find out whether they've cause for their concern."

She held his gaze. "And?"

"We'd like you to tell him that there won't be any rising. Or at least not unless they introduce conscription here, and our sources over there tell us that's unlikely to happen anytime soon."

Caitlin now knew where the phrase "heart in mouth" came from. What was fate dishing up for her? Ever since the conversation with Kollontai, she'd been mentally flirting with the idea of meeting him again, knowing full well that she'd never, ever seek him out. And now here he was, served up on a republican plate.

Too many feelings, too many thoughts — she retreated into practicalities. "I can only think of one reason you'd want the British believing that a rising's not in prospect."

Mulryan just smiled at her.

Caitlin shook her head, as if that might restore some order to her thoughts. "Why would he believe me, for heaven's sake? If you know I know him, you know why we fell out. Am I supposed to have had some Damascene conversion and suddenly realized how wonderful his wretched empire is? He's not a fool. If I tell him what you want me to, he'll see through it in an instant and assume that the opposite is true. I can't see how that would help you." Even as she spoke, the thought of seeing him again was inducing a silent paroxysm of contradictory emotions. "I will have that drink," she decided. "A whiskey, please."

Mulryan ordered three.

"Give us some credit," Mulryan said once the drink had arrived. "We're hoping you can convince the man that you've forgiven him and are willing to give him another try."

Her eyes widened. "You want me to sleep with the bastard who put my brother in front of a firing squad?" She didn't know whether to slap the man's face or applaud him for his gall.

"Lovers tell each other secrets," McEvoy muttered behind her, as if revealing some great philosophical truth.

"Perhaps we're asking too much," Mulryan said more diplomatically. "Only you could say how much you would do in your brother's memory. But I can tell you this — you will have your revenge. There are men in Dublin who want nothing more than to see this McColl dead. Friends and brothers of those who died with Colm. Whatever you say to us now, he won't leave Dublin alive."

That shocked her anew, and so did the feeling of panic it induced. "Killing him won't bring Colm back," she said briskly, for want of anything better. "And it was the British government that killed my brother, not Jack McColl." With more than a little help from Colm himself, she reflected bitterly.

Mulryan shrugged. "The enemy's the

enemy. Will you at least give the matter some thought?"

"I will," she said, surprising herself. But then why not see him again? What did she have to lose? If he was still crazy about her, she wouldn't have to sleep with him, just give him hope that she might. And there was a certain poetry to rewarding deception with deception. She could do what Mulryan asked and discharge her debt to Colm, then give McColl the same chance of escape that he had given her brother and pay off that debt, too. And be free of them both.

Never kid a kidder, her father had used to say.

She knocked back the rest of her whiskey. "So where is he staying?"

Mulryan gave her the name of McColl's hotel. "Then you'll do it?"

"I told you I'd think about it," she said, more to annoy him than because there was any real doubt in her mind. On the walk back to Maeve's house, she asked herself why she wanted to do this. And the simple answer was that if Kollontai was right and he was unfinished business, then surely this would finish it. Since she'd met him, Jack McColl had conjured up just about every emotion there was in her heart, with the possible exception of indifference. And all of them seemed to come and go, to rise and fall, pursuing a logic completely their own. She'd tried to convince herself that it didn't matter, because love was one thing, life another, and whether or not he'd betrayed their love, sooner or later the lives they'd chosen would have set them apart. But he *had* betrayed her, and she wanted him to know how wrong he'd been.

She wanted to hear his explanation — the one she'd been too angry to listen to that day in his London flat — and tear it asunder line by line.

As for assuring him that there wouldn't be a rising, she would find some way to convince him that she was acting in good faith. She had no qualms at all about lulling the English into a false sense of security — if a thousand years of Irish tears and anger hadn't taught them to keep looking over their shoulders, they had only themselves to blame. Which didn't mean an armed insurrection was a good idea. Surely one couldn't succeed? And if that were true, then what was the point? To show that Ireland still bridled at English rule? There were dozens of newspapers and organizations providing constant reminders of that. Did people have to die?

As she crossed Liffey Street, the thought

passed through her mind that the number of dead would hardly compare with the carnage in the trenches. But what did that matter? She remembered the families of Colm's comrades, all still coping with grief long after the deaths.

Kollontai had half convinced her that people would have to die for real change to come, but would even a successful rising bring real change to Ireland? If Connolly was in charge, perhaps. But the Volunteers? All they wanted was a change of flag.

Caitlin let herself into Maeve's house, put on the kettle for tea, and stood by the stove examining her own position. She had believed — or wanted to believe — that a line could be drawn between political activism and journalism. A blurry line, but a line nevertheless. Now she wasn't so sure. Whether or not she reported that a rising was imminent, she would be playing a part in the way events unfolded. If all she did in print was analyze how popular or successful a rising might be, she would, at least potentially, be influencing those involved in deciding whether or not to rise.

Her certainties seemed to have vanished, and she found herself envying Kollontai, who accepted that very few judgments were wholly right or wrong but still insisted on acting as if they were. There were two political responsibilities, she had told Caitlin: one was finding out all you could about any particular issue, and the other was refusing to be immobilized by the complexity of what you discovered.

Maeve's key was turning in the lock, so Caitlin put the kettle back on. Up until this moment, as far as she knew, the two women had told each other everything, but her conversation with Mulryan had put an end to that.

When McColl arrived back at his hotel on Saturday evening — he had taken the Ford for what he hoped would be a thought-clearing ride in the Wicklow Mountains — the receptionist called him over. "A Miss Hanley telephoned," the man said, scrambling any thoughts that might have been cleared. "If it's convenient for you, she would like to meet at eleven tomorrow morning. In the cafeteria at Kingsbridge Station."

McColl was struck dumb for several seconds. "And if it isn't convenient?" he eventually asked. "Did she leave a number?"

"No, sir, she didn't. In the event that you couldn't be there, she asked that you send word to eleven Mary Street."

"Thank you," McColl said automatically, and almost sleepwalked his way up the stairs. This had to be more than coincidence. How did she know he was in Dublin? Unless she'd seen him on the street — which was somewhat unlikely — someone else must have told her. Which raised all sorts of disturbing possibilities, because the only people likely to know were colleagues from the Castle and Irishmen who wanted him dead.

At least she had spared him the task of arranging a meeting. He called Dunwood to pass on the news, stopped off in the empty hotel bar for a couple of sleep-assisting doubles, and finally went to bed, where his wildest hopes and direst fears took turns keeping him awake.

After spending more time than usual in front of the bathroom mirror — had India actually aged him? — McColl left the hotel at half past nine. The sun was shining for the first time in days, and he decided to walk the two miles. He was carrying a revolver in his coat pocket but couldn't believe he would need it — if she was the bait in a republican trap, why suggest such a public space?

Walking west along the Liffey, he passed a

series of families in their Sunday best, but the square outside Kingsbridge Station held only a few hopeful cabs. He passed through onto the concourse, where a very ragged queue was waiting to board a Limerick train. The cafeteria was off to his right.

He was early, but she was earlier, sitting on the far side of the room nursing a cup in both hands. He stood there for a moment, looking at her. She was wearing the same dark coat and skirt but had unbuttoned the former to reveal a pale lilac blouse. As he started across the room, she turned her face toward him, and the merest ghost of a smile crossed her lips, only to be swiftly suppressed. He looked much the same, Caitlin thought, his deep tan even more eye-catching among the pale Irish complexions. He wasn't a big man, but there was strength in the way he moved, in who he was — she had felt that since their very first meeting in the Peking embassy. He arrived at the table, wondering whether to offer his hand or even risk a kiss on the cheek. As both seemed equally absurd, he just sat down in the opposite chair.

"Hello, Jack," she said, with what felt like admirable control. God, she thought, this is going to be hard.

"It's good to see you," he replied. So good

that he was finding it hard not to smile at how lovely she was. "I was surprised to get your message," he added. Was he imagining it, or was her Irish accent more pronounced?

The waitress arrived to take their order, one coffee for him and a second for her. Out on the platform, a whistle shrilled, presumably announcing the departure for Limerick.

"I heard you were in Dublin," Caitlin said. "And I decided I wanted — needed — to talk to you. So I rang round the hotels until I found out where you were staying." Her voice sounded false to herself, but then *she* didn't deceive people for a living.

"I'm glad you did," he said, adding two spoons of sugar to his coffee and wondering whom she'd heard it from. He deemed it wiser not to ask.

Now for the hardest bit, she told herself. "The day before he died, Colm told me that you offered to let him escape."

So her brother had told her. "I did, but he refused." She was avoiding his eyes, and he guessed that she was finding it hard to keep her composure. Or to keep from slapping his face.

"Well, thank you for trying," she said quietly.

"I'm sorry I didn't succeed."

"Yes, well . . ."

He wanted to lift her eyes from the table. "I hear you met Jed in France."

The smile that briefly lit her face was the one he remembered. "Yes. It was good to see him again. I wanted to talk to someone I knew," she added, as if he'd asked for an explanation. "Someone who might tell me the truth about the trenches."

"I read your piece."

"Did you?" She sighed. "It's hell on earth. He said you look at someone you thought you knew and all you see is a bag of blood."

"Yes," McColl murmured, as much to himself as to her. The smell of blood always took him back to the night he'd spent on Spion Kop, badly wounded and pinned to the ground by the weight of a dying man. "At least he's still alive," he said, before he realized how crass that sounded. "I'm sorry . . . I wasn't thinking."

She placed a hand on top of her head, as if that might keep it from flying off, and looked him straight in the eye. "Why did you deceive me? I know you tried to say something when I came to your apartment, but I was far too angry to listen."

He took a deep breath. Was he being offered a second chance? "I . . . I was going to tell you I had no choice . . ." He sighed.

"But of course I did. When I met you, when we . . . when I fell in love with you, well . . . secret agents are supposed to be secret — they're not supposed to tell each passing girlfriend who they are. And you made me believe — you were very clear about it — that we would have our affair and then part with no regrets."

"Yes, but . . ."

"When I met you, I was just a part-time spy — I was a businessman who did odd jobs for my government, partly out of patriotism, mostly because it helped pay the bills and I enjoyed it. The thrill, I suppose. Boys' games and all that."

She gave him a strange look, as if surprised, but didn't say anything.

He plowed on. "In San Francisco I was supposed to investigate links between the German embassy, the local Irish republicans, and Indian exiles. That led to me Father Meagher and your family . . ."

"That's when you should have told me." And if only you had, she thought.

He nodded. "I know. Either that or tell my boss that I wasn't prepared to spy on you or your family."

"But you didn't do either."

"I told myself I wouldn't have to choose between you and the job, that since no one in your family would be involved in the plot I was investigating, I could carry on doing my job without losing you."

Caitlin took a deep breath. She didn't feel ready for forgiveness. "And when did you learn that Colm was involved?" she asked, staring into her empty cup.

"Not until I got back to England. No, that's not completely true. I found that Seán Tiernan was involved in some sort of plot while I was still in New York, and I guessed that Colm must be, too. But then I was taken off the investigation and sent to Mexico. It was only when I got back to England that I found out they were both in Ireland."

She looked him in the eye. "You're being remarkably frank."

He held her gaze. "I won't lie to you again."

That surprised her. "Really? What are you doing here in Dublin?"

"I'm supposed to find out whether the republicans are planning an insurrection. My boss reckons that with all the republican contacts you've made over the last year, you may know, and that you might be willing to tell me."

"So *you* were going to get in touch with *me*," she said, as much to herself as him.

Was fate trying to tell them something?

"Yes," he said simply.

"And why in heaven's name would you think that I would betray my Irish friends?" she asked angrily.

"I don't believe you would," he said. "It was my boss's idea, and I went along because . . . well, because I wanted to see you again."

She chose to ignore that. "Why would *he* think I'd betray my friends? And to you of all people?" '

That hurt, but he persisted. "You might oppose a rising on pacifist grounds, and warning the British government — through me — might save a lot of lives, including those of friends. Or — and this is his reasoning, not mine — you might still hold a torch for me and be willing to tell me anything I wanted to know."

Lovers tell each other secrets, she thought. This was more than she'd bargained for. "And what do you think?" she asked after a long moment's hesitation.

"I've never stopped holding a torch for you."

"I . . ." she began. "I meant about the chances of my telling you Irish secrets."

He shook his head. "I'm not going to ask you."

She felt bemused. Here she was racking her brain for a credible way of passing on the false news, and here he was holding out both hands. "What will you do — does one resign from whoever it is you work for?"

"Oh, I shall still investigate — I'll simply leave you out of it. I'll say you just laughed in my face when I begged for your help." He smiled. "As I'm sure you would."

"Probably. But aren't you afraid I'll go back to all these republican contacts and tell them what you're doing here?"

"I expect they know already, but . . ." He shrugged. "It's a risk I'm prepared to take."

"You seem very sure of yourself," she said.

He smiled at that. "Far from it."

She felt like she was walking a wire. What was she going to do?

"What are you doing here?" he asked. "I mean, I presume you're here for your paper."

She explained what she was working on and about Cumann na mBan, glad that he'd changed the subject. As ever, he was a good listener.

What he heard was the passion in her voice, the passion she brought to everything, the passion she had once brought to him.

Seeing that in his eyes, she felt the sense of panic return. This was all too confusing

— she needed time and space to think. "I have to go," she announced abruptly. "I'm meeting someone."

"Oh. Of course."

But she still had Mulryan's message to deliver, and it wouldn't sound very convincing as part of a hurried good-bye. Kollontai's judgment, that this was unfinished business, suddenly reared up in her mind, both appalling and arousing. She was wondering how to broach the possibility of another meeting when he beat her to it.

"Could we meet again?" he asked, fully expecting rejection.

This surprised her even more. Was he doing it again, this time relying on apparent honesty to deceive her? "What for?" she asked. "If you're not going to ask me any questions . . ."

"We could always talk about something else."

She made a show of considering the idea. "All right," she said. "For old times' sake. How about Saturday?"

"All right," McColl agreed, as surprised as he was pleased. "How about a drive?"

"Yes," she said. "A drive would be nice. Let's go to the sea."

On the hansom ride back into town, Caitlin

wondered what on earth she was doing. A drive, for God's sake — why hadn't she suggested somewhere more public, like a bar or another cafeteria? Why hadn't she just accepted the opportunity he'd presented, claimed her pacifism prevented her from supporting a rising, and told him what Mulryan wanted London to know? It would be over, and she'd never have to see him again. Finished business.

Except it wasn't, and after the last hour she knew that more surely than ever.

Back in the house on Mary Street, she said nothing to Maeve about her rendezvous with McColl or their plans for another. She did arrange to meet Mulryan in the Imperial's bar, and this time he came alone.

"McColl's here for the reason you thought," she told Mulryan.

"And did you tell him there's no need to worry?"

"Not yet. He wouldn't have believed me if I had. I'll need time to get his trust back." She noticed a look of disapproval come and go on the Irishman's face — he would ask her to sleep with the enemy if the situation required it and then condemn her for agreeing to do so. "But there's one thing I want from you."

"And that would be?"

"Your word that my part in this business is kept secret. I don't want every republican in Dublin thinking I'm a whore."

"They wouldn't be thinking that."

"Oh, yes they would. And that wouldn't be in your interest. You don't want one of your foreign allies discredited like that."

Mulryan shrugged. "Very well, then — I give you my word."

"All right. I'll let you know when I've told him. And more to the point, when he's told his bosses in London. If your boys take their revenge before he passes it on, it'll all have been for nothing."

As Caitlin walked out of the bar, she caught a glimpse of herself in one of the mirrors — a stern-faced young woman with a confident step and no hint of the turmoil within.

McColl was less than frank with Dunwood. He meant to tell the MI5 man that Caitlin had sent him away with a flea in his ear, but he changed his mind. It was all very well telling Caitlin that he could investigate a possible insurrection without her help, but in truth he had no other contacts, and if she was out of the picture, Cumming would expect him to leave the whole business to Dunwood and his colleagues.

McColl had no intention of being recalled just yet. He hadn't been able to read Caitlin at their strange reunion but supposed that that was an improvement on their previous meeting, where he'd been left in no doubt about her feelings. He hadn't expected her to agree to another meeting and was still searching for a reason that made sense. One thing he was sure of — she would never betray her Irish friends. So why meet him again? Was it remotely possible that she might be willing to give him another chance?

He told Dunwood that he was still hoping to win her over, told himself that he was taking a well-deserved holiday. Who knew? Perhaps deceiving the Service for her would turn out better than deceiving her for the Service.

THE ROOM AT THE
ROYAL HOTEL

As he drove the Model T across the city on a cold but sunny Saturday morning, the thought crossed McColl's mind that this was the day she could avenge her brother, by luring him out to some lonely byway where armed republicans lay in wait. He told himself he didn't care. If he was that wrong about her, it didn't much matter if he lived or died.

Drawing up in front of the house on Mary Street, he remembered the day he had collected her on Shanghai's Bubbling Well Road for another drive in the country. It was the day after that when they'd first become lovers.

Caitlin answered the door. She was glad that Maeve was out on one of the Volunteers' frequent weekend exercises, because she wouldn't have to make up some story to explain her assignation with one of the enemy. "Where are we going?" was the first thing she asked after settling into her seat.

"I thought Howth for a start," he said. "Then on up the coast if the weather holds."

"Okay," she agreed.

She seemed unsure of herself, McColl thought as he worked their way out of the city. In the past, questions about her work had been almost guaranteed to provoke a vigorous response, but not this morning.

"I've been thinking," she said as they finally reached open country, "that you have me at a disadvantage. All I know about what you've been doing is what I gleaned from Jed, but you probably know everywhere I've been in the last year and everyone I've talked to."

"I was shown your file when I came back from India," he conceded. "It didn't have quite that level of detail, but I do know about your job, and your friendship with Sylvia Pankhurst, and that you spent the summer in Europe."

"I should have known there was a file," she said. "I'd love to see it."

"That *would* get me fired."

"It might be worth it. I suppose you know about Michael Killen, too?" She knew she was trying to hurt him and thought a little less of herself.

He maneuvered the Ford round a slow-moving hay cart. "I know who he is and that you spent time together. I don't know how you felt about him."

She resisted telling him. "No, you couldn't learn that from a file. But you probably know that I haven't seen him lately." She refrained from adding what Maeve had told her, that Michael had recently announced his engagement to another member of Cumann na mBan.

"No, I didn't know," he replied. "You're not being followed anymore," he added.

"Do I have you to thank for that?"

"Not only, but I'm happy to take the credit."

She stared out the window for a few moments. "So can you tell me what you were doing in India?"

"Trying to track down terrorists." He explained about Jugantar and told the story of his and Tindall's pursuit of the group, which had reached some sort of conclusion with Jatin Mukherjee's death.

"You sound as if you admired him."

"I did. But not his methods. Too many innocent Indians died."

"Sometimes it can't be helped, if anything is going to change."

"Maybe, but I don't think that's the case in India. Not yet anyway." He smiled. "I met Mohandas Gandhi again."

"How?"

McColl explained how he'd stopped off in Ahmedabad en route to Bombay.

"He disappointed me," Caitlin said. "How can he recruit young men for this war after everything he's said and done? I don't understand it."

"Me neither. I asked him, but I can't say I followed his argument." McColl tried, without much success, to repeat the gist of what Gandhi had said. "But I can still see why Indians want to follow him. And once the war's over, I suspect he'll give us a run for our money."

"Once the war's over, I think all hell will break loose," Caitlin declared. "I don't suppose you've heard of Alexandra Kollontai?"

"No."

Caitlin explained who Kollontai was, where she came from, and what she stood for. Listening, McColl felt as if he were back on the *Manchuria,* where she'd first introduced him to a world he knew nothing about, a world of women intent on radical change. Some just wanted the vote, but most wanted so much more, from easy contraception to unrestrictive clothing, equal opportunity to equal pay. Kollontai apparently believed that the road to women's liberation led through world revolution, and it seemed as if Caitlin agreed with her.

There were a few more clouds in the sky by the time they reached the small fishing port of Howth, but it was still a beautiful day. "This is where they brought the guns ashore last year," Caitlin said as McColl pulled the Ford up alongside the harbor.

"I know, I was here," he said without thinking.

"You were?" she said, surprised.

He paused, silently cursing the way that so many things led them back to Colm. "I was looking for Tiernan and Brady and your brother," he admitted. "I'd been looking for weeks, turning up at any republican event I heard of."

"Did you find them?"

"No." He refrained from adding that spotting Brady in Dublin later that day had set them on the plotters' trail. "But I watched them unload the guns and joined the march back into Dublin." He smiled. "It ended badly with the shooting in town, but up until that moment it was a pretty amazing day. On the way back, some soldiers tried to disarm the crowd, and you could see men disappearing through hedges and hightailing it across the fields clutching their new rifles, and all the soldiers could do was watch them go."

"I wish I'd seen that." She pointed at the cliffs away to their right. "That looks like a good walk."

They left the Ford at the foot of a path and started to climb, McColl carrying the sandwiches and beer he'd brought along for their lunch. As the path curved round to the south, the Irish Sea spread out before them, silver blue in the early-winter sunshine. The one visible craft was a yacht heading into Dublin Bay, tacking against the westerly breeze.

They reached a wooden bench overlooking a precipitous drop. "Do you want something to eat?" McColl asked.

"No, I want to be kissed," she said, surprising both of them.

He did as she bid, and after only the slightest hesitation she responded. And once started, they seemed unable to stop, pressing against each other as fiercely as the need to breathe allowed.

And then they were simply holding each other, her head resting against his shoulder.

"I love you so much," he told her. Wise or not, it was something he had to say.

She wiped away a stray tear. "God only

knows why, but I can't seem to stop loving you."

"I know I —"

"No," she said. "No more explanations. I just want to make love."

"There are hotels in Howth."

"Then let's go to one."

They walked back arm in arm, hardly speaking. What was she doing? Caitlin asked herself. What she wanted to do, was the answer. She wanted to lie with this man again, to have Kollontai's waves of passion sweep over her, to drink from the Russian's cup of love's joy, however deep it might be. Tomorrow was tomorrow.

The first hotel had empty rooms in abundance. McColl signed them in as Mr. and Mrs. McNally and tried to ignore the knowing smirk on the desk clerk's face.

Their room was large, with a splendid view, which they didn't stop to admire. He helped her undress, unclipping her modern brassiere at the back and lifting it off her shoulders before gently cupping each breast and kissing her on the neck.

The first coupling was short, almost desperate, and oh, so sweet. They came together and collapsed together, laughing at the absurd perfection of the moment.

Then, and for most of the next two days,

it felt to them both as if nothing had changed since their New York parting, that all the guilt and anger had somehow been magicked away.

They also both knew that this wasn't true, but for now only love and desire seemed to matter.

After the weekend in Howth, they restricted their trysts to the hours of darkness, sharing his bed at the Royal. Their passion showed no sign of waning, and, lying cradled in his arms, Caitlin asked herself why it was so much better with him than it had been with other men. It was almost as if those idiots who claimed there was only the one perfect partner were actually right.

She also wondered why a reasonable God would give all this with one hand and threaten to take it away with the other. Ireland clearly divided them, and even if she could fully forgive him for Colm, her brothers' friends would not. And was there any place on earth where a radical journalist and an agent of the British Crown could happily coexist?

On Wednesday she was waylaid in the Imperial lobby by an impatient Mulryan, who asked her "how many nights" she thought it would take to regain the Englishman's trust. She could tell he wanted to say it more crudely, that as far as he was concerned each extra "fuck" was a further betrayal.

Still, she knew she couldn't delay much longer. A few more days, perhaps. "I'll tell him this weekend," she told the Irishman.

McColl spent the days pinching himself. Was this too good to be true? He occasionally saw something in her eyes that sent corrosive shivers of doubt racing up and down his spine, but then a look of love from the same green eyes, a look he couldn't believe was faked, would bring him back to his senses.

On the Wednesday he saw Dunwood and gave him an edited version of what was happening. The "laughed in my face" story was obviously not going to work, so he invented another, one that had her refusing to betray her friends. "I don't think she's going to tell me anything," he confided to Dunwood. "Maybe it's time we started looking for other sources."

In the meantime he relished the moment. Double lives were usually short ones, and even if the two of them could sustain this daily pattern of Dracula-like transformations, changing from lovers to foes with each rising of the sun, it seemed cruelly inevitable that sooner or later their jobs would pull them apart. She had already told him that her paper was keen to see her back in London.

As it happened, it was McColl's boss who called time. "You have the rest of the week to get something out of her," Dunwood told him at a hastily arranged meeting. "Cumming needs you back in London by Sunday. Another job's come up."

"Do you know where?" He'd known that this moment would come, but leaving her again was hard to accept, even though they'd both agreed that their work would have to come first until the war was over.

Dunwood laughed. "You think he'd tell me?"

He told her that evening, as they lay in bed with the rain beating down outside. "I'm going to Glasgow soon," she told him. "To report on the rent strikes. I thought I might go and see your mother and tell her about my meeting with Jed."

"She'd like that. What will you say about us?"

"I don't know. Nothing, I think. I don't want to jinx things."

■ ■ ■ ■

It was raining again two nights later when she told him he had to leave Dublin. "As soon as you can, but by Friday night at the latest. Don't ask how I know, but there are plans to grab you off the street sometime over the weekend. I know the men involved — they're relatives of boys who were shot in the Tower — and they mean to take you off somewhere for some sort of trial and then shoot you."

"I —"

"I know you're going to say you've got a job to do," she interjected. "Well, I don't want to read about your body washing up in Dublin Bay, so I'll tell you what you want to know. There'll be no insurrection."

"How do you know?"

"I just know. I'm a journalist, I have sources, and I know people through Colm. I'm not going to give you any names, am I? If you pass them on to your bosses, then I've betrayed them, and if you don't, then you wouldn't be doing your job." She was finding it easier to look him in the eye than she'd expected, but deceiving him still felt bad. She was beginning to understand how difficult he must have found all those weeks of deceiving her.

He was asking why they'd decided against a rising. "Because there's not enough support," she told him. "Because they haven't got enough weapons. If your government decides to bring in conscription here, the first might change, but not the second. And they've given up hope of help from the Germans." All of which was true, she thought, yet still they planned to fight. God help them. "So you've no reason to stay here."

"You're a pretty good reason."

"I'm off to Scotland tomorrow," she lied, "so there's nothing to keep you."

"Oh."

"Promise me you'll leave," she said, putting her hands on his shoulders. "I don't want to lose you again."

He kissed her. "I promise."

"But God knows when we'll next see each other," she added. Or if, she thought. His tale of the Indian gun that jammed still brought a chill to her heart.

"But that is what you want?"

"Yes," she said simply. She remembered Kollontai's admonition, that when the cup of love's joy was empty, you threw it away without regret and bitterness. Well, this cup wasn't empty. There were times she thought it never would be.

Next morning McColl passed the intelligence on to Dunwood.

"Do you trust her?" the Irishman asked.

"What she said made sense."

Dunwood pulled a face. "Well, it would have to make sense, wouldn't it? What if it's a setup, designed to put us off our guard?"

This possibility had already occurred to McColl, and he had forced himself to examine it. "She was in Dublin before I was, and at that point no one knew I was coming."

"The republicans might have seen you arrive, known she was here, and decided to use your past against you."

"I suppose that's possible . . ."

"But not likely," Dunwood agreed.

"No. And look, we agree that any insurrection would be doomed from the start, don't we?"

"We do."

"And she's told us that they've decided against it for just that reason."

"True."

"So why look a gift horse in the mouth?"

She was tired of the Imperial's bar. "I've told him," she informed Mulryan late that same afternoon, "and I'll let you know when he's passed it on."

Mulryan smiled at her. "No need, my dear. Your work is over."

"What do you mean?"

"He has passed it on."

She suddenly felt a chill reach up her spine. "How do you know?"

"How do you think? We have people in Dublin Castle. McColl told his friend Jimmy Dunwood when they met up this morning." He gave her a sharp look. "I thought you'd be pleased — you can't have been enjoying these past few days." There was the slightest hint of a question mark attached to the final sentence.

"What do you think?" she retorted. "But I owed it to Colm," she added flatly, picking up her bag. "And now I must go."

"Ah, don't rush off. Let's have a drink to celebrate."

"Some of us have work to do," she snapped, leaping to her feet. She managed a steady walk to the door, then almost ran to the curb, scanning for the street for a taxi. There wasn't one in sight.

She walked hurriedly south toward the river and managed to catch one emerging from Lower Abbey Street. "And please hurry," she told the young driver, who took her at her word, almost knocking down a cyclist as they crossed the O'Connell Bridge. After he'd screeched to a halt outside the Royal, she passed him a generous handful of coins and rushed up the steps, praying she'd find McColl gone.

And yes, he had checked out, the desk clerk told her. But as he'd already paid for the week, he'd left his suitcase up in his room, for collection later that day. As madam presumably knew, the gentleman had booked a passage on the night ferry to Liverpool.

Mind racing, Caitlin sat down in a lobby chair and tried to decide on the best course of action. She couldn't just wait there for him to return — Mulryan's friends might already be on his trail. She had to try to find him, hopeless as that seemed. And leave a message at the desk in case he returned.

Make that *when* he returned, she corrected herself, reaching for a sheet of the hotel notepaper.

After leaving Dunwood, McColl strolled down Sackville Street, half hoping to see her one more time. Their parting that morning had brought back the one in New York, when she'd been starting her new job and he'd been Mexico-bound. At that time

400

everything had been colored by his lack of honesty, and now it felt so good to be truthful. If Cumming found out, he might be dismissed from the Service, but there seemed no reason he should, and if he did . . . well, that was a price that McColl was willing to pay. There had been a shift, slight but still important, in his priorities. His own experiences in India, what he knew from others of the wider war, had nibbled away at his notion of who and what he was serving and with that at his sense of duty. He was still convinced that a British victory would be better for the world, and he would play what part he could in bringing that about. As long as Jed — and all the thousands of others — were going through hell in the trenches, he felt morally obliged to put his own life at risk in the British cause.

But — and it was a big but — he'd been given a second chance with Caitlin, and he wasn't about to throw that away. If he had to choose between her and the Service, then Cumming would be the jilted party.

He reached the O'Connell Bridge and paused there for a moment, leaning on the balustrade and gazing downriver. It was another beautiful day, and he didn't want to spend it cooped up in his hotel or sitting in the departure shed at Kingstown. And even if his enemies were waiting for Saturday, he didn't want to wander the streets.

A film, he thought. That would fill an hour or so.

The first cinema he passed was showing Chaplin's *Tramp,* which he'd already seen; the second had a film that he knew divided opinions, *The Birth of a Nation.* A fellow passenger on the *Marmora* had thought it absolutely wonderful, but Caitlin had told him how progressives had picketed American cinemas to protest the film's depiction of Negroes.

He decided to make up his own mind. The cinema was almost empty for the early-afternoon show, and he opted for a seat in the farthest corner, where he couldn't be approached from behind.

By the time the film ended, he could see both points of view. There was something startlingly original about it, in the way the camera moved, perhaps — he couldn't be sure. The story rattled along, and it all seemed bigger, more extravagant than the films he was used to — the makers must have put half the men in Los Angeles in either a blue or a gray uniform. That said, he could see the boycotters' point. The Negroes — white actors with blacked-up faces — circled the film's white women like sex-mad sharks, while the vigilante Ku Klux Klan — "hooded cretins," Caitlin had called them — seemed unlikely saviors of civilization. *Birth of a Nation* might be good drama, but as a representation of American history it left a lot to be desired.

As he emerged onto the street, eyes narrowed against the afternoon sun, a rumbling in the stomach reminded him that he hadn't had lunch. By the time a worker's café off Grafton Street had supplied the necessary, it was gone four — time, he thought, to head for Kingstown.

He was halfway across the Royal's lobby when the desk clerk called him over. "The lady left a message for you," he said, and passed McColl an envelope. Hoping for a fond farewell, and dreading an unexpected brush-off, he tore it open and read the two short sentences. "They're not waiting for Saturday. Go at once."

Heart beating a little faster, he put the note back into the envelope and the envelope into his pocket. "Has anyone else asked for me?" he inquired of the desk clerk.

"No one, sir."

"I'll just go up for my luggage, then," McColl said. It seemed sensible to advertise the fact that he was going to his room.

He took the four flights slowly, stopping

at each landing to listen for noises above. But the hotel was quiet, and his corridor, when he reached it, was empty.

He tiptoed to his door and stood for almost half a minute with an ear pressed to the wood. The only thing he heard was a ship's horn out in the harbor.

He put his key in the lock, clicked it open, and pushed the door back slowly, gun out and ready. The room had been cleaned, the bed made. His suitcase was by the window, where he'd left it.

As he stepped across the threshold, something cold and hard pushed into the side of his neck, and a soft Irish voice invited him to "step right in."

Caitlin hurried up Grafton Street and along the Liffey, scanning the roads on either side with increasingly anxious eyes. Where could he be? Signing off at Dublin Castle, perhaps. They had made a pact never to discuss their work in Ireland, so she had no idea if that was where his superiors were based. She could hardly go banging on the gate for him.

Nevertheless, she made her way down Parliament Street to the corner of Cork Hill and stood there staring at the ancient seat of English rule. Stood there too long, in fact, according to the policeman who came over and politely asked her to move on.

Fuming, she walked back to the river and east along the northern side until she reached the bottom of Sackville Street. Which way now? she asked herself. This really was like looking for a needle in a haystack.

A café across the way caught her eye — if she sat in the window looking out on the busiest street in the city, there seemed a fair chance he might walk by. But she reckoned without her own impatience. After watching people pass for what felt like an hour, but which the clock insisted was only fifteen minutes, she could sit there no longer. It was growing dark, and soon he would have to return for his luggage, if he hadn't already done so.

She recrossed the river and started down Westmoreland Street, walking so fast she was almost running.

There were two of them behind the door. The one holding the gun to McColl's neck was about forty, with curly brown hair and a round face; he wore a cheap gray suit and a collarless shirt. His partner was younger and thinner, with a sharp face and short black hair; he was wearing a rough jacket over workingmen's overalls. The latter's face

405

looked familiar to McColl — one of the men captured in 1914 had shared similar features. Kieran Breslin had been his name, and this must be a relation.

The older man had relieved him of the Webley and was now giving him the sort of look a cat might give a saucer of milk.

"Who the hell are you?" McColl blustered like an innocent. "And what the hell do you want?"

The older man laughed. "It's just your past catching up with you, Jack McColl. The way we see it, this is not your country. And spies in other people's countries are usually taken out and shot."

The only point in arguing was in winning a few seconds' grace, but that was point enough. "Another few years and we'll be gone, and you'll have your country back. But not yet. You're the outlaw here."

"One with a gun," the Irishman agreed. "And you'll have your chance to split hairs in front of a judge."

"And then we'll shoot you," the younger man added coldly. He turned to his partner. "How about we stop all the yapping and get moving? It must be dark enough by now."

The older man glanced at the window. "We'll give it another ten minutes or so. Jack's in no hurry, I'm sure."

They were presumably going to take him down the fire escape, McColl thought. There might be a car waiting, or perhaps they intended walking him to the republican stronghold down by the docks. He had a mental picture of Killoran's Tavern dressed up as a courtroom, with the regulars forming the jury and the barman pronouncing sentence.

The younger man had pushed up the lower sash on the window and was peering out. "It's dark enough now."

"Patience!" his partner insisted. "I've no desire to spend five years in Kilmainham Gaol just because you couldn't bear to wait a few minutes."

"I need a piss."

"The toilet's down the corridor," McColl said helpfully.

"Can't you wait?" the older man said wearily.

"I've been waiting for two hours already. What's the problem — you've got the gun, haven't you?"

"Jesus Christ! Be quick."

Once the younger man had slipped out through the door, they could hear him whistling his way down the corridor.

"Don't try anything," the older one warned. "I wouldn't like to deprive you of your day in court, but if needs must . . ."

McColl had few doubts on that score, but this was likely to be his only chance. Above him, as he knew from the hours he and Caitlin had spent in bed, were four shaded lamps arranged on the ends of a metal cross, which hung from the ceiling on a single vertical rod. If he reached up on tiptoe, grabbed the cross, and pulled down hard, the light would surely go out. If it didn't, he hadn't lost anything, unless the man in front of him started blazing away. Would he do that and probably thwart his own chances of escape? Or would he simply take the couple of steps needed to reach the door and make use of the corridor light? If he chose the latter course, McColl would have only two or three seconds of darkness in which to rearrange the odds.

Was it worth the risk?

He couldn't decide. And then he heard whistling in the distance and knew the younger man was coming back. He turned his eyes upward, reached for the cross, and pulled himself up off the floor. For a split second, he thought it would take his weight, but then the whole fixture came out of the ceiling in a shower of plaster. He had a fleeting glimpse of the other man's indecision before the room was plunged into darkness.

After dropping into a crouch, he quickly moved to the right. No shots were fired — the Irishman, as McColl had half expected, was reaching for the door. As he crossed the thin line of light seeping in around its edges, McColl hit him with his shoulder, driving him into the wall. The thud of something hitting the carpet had to be the gun.

Outside in the corridor, the whistling had stopped.

McColl moved toward the window, the pale square growing lighter as his eyes grew accustomed to the dark. Throwing a leg across the frame, he ducked his head and wriggled out, just as the corridor door swung open, flooding the room with light. The young republican was silhouetted in the doorway, the older one still on the floor, reaching for his gun.

McColl slammed down the sash, took a second to get his bearings, and then scrambled, almost tumbled, down the first flight of iron stairs. He had just reached the next landing down when the window above him crashed open, letting angry voices out. As he hastened down the next flight, McColl expected the pounding of feet in pursuit, but what he heard was a drawn-out scream of surprise as someone flew past him only a few feet away. The scream gave way to a thump and a crack when whoever it was hit the ground.

And now feet were crashing down the steps above. As he continued his own descent, McColl wondered what the hell had happened to send one of them over the rail — a jostle for the lead?

Seeing movement below, he realized he had more important things to worry about. There was an automobile parked by the back gates and a man standing beside it staring into the yard, as if unsure who or what had just come out of the sky.

More lights went on in the back of the hotel, casting the yard in a pale yellow glow, and the man by the car broke into a run, crossing the yard and sinking to his knees beside the spread-eagled body. He cradled the head in his arms, oblivious to both McColl and the shouts of his other comrade.

As he reached the foot of the fire escape, McColl hesitated for a second, half expecting the man to pull out a gun and confront him. He didn't. A door opened, revealing curious watchers, and a police whistle sounded not far away, but neither caused the man to lift his head.

McColl hurried past him, out through the gate and onto Leinster Street, not slowing his pace to a walk until certain there was no one behind him.

Caitlin arrived at the same time as the ambulance and spent a very long minute fearing the worst. When she finally got a view of the victim's face, she almost retched with relief.

The man on the stretcher was a Breslin, and so was the younger one holding his hand. Despite falling forty feet, the victim had survived; he was, someone told her, unconscious but breathing. But even laid straight on the stretcher, he looked terribly misshapen.

She tried to find out what had happened, but no one seemed to know. "His brother said he was pushed," a woman was saying, "but his friend said he fell."

Caitlin looked up at the window of the room she knew so well and wondered where Jack was at this moment. On his way to the boat, she hoped, because Dublin was certainly death for him now.

TRAPDOOR INTO BELGIUM

"You don't seem very popular in Dublin," was all Cumming had to say about McColl's lucky escape from the Royal Hotel. They were sitting in the Service chief's Whitehall office, where the glow of the gas fire lent an air of coziness to the proceedings. Outside the window a curtain of mist veiled the river beyond.

"I don't suppose the man survived?"

"He did, actually. But I'm told he won't ever walk again."

"Oh." McColl wouldn't wish that on anyone. "I still don't understand how he fell."

"He just slipped and went over, according to the other man."

"They're both in custody, I presume."

Cumming grimaced. "Not any longer. There was nothing to hold them on. They admitted they were chasing you, but only because they wanted a friendly chat."

"About what?"

"Your immoral behavior with you-know-who," Cumming said. His tone suggested he might even share the censure, but McColl doubted that was so. The Service chief's reluctance to name Caitlin or discuss the role she'd played in recent events was more likely down to prudishness. Fast machines might not scare Cumming, but fast women probably did.

Which was fine by McColl. There might come a time when he had to report the rekindling of the relationship, but for the moment he thought it wiser to keep quiet. In one moment of love-induced naïveté, he had offered Caitlin the use of his London flat, only for her to sweetly ask him how, after what had just happened, he expected either his superiors or her republican friends to view such an arrangement.

Cumming picked up his pipe, stared at it for several seconds, then put it back down again. "Let's move on," he said with typical brusqueness. "I'm sending you to Belgium — the occupied bit. I know you speak fluent French, and I'm told that the Belgian version is very similar, with just a few distinctive differences that you'll have to be aware of. I've arranged a meeting for you tomorrow with an expert in the field — a man named Thistlethwaite."

"What's the job?" McColl asked. The thought of operating behind enemy lines both intrigued and worried him. There was no doubt about it — his life seemed a lot more precious than it had a fortnight before.

"There are two. What do you know about our train-watching networks?

"Only that we have them."

"We do. Or in some cases did. And when I say 'we,' I should be more precise. The French Deuxième Bureau have people in occupied Belgium, and so, believe it or not, do the Russians. Both of them have managed to retain a single command structure. We had three until a few months ago, and we still have two — an army outfit run from France and our own, which our man Richard Tinsley runs from Holland. Too many cooks, as you can imagine. Anyway, there was a meeting a couple of weeks ago, and some lines were drawn on the ground." He pulled an atlas onto his desk and found the appropriate page. "The one in Belgium runs south from Antwerp to Brussels," he said, tracing it with his finger. "And then on down to Namur. Everything east of that line is ours."

"You implied that there have been some setbacks."

drop into enemy-occupied territory was far from appealing. "When do I leave?" he asked.

"As soon as you're ready. You've Thistlethwaite to see, and you need to talk to our man Staunton — he knows the situation in Belgium best. And there's some stuff here for you to read," he said, handing over a thin folder of papers. "Dorothy will find you somewhere to sit. There are codes to memorize, your cover story, identity cards . . . oh, and the railway map — I almost forgot your second task. You'll see on the map that certain stretches of line have been marked. We'd like you to take a proper look and find out where they're most vulnerable. The bridges farthest from German garrisons, the ones with no guards or only a few."

McColl examined the map. "With destruction in mind?" he asked.

"Not always. There are some bridges we wouldn't dream of destroying, because we have good watchers on that line and would be shooting ourselves in the foot if we forced the Germans to divert their trains. But in the event of a major push, a few downed bridges would certainly slow the flow of German reinforcements to the sector in question."

McColl stared at the web of lines, wondering how on earth he was going to memorize it.

Judging by the conversations Caitlin overheard in the twenty-four hours that followed McColl's disappearance, the story of his escape was all over Dublin. Opinions differed as to whether young Dermot Breslin had fallen or been pushed, but all agreed that the G-man from London had gotten clean away. And that seemed to be that. The police were pretending that no crime had been committed, and the republicans looked eager to forget what appeared to be an embarrassing failure.

But the latter was not the case, as Mulryan told Caitlin the following day, falling into step beside her as she walked down Henry Street. "We were thinking an apology was in order," he told her.

"I expected better," she agreed, diluting the bitterness with more than a hint of resignation.

"And so you should have," he said with a suitably shame-faced expression. "I don't suppose the man will dare show himself in Dublin again, but if he does . . ." He left the promise hanging in the air.

"Well, you got what you wanted," she told him. "They won't be expecting an insurrection anytime soon."

"We hope not."

She stopped and turned to face him. "Come on, you can tell me. When will it happen?"

He looked almost alarmed. "Oh, that hasn't been decided. Not yet."

They walked on in silence, parting company at the junction with Sackville Street. Caitlin had moved back in with Maeve, who was obviously burning with curiosity as to where, and with whom, her houseguest had spent so many nights, but she had so far shown a welcome disinclination to pry. Of course she might already know, but as far as Caitlin could tell, the republicans kept their cards pretty close to their collective chest.

She turned in through the doors of the GPO and walked across to the telegraph counter. On the previous day, she had cabled her editor saying she had a big story and asking permission to spend a few more days in Dublin. The reply was waiting — he was willing to trust her judgment. The postscript — "Please remember war declared in Europe" — was just a warning shot.

And it really was a big story, albeit one she couldn't yet tell. If she did discover the date of a projected rising, there was no way she was going to give the British authorities advance notice in her newspaper, but she was determined to be here in Dublin, ready and waiting, when the first shots were fired. She needed the date and was pretty sure she wouldn't get it from Mulryan.

An insurrection required troops, and there were two obvious sources of these — the small, well-trained, and highly committed Citizen Army and the far more numerous, but much less reliable, Volunteers. None of the leaders of either organization was going to tell her anything deliberately, but if she loitered in the right places, someone in the know might let something slip. Maeve and other contacts gave her access to Liberty Hall, and that weekend there was a Volunteer exercise involving most of the Dublin groups. She would spend the next few days asking people questions they wanted to answer and hope to hear something more in the spaces in between. Eavesdropping might be a vice for others, a New York editor had once told her; for reporters it was surely a virtue.

Walking on toward Liberty Hall, where she was picking up Maeve for lunch, Caitlin realized it was almost an hour since she'd last thought of Jack. It had occurred to her that morning that she was now one of those women who spent part of each day wondering whether their man would survive. The thought had infuriated her, mostly because it was true. But why not? she thought now. He was in more physical danger than she was, and it was only natural that she should worry.

The week they'd just shared — the nights, to be precise — had been . . . well, "wonderful" was a word that seemed to fit. She had felt no ambivalence, but that was hardly surprising. They'd been living in a bubble — one room, one bed, a finite number of nights. She didn't doubt their love for each other, but could they carry it over into their normal lives? Lives that both of them liked, work that both of them valued. Had anything really changed?

The Channel crossing was a somber affair, partly on account of the cold gray skies but mostly because the converted ferry was crowded with soldiers confronting the prospect of winter in the trenches. If McColl had received a penny for each pair of eyes staring wistfully back at the white cliffs of Dover, he'd have been a very rich man.

He couldn't say he was looking forward to the next few weeks himself. After two days of cramming, he was well equipped to pass himself off as a Belgian, but first there was the minor matter of surviving the journey. He knew that the one-legged Cumming would happily have swapped places with him, but his chief was a trifle deranged where newfangled modes of transport were concerned. Cumming probably would have let the Royal Artillery fire him into Belgium if there was even the slightest chance of survival.

Boulogne looked thoroughly woebegone, and McColl was pleased to leave it behind, traveling south across the Pas de Calais with a group of returning young officers. The guns had been audible since the ship cleared Dover Harbour and were now rumbling and cracking above the sound of their mud-spattered Cottin & Desgouttes saloon. As darkness began to fall, McColl noticed an ominous red glow slowly deepening above the eastern horizon.

His was their first stop, outside the gates of the sprawling Royal Flying Corps's Saint-Omer HQ. The field was unlit, but as a corporal walked McColl to his sleeping quarters, he could make out a line of parked airplanes stretching into the distance. "Does it ever stop?" he asked his escort.

"What? Oh, the noise. After a while that's the only time you notice it — when it stops."

McColl's bed was a lower bunk in the mainly empty barracks. Most of the pilots were in the canteen, playing cards and drinking tea. They seemed appallingly young to McColl, but no more so than Jed. He was still hoping to see his brother but doubted there'd be time.

After breakfast next morning, he reported to the squadron leader, a man named Plumley with an accent to match and a mustache so extravagant that McColl thought he must have nightmares about catching it in a propeller. He also had a very soft voice and struggled to make himself heard above the constant roar of distance guns that poured through the open window. McColl asked how far away the front was.

"About thirty miles," Plumley told him. "Look, we can take you where you want to go, but we'll have to get a move on. The moon's on the turn already, and once it's passed its quarter, long flights get a little too risky. We could always take you out when there's decent cloud cover, but that would mean a drop in total darkness, and they're always a bit of a lottery."

"A drop?" McColl asked, already feeling it in his stomach.

"Ah, yes. We won't be landing you, I'm afraid. We don't know enough about the area for one thing, but even if we did . . . The Boche have a new kite, a Fokker monoplane, and they've put us at a bit of a disadvantage. They have machine guns," he added sadly, as if the enemy weren't quite playing the game. "And we've had so many losses in the last couple of weeks that landings behind enemy lines have been ruled out."

"I thought a landing only took a few minutes."

"It does. But taking off is a noisy business, and once the Germans know there's a kite headed home, they send half a dozen up to intercept it. But don't worry — we'll get you on the ground. Have you heard of the Guardian Angel?"

"No."

"It's a new parachute, works like a charm. We've only had one failure."

Wonderful, McColl thought. He hoped the man who'd been unlucky appreciated his comrades' good fortune. The thought of clambering out of a cockpit a mile from the ground, encumbered by heaven knew how many square yards of fabric, was enough to send a whole army of shivers marching down his spine.

But as the other man explained, there'd be no need to clamber.

"There's a seat like a sidecar slung under the fuselage," Plumley told him. "With a sort of trapdoor. At the appropriate moment, the pilot pulls a lever and you just drop through the hole, count to three — two if you're nervous — and then pull the cord."

"And nothing more to worry about until I hit the ground," McColl murmured.

"Exactly so," Plumley agreed with a grin.

"I don't suppose there's much point in a practice run?"

"Can't spare the fuel, old man. And anyway, why go through it twice?"

Why indeed? McColl thought wryly. There was nothing to be gained from waiting around at Saint-Omer and much to lose with the moon shining brighter each passing night. He might as well get it over with. "So the sooner the better," he said. "How's the forecast for tonight?"

"Not good. But tomorrow's looking better."

McColl spent the day either reading in the canteen or walking around the airfield. The weather was clear and cold, and the blazing sunshine seemed freshly inappropriate each time a heavily loaded ambulance trundled past on the road from the front. On several occasions McColl felt like dashing out in front of one of these vehicles, holding up a hand, and asking to see if his brother was lying inside.

He was introduced to his pilot a couple of hours before the scheduled takeoff, and the two of them pored over maps together, the large-scale one of the upper Meuse Valley that McColl had brought with him and two others that the squadron used for planning its flights over Belgium. His first point of contact with the Belgian underground was a bookshop in Huy, and his briefer in London had suggested a landing halfway between there and Andenne, a smaller town seven miles farther west. With most of the night still ahead of him, McColl should have no trouble reaching the outskirts of Huy before dawn.

The pilot, a young man in his early twenties named Rob Lansley, had already flown similar missions and clearly lived to tell the tale. His passengers had not been so lucky. Both had been intercepted by German patrols on the night of their arrival, one arrested, the other shot dead when he made a run for it. "It's those first few hours," Lansley explained. "The Germans hear an airplane and they don't hear any bombs exploding, so they know that someone's been landed or dropped." The pilot smiled. "So we've started carrying a couple of twenty-pounders. Once I've pulled the plug on you, I'll fly on to Huy and throw the bombs at the local castle. That's where the Boche are billeted," he added in explanation. "I don't want any Belgians on my conscience."

As the pale November sun sank below the hedges lining the airfield, the two of them ate an early dinner in the canteen. Lansley was from Bristol and had two brothers in the army, one up near Ypres, the other out in Mesopotamia. "And Mum's just had another boy. Insurance, I reckon."

There was one slight delay while the pilot went off in search of a thicker coat for McColl — "It's bloody cold up there!" — and another when Plumley arrived to wish them luck. Eventually McColl and his suitcase were squeezed into the underslung sidecar, Lansley and his bombs into the B.E.12's single seat, the propeller set in motion. The biplane drove steadily across the field, suddenly accelerated, and seemed to almost leap into the sky. As it climbed and turned, McColl could see the distant rows of lights that marked the two front lines.

It was indeed "bloody cold," and the exposed area of skin between flying cap and scarf soon felt coated with ice. McColl clasped his collar shut in front of his throat and tried to look on the bright side — he might be freezing to death, but at least he was still aloft, with an hour's respite until the dreaded moment arrived. Or moments. If the chute surprised him and actually opened, there was still the small matter of getting down in one piece.

At least he didn't have a basketful of restless pigeons in his lap, as most of his predecessors had done. According to Lansley, hundreds had been taken into occupied Belgium, each with a tightly rolled piece of paper containing a list of questions about the occupation, which locals were asked to answer and return with the homing bird. The pilot had also told him, with a perfectly straight face, that scientists in England were trying to crossbreed pigeons and parrots, so that verbal reports might be delivered.

They were over the British trenches now, the line of Very lights stretching away to north and south. Guns were still audible in the distance, but silence reigned in this particular sector. Looking down at the dark expanse that separated the two lines, McColl wondered if men were out on patrol, mapping the enemy's defenses, recovering the dead. "Shoveling them into bags," as one soldier had said, in an exchange he'd overheard during the Channel crossing.

In both British and German trenches, brief flares announced the lighting of cigarettes, and no doubt men of both nations were filling their dugouts with the same noxious gases that army food produced. Or maybe not. Maybe sauerkraut and bully beef generated subtly different farts. High above the fray, it was hard to believe that much else distinguished the armies below.

The illuminated front gave way to darkened fields and woods. Behind the biplane the cloud-veiled quarter moon was still casting a faint light across the earth below; it would set in just over an hour, giving him time to land, hide his parachute, and work out where he was before the darkness deepened.

The airplane's engine droned on. It was too dark for him to read his watch, but he guessed they'd been flying for almost half an hour and would have crossed the Belgian frontier. There seemed to be more lights scattered below — villages, no doubt. Looking back over his shoulder, he caught a flash of moonlight reflected in a river or lake.

God, it was cold. He rubbed his gloved hands together, hugged himself fiercely, and started counting seconds to pass the time. Hearing what sounded like a train, he scanned the earth below, and there it was, a shadow curling like a snake, one flickering orange eye where the blackout tarpaulin had been carelessly tied. At this hour it was probably an army train, and McColl wondered whether one of Cumming's local watchers had already recorded its composition.

How else could he take his mind off what felt like incipient frostbite? Practice his Belgian French?

Professor Thistlethwaite had been much younger than McColl had expected, barely thirty in all probability, with a congenitally twisted foot that ruled out military service. They had talked for an hour in his university office, while rain ran down the windows and thunder rolled in the distance. Some of what Thistlethwaite had told him — the Belgian habit of making a stronger distinction between their short and long vowels — had been hard to grasp in the abstract but would probably become clearer once he was there. Other differences were easier to remember. What sounded like *"vagon"* in French was the English-sounding *"wagon"* in Belgian French — something a train watcher might need to know. And if counting the number in a train, then he should use the Belgian *"eptante"* and *"nonante"* not

430

the French *"soixante-dix"* and *"quatre-vingt-dix."*

Meals were different, too. "Breakfast" in Belgium was *"déjeuner"* without the *"petit."* And *"souper"* was any evening meal, not one taken late after seeing a show.

It was all very interesting and might prove crucial. The German occupiers were unlikely to appreciate such linguistic quirks, but Belgians in their pay would be listening for such slips.

The moon behind him was almost down. They must be getting near the drop zone.

He wondered where Caitlin was at that moment. In bed, he supposed, and a damn sight warmer than he was. It crossed his mind that now that they had found each other again, dying would not be so bad. A morbid thought, but true. And death was certainly all around — so many millions of men, who only eighteen months before had barely given it a thought, were now contemplating their own mortality on an hourly basis. Would knowing how easily life could end encourage survivors to make fuller use of their own? Would those who had lived in constant fear ever be able to shake it off?

He had always believed that his own near death on Spion Kop had made him more inclined to seize those opportunities that presented themselves. That might be the way most young men reacted. He hoped so.

It was something he and Caitlin shared, he thought — a willingness, an eagerness almost, to take leaps in the dark.

Though he didn't feel that keen to take this one.

As if on cue, Lansley's foot tapped out the prearranged signal on the floor of his cockpit. Three taps to say good-bye, thirty seconds to prepare himself, and down he would go.

Or fewer than thirty. He had only counted to twenty-one when he heard the scrape of the lever and, with appalling but thoroughly predictable suddenness, found himself plummeting earthward. The plane had vanished from view, the sound of its engine swiftly fading, before he remembered to pull the cord. After what seemed a very long second, the Guardian Angel jerked open above him and his speed of descent abruptly slowed, though not quite as much as he would have liked.

It was only about ten seconds later that the grayness below him took form and shape and he knew he was falling into trees.

WATCHING THE TRAINS GO BY

Caitlin's extra few days of research in Dublin did nothing to undermine her belief that some sort of rising was under active consideration. A day at the central library, whose excellent stock of seditious material bore testament to either great tolerance or great stupidity on England's part, offered ample confirmation that Irish republicans certainly talked a good game. In article after article that year, the Citizen Army and union leader James Connolly had lambasted the Ulster Volunteers for their timidity. In only the last few days, he had suggested that "if Ireland did not act now the name of this generation should in mercy to itself be expunged from the records of Irish history."

It was true that the Volunteer leaders sounded less eager to take the military plunge. The previous May even the fiery Patrick Pearse had written that such action would make sense only if taken in self-defense, should the London government try to introduce conscription, or repeal the Home Rule Act, or attempt to disarm the Volunteers. And though Pearse himself had upped the rhetorical ante in recent months, other leaders like Eoin MacNeill and Bulmer Hobson still seemed firmly opposed to any sort of insurrection.

But there were counterrumors swirling around in republican circles. According to one that reached Maeve, MacNeill had stumbled across a letter from Pearse to a Volunteer unit in Kerry that showed that military contingencies were already under discussion, but he had then decided not to investigate further. Why would he do that, unless he knew that a rising was off the table?

And yet, and yet. Why try to lull the British authorities into a false sense of security if nothing was planned? Could Pearse and his friends be keeping other preparations from MacNeill and Hobson?

There was no way to know. On Saturday she watched the Citizen Army march off down Marlborough Street lustily singing, "The Germans are winning the war, me boys!" On Sunday she followed Pearse and around a thousand Volunteers out to the site of an old obscure Fenian victory, where they drilled and listened to the sort of rousing speech that most must have heard a hundred times. The two watching G-men at the second event seemed by turns amused and contemptuous. As one told Caitlin, "Ireland's real fighting men are in France — these are the mummy's boys."

She didn't share the opinion, but it was hard to refute the implication that this ragged bunch offered little real threat to what Connolly called the "Robber Empire." What could fewer than two thousand men do against the British army? If a rising was under consideration, then surely a defeat was, too. A glorious one, no doubt, but how many of the young men parading before her were ready to embrace martyrdom?

The voices were German. Two of them, talking about something called "Hilde's Heaven." A dancer called Greta, with breasts like melons.

McColl had a terrible headache and a throbbing pain in his right leg. When he tried to flex the latter, the shaft of agony almost took his breath away. He remembered the sound of splintering as he'd fallen through the branches and wondered how much damage he'd done to himself.

He opened his eyes to a darkened room.

Two pale washes of light at either end of a curtained window suggested that the night was over but offered little in the way of illumination. He wondered what sort of jail had curtains. A makeshift one, perhaps. There was probably a guard outside the door.

The German voices had gone, and he wondered whether he'd imagined them. Not to mention Greta. But now there were footsteps nearby, the sound boots made on stairs.

The opening door admitted no light, but the shadowy figure that crossed the room pulled back the curtains on a slate gray sky. The silhouette was female, the woman who turned toward him young and pretty, with dark, wavy hair that tumbled to her shoulders. The way she hugged herself reminded McColl how cold he was.

She walked across to the bed and looked down at him. Her eyes seemed less than friendly. "I am Mathilde," she said in French.

"I am Jack," he replied, raising a hand.

After only a slight hesitation, she took it.

"Where am I?" he asked. "And how did I get here?"

She shook her head. "I ask the questions. Where were you supposed to go in Huy?"

It was his turn to demur. "How do I know you're not working for the Germans?"

She nodded. "A fair point. So just tell me the password. If I'm working for the Germans and I don't already know the address, that can't help me."

As far as his aching head could determine, that seemed to make sense. "I was to ask for a copy of Zola's *Au Bonheur des Dames.*"

"Good," she said.

"And the reply should have been?"

"We only have a first edition, which monsieur might find expensive."

"So how did I get here?" McColl asked.

She sat down on the edge of the bed. "Your parachute was seen coming down, and we managed to get you out of the tree and bring you here."

"Which is where? I thought I heard German voices."

"You are in Huy. The Germans were probably soldiers who had just had their breakfast in the café downstairs. A lot of them use it, because the food is better than the swill they are given at their barracks."

McColl found that somewhat alarming. "That doesn't sound very safe. For me or you."

"It isn't, and we will move you as soon as we can. But now we are waiting for the doctor. We think you have broken your leg."

"Oh."

"He may be some time," she added. "He is visiting the district where your airplane dropped its bombs."

Her tone was enough, but he asked it anyway. "Was anyone hurt?"

"A girl was killed, her father injured."

"He was supposed to drop them over the citadel," McColl said, as much to himself as her.

"He didn't."

McColl felt terrible and knew that Lansley would, too.

His look of distress appeased her a little. "Such things happen," she conceded.

There were more footsteps on the stairs. The man who entered was about thirty and carrying a traditional doctor's valise.

"The idea was to bomb the citadel," Mathilde told the new arrival.

"Why bomb anything?" was his curt response.

McColl repeated what Lansley had told him. "If the Germans hear a plane and there aren't any bombs, they assume that someone has been dropped behind their lines."

The doctor just shook his head and leaned over McColl. "Let's get his trousers off."

The two of them pulled them down. They

clearly tried to do it gently, but suppressing the urge to cry out took everything he had. "This will hurt," the doctor now told him, reaching for the damaged leg.

McColl braced himself.

The fingers probed away at his calf for what seemed an eternity. Any longer and he would have passed out.

"The bone is broken in two places," the doctor told him. "I've reset it, and this afternoon I'll come back with splints to hold it in place. Until then try to keep still. Do you have any other problems?"

"A bad headache."

The doctor took a look at his head, then shone a small flashlight in his eyes. "I have aspirin," he said, reaching for his bag. "Other than that we'll just have to wait and see."

"How long before I can walk again?"

"Six to eight weeks, maybe longer."

"But . . ." McColl let the implications sink in. He could hardly expect Mathilde and her friends to feed and hide him for all that time, but what other option did they have? They could hardly cart him to the frontier and toss him across. Or deliver him up to the Germans.

"We'll sort something out," she said once the doctor had gone. "I expect you'd like something to eat. And we'll fix you up some sort of toilet."

Caitlin reached Glasgow's St. Enoch station on the morning of November 17, deposited her suitcase in the left-luggage office, and hired a taxi to take her across the city. The different columns of rent-strike marchers were due to merge in George Square, but by the time Caitlin's taxi reached the area, the crowds were already proving too much for the traffic and she had to walk the last two hundred yards. As she reached the square, a swelling chorus of drums, whistles, and shouts announced the arrival of the main column from Govan, Mary Barbour at its head.

After searching for a while, Caitlin came across Helen Stephens. A legal discussion was under way inside the Sheriff Court, which was just round the corner — the thousands now filling the surrounding streets were there to offer moral support and exert political pressure. There would be plenty of speeches.

Once poster boards had been borrowed from shop fronts and hoisted across a line of shoulders, speakers were lifted up to address the crowd. Over the next few hours, Caitlin watched a succession of men and women — some famous, some not — sway to and fro on this makeshift platform, only a careless gesture away from losing their balance and tumbling into the crowd.

It was heady stuff, but the real business was being done behind closed doors. The landlords had the law on their side, the tenants only justice. That and the crowd outside, and the threat of downed tools in the shipyards and armament factories, and the pressure of politicians who wanted to keep their war on the road. Soon after noon the word slipped out that the landlords had accepted defeat and had only asked that the tenants refrain from gloating.

The crowd dispersed almost as quickly as it had gathered. The women had won their yearlong battle.

Caitlin spent the evening in her hotel room, compressing it all into a thousand heartfelt words. Not since the Lawrence strike had she felt such a warm glow of triumph, such a sense of hope for what could be achieved.

She still felt full of joy on the following morning as she approached the address that Jack had given her. All the houses on Oakley Street were terraced, but she had seen far worse areas in Glasgow, and the one his parents rented looked neat and well kept.

The woman who answered the door was in her late fifties, small but sturdy-looking, with lovely blue eyes and a mouth like Jack's.

She seemed in high spirits, and Caitlin soon found out why.

"I noticed you yesterday," Margaret McColl said as she ushered her guest inside and hung up her coat on the rack. "Though of course I didn't know who you were. Wasn't that a wonderful morning?"

"It truly was."

"Come through to the parlor, and I'll make us some tea. This is Jack's father," she added as the elderly man struggled to his feet.

He nodded but said nothing and after shaking Caitlin's hand sank back into his chair with obvious relief.

"Jack wrote to say you were coming, but he didn't say much else," Margaret McColl confided as she waited for the kettle to boil. "Only that you'd seen Jed in France."

"Jack and I met in China," Caitlin told her and her husband, whose eyes were now closed. "If it wasn't for the war . . ." she added vaguely. She had no desire to explain the previous year.

"This stupid war," Jack's mother said, in sadness rather than anger.

442

Her husband shook his head, though whether at her or the war wasn't clear.

"I had a letter from Jed yesterday," Margaret said, putting the tea down in front of her. "I'll read it to you."

It was a cheerful missive, full of family jokes, anecdotes of military life, and mockery of the French. "I know he doesn't tell me anything real," Margaret said, "and that he doesn't want to worry me. Men often say that when they can't be bothered, but Jed really doesn't. He's always been a good boy."

"Like his brother?" Caitlin asked mischievously.

Margaret smiled at that. "Jack was never a bad boy. But older brothers . . . well, they always need to prove their point."

"Perhaps. I suppose my elder brother was a bit like that."

"So how did you find Jed?" Margaret asked a trifle bluntly.

Caitlin decided to be honest. "It was only a year since I'd seen him, but he seemed a lot older. Not physically — he looks exactly the same — but in the way he talks, the way he is. He's grown up. He's not happy, of course — who could be in such circumstances? — but he seemed — how can I put it? — he seemed at ease with himself. The things he worries about — like getting killed or losing friends or being hardened by all the things he's witnessed — they're the things any sane young man *would* worry about."

His mother absorbed all this in silence, sadly shook her head, and finally managed a smile. "And how about Jack?" she asked. "Where is he now?"

"I've no idea. He's off on a job, but he didn't know where it would take him. I don't think he could have told me if he did know."

"He went to war, too, you know. He was even younger than Jed. And it changed him, too, but not for the worse, I think. So there's hope for Jed. I just pray they both survive it."

"And I."

Margaret insisted that Caitlin stay for lunch, a thick and delicious vegetable soup. There was no shortage of conversation between the two of them, but Jack's father was mostly silent, confining himself to polite, almost obsequious requests for one thing or another. The man Jack had described on the *Manchuria* was conspicuous by his absence.

Caitlin's journey south the following day was both long and uncomfortable. After weeks in Dublin and days in Glasgow, a cold, damp London felt profoundly anticlimactic, and the news that the American socialist and songwriter Joe Hill had finally been executed in Utah depressed her deeply. She had met him in prewar days, and on one memorable night in Brooklyn he had dedicated his song "The Rebel Girl" to her.

Staring out her lodgings window at a foggy Clapham Common, she was reminded of the previous winter, when her life had still revolved around a brother awaiting a similar fate to Joe Hill's.

Over the next few days, she cajoled herself back into work, seeking out stories that offered a blissfully ignorant American public glimpses of what the war was doing to Europe, away from the obvious battlefields. And work was fine — it was the rest of her life that left her feeling increasingly lonely. Sylvia was her best friend in London, but she didn't feel she could talk to Sylvia about Jack. Her friend was still mourning Keir Hardie, and it felt almost cruel to have a man who might very well come back.

McColl spent five days above the café, five that felt like fifty. The broken leg made it hard to sleep, and the doctor freely admitted a reluctance to use up all his painkillers on one patient. So the days dragged by, and the icy nights seemed even slower.

He had a great deal of time for reflection. Those who thought that only the threat of death could parade one's life before one's eyes had never spent a week confined in a freezing Belgian attic.

He thought about Caitlin a lot, mostly with thanks in his heart, though sometimes in the predawn hours he found it hard to resist the conclusion that they would never be together in the normal way. The idea of having children with her seemed as unrealistic as it was enticing.

Once the doctor had been back to put his leg in splints, Mathilde was the only person he saw. She brought him food and drink three times a day and emptied the ancient commode he managed to reach with the aid of a crutch. It wasn't until the fourth evening that she stayed long enough to offer a rundown of the local situation.

There was a small German garrison in Huy, most of them middle-aged *Landsturm,* and a rest camp for soldiers some ten miles up the river, about halfway to Namur. Neither posed much of a threat to those Belgians actively resisting the occupation, either on their own government's behalf or in collaboration with the Allied intelligence

446

services. The real danger came from two German police forces, the military and the secret. Each area of occupied Belgium had a branch of the former, which reported to army headquarters. The latter had their own HQ in Brussels, attached to the staff of the German governor-general. The two organizations often worked together, but relations between them were rumored to be poor.

They had three main methods when it came to uncovering resisters and spies. The first was the sudden raid, in which whole streets or districts of towns were blocked off and every dwelling within the cordon searched. The second was a rigorous restriction of movement. People were not allowed more than ten kilometers from their homes without copious proofs of purpose and identity, and even the shortest journey required some sort of pass. Third, and most potent of all, was the German use of paid informers, which according to Mathilde accounted for nine in ten arrests. In Huy several active collaborators had been identified and dealt with, but no one expected the supply of traitors to suddenly dry up.

What the informers and their German paymasters sought were the train watchers. They had caught quite a few and intercepted their reports — they knew what sort of information was reaching the Allies and how crucial it was that the flow be stopped. By keeping tabs on German train movements, Belgian watchers made it impossible for the German army to mount a surprise offensive.

And McColl would be one of them, Mathilde announced on the following evening. "Tomorrow night we will move you to a house on the other side of town," she told him, "one with a fine view of the railway line. It's a special house, as you will see. And there you can start to earn your keep," she added with a smile. "It will be much less boring than lying here and staring at the ceiling."

His training would begin as soon as he reached the new address.

They moved him the following evening, carrying him down and out through the back door to where a horse and cart were waiting. Buried under a load of furniture and with every rut in the road shooting pains through his leg, he spent the twenty-minute ride praying that each halt was the last. When they finally arrived at his new home, he had a fleeting glimpse of a tall, gabled house silhouetted against the night sky before they lifted him out and in. Three staircases, one incredibly narrow, brought him and his burly Belgian bearers into a cramped space between roofs. "The false roof and hidden steps were built by smugglers," Mathilde told him. "They used it to store tobacco. And they made holes for watching the attic below and the street outside," she added. "The railway is about a hundred meters away, behind the houses opposite."

There was a watcher on duty, an attractive middle-aged woman named Yvette who lived downstairs with her husband and children. She was surrounded by bowls of beans.

"Chicory for horses, haricots for soldiers, coffee for guns," Mathilde explained. "Some women use knitting — a stitch for men, a purl for horses. You can use whatever method suits you, as long as you end with something like this." She showed McColl a written report, with a first entry that read *2201 1VOF 28WSL&CHV 4W+4CN/5W 12CAIS*. "That's the time the train passed, along with its composition — one officers' carriage, twenty-eight wagons for soldiers and horses, four wagons with guns, and five with artillery caissons."

The men who had carried him up were gone, and over the next half hour Mathilde gave him a lesson in trains. Infantry trains, cavalry trains — "nearly all horse boxes" — hospital trains, food trains, and leave trains — "when *they* stop, we know an attack is imminent." Mathilde had pages of them in silhouette, showing the various types of vehicle. An artillery train, for example, usually comprised one proper carriage for the officers, nine boxcars for the lower ranks, twenty-one horse boxes, and around ten flat wagons for the guns and ammunition.

"Who drew these?" McColl wondered out loud.

"Your people in Holland," Mathilde told him. "Once the watcher has compiled a report," she went on, "someone else copies it out on *papier pelure* — that's tough but very thin — in writing as small as they can manage. We have one man who can fit a thousand words on the back of a postage stamp. No one else can match him. You must just do your best."

"I thought you said the watchers and copiers were different people."

"Usually yes, but in your case we're going to make an exception. It's not as if you have any other work."

"I guess not. And after the reports have been miniaturized?"

"They're rolled up tight and wrapped in a piece of rubber — a *préservatif,* usually. I think you English call them 'French letters.' Then they're dropped off at a prearranged address and eventually collected by those who take them across the border."

"With each person isolated from the next one up the chain?"

"That's the ideal, but it's not really possible. All we can do is minimize the contacts so that each person caught only leads to one more and gives us time to get others into hiding."

"What do the Germans do to those they catch?" McColl asked, expecting only one answer.

"They shoot most of us," Mathilde said, not disappointing him. "A few they turn and use against us, and then it's we who pull the trigger. I hope that doesn't shock you."

McColl shrugged. "Not at all." Killing a man for serving his country in the way you would serve your own had always struck him as slightly absurd, but that was the way it worked.

"There's a train coming," Yvette said softly, and soon he could hear the steady chuff of an engine climbing the valley. There wasn't room for more than one pair of eyes at the spy hole, so he and Mathilde just listened to it pass and watched Yvette's fingers sort beans into plates with a dexterity born of practice. "An infantry train," Yvette said, once it had gone. "That's three this evening. If it's a regular division," she told McColl, "we can expect fifty-two trains over the next four days."

"But there's no way of knowing which division?"

"We'll know if it's from the east," Mathilde answered him, "because the trains will be more spaced out. And most of them stop in Liège to take on fuel and water, so our people there should get a look at the markings on the wagons and the soldiers' shoulder straps. By the time a division reaches the area behind the front, London should know where it is and what it is."

In London, Caitlin busied herself with work. There was no shortage of interesting stories on the home front, and many concerned the war's impact on women. Some developments, like the possibilities opened up by the absence of so many men, were mostly positive, while others, like the bad treatment often meted out to wives by returning soldiers, were clearly not. With a few it was hard to say. The billeting of thousands of young soldiers in towns and villages throughout the country had alarmed some influential women — notably those in organizations representing headmistresses and university women — who saw their presence as a dire threat to the morals and reputations of local girls. To counter this invasion of lustful young men, these women had set up hundreds of Women's Patrols, who shone their flashlights at couples in parks and doorways and tried to persuade cinema managers that their lights should never be off.

Caitlin wasn't sure what to make of it all. The patrols were probably saving a few girls from being raped, which was no small matter. They were also — as several complainants reported — preventing other women from making love where and when they wanted to and thereby "saving them from themselves." After joining several patrols in the big London parks and noting how many angry couples they left in their wake, she couldn't help concluding that there had to be better way.

The same could be said of the war, now ensconced in its second winter. The two main fronts were quiet, but the Allies seemed in retreat almost everywhere else: the evacuation of Gallipoli was imminent, the campaigns in the Balkans and Mesopotamia apparently going no better.

Christmas arrived, out of place amid all

the gloom. Caitlin spent the day in the East End, helping out at Sylvia's café, where families were fed in shifts and sackfuls of volunteer-made toys were handed out by female Santas. Over the next few days, she tried to find out whether the troops at the front had revived the no-man's-land fraternizations of the previous Christmas, but no such reports came in. Either Jed had been right, and the higher ranks had forbidden it, or the news had been suppressed.

There was none from Ireland either. If a rising had been planned, it hadn't been for Christmas.

On New Year's Eve, she received a long letter from Aunt Orla. Caitlin's father had been ill but was recovering; her sister was pregnant again. The family was having a Mass said for Colm at St. Saviour's on Christmas Eve. Orla herself had been "a bit under the weather" and, though she would never say so, was clearly hoping that Caitlin would soon come home.

The letter made Caitlin feel homesick and changed her mind about attending the embassy party, to which all the American correspondents had been invited. It was a drunken affair, and the chore of removing hands from her shoulder, waist, and worse soon became as irritating as their owners' conversation, which seemed overripe with cynicism. She found herself missing Jack Slaney, who had earned the right to be cynical and who, God help him, actually cared.

She left soon after midnight and, failing to find an available cab, ended up walking west. She had heard nothing from McColl, and now, standing outside his flat in Fitzrovia, all she could remember was the day she'd stormed out, vowing never to see him again. That day she'd reached a bench in Red Lion Square before breaking down and weeping. Several people had stopped to ask if she needed help — say what you like about British reserve, they wouldn't leave a woman to cry in peace.

She was, she realized, feeling thoroughly sorry for herself. Which, given what others were going through, was more than a little ridiculous. Maybe 1916 would be better, but somehow she doubted it.

In Huy, December went by, flurries of snow filling the sky and painting the slopes of the valley an aching white. McColl soon had the hang of train watching and found some pride in squeezing ever more letters onto the small sheets of *papier pelure,* but the days still passed by at a crawl. His leg was less painful, movement with the aid of crutch somewhat easier, and after a couple of weeks he found he could negotiate the stairs to the room below, which wasn't much more comfortable but at least offered some relief to his latent claustrophobia.

He'd been given the night shift, and sometimes an overcast sky made the trains hard to see, let alone categorize. On clear moonlit nights, by contrast, they were silhouetted against the snowy hillside like reproductions of the drawings sent from Holland. There seemed more of them as the month went by — perhaps the Germans were using the winter breather to move their troops around. Or maybe not. There was no way of deducing the bigger picture from an attic space in Huy — for all McColl knew, the enemy was simply using this line more and other lines less. He was just one cog in a very big machine, one that was sometimes jerked awake by a helpful driver's whistle.

When off-duty he either read, dozed, or did exercises to keep himself fit. A steady supply of books was provided by the *bibliothèque* in town, and by mid-December he had waded his way through several Zola novels and a large chunk of Balzac's *Comédie Humaine.* Dumas romances and a book of Sherlock Holmes short stories in English provided some light relief, a French translation of Gogol's *Dead Souls* some very dark comedy.

The Deflandres family downstairs seemed decent people. Yvette was always ready for a friendly chat and removed his waste day after day with a cheeriness that McColl suspected he would find hard to match. Her husband, Eric, was more withdrawn at first, but a natural friendliness soon showed through. His dream was to travel, and he seemed both awed and astonished by the amazing places his guest had seen. On Christmas Day the couple invited McColl downstairs for lunch with themselves and their eight-year-old son, Philippe. The main dish was a scraggly chicken that Yvette had collected from a relative in the hills, smuggled back into town beneath a load of firewood, and roasted that morning. The smell was so delicious that McColl half expected German troops to come knocking.

They did so two days later. The thunderous bang on the door wasn't a surprise — by then the whole street was aware that both ends were blocked off by soldiers, while an assortment of uniformed and plainclothes officials worked their way down each side. And something of this sort had been expected — the Germans knew that their train movements were being reported, and there were only so many streets in towns and villages with a decent view of the tracks.

The on-duty Yvette had hurried downstairs, leaving McColl the use of the spy hole. Watching the street below, he found hope in the fact that the Germans were visiting every house. This was a fishing expedition, not the result of someone's betrayal.

Only a minute or so elapsed between the knock and the sound of movement below. The entrances to the attic and the roof space were in the same room, one obvious to anyone, the other concealed between one of the large cupboards that occupied two corners. McColl could hear voices now, one of them Yvette's, and knew they were climbing the steps.

Straining to be still, he found himself recalling games of hide-and-seek with his cousins in Fort William. Games in which the losers were not arrested and shot. His breath and wildly pumping heart sounded alarmingly loud.

In the room below, a man was speaking French with a German accent. McColl couldn't make out what he was saying, but the tone was typically Prussian, impatient and condescending. And then there was Yvette's familiar voice, insisting that their attic had no window and couldn't be used for watching the railway. "And we cannot see it from downstairs either," eight-year-old Philippe chimed in. What was he doing there? McColl knew that the boy wouldn't give him away on purpose, but would he be able resist a telltale glance at the ceiling?

The voices receded — they were going back down. McColl gave them a minute, then quietly eased himself across to the spy hole to see if the Germans were leaving. One minute passed, then another. What were they doing? Were they searching the room below the attic? If they found the hidden steps, he'd have nowhere to go, but there was no point in surrender. He would shoot whoever came up, take his chances going down, and try to escape out the back. He probably wouldn't get far, but what did he have to lose?

He sat there gripping the Webley, dreading the sound of feet on the steps. The thought crossed his mind that this was what it must be like in the trenches, waiting to launch or repel an attack, fearing that this might be the end. How could they stand it? What else could they do?

Hearing a sound on the steps, he raised the Webley and aimed it at the opening. Someone was coming up.

And then relief spread through his body. Those weren't soldiers' boots on the stairs.

"*Maman* says to tell you they're gone," Philippe said nonchalantly after sticking his head through into the space.

He was gone in an instant, whistling his way downstairs. McColl wondered if the boy had any notion how close he'd come to being an orphan.

Two Oaks

On January 27, 1916, the British government announced that it was introducing conscription. The Military Service Act stated that all single men between the ages of nineteen and forty-one, and all of a similar age who had married since the previous November, would be liable for military service from this coming March. No reason was given that this should be necessary, but then none was really needed — the army was hemorrhaging men, and the supply of volunteers had dried up. As Caitlin noted sadly in the piece she wrote home, three million had not been enough.

Ireland remained exempt, though nobody knew for how long.

Visiting Sylvia Pankhurst in the East End, Caitlin found her busy with antiwar work. Sylvia still received many letters from soldiers at the front and, despite a barrage of government threats, continued publishing them in *The Women's Dreadnought.* An increasing number concerned the executions of soldiers accused, often on the flimsiest evidence, of desertion or cowardice under fire. And this was an army, Sylvia said bitterly, that men had no choice but to join!

It was two days later that Caitlin came home to a letter from Maeve. The envelope showed signs of having been opened, which wasn't promising, but the letter was still inside and apparently unmarked. The interceptor had probably been bored by the latest goings-on among Irish women auxiliaries and either missed or misunderstood Maeve's report of the "mystery surrounding our friend Jimmy," which was now "the talk of the town." Since they had no Jimmy in common, Caitlin could only assume that Maeve was referring to James Connolly, and any mystery surrounding him seemed likely to be newsworthy. She spent the rest of the evening finishing a piece on military executions and wired it off next morning en route to Euston station.

In Dublin, Maeve was only too happy to tell all she knew. Around ten days earlier, James Connolly had vanished from his usual haunts without a word, only to reappear three days later without any explanation. Or, more precisely, without one that made any sense. When Connolly had still been missing, some had suggested he might have been kidnapped, but no one believed that now — the thought of the ICA leader receiving such treatment and uttering no complaint was simply inconceivable. Connolly reportedly told one colleague that he'd been on a walking tour, something he always "liked to do in the spring." This might have been believable in March, but not in midwinter, and Connolly apparently realized as much — asked again where he'd been, he'd replied that "that would be telling."

The day before Caitlin's arrival, Maeve had heard a new explanation. A male acquaintance at Liberty Hall had overheard a conversation between two of Connolly's aides. According to his account, one of the aides, worried by his chief's disappearance and sharing the fear that he'd been kidnapped, had gone to ask the rival Volunteers what they knew of Connolly's whereabouts. The Volunteer leaders had pleaded ignorance and suggested, very unconvincingly, that perhaps the English had him. Now certain that the Volunteers had kidnapped his chief, the aide had given them two days to set Connolly free or face the wrath of the Citizen Army.

"And two days later, there he was," Maeve concluded.

It was a mystery, and Connolly himself showed no inclination to solve it. Caitlin spent the next three days asking all the journalistic and republican contacts she had if they could help her unravel the story, but if any were able, none were willing. She didn't doubt that he'd been with the Volunteers, and probably of his own free will. But why and what for? The two organizations had spent a lot of energy sniping at each other over the last year, but it wouldn't have taken three days to iron out their differences. There had to be something more. Some sort of military alliance, perhaps. They might even have been setting a date.

She had planned to take the ferry back to Holyhead, but it wasn't running on the day she wanted, so she took the Liverpool boat instead. This arrived late, forcing her to take a hotel room for the night, and she was just getting ready for bed when shouting outside brought her to the window. On the street below, people were pointing up at the sky. Craning her head out, she saw nothing but stars — and then the word "Zeppelin" reached her ears.

After hurriedly throwing some clothes back on, she reached the street in time to see two black shapes gliding across the star-filled sky. Sausages with tail fins, someone had called them, but they looked more like whales to Caitlin. Killer whales.

As she watched, light flashed above the roofs to her right, swiftly followed by the boom of an explosion. And then another, and another. Within seconds bells were clanging on nearby streets and orange flames were licking up. Caitlin hurried down the street in their direction, keeping an eye on the dark shapes above, which were heading out across the Mersey.

The first bomb had destroyed two houses and probably killed all their occupants — as Caitlin arrived, a small body draped in a sheet was being stretchered out of the wreckage. With the emergency services already there in force, there was nothing she could do but watch and mentally write her report.

This was the future, she thought. Murder from above, indiscriminate and unforgivable.

Two days later, walking down a street in Stepney, she saw a poster on a police station's wall. The illustration was of a floodlit Zeppelin hanging above a darkened London; the words were intended to frighten. IT IS FAR BETTER TO FACE THE

BULLETS THAN TO BE KILLED AT HOME BY A BOMB, a government propagandist had written. JOIN THE ARMY AT ONCE AND HELP TO STOP AN AIR RAID. GOD SAVE THE KING.

Lie upon lie, she thought. The whole war was a lie. And if by some strange chance a God existed, Caitlin hoped she had better things to do than save the King of England.

By the end of January, McColl was walking without crutches. His leg sometimes hurt like hell, but the doctor was certain that the bone had knitted and foresaw no lasting complications. Once he could get himself up and down the hidden staircase with relative ease, he was able to spend more of his off-duty time in the rooms downstairs, and one cold evening in mid-February he went for his first walk outside. His eagerness almost cost him dear, when his other foot slipped on an icy patch and tipped him over, but this time the luck was with him and no new damage was done. He just lay there for several seconds, looking up at the heavens, lamenting his own stupidity.

About two weeks later, Mathilde came by with a message from London. The train-watching networks had been reconstructed without him, but the other job he'd been given three months earlier — that of checking out bridges between Namur and Liège — still needed doing. And assuming he was well enough, Cumming would like him to get on with it.

Mathilde was already preparing the ground. New papers were being forged, she told him. And he would be moving again, to Namur. There was a family there that owned a garage and could use a new mechanic to help the son and his ailing father. "You have some experience in this line of work?"

"Some."

"Well, you are the owner's nephew. You used to live in Louvain — you know what happened there?"

"The Germans burned down the famous library, along with half the town."

"Including the records office," Mathilde said. "So it's hard for them to prove that someone didn't live there."

"All right," McColl said.

"And the other important thing," she was saying, "is that the Germans are short of mechanics. They have called this man and his son out on several occasions, to check their vehicles in different camps. Which is why the owner has been given permission to bring you from Louvain and why you will have a pass that allows you to travel between there and Namur on the weekends."

"That sounds perfect," McColl agreed. The idea of visiting a German military base to fix up a *Kraftwagenmotor* or two had a certain perverse appeal.

"Not quite," she demurred. "It will allow you to take the train down the valley, but if you're caught getting off, you'll still need a good reason. And if they catch you drawing bridges, they won't even bother to ask for one."

A week later she was back with papers for Jacques Crasson, mechanic. McColl said good-bye to the Deflandres family, and took the local train from Huy to Namur. His papers were examined at the platform exit by a posse of Belgian and German officials and clearly passed muster. Following Mathilde's directions, he walked to the garage.

His new hosts proved as welcoming as Monsieur and Madame Deflandres had been, although he did detect a certain nervousness on Madame Crasson's part. He was given the room over the garage to sleep in and started work next day; he was hoping there were no German calls for assistance until he was back up to speed — it had been almost two years since he'd put his head under a hood.

The owner's son, Martin, was about twenty, and his amiable disposition reminded McColl of Jed. There was a fair amount of work — McColl had expected the Germans to commandeer any usable vehicles, but special dispensations had been liberally distributed, particularly among those who collaborated, and several times in that first week he and Martin were sent out to repair a local bigwig's pride and joy.

The first German call for assistance came toward the end of his second week. He and Martin drove out to a rest camp near Charleroi, where a general's staff car was making strange noises. While his partner put things right, McColl stood there watching the German soldiers and listening to the rumble of the distant guns. When Martin was done, the sense of relief was short-lived; the Germans, McColl now discovered, were keen to show their gratitude by offering up free meals. Luckily, none of those they encountered spoke more than a few words of French, and the food was surprisingly good.

The weeks went by. Mathilde visited him twice, with jobs she needed doing in Liège. The first was simple enough: he had to drop off a sheaf of reports at a dead-letter office in one of the town's industrial suburbs. After making doubly sure he wasn't being followed, he approached the address he'd been given and tapped thrice, then twice, on the designated ground-floor window. The sash flew up, a hand grabbed the envelope, the sash slammed down.

The second proved more complicated. Cumming had somehow heard that a Belgian group run by his army rivals were planning to blow up a bridge on the line running south from Liège to Jemelle and wanted McColl to dissuade them. That line was apparently one of the best-watched in Belgium, and Cumming was keen that the Germans kept using it. McColl spent several hours in a dingy riverside bar explaining this to two young Belgians, who were reluctant to abandon their long-cherished plan. In the end the only way McColl could win their acquiescence was by promising them other targets. Whether Cumming would *have* any was another matter.

On the weekends he cautiously explored the Meuse Valley between Namur and Liège, noting the bridges against the kilometer posts from the train, then getting as close as he dared on the ground. Those that carried the tracks across the Meuse were substantial girder affairs, with commensurate protection, but there were many smaller bridges over roads and streams that didn't seem guarded at all.

He finished the report in the first week of March and took it to the window in Liège. He wasn't expecting a reply in anything less than a fortnight, but when one eventually came, he hoped it would call him home.

Toward the end of February, Jack Slaney turned up out of the blue and insisted on taking Caitlin out to dinner. "Despite rumors to the contrary," no one had actually asked him to leave the Kaiser's realm. But the authorities in Berlin had grown "a little tetchy" in recent months, and an extended furlough had seemed advisable. Having reached England from Holland, he was stopping a few days in London before going home for a couple of months.

The restaurant he'd chosen — a small one near Leicester Square — had been recommended by a friend at the embassy, but Slaney found the fare disappointing. "I've eaten better in Berlin," he said crushingly. "The U-boat campaign must be working."

"If it is, the British Admiralty's not letting on."

"They wouldn't. And it'll get worse. Did the press over here carry that German announcement about armed merchant ships being fair game after March first?"

"Oh, yes. The English wouldn't miss an opportunity to remind everyone how utterly beastly the Germans are."

Slaney mopped up some gravy with a hunk of bread. "They're all beastly, but I have to admit that the Germans take some beating. Have you been following what's happening around Verdun?"

"The latest big push. After watching the English and French bang their heads against walls for over a year, you'd think the Germans would know better."

Slaney grinned but shook his head. "It's worse than that. I talked to a lot of General Staff people over the last few weeks — all off the record, of course — and even some of them are appalled. What do you think the Germans are hoping for at Verdun?"

She shrugged. "The usual elusive breakthrough?"

"Oh, no. They'd take one if they got it, naturally, but that's not the point of the exercise. General Falkenhayn actually spelled it out. He said that Verdun, with all its forts, was the one place the French could not afford to lose, the one for which they really would fight to the very last man. And that's the German plan, to keep sucking

Frenchmen onto their guns until there aren't any left."

"I see."

"Do you?" Slaney was angry now, though at what or whom was harder to tell. "It means that men really are being taken like lambs to the slaughter. That the life of an ordinary man is not of the slightest interest to the bastards in charge. And I'm not just talking about the Germans."

"I didn't think you were."

"The point of the U-boat campaign is to starve the British into submission. Not the British soldier — the British. And the point of the British blockade is starve the Germans. Men, women, and children."

"I know."

"I know you do — I've read what you've written. And you've probably already realized what I'm going to say next, but just in case . . . There's only one reason that we've been allowed to put such thoughts in print, and that reason is American neutrality. The moment Wilson drags us into this war, the shutters will come down. Look at the US papers now and you'll still find journalists writing that this war is as stupid as any and more so than most. You'll still find people saying that both sides have a case and that compromise is the only sensible way to end it. The moment we come in, that'll all disappear overnight and journalists like you and me will have to go on long sabbaticals or do all our real writing between the lines. Because if we carry on telling the truth, things are going to get ugly."

An hour or so later, after he had seen her off on the Number 4 tram, she sat staring out at the houses on Kennington Park Road, feeling more depressed than she had for months. A part of her wanted to get away from it all, from Europe and all its self-inflicted sadness, to book a passage on the ship that Slaney would be catching in a couple of days. But she knew that she wouldn't. Her work — her life — was here.

The next message from London did summon McColl back to England, but not at once, and not in the way he expected. Mathilde arrived with it early one evening, and they spent most of an hour in his room above the garage discussing Cumming's requests.

The Service chief wanted three bridges destroyed, preferably on the same night. Looking at the list, McColl remembered each one and noticed the common factors. They were all relatively small, far enough from the road to complicate the business of repair, and quite a distance from one another. Bringing them all down on the same night would both stretch the Germans' resources and maximize the saboteurs' chances of getting away — if different nights were chosen, those going last would find the authorities on maximum alert.

The explosives would be brought in by plane, either on the night of April 9–10 or on the next one fit for flying. The chosen landing ground was a field southwest of Huy that according to Mathilde had been used on a couple of previous occasions. McColl was to help with the necessary preparations and then return with the airplane, leaving the Belgians to carry out the operation.

"Do you have three men who can handle explosives?" he asked her.

"I will find them," she answered firmly. "And at least six people will be needed to light the fires for the airplane and to douse them once it has landed. The less time they're lit, the better."

"You'll need at least two for each bridge, one to keep guard while the other plants the explosives. So that's six already, and I'll be there, too." He almost regretted missing the action, McColl realized. It would be more exciting, and probably much less dangerous, than spending another three hours aloft, a frozen sitting duck.

"We will need to revisit these three bridges," Mathilde said. "As near the time as possible."

"I will do that," McColl promised. He had not been idle since his leg mended, but he still felt in debt to her and her people. Given the risks they ran, and the terrible cost of capture, he often wondered why more of them didn't just keep their heads down until the war had run its course.

On March 24, Caitlin was back in Dublin, talking to Maeve's friend Helena Molony on the first-floor landing of Liberty Hall and trying to enlist her help in arranging a quiet chat with James Connolly. Molony, an attractive no-nonsense woman in her mid-thirties, had once been Connolly's secretary and now held that post in the Irish Women Workers' Union.

Their conversation was interrupted by the raising of voices below.

"Excuse me a moment," Molony said over her shoulder, hurrying off down the stairs.

Keeping pace behind her, Caitlin saw two young men by the front door gesturing toward the basement stairs. "G-men," they whispered. "Four of the buggers."

Molony hardly missed a stride and, much to Caitlin's astonishment, pulled a gun from her pocket as she started down the next set of stairs.

Caitlin went after her. At the bottom Molony stopped for a second, then marched along the corridor that led to the room with the presses. She strode straight in, raising her gun as she entered to point it at the intruders.

One man had already gathered up an armful of papers.

"You can't take those," Molony told him, waving the gun to and fro along the line of potential targets.

Two of the men wore nervous smiles; the other pair just gaped. Presumably all four were armed, and Caitlin found it hard to imagine them letting a woman — even one pointing a gun — hold them there for long. For a few tense seconds, no one moved or spoke.

Then Connolly walked in, brandishing his Colt .45. "Drop those," he told the man with the armful of papers.

The pile hit the floor with a thud. Copies of *The Gael,* Caitlin noticed.

The two sides stared at each other, rather like children disputing ownership of a playground.

"You can hurry along now," Connolly said at last. "But don't come back here for any newspapers, no matter who sends you. Or next time we'll carry you out." Stepping aside from the door, he showed them the way with an open palm.

Four sullen faces filed out, eight feet clomped up the steps. Once the G-men were out of the building, Connolly and Molony shared looks of astonishment, then burst out laughing. "We'd better get the boys in," Connolly said eventually. "The Castle might feel the need to respond."

The next few hours were frenetic, as young men from all over Dublin answered the summons, leaving their work and grabbing rifles to stand in defense of the hall and its leaders. There were few signs of nervousness, Caitlin noticed; on the contrary, the mood seemed euphoric, as if everyone were happy that a gauntlet had been thrown down. As the evening progressed and it became abundantly clear that the British were taking no action, the republicans' confidence grew and the thought that a rising might even succeed didn't seem quite so outrageous.

Caitlin finally managed to interview Connolly in his office on the following morning. He still seemed energized by the events of the previous day and would occasionally leap from his seat to check on the square outside, where his men were busy drilling. "I think they've decided that arresting Helena and me would do them more harm than good," he said, as much to himself as to Caitlin. "But who knows?" he murmured. "Our rulers are stupid one moment, cunning the next. So how can I help you?" he asked at last. "Helena says you have a proposition."

"I have a request," she said. "But before I tell you what it is, I need to tell you who I am. Not to put too fine a point on it, I need to tell you whose side I'm on."

"You're a journalist," he said, a statement, not a question.

"Yes. And I need to stress that this discussion is off the record."

"All right."

"I believe in Irish independence," she began. "My brother died for it, as you know. I would never betray you or help the English. But if Irish independence were all I wanted, I might just as well talk to Eoin MacNeill, or any of the other Volunteer leaders. It isn't. I'm also a socialist and a feminist, and I believe that the Citizen Army embodies these ideals. And last but not least, I am a journalist. A good one, I think, though others would be the best judge of that."

"No doubt," Connolly agreed.

"And it's as a journalist that I can best serve my brother's memory," she went on.

"Yes?" Connolly looked a little bemused, as if uncertain where all this was leading.

She took a deep breath. "I believe — I *know* — that an insurrection is planned, in which the Citizen Army and the Volunteers will fight together. What I don't know is when. I want to be here when it happens, but I can't just wait here in Dublin — my newspaper needs me in London —"

"Where did you come by this information?" Connolly asked coldly.

"I was asked by the Volunteers — by a man named Mulryan, to be precise — to help feed false information to an Englishman I know. They wanted the English to believe that no rising was planned, and I managed to convince the man that this was the case."

"Ah. I was told about this. Not the details, mind," he added, though Caitlin could see from his face that he knew the whole story.

"I have proved my loyalty," she said, pressing the point. "And you will not find a more sympathetic witness."

He mulled that over for a few seconds.

"Assuming you are right and a rising *is* on the cards, you surely don't expect me to give you a date?"

"No, of course not. What I want is time to get here — a day's warning, that's all."

He shook his head.

"Mr. Connolly, you are an intelligent man, and you used to be a soldier. I doubt you think you can win. So the only point of your insurrection will be to show the world that the Irish still want their independence and will give their lives to gain it. But what if the lives are given and the world never learns what really happened, because the English have kept out all the reporters who might have told the truth? You need someone like me, who writes for a big paper and whom you can trust to tell the true story. And I need to be here the moment it starts."

He shook his head again, but this time with a smile. "You make a good case," he admitted. "But why not just stay on in Dublin? Then you could be certain you wouldn't miss a thing."

It was the first thing he'd said that disappointed her. Only a man would think she had nothing but time on her hands. "I'm a *European* correspondent," she told him, barely controlling her anger. "I can't just sit here in Dublin for weeks on end."

He gave her a thoughtful look. "You're asking me to take a huge leap of faith," he said.

"I'm asking you to take a very small risk for a very big gain. Here I am, an Irish martyr's sister, who's in a position to help you make your point to the world. And all I need from you is one day's notice."

He inclined his head. "I'll think about it. How can you be reached if I decide to do as you wish?"

She was ready for that. "This is my address," she said, passing it across, "and a phrase you could use to alert me."

"Kathleen Brennan has returned from America," he read, "and is willing to be interviewed next time you're in Dublin. Maeve." He grinned. "That sounds innocent enough."

The six piles of hay were ready for lighting, along with sundry containers of water for dousing the subsequent blazes. A man with matches stood waiting by each pile, McColl and Mathilde at the northern edge of the wide clearing, scanning the western sky for the prearranged signal.

It was a minute past midnight when they saw it — a couple of starlike flares floating down from heaven above the next town up the valley. The plane would be here in three or four minutes.

Mathilde waited two, then shouted out that the fires should be lit. In quick succession the mounds of hay caught fire, and as the last one ignited, McColl heard the drone of the engine.

It was almost on them before they saw it, a falling shadow against the starry sky, throttling down as it crossed the bushes that bordered the northern end of the field. A little too high, was McColl's instant judgment, and the pilot seemed reluctant to land, hanging for what felt like an age about thirty feet above the grass, dipping, then rising again before touching down only twenty yards from the line of trees. In McColl's estimation the plane was still going fifty miles an hour when it plowed between two oaks, catching a wing on each.

McColl expected an explosion, but none came. He started running toward the plane, the field around him darkening in stages as each new fire was extinguished.

The boxes of explosives were still tightly wedged in the empty observer's seat. The pilot looked equally undamaged, save for a head that hung much too limply. He had no pulse; the force of the impact had broken his neck.

The Belgians were already lifting out the explosives. "Let's go," Mathilde urged McColl. "There's nothing you can do for him."

She was right. McColl leaned over and closed the young man's eyes, then stepped back down to the ground. The tail of the plane was barely protruding into the field — there was a good chance it wouldn't be spotted from the air, and if the Germans hadn't seen the craft descend, they were unlikely to stumble across it. He wouldn't be going home, but those charged with blowing up the bridges might still have surprise on their side.

SAFETY PINS

Two nights after the fatal landing, McColl was crouched inside a stand of trees looking down at the lines that followed the river. The Meuse rolled slowly westward a hundred yards beyond the tracks; the girder bridge that carried them over the tributary was slightly to his right. About half a mile to his left, only one light was showing in the village that lay between railway and river. This was the house where the German guards were billeted. The current man on duty was leaning against the bridge's parapet and looked like he might be dying of boredom.

It was a warm night, with only the faintest of breezes to stir the branches above. A waning moon played hide-and-seek behind slow-moving clouds.

"It's time," the man beside McColl decided. Emile Mertens was well over six feet tall, with a bulk to match his height, a fairly extravagant mustache, and surprisingly cold blue eyes. His job was to deal with the sentry, McColl's to plant the charges.

When Mathilde had turned up that morning, he'd expected her to say that she'd found a *passeur* to take him across the border. What she'd actually told him was that one of her three explosives experts had backed out of that night's operation. "His wife's both ill and hysterical," she said. "Can you take his place?"

He hadn't considered refusing.

As Mertens got to his feet, McColl's ears picked out a noise in the distance. A train was approaching from the west.

Mertens heard it, too, and hunkered back down with an irritated sigh.

Not much more than a minute went by before it steamed past on the line below — the trains that were heading down the valley, McColl had long since realized, made much less noise than those that were climbing. As this one rumbled past he caught himself noting its composition. Old habits.

The taillight swayed past the cluster of houses and disappeared around the next bend. The sentry on the bridge stared after it, as if he wished that he were homeward bound.

They started down the slope, McColl carrying the bag of explosives, Mertens a rifle and a fearsome-looking knife. Keeping close to the trees that curved down to the bank of the tributary, they reached a position some twenty yards from the tracks. The German sentry had his back to them, having resumed his contemplative stance by the parapet.

Mertens handed McColl the rifle and began walking toward the unsuspecting German. McColl put the stick against his shoulder and took aim, just in case the sentry turned round. There was a fair chance that the sound of the shot wouldn't reach the soldier's billet, but if it did, they would just have to make a run for it. These days McColl's leg felt almost as good as new, and the woods above were big enough to hide in.

Mertens was light on his feet for a big man, but Nijinsky would have had a hard job traversing two ballasted tracks without making a sound. A final dash was the Belgian's only hope, but the sentry had just enough time to evade the plunging knife, and both men crashed to the ground in a welter of arms and legs. Staring down the sights of the rifle, McColl knew that he couldn't risk shooting and hitting his partner.

He dropped the rifle and rushed to the

Belgian's aid, thinking to use his Webley on the bareheaded German. There was no need. As he reached the two men, Mertens was staggering to his feet, the sentry covered in blood and clearly breathing his last. Before McColl could do or say anything, the Belgian had lifted his victim onto the balustrade and tipped him over. There was a loud splash and the briefest glimpse of a white face before the body tumbled off downstream.

Mertens picked up the German's helmet and forced it onto his own much larger head. McColl collected his bag and set to work. He had done a training course in fixing explosives before his assignment to India, and one of the Belgians had given him a refresher course the previous night. At the Belgian's suggestion, the slabs of gun cotton had been fixed to short lengths of wood, through which holes had been drilled for the detonators. Under the bridge McColl now set about tying these to the girders and connecting them via fuses to the track above. It had already been decided that the flat detonators would be clipped to the rails of the westbound tracks, as only trains in that direction were likely to carry ammunition.

As he worked, it occurred to McColl that

Colm Hanley had been shot for trying to blow up a bridge, on what he at least believed was enemy territory. Could Caitlin ever forgive him for what had happened to her brother? During that week in Dublin, it felt as though she had, but he might be kidding himself about that. So might she.

The slabs were lashed to the girders, the fuses threaded through to the side of the rails. As he clambered back up the slope, he saw Mertens peering down the tracks with what seemed rapt attention. Following the Belgian's gaze, he saw the reason. What looked like an electric flashlight was flickering to and fro. The dead sentry's relief was on his way.

"Are you done?" Mertens asked.

"A few more minutes," McColl said, lowering himself onto the sleepers.

"Shit!" the Belgian muttered. "They'll be here in two."

McColl tried to concentrate on the job at hand. For several seconds all his fingers felt like thumbs, and he had to force himself to take things more slowly.

The flashlight was still some distance away — Mertens's estimate had been pessimistic. McColl was taking comfort from this when the signal beyond the bridge clanked itself to go. A train would soon be with them.

One fuse was done, the sentry's relief still two hundred yards away. But now McColl could see that there were two of them. And if they weren't dealt with, they would notice the detonators and stop the train.

The second fuse fixed, McColl glanced up and down the line. In one direction the two German soldiers, now some eighty yards away, in the other a distant plume of moonlit steam announcing the oncoming train.

"A beautiful night!" the German without the flashlight cried out, spreading his arms to encompass it.

Mertens didn't answer, and McColl stayed prone on the ground, not wanting to give the game away.

"Are you growing deaf, Erich?" the same German shouted. He was obviously in a good humor.

This time Mertens replied, raising the captured rifle and pulling the trigger. Whichever man he was aiming at, it was the one with the flashlight he hit, throwing him backward across the rails.

His companion responded instantly, sinking to one knee, raising his own weapon, and firing at Mertens.

The Belgian collapsed with a grunt, his rifle clattering onto the ballast.

By this time McColl was running toward him, Webley in hand. As the barrel of the surviving German's rifle swiveled in his direction, he threw himself forward, and the subsequent shot went over his head. Steadying himself, he took aim at the helmeted shape ahead and pulled the automatic's trigger.

The German fell back without a sound.

"I'm finished," Mertens was telling himself and the sky.

McColl scrambled across the few yards that separated them, aware of the train growing louder behind him. Mertens had been right about his prospects — McColl had never heard a death rattle, but the sounds coming out of the Belgian's throat were the ones he had always imagined.

The approaching train couldn't be more than a minute away. Where Mertens was lying, he would be hidden by the bridge abutment, but one of the sentries was in the middle of the tracks. McColl sprinted the thirty yards, hoisted him clear, and rolled first him, then his partner, down the slight embankment.

Turning, he saw the engine round the bend beyond the bridge, less than half a mile away.

He was tempted to just head up the slope

toward the forest, but that would leave him on the same side of the tributary as the other Germans.

He ran back toward the bridge, toward the oncoming train, praying the driver wouldn't see him in the darkness. Across the sleepers he sped, conscious that one missed step could plunge him through the girders and into the river, where the train would probably land on his head. The bridge seemed three times longer than he'd thought, but at last he was clear of it and starting up the slope toward the trees as the locomotive pounded past.

He saw the explosions reflected in the trees and couldn't resist turning to see the consequences. As the bridge collapsed beneath the locomotive, both slid down toward the opposite bank, and the wagons behind crashed and thundered into the gap, piling into one another like a line of huge iron dominoes, until one exploded with staggering force, throwing McColl to the ground and turning night into garish day.

The long walk home was a fraught affair. Sporadic shots in the distance offered proof that a hunt was under way, and on one occasion a sudden tumult of baying dogs almost gave him a heart attack. But they weren't as close as he feared, and it was only the darkness — almost complete now that the moon had set — which actually slowed his progress. The birds were singing by the time he reached the outskirts of Huy and carefully worked his way round the still-sleeping town to the house of his Belgian hosts.

Mathilde had agreed that he should leave for Holland as soon as that was practical, but both of them knew that their work that night was likely to delay matters, and with a wait of unknown duration in order he found himself back in the familiar space between roofs. At least it wasn't as cold as it had been in the winter.

During the first day, Yvette Deflandres brought him regular bulletins: all three bridges had been destroyed; Mertens had been the only casualty among the saboteurs, but two other Belgians had been shot by the Germans, allegedly for fleeing when challenged. So far the Germans had not taken hostages, as they had elsewhere in similar circumstances.

But they were moving heaven and earth to find the perpetrators, as Mathilde told McColl on the following afternoon. They were all over the valley, hundreds of them, searching houses and farms, questioning anyone out on the roads. Even if the trains started running again, things would need to calm down before McColl could safely venture out.

With no new books to read, he started rereading the old ones. Thanks to himself and the others, there weren't any trains to watch.

In London, Easter Saturday was warm and bright, fluffy white clouds in formation dotting the deep blue sky. After treating herself to bacon and eggs at a café on the Clapham High Road and forcing herself to peruse the war reports, Caitlin took a walk in the park and reread the latest letter from Brooklyn. Aunt Orla had lots of news, both national and domestic, from Mexican rebel Pancho Villa's invasion of the United States to the latest in the long line of Caitlin's old school friends who had beaten her to the altar. Though the tone was unremittingly cheerful, there was a hint of wistfulness somewhere in the mix, as if her aunt had finally realized that the life she had wanted for Caitlin, the one she herself had given up, might come at too high a cost.

Caitlin sat there on the bench listening to the birds in the blossoming trees, wondering if it really was time she went home, if only for a couple of weeks — her editor would surely agree to that. She had been telling herself it was the job that kept her in London, and to some extent that was true, but there were other jobs, other stories. If Slaney was right, those Americans opposed to joining the war would need all the help they could get over the next twelve months.

No, it was Jack who was keeping her here, the fear that he might turn up the moment she was gone. If she was here to welcome him back, they could have some time together and then go their separate ways again.

She didn't think he was dead, though that was always possible. They'd broached the matter in Dublin and thought of asking Cumming to let her know if Jack was killed, but after a little more thought that hadn't seemed such a great idea. McColl had promised to think of something else, and probably he had. So no news was most likely good news.

She got up from the bench and started walking back across the grass. On a sunny day like this one, the women in black seemed sadder than usual, and each day there seemed to be more of them.

As she passed her landlady's door, it suddenly swung open and the woman in question thrust an envelope toward her. "Delivered by hand," her landlady said. "About half an hour ago. He had a Galway accent," she added with a Connemara native's condescension.

Caitlin opened it in her room, unsure whether dread or excitement was the appropriate response. The single sentence was all in capital letters, scrawled with a green colored pencil. *KATHLEEN BRENNAN HAS RETURNED FROM AMERICA.*

It took the Germans six days to repair the damage, the first train passing through Huy early on Good Friday morning. McColl and Yvette Deflandres were downstairs, Eric on duty in the roof space, when Mathilde arrived twenty-four hours later with the bad news. "Jules has been arrested," were her opening words. Jules was the man who had fixed the charges on one of the other bridges.

"When?" Yvette asked.

"Late last night."

"He won't tell them anything," Yvette insisted.

"He won't want to. They're using truth drugs now, so he may not have a choice."

"Then what do we do?"

"Nothing," Mathilde told her. "He doesn't

know about you and Eric. You only need to start worrying when I'm arrested," she added, trying to make a joke of it. "But you're leaving today," she told McColl, "and not for Namur. You're going home. Liège today, then over the border to Maastricht. There should be a train in half an hour. I'll go with you to the station — a romantic send-off will look less suspicious. I've got nothing to lose," she added when McColl tried to dissuade her. "I'll be organizing my own exit next."

In the event, Huy Station was strangely devoid of German or local police, the train was on time, and all he got was a kiss on the cheek.

"Safe journey," she said.

"And you."

Half an hour later, the train inched across the bridge they'd built to replace the one he'd blown up. The river below was still partly dammed by sundered rolling stock, but the locomotive had been taken out and away. It was hard not to admire German efficiency where engineering was concerned, and McColl found himself wondering whether six days' worth of canceled trains was worth three lives.

He recognized the ticket inspector who got on at Flémalle, but not the German who accompanied him. As he watched them work their way down the carriage, he considered his chances. If Jules had talked, then McColl's papers would give him away, and he would either have to go quietly or do something very rash, like pulling out the Webley and jumping off the moving train. The thought of the latter sent a painful twinge down his recently broken leg.

Play it by ear, he told himself. Stay calm.

When they reached him, he smiled at the Belgian and tried not to notice the German's fierce stare. The Belgian returned his papers with a smile; the German looked disbelieving but followed his colleague on to the next.

McColl sat back with a mental sigh of relief. They were only twenty minutes from Liège, so another inspection was unlikely.

The line crossed the Meuse on a long bridge, then hugged the right bank through the series of coal-mining villages on the southern approach to Liège. Longdoz station seemed full of Germans, but the Belgian who checked his ticket and papers there hardly bothered to look at them. Clutching the copy of *Comédie Humaine* that was supposed to identify him, McColl began slowly traversing the concourse. He was about halfway across when a slim, dark-haired woman in her thirties materialized in front of him and warmly embraced him. "I am Monique," she said, taking his arm and steering him out onto the busy Rue Grétry.

She led him north across the two river bridges and into the heart of the city, saying nothing but keeping a grip on his arm. She had a serious, almost stern face, which seemed slightly at odds with her rose-scented perfume.

"Where are we going?" he asked once the Meuse was behind them. The sun had sunk below the buildings now, and it was rapidly growing dark.

"To a bar," she replied. "It's not far."

A few minutes later, they entered the Café de Tongeren, a large, smoke-filled room lined with booths and lit by flickering gaslights. It was crowded with early-evening drinkers and smelled of sweat and beer.

Monique looked round the room, failed to find the face she was seeking, and guided them to an empty booth. When the waitress came over, she ordered beer for him and pastis for herself.

While they waited for their drinks, McColl examined the clientele. It was overwhelmingly male and seemed mostly composed of neatly dressed clerks stopping off on their way home from work, though one table was occupied by young men in workers' overalls. There was also a solitary man at the bar who kept throwing stares in his and Monique's direction. He was around forty, stocky, with a thin mustache, and obviously fond of himself. McColl hoped the stares were for his companion, who had her eyes glued to the door.

A German captain walked in, his shoulders glistening with raindrops. Much to McColl's surprise, he exchanged greetings with several Belgian customers. He seemed particularly friendly with the stranger at the bar, which increased McColl's suspicions, so he asked Monique if she knew who the stranger was.

"He's been hanging round here for several weeks. He says his name is Delors, but no one knows who he is."

That didn't sound good. "How long do we wait?" he asked her.

She shrugged. "Another half an hour?"

"Do you know who we're waiting for?"

"Yes," she said simply, keeping her eyes on the door. She hadn't touched the pastis.

Another five minutes had passed when the second German came in. This one was wearing a military police uniform, and the only greetings he received were a drop in the level of conversation and a bevy of hostile glances. Apparently unperturbed by these signs of unpopularity, he stood by the door scanning faces, found the one he wanted, and advanced across the sawdust floor to the table with all the young men, where he hovered over a tousled-haired boy with a strikingly beautiful face.

"Papers!" the German demanded.

The youth offered them up. His smile looked like so much nervous bravado.

The German examined the papers and seemed to find nothing amiss, but as one hand returned them, the other shot out like a striking snake and turned back the young man's collar. On the inner face, two safety pins were visible, side by side at a slant.

Still gripping the collar, the German yanked the boy to his feet. "You come with me," he said in passable French.

"Do nothing," the woman whispered to McColl, as if she feared he might intervene.

The idea had not occurred to him, but it had to the man called Delors. He walked across to the German and politely asked for a word.

As the other man turned toward him, Delors's arm jerked upward. After making a few feeble gropes at the knife now buried in his chest, the German fell back across the nearest table, splintering wood and cascading glass.

The German captain was having trouble freeing his gun from its holster. After shouting, "Jean, get out of here!" Delors picked up a convenient bottle and smashed it into the side of the German's face. "Now!" he added, since Jean was still rooted to the spot.

Needing no third bidding, the young man vanished through the door. Delors took his time pulling the knife from the dead German's chest and wiping it on the man's uniform before taking his leave at a stroll.

"Come," Monique told McColl, "we must go. The police will be here in a few minutes."

It was no longer raining outside.

"This way," she urged him, heading downhill, just as two uniformed Germans hove into sight farther up. "Run!" she ordered, hitching up her long skirt to do so.

McColl obeyed but was not surprised when the Germans shouted "Stop!" It might have been wiser not to draw attention to themselves, he thought as the first shot whistled a few feet wide, gouging slivers of stone from a house façade.

Ten yards ahead Monique was already turning a corner. He took it a few seconds later, skidding on the rain-greased cobblestones as another bullet zinged harmlessly past. The new road was empty of people, barely lit, and lined with small workshops. She ducked between two of these and raced off down another short alley, which ended in an archway. McColl was slowly losing ground, his leg beginning to throb, but he managed to reach the end before the Germans came into view.

A square lay on the other side of the archway, with a church on one side, restaurants and shops on the others. A fountain sat in the middle, surrounded by small trees and benches. Best of all, it was crowded with people. The woman hurried him across and pulled him down beside her on one of the rain-soaked seats. After taking a bright red scarf from her pocket and wrapping it around her head, she snuggled into the crook of his shoulder, filling his nose with the scent of roses.

He liked the perfume and briefly contemplated buying a bottle for Caitlin. Briefly because he didn't think there'd be much time for shopping.

Across the square the two German policemen appeared. After looking this way and that, one started forward only for the other to call him back. "It's not worth it, Fritz," McColl murmured, imagining what the German had said.

With admirable synchronization the two men spun on their heels and vanished back up the alley.

Monique sat up straight. "So far, so good," she said in a less than confident tone.

"What now?" he asked.

She just stared into space for a moment, then seemed to make up her mind. "We must get you inside. Come."

They headed away from the square and zigzagged their way down several dark streets. McColl's leg felt worse with each stride, and he was about to beg a few moments' rest when they reached their destination, a fairly anonymous house in one of the city's older quarters. The woman who opened the door was clearly not happy to see them but was welcoming nevertheless. Once inside, McColl leaned back against the door while the two women talked. Monique was promising that it would be for only one night.

She turned to him. "You will stay in the cellar," she said. "It will be safer for everyone."

"It's not very comfortable, I'm afraid," the other woman said. "But I will bring you some food and water."

Monique took him downstairs. The cellar was almost bare, with a damp earthen floor, but at least it wasn't cold. She walked across to the only window, which looked up toward the street. "If the Germans find you, you must say that you broke in," she said, forcing the window open and then closing it again. "And I'm afraid there won't be any bedding — if the Germans found you with blankets, they would know that you got them from the people upstairs."

"I'll be fine," McColl told her.

After his hostess had brought down bread, jam, and water, both women left, bolting the cellar door behind them. McColl ate the food, found an empty paint tin to piss in, and sat down with his back to the wall. Rain was drumming on the window and, hopefully, keeping the Germans indoors.

There were quite a few army officers lining the deck of the Dublin boat, men on leave from their units in France, expecting a week or more's rest and recuperation in the bosom of their families. As the boat edged into the Dún Laoghaire dock, Caitlin found herself feeling sorry for them, especially those in obvious need of convalescence — the country that awaited them would not be the one they expected. They might have a few days' grace — no date had come with her tip-off, and the Holyhead evening papers had carried no hint that a rebellion was already under way — but Caitlin had heard whispers of "Easter" more than once in the corridors of Liberty Hall.

The inspection shed looked much the same. A couple of uniformed policemen were sharing a joke in one corner, a probable G-man scanning faces with bored eyes and a cigarette drooping from his lips. If Dublin was in the throes of an insurrection, the news had not reached Dún Laoghaire.

Was it a false alarm? The clock in the hall said it wasn't yet nine, so there was plenty of time. She remembered that the Volunteer and ICA exercises usually started late in the morning, and she guessed that these would serve as cover for a rising. As one Liberty Hall man had told her back in March — "Someday this will be for real."

On Sunday the trains into Dublin were few and far between, and it was gone half past ten when she arrived at Tara Street station. Outside, the streets seemed quiet, with only a few families enjoying the traditional Sunday-morning stroll along the Liffey. Caitlin walked across Butt Bridge, under the shadow of the railway arches to the end of Lower Abbey Street, and down to Liberty Hall.

There were no men milling outside, but

the young men guarding the doors did seem unusually edgy and wouldn't admit her without permission from inside. Luckily for Caitlin, Maeve McCarron was there. As they walked up to the Cumann na mBan office, several open doorways offered glimpses of silent men sitting in chairs or standing by windows. Everyone seemed to be waiting.

"The Military Committee are meeting in the commandant's office," Maeve explained when they reached their destination. "They're deciding whether to go ahead."

"Why?" Caitlin wanted to know. "I assumed it was on."

"Yesterday I did, too. It's been mad these last few days. First it was on, then off, then on again. And now it's off again — Eoin MacNeill has revoked all the mobilization orders."

MacNeill was the Volunteer leader. "Why? Did he get cold feet?"

"No, we can't accuse him of that. He only discovered a few days ago that a rising was planned."

"Oh, my God. I always assumed . . ."

"So did everyone," Maeve agreed. "But the Military Committee thought it prudent not to tell him. People like Tom Clarke were afraid he'd say no."

"And he has."

"Yes, but the committee are furious, and I think they'll go ahead anyway."

"Doesn't MacNeill have a lot of supporters, though?"

"Sure he does. But the feeling is that once the whole thing starts, no one'll want to miss out."

Caitlin shook her head. "That seems like a terrible gamble."

Maeve smiled. "It always was."

"I suppose so." Caitlin walked over to the window and looked out at the empty square. She was about to ask how long the meeting had been under way when a distant chorus of cheers echoed through the building.

"I'll go and see," Maeve said. "You'd better wait here."

More cheers went up every now and then, and when Maeve returned, her news came as no surprise. The rising was back on. Everything planned for today would now take place tomorrow.

"I'm going to be busy this afternoon," she said, "but later —"

"You don't need a houseguest at a time like this," Caitlin said. "I'll go to a hotel."

"Don't be silly. Once it starts, heaven knows when I'll be home, and you can look after the place. Here, I'll give you my key.

I'll pick up the spare tonight." She sat down, then stood up again. "I can hardly believe it," the Irishwoman said, her expression suddenly serious. "I haven't felt this frightened since I was five and my father put me up on a horse in Phoenix Park. I'm excited, too, of course I am. But oh, Jesus, I'm frightened."

Caitlin put an arm around the other woman's shoulders but could think of nothing useful to say. "You could always walk away" was pointless and "You'll be all right" just fatuous. Truth be told, she felt frightened herself, and unlike Maeve, she wasn't going to war.

Georges and Didier

McColl hadn't harbored much hope of sleep, but he woke with a start stretched out on the earthen floor. Turning his watch toward the one small window, he discovered it was almost five o'clock. His neck and back were painfully stiff, but he told himself there was good news, too — the Germans hadn't shown up in the night, and, as far as he could tell, their precipitate flight hadn't caused his leg any further damage. He had hardly eaten on the previous day and felt really hungry now, but his bowels seemed unaware they should be empty.

After relieving himself in a bucket that he'd failed to spot the night before, he settled down to wait, eyes on the brightening window, ears cocked for signs of life upstairs. It was half past seven when the bolts were thrown back and his friend from yesterday reappeared, wrinkling her nose as she came down the steps.

"I had to relieve myself," he said apologetically.

"Of course. Are you ready to go?"

"Oh, yes."

There was no one to thank in the house upstairs, and McColl felt absurdly guilty for leaving them a bucket of shit. Outside, the streets were dry, the sky threatening rain.

"How far this time?" he asked her.

"Cinq minutes," she told him. Today a red beret was perched on her dark brown hair, but the long black skirt and sturdy shoes were the same.

Their destination was a backstreet milk depot. As they arrived, a cart full of churns was coming out through the gates, and many more were parked in the yard. Several of the attached horses were stamping their hooves on the cobbles, as if eager to be gone.

They walked across to the office, where two men greeted McColl's companion with kisses on the cheek. One was the depot foreman, the other a dairy farmer. All four of them watched through the window as the yard slowly emptied, until only the farmer's cart remained.

After the foreman had closed the gates, he and the farmer removed what had looked like the floor of the cart, to reveal a hidden space beneath in the shape of a shallow coffin.

The farmer waved a hand, inviting McColl to climb in. "Just until we get clear of the city," he promised.

McColl turned to the woman. "Thank you," he said. "And please thank the people who own the house."

She nodded.

McColl clambered up and laid himself out in the narrow space. Once the false floor had been replaced, it was only an inch from his nose, and he endured a momentary flash of panic when the empty churns were lifted on, causing his new ceiling to noisily creak with the strain.

He felt the farmer climb onto the seat and heard him gee the horse into motion. As they rattled out onto the street, he decided to look on the bright side and dwell on how impressed his grandchildren would be when he told them the story of his daring escape from Belgium.

If he escaped. The journey out of Liège seemed to take forever, and each time the cart halted without releasing him, he felt like crying with rage. When the first churn was finally lifted off, he could have wept with gratitude. Once the planks had been removed, he painfully extracted himself from his hiding place, gingerly lowered himself to the floor, and leaned, somewhat unsteadily, against the side of the cart. They were parked by the side of an empty road, the horse serenely munching on a clump of wild grass.

The farmer put his cart back together, and the two of them loaded the churns.

"About a kilometer in that direction," the Belgian told him, pointing down the road, "there's a house that nobody lives in. It's the first one you come to. On the left. The husband and son are with the King's army, the wife is with her sister in Brussels. And this is the key," he said, taking it out of his pocket. "Now, listen. In the main room downstairs, there's a big stone fireplace, and on either side of that there are big cupboards. If you go into the one on the right and push hard against the bottom of the opposite wall, it will swing open and let you into the secret room. There are regular patrols on this road," he added, glancing up and down it, "so you'd be wise to hide yourself in there until the *passeur* comes to pick you up."

"And when will that be?" McColl asked.

"There's some bread and water waiting for you," the farmer answered. "And if he doesn't come tonight, someone else will bring you more." He gave McColl an encouraging thump on the shoulder. "Now I must be getting home."

After watching the man turn his cart and drive it back the way they'd come, McColl started walking, keeping close to the trees that bordered one side of the road. He'd been walking ten minutes when he saw another cart in the distance and crouched down in some bushes to watch it go past, loaded with spring cabbages. Continuing his journey, he came on the house quicker than expected, let himself in with the key, and found the door to the secret room. The bottom flew back when he shoved it, causing the top to come down on his head. A detail to spare the grandchildren, he decided, rubbing his scalp and looking round the room. It was empty, save for the bread and the bottle of water in the middle of the floor.

He relocked the front door, closed the secret entrance, and settled down for another wait. The Belgians had all been wonderful, but the life of a human parcel was somewhat undermining. He had only the vaguest idea where he was — the Dutch border could be one or fifty miles distant, and heaven knew in which direction.

The hours dragged by with few diversions.

He heard vehicles and voices on several occasions, but none of the latter were German, and the light seeping through the boarded-up windows slowly began to fade. With the bread and water long gone, he felt increasingly hungry and thirsty, and when the *passeur* arrived just after midnight, McColl almost fell on the food he brought.

"Call me Jacques," the man told him. He was probably in his forties, with stubble for hair, sharp blue eyes, and the general demeanor of a theatrical villain. "What's your name?"

"Jack," McColl told him.

"Two Jacks!" the man said, clearly amused. "I have two friends outside who will come with us."

"How far is it?" McColl asked.

"Ten kilometers. But no need to hurry. The moon will not be down for several hours."

The men outside were younger. They greeted McColl with smiles but didn't introduce themselves. One was holding a canvas haversack, which he passed to Jacques.

The first stage of the trek took them across numerous moonlit fields and through several moon-dappled woods and would have been enchanting in other circumstances. No one talked, and Jacques, in the lead, would occasionally stop to listen, then offer up a reassuring nod before moving on. McColl had questions he wanted to ask — were there patrols this far from the border? — but managed to restrain himself. No one liked a talkative parcel.

They came to a wide stream. According to Jacques it marked the boundary of the "verboten zone" — anyone found between here and the frontier would be shot on sight. The four of them waded across and were soon out in the open, traversing a broad stretch of heathland. After a while McColl noticed shifting patterns of light on the distant horizon. Searchlights.

They entered another stretch of woodland, walking along a well-used path until they reached a large clearing, where Jacques's two helpers started rummaging among the pile of dead branches that lay in one corner and eventually pulled something clear. It looked like a window frame.

"We will wait here until the moon is down," Jacques told McColl. "Maybe half an hour," he added, gazing through the trees at the sinking yellow disk.

A breeze had risen, and the noise it made in the branches above was loud enough to mask their conversation. "Tell me about the frontier," McColl asked. "How well guarded is it?"

"A man every hundred meters, lights every four hundred."

Wonderful, McColl thought wryly. There wouldn't be a section out of eyeshot.

"And then there's the electrified fence."

"And how do we get through that?"

Jacques smiled. "You will see."

With the moon gone, the last lap was difficult, but the deeper darkness at least offered hope of an unseen approach. Or so McColl thought until they arrived. When they reached the edge of the trees and looked out across the fifty-yard strip that the Germans had cleared, one of the searchlights was bathing it all in a pale yellow glow. When the beam moved on, the light dramatically faded, but the resulting darkness was far from complete.

Two sentries were visible, one quite close, now walking away to the left, the other much farther away but apparently approaching. More worryingly, McColl had noticed two dark shapes on the glinting wires. Human shapes.

"What's that on the fence?" he asked in a whisper.

"Georges and Didier," was the terse reply. "The Germans leave bodies on the wire to discourage the rest of us, so of course we cross as close as we can. Just to show the bastards we're not afraid." As he talked, the Belgian had taken two balls of string from his haversack and started winding an end around each wrist. That done, he handed a ball to each of his two partners, both of whom gave McColl a friendly pat on the shoulder before slipping away in opposite directions, trailing string behind them. "You're lucky you're on your way out," Jacques said.

"Why?"

"Because coming in, you can't afford to be seen, or the Germans will hunt you down. Going out, even if you have to shoot a sentry, once you're across, there's nothing more they can do."

Gazing at the fence and its victims, lit again by the moving light, McColl didn't feel that lucky. "How do I get through the wire?"

Jacques reached for the window frame, which was actually four lengths of wood screwed together to form a square. Grooved strips of rubber had been fixed to opposite sides. "We slide this onto the bottom strand of wire and push down until we can slip the other side into the next strand up. Then you just squeeze through." He took a pair of wire cutters out of one pocket. "You'll need these for the second fence. It's a hundred meters beyond. But not electrified. Or at least it wasn't," he added with a grin. There was a tug on one of the lines. "Maurice is in position. And so is Albert," he added a few moments later. "They will tug each time their sentry is farthest away from us. When both tug within a few seconds, we go."

"And the searchlight?"

"It only shines on this stretch of fence for a few seconds, and as long as we hold still, there's a good chance of not being seen."

Which all seemed reasonable enough, McColl reckoned, until you considered the corpses fused to the wire. Or had they just slipped?

"Sometimes we have to wait a long time," Jacques warned him.

But not on this particular night. One sentry had been swallowed by the darkness much earlier than the other, but he must have stopped for some reason — a piss, maybe, or a chat with the next man along — because both strings tightened at almost the same moment.

"Let's go," Jacques hissed, and, picking up the insulated frame, he started toward the fence.

The light was swinging their way, and both

men fell face forward into the grass, scrambling back up as soon as it receded.

The fence was about ten feet tall, the wires around nine inches apart. Having donned rubber gloves that he took from his bag, Jacques arranged one grooved side of the frame across the second-lowest strand and invited McColl to help push down. Both men put their weight into it, McColl realizing that if it slipped out, they would probably both fall onto the wires and join the two a few feet away.

When they had a half inch to spare, Jacques maneuvered the opposite groove onto either side of the wire above and slowly let them entwine. "Go," he said.

As McColl stooped to squeeze himself through, the searchlight beam swept over the contorted faces of Georges and Didier and seemed to hover over himself and Jacques. There was a shout away to his right.

Refusing to panic, he inched his way through, petrified that any misstep might dislodge the frame. As he eased his head under, a shot rang out and there were more shouts father away. The moment he'd pulled his second leg through, he was off and running, pursued by the questing searchlight. More shots were fired without apparent effect, and he found himself back in darkness, approaching the second fence.

Jacques had assured him that this one wasn't charged, but the first safe contact was still a relief. As he rapidly cut a flap in the wire, the searchlight was sweeping back in his direction, arriving just as he wormed his way through and slumped to the ground beyond.

The operator overshot, and McColl was up and running into Holland. As the yards flew by, he waited for the searchlight to pin him again; when it didn't, he knew he must have passed beyond its range.

After another hundred yards, he felt able to stop, crouch down, and give his heart and lungs a chance to recover. Far behind him more shots cracked out. He hoped Jacques and the others had gotten away but knew he would probably never find out.

He walked on until he found a farm track, tossed a mental coin, and followed it north-ward. When dawn broke, he was overtaken by a Dutch farmer in a mud-spattered Model T and offered a lift into Maastricht.

Arriving home after midnight, Maeve was on her way out by eight, looking both nervous and proud in her Cumann na mBan uniform. "Be outside the GPO at noon," she reminded Caitlin from the doorway.

It was a long morning. Soon after eleven, Caitlin secured a seat in the Imperial's bar, which offered an excellent view across Sackville Street of the colonnaded post office, and settled back to watch and wait. Noon came and went, and she began to think that the rising had again been postponed. She felt disappointed and, much to her own surprise, even a little relieved. Maybe, as Maeve had feared, MacNeill's intervention had confused or deterred too many Volunteers and the members of the Military Committee had decided they lacked sufficient men to implement their strategy.

But then Caitlin heard the clump of boots and, pressing her eyes to the window, could see a column approaching.

She hurried out onto the pavement.

There weren't that many rebels — fewer than two hundred, she thought — and one small group broke away as she watched and marched off in another direction. Some men were in uniform, others not, and the weapons they carried ranged from modern rifles to crowbars and medieval-looking pikes. Patrick Pearse and James Connolly were at the front, and as they approached the GPO, Caitlin saw two other leaders she recognized

— Seán McDermott and Thomas Clarke — climb out of a car nearby.

On the pavement a few feet away, a British soldier was laughing at them. "What a motley crew!" he cried out seconds before a raised Irish voice bellowed the order to charge. There was some hesitation, then another shout: "Take the GPO!" At which point they all turned and ran for the entrance, causing the lone policeman on duty to throw up his arms in surrender.

Now there was silence out on the street, and faces full of surprise. What was happening here?

For more than a minute, those in the street just stood there, waiting for some sort of sign. And then a shot was heard inside the building, suddenly making it real.

Before too long, customers and employees were being hustled out through the doors at bayonet point, some clearly scared, others more bemused. Minutes later there were signs of activity on the roof, and then, one after the other, two new flags were raised in place of the Union Jack, the first one green with a golden harp and the words "Irish Republic," the second a tricolor in green, white, and orange. On the street these received a mixed reception — cheers and jeers in more or less equal measure.

In keeping with this transfer of power, a rebel was tearing down those British recruiting posters that adorned the GPO façade and taking great delight in trampling them underfoot.

The watchers, still no more than a couple hundred strong, waited and wondered. What was happening inside? Would anyone come out to tell them? Surely a speech was called for.

At around twelve forty-five, the doors opened and Patrick Pearse stepped out, a single sheet of paper in his hand. James Connolly followed and took up position at Pearse's shoulder, one hand on his holstered gun.

The crowd fell silent as Pearse began to read. He was speaking, he said, for the Provisional Government of the Irish Republic and to all the people of Ireland. "Irishmen and Irishwomen," he began. "In the name of God and of the dead generations from which she receives her old tradition of nationhood, Ireland, through us, summons her children to her flag and strikes for her freedom."

As he read on, explaining and defending their action, Caitlin, almost despite herself, found herself falling under his spell. She had never felt more Irish; she could almost feel the joy of those dead generations, whose struggles had finally come to fruition. How happy Colm would have been to witness this, how proud her father would be.

She realized she was being swept along by the moment, but in that moment she didn't care. Pearse's naming of Irishwomen alongside Irishmen was a wonderful bonus, proof that she'd been right to trust the republican leadership in matters of gender. Things would not change overnight, but what a start this was.

Pearse was still speaking, promising fair treatment for all on the island and votes for men and women alike. He insisted that the rebels would defend their new republic with honor and make whatever sacrifice was necessary for the common good. Young men were already passing out printed copies of the declaration, and once he had finished reading, Pearse turned and walked back inside.

Connolly was more reluctant to leave, and Caitlin took a chance on approaching him as he stood there surveying the street. A rebel quickly moved to head her off, but seeing who she was, Connolly told him to let her through. "A great day," he said. "I'm glad you could make it."

"So am I," she replied. An idea suddenly

came to her, both sensible and cheeky. "Mr. Connolly, wherever I've worked as a journalist, I've needed accreditation from the local authorities. Now that Ireland has a new government, perhaps you could give me something in writing. It would make it easier for me to get around."

Connolly laughed. "Why not? Come with me — I'll do it now."

Inside the post office, it sounded like a construction site as the rebels readied the building for defense. Following Connolly up the stairs, Caitlin found herself hoping that they weren't just going to sit behind barricaded windows and wait for the English. Surely there was no future in that?

Connolly had already set himself up in the manager's office. Seating himself at the desk, he reached for pen and paper. "I can't say I have much experience in this sort of thing," he said. "Perhaps you'd care to dictate?"

After she'd done so, he passed across the finished article, having signed it "James Connolly, on behalf of the Provisional Government." One day she'd have it framed, Caitlin thought. "Can I ask what happens next?" she said, placing it in her bag. "I assume you've taken other positions."

He reeled them off. The four Volunteer battalions had HQs at the Four Courts, Jacob's Biscuit Factory, Boland's Bakery, and the South Dublin Union; the Citizen Army had been sent to Dublin Castle and St. Stephen's Green. "I can't tell you what happens next until I hear how everything's gone." He gave her an impish smile. "For all I know, the English have already surrendered."

"Well, armed with this" — she raised the letter — "I shall go and see."

There was still a host of onlookers outside, and as she emerged, Caitlin was briefly the focus of their attention. They were like theatergoers at intermission, she thought, waiting impatiently for another act to begin.

Walking south toward the river, she found herself back in the usual Dublin, albeit one whose policemen were all on leave. There were no surging crowds, no scurrying troops, no rattle of gunfire or plumes of smoke.

After crossing the Liffey on the Ha'penny Bridge, she worked her way toward Dublin Castle, the seat of British rule. The crenellated battlements were looming above the roofs ahead when she turned a corner and found herself facing a British army barricade.

"You'll have to go back, miss," a sergeant told her.

"Why's that?" she asked indignantly.

"Because there's rebels on the roof of City Hall," he told her. "And they're shooting at anything that moves."

"Have they taken your Castle?" she asked innocently.

"No," he told her. "They just shot the poor bugger on the gate and bolted into City Hall."

Connolly would be disappointed. She didn't place any credence in the soldier's description of how it had happened, but she instinctively knew he was telling the truth about the rebel failure to take the Castle. Looking up, she could still see the wretched Union Jack fluttering against the sky.

Her next three ports of call offered more in the way of encouragement. She saw no sign of British troops on the mile walk to Boland's Bakery, and the men who had occupied it, though seemingly few in number, were all in high spirits. Their leader, Éamon de Valera, pointed down the road that ran southwest to Dún Laoghaire. "If they come, they'll come that way," he told her. "And all my best marksmen are in these buildings," he added, indicating several with excellent lines of fire.

At St. Stephen's Green, a mile to the south, she discovered that another policeman had been shot dead, this one by Countess Markievicz, whom Connolly's man Mallin had appointed as his deputy. Beyond the congealing pool of blood, Caitlin could see men digging trenches out on the green. When she asked a Citizen Army officer why, he just shrugged, which only increased her doubts. Why would any army dig itself into a space surrounded by high buildings? She hoped there was a good explanation but found herself remembering her talk with Jed McColl and his disdain for the military mind. Why should the good guys be any less stupid?

Jacob's Factory gave her fresh grounds for hope and despair. It was full of eager young men, "walking on air" as one lad described it, all fighting together for what they believed in. And outside on the pavement were a crowd of barracking women, all shouting that the rebels should be fighting the Germans, the way their husbands and sons were. Both sides considered the other traitors, and after all she'd learned from the working-class women of Lawrence and Paterson, Caitlin found it distressing that Dublin's poorest were the rebels' bitterest foes.

By nightfall she was back at the GPO, having put off visiting the other strongholds until the following day. By this time a detachment of Cumann na mBan had joined the garrison, Maeve among them. Most of the women, her friend admitted to Caitlin, had been sent to either the kitchen or the first-aid room, but some, herself included, had been chosen to serve as messengers between the different battalion HQs. "I know it's not perfect," she said defensively, "but if we get our chance to fight, we'll take it, believe me. And it could be worse — down at Boland's Bakery, de Valera has refused to admit any women at all. He wants to spare us the horrors of warfare," she added contemptuously. "Well, we never thought it would be easy."

A series of shots outside drew them to the shuttered window.

"They're just trying to scare off the looters," Maeve decided after looking through the slit.

"Looters?" Caitlin said, surprised.

"I'm afraid so — it's been getting quite ugly out there. You should be off before it gets worse."

Caitlin hadn't given any thought to where she would sleep.

"The English might come in the night,"

Maeve said. "And you won't be much use to us trapped in here."

Which made sense. Caitlin gave her friend a good-bye hug and, at the suggestion of one of the rebel sentries, left by the Henry Street entrance. Out on Sackville there were shadows moving inside the looted shops but no sign of police or soldiers, and along the banks of the Liffey the bars were still serving drinks as if nothing had happened. Caitlin had half-pints of Guinness in two of them and listened to stray conversations, trying in vain to discern whose side the city was on. Feelings were mixed — it was as simple as that. Heroes or "idjits" or something in between.

Back at Maeve's she reread the proclamation and decided her own feelings were mixed as well. She loved the words, had no quarrel with the aims. But several times that day, she had found herself doubting the political and military sense with which those aims were being pursued. Perhaps tomorrow would prove the rebel leaders right and herself wrong. She hoped so. The men they led were so few.

After seeking out the British consul in Maastricht and securing the wherewithal to buy himself a ticket, McColl took a northbound afternoon train. It was less than two hundred kilometers to Rotterdam, but a lengthy stop at Eindhoven and a surprisingly funereal pace ensured a late arrival. He took a cab to the Maas Hotel, where he'd stayed on his only previous visit and which he knew was only a short walk away from the Service's local office. The bar overlooking the river sounded lively enough, but he decided in favor of an early night.

At breakfast the next morning, two of the adjoining tables were occupied by Germans, but the nationals who had seemed so intent on killing him forty-eight hours earlier were now more interested in sharing his marmalade. He smiled and passed it over.

Outside, the sun was shining, the word IERLAND plastered across the billboards that lined the newspaper kiosk. Dutch wasn't one of his languages, but Ireland seemed a pretty good bet. Had Cumming's fears proved founded?

The local office occupied an entire floor of a sizable building. This was divided only by thin, head-high partitions, which offered panoramic views of the Maas River to the south and the docks to the north but made it impossible to conduct private conversations in anything louder than a whisper.

Cumming's man Richard Tinsley was

short and broad-shouldered, with complexion and eyes that suggested an outdoors past. "Let's have coffee in one of the hotels," he suggested.

"I'm staying at the Maas," McColl told him.

"You and a dozen German agents," Tinsley noted dryly.

They went to the nearby Weimar. Tinsley ordered café au lait and pastries for them both, then sat back and listened, a worried look on his face. "Well, at least the group in Liège is still operational," he said once McColl had finished with a brief account of his last few days. The unstated implication, that other groups had not been so lucky, was left hanging in the air.

"I assume Cumming wants me back in London," McColl said.

"As soon as possible," Tinsley concurred. "And you can take some reports back with you. There's a ferry this afternoon, and the train for the Hook leaves at one, so I'll get them to your hotel by noon. They'll be heavy," he added with a wry smile. "A few months ago, I sent another batch of reports with a messenger. When the Germans boarded the ferry, he had the wit to throw the package overboard, but the damn thing didn't sink. So now we add some weight."

As they were getting up to go, McColl remembered the kiosk headlines and asked what Tinsley knew.

"Oh, some sort of fracas in Dublin," he said dismissively. "Some hotheads seized the General Post Office for some reason. Maybe they're stamp collectors. It'll all be over by now."

HUMAN SACRIFICE

It was barely light outside when Caitlin was awakened by gunfire. A single machine gun, she thought, and several rifles. Somewhere south of the Liffey.

It wasn't yet five o'clock, and she lay there for a while, unwilling to get up and face the day. It seemed all too likely that the Rising's finest moment had already been and gone, and the thought of witnessing a long and bloody fall from grace was painful to contemplate.

When the guns fell silent and a bird outside the window filled the gap with song, she found herself dabbing tears from her cheeks.

It was still mostly quiet when she finally left the house and walked down an empty Mary Street toward the GPO. Every now and then, a single shot was audible in the distance, but the area around the post office was almost deserted. Yesterday's looters were probably sleeping off the excitement, the authorities still holed up in their Castle, busy making plans. No trams were running on Sackville Street, but a few pedestrians were presumably headed for work. Much to Caitlin's surprise, *The Irish Times* had been published that morning; rather more predictably, it hardly mentioned the Rising.

With Connolly's accreditation, she had no trouble getting into the GPO. Yesterday the building had felt like a human anthill, with people rushing in every direction, but eighteen hours of organization had worked wonders. Every street-facing window was now barricaded and guarded, and the various weapon caches had been sorted and stored in several rooms. Fire extinguishers were everywhere, and out in the backyard several men were shoveling sand into mailbags. A makeshift hospital had been set up and the staff canteen turned into a mess hall for feeding the rebel garrison. At one table she saw Patrick Pearse and Seán McDermott deep in conversation, their breakfasts growing cold.

According to another Cumann na mBan woman, Maeve was out on messenger duty, so, more in hope than expectation, Caitlin dropped by Connolly's office. As usual the door was open, and, seeing her standing there, he gestured her in. "What's it like outside?"

"Quiet," she said. "But there was a lot of firing earlier. Across the river somewhere."

"The British captured City Hall during the night," he explained. "And there's been quite a battle at St. Stephen's Green. We've had to give up some of the park." He sounded less worried than she would have expected.

"Will you able to hold the Green?"

He didn't answer that. "What are people saying?" he wanted to know. "Do you think most people support us?"

"A lot do," she said. "But many don't. Many have sons and fathers in France."

"I know. And if I were them, I might feel the same. We shall certainly have to earn their good opinion."

"And how will you do that?"

Connolly smiled. "By the way we conduct ourselves in the coming days."

Like her, she realized, he harbored no illusions of victory.

"Where are you off to this morning?" he asked.

"After what you've just told me, St. Stephen's Green."

"Well, be careful," he said, getting up. As they shook hands, he had a thought. "Would you consider it compromising to carry a message to the CO down there? His name's Mallin — you probably know him."

"I know him by sight." She hesitated. Acting as Connolly's private messenger would dent her journalistic integrity in many people's eyes, but it wouldn't change what she reported. And it might help her get through any rebel barricades. "I'll take your message," she told him.

He hurriedly scribbled it down.

Outside, a decent crowd of onlookers was slowly coalescing, but there was still no sign of police or soldiers. She walked south toward the river, the sealed envelope safe in her bag. The fact that Connolly had trusted her with it seemed touching and faintly absurd. And wonderfully Irish.

The sounds of battle were louder on the other side of the Liffey, but there were plenty of people out on Grafton Street, strolling along and inspecting shop windows as if nothing else were amiss. As she neared St. Stephen's Green, two rebels with rifles shouted for her to go back; she had to show them Connolly's letter before they would let her pass. One rebel agreed to escort her, and after a tour of alleys they arrived at someone's back door. "This is the College of Surgeons," he told her. "You'll find

Micky Mallin upstairs."

She found him on the top floor, looking out through a slit in a barricaded window. He took and read Connolly's message, carefully folded it, and placed it in a pocket. "How are things at the GPO?"

She told him, then asked about his own situation.

"Have a look," he invited her.

The park had been mostly abandoned, and at a very obvious cost — there were several corpses out in the open, and heaven knew how many more among the shrubs and trees. "The English took the Shelbourne Hotel in the night," Mallin explained, "and put a machine gun up on the roof. We only found out the damn thing was there when it opened up."

He had no problem with her talking to his men — "You won't find any who regret being here" — but warned her against leaving by the front door — "Likely as not, one of their snipers will pick you off or at least have a damn good try."

She talked to three of the rebels, one alone and two together, and all seemed unrepentant. After leaving by the back door, she made her way to the nearby Jacob's Factory, where the "separation women" were still crowding the pavement outside and still hurling abuse at those within. There was no sign of the authorities.

She interviewed several rebels and spoke to their raucous critics outside before heading back toward the Liffey, in hope of visiting the rebel-held Mendicity Institute. But after cautiously trying several approaches, she was forced to concede defeat — all were covered by men on the ground or snipers on the roofs, and if she managed to find a way in, there seemed little chance she would ever get out.

The Four Courts was a relative oasis of peace, and she was able to share a late lunch with its Cumann na mBan contingent. Here, as everywhere else that day, she heard only the faintest echoes of her own doubts. How could they win? For some the answer was easy — help was on the way. The Germans had landed in the west and were even now marching on Dublin; the countryside had risen, and volunteers were boarding trains and buses, even walking to their aid. The wisest among them were much more skeptical but generally held their tongues — as one young man told her the latest "news," a friend behind him rolled his eyes.

As everyone knew, Casement had been arrested the previous weekend, not long after stepping ashore from his German U-boat. The weapons he'd brought with him were now at the bottom of Queenstown Harbour. Caitlin was surprised he'd gotten as far as he had, and the thought that another shipment was on its way — this one with German troops — seemed sadly implausible. As for the rest of the country . . . well, so far only a few Volunteers had made their way to the capital. Most Irishmen and -women seemed disinclined to play a part.

There was certainly no sign of Dublin rallying to the rebels' cause, as she found that evening touring the still-open pubs. A few old souls were wearing smiles that could light up the darkest tavern — for them the rebellion was a thing of beauty, no matter how well or badly things went. Others were really angry. Why not wait for the promised Home Rule? Why cause all this heartache for the sake of a stupid flag?

These were the two extremes, and much to Caitlin's dismay there seemed more support for those saying no than for those with the shining eyes. Most people, of course, just wanted the whole thing over, the trams back running and the bakeries baking. Until that joyful day arrived, they would grumble and keep their heads down, cursing the inconvenience caused. And a few, as she noticed on her way home to Maeve's, would make the best of a very bad job and help themselves to some restitution from the many unguarded shops.

The cross-Channel voyage was pleasantly uneventful, and those passengers of nervous disposition who took up station close to the lifeboats and trained their eyes on the fog-shrouded sea saw nothing to further alarm them — no German ships, no questing periscopes, no monsters of the deep. But the boat had been late in leaving the Hook and was even later arriving in Harwich, so by the time McColl reached Liverpool Street, it was almost ten in the evening. He took the Underground to Great Portland Street and was climbing the stairs to his flat before he remembered he hadn't a key. A vague memory of leaving one with the married couple downstairs slowly percolated up through his tired brain, and a ring on their bell eventually brought the sleepy-eyed husband to the door in dressing gown and pajamas. Yes, he did have a key, though he was damned if he knew where it was. Five grumpy minutes and several drawers later, McColl was turning it in his lock and wading through the mail on the mat.

There was nothing from Caitlin. Though

they'd agreed that her writing to him there was foolish, he still felt slightly disappointed. He dearly hoped there'd be letters waiting at the King William Street post office, which they'd chosen as their poste restante. If not, he would visit her lodgings in Clapham.

The flat felt stuffy, so he opened all the windows before running himself a bath. Soaking in the tub, he thought about his months in Belgium. The last few days had been somewhat fraught, and he couldn't say he'd enjoyed the first three months — the absurd manner of his arrival had precluded that — but working with the resistance had been a pleasure and an honor. In Belgium he'd been on the side of the angels — he had no doubt about that.

Next morning he walked south toward Whitehall, saving the poste restante for after his meeting with Cumming. On Charing Cross Road, he saw the word DUBLIN emblazoned on a news vendor's stand and stopped to buy a paper. Tinsley's fracas had grown into a full-scale rebellion.

Something like a cold compress seemed to settle on his stomach. Was Caitlin over there?

He hurried on down Whitehall, wondering what, if anything, he should say to Cumming. Taking the familiar lift up, he emerged in the top-floor warren that housed the Service HQ. After handing Tinsley's package to the duty secretary, he took a seat in Cumming's anteroom and skimmed through several boating magazines. Eventually a man in an infantry captain's uniform emerged from the inner sanctum and offered a polite smile in passing. A few seconds later, Cumming's raised voice called him in.

It was almost six months since McColl had seen the chief or his office, but neither seemed changed. "So parachuting didn't agree with you?" was the first question fired across the over-crowded desk.

"I might like to try it in daylight," was McColl's wry response.

Cumming grinned. "You don't seem to have done any permanent damage."

McColl couldn't help glancing at the chief's artificial leg, the legacy of driving into a French tree eighteen months earlier.

"Some days I almost forget it's not real," Cumming said equably, having noticed the look. "So how's Tinsley?"

"Very worried. I brought a bunch of reports back, but he didn't tell me very much. I got the impression that things are going pretty badly in Belgium."

"They are. The Germans have rolled up half our networks in a matter of weeks."

McColl shook his head. "That's a shame. The Belgians I met were an impressive bunch."

"Oh, they're a plucky lot, all right. We've let them down, I'm afraid, with some really basic errors. Putting too many eggs in one basket, that sort of thing. But we're going to reorganize the whole business. I'm sending Tinsley some help — you probably saw him leave. Impressive chap. I think he'll sort things out."

"That's good," McColl said automatically.

"I haven't made up my mind where to send you next," Cumming was saying, "but I expect you could do with a few days off. Visit your family, perhaps."

"Yes," McColl agreed. "I see there's trouble in Dublin," he said impulsively. "Is it serious?"

Cumming grunted. "Treason is always serious. But it won't take the army long to sort these rebels out."

"What have they done, exactly?"

"Oh, seized a few buildings in Dublin. The post office, the Four Courts, a bakery — about eight in all. Now they're sitting inside them waiting for the army to roust them out. It'll be over in a few days, and then there'll be a reckoning."

"A reckoning?"

"We'll need to make examples. This sort of treachery would be bad enough in peacetime, but when the country's at war . . ."

"How many of them are there?"

"Around fifteen hundred, we think. Maybe fewer." Cumming must have read something in McColl's expression. "Your old girlfriend Miss Hanley lied to you last autumn," he added. "And maybe worse than that. We still don't know how those republicans tracked you to the Royal Hotel."

"Perhaps they fooled her, too," McColl said, ignoring the last suggestion. "Maybe they had no plans back then."

"She took the boat across on Saturday night," Cumming said. "Which might have been a coincidence if she hadn't received a highly suspicious message that morning."

"What sort of message?"

"One that read like a prearranged signal."

"Journalists get tip-offs."

Cumming gave him a stern look. "You're not still carrying a torch for this girl, are you?"

"No, of course not," McColl said, trying to sound offended.

"Good. Not that I'd dream of sending you back to Dublin. The bastards almost killed you on the last two visits, and being Irish they probably believe in third time lucky." Cumming smiled at the thought. "Take a break and report back here on Monday week. By then I'll have found you something to do."

McColl nodded and took his leave, hoping the Service chief hadn't noticed his emotional turmoil. After buying two papers from the newsstand outside Charing Cross Underground, he dodged across the busy embankment and read through the news from Dublin on the first empty bench. Cumming had sounded disgusted by the rebels' treachery, and McColl could understand why. Most British people — and especially those with men in the services — would consider this a stab in the back. But McColl had spent enough time in Dublin — and enough with Caitlin — to know that things were not that simple.

The tone of the newspaper reports veered between paranoia and complacency, as if the reporters were uncertain of their role — did patriotism require that they exaggerate or play down this threat to the empire? There was no shortage of paragraphs, but details were surprisingly thin on the ground. How much danger was she in?

However much she wanted to be, was the

obvious answer. He couldn't believe she was actively involved in the rebellion — whatever her sympathies, she saw herself as a journalist first and foremost.

A journalist who would seek to put herself wherever the action was.

And that was her choice. It was not for to him to decide what risks she took with her life.

Provided, of course, that she knew what they were. Cumming's "need to make examples" sounded ominous. And she probably had no idea that Kell and his people were still watching her and reading her messages. If he didn't tell her, no one else would.

Out on the Thames, a tug was pulling a chain of barges downstream. Had she lied to him about the prospect of a rising? Probably. He didn't blame her if she had. If anything, he found the thought of her deceiving him almost gratifying, as if that might make his earlier deceiving of her a tad less inexcusable.

But he would never believe what Cumming had implied, that she had led his republican enemies to the Royal Hotel. No one could act that well. And he knew she loved him. Despite Colm, despite Ireland, despite his job as a hired gun for the British Empire.

He had to go, but how was he going to get there?

In a travel agency on the Strand, a serious young woman informed him that the ferries to Dublin and Rosslare had been suspended until further notice, but that as far as she knew, those from Scotland to Ulster were still running. When he expressed interest in the latter, she consulted her Bradshaw and found him an afternoon train to Stranraer. If he spent the night there, he could catch the early-morning boat.

Emerging onto the busy pavement, he looked at his watch. The train left in two hours. He had time to visit his bank and the post office and pack himself a change of clothes.

As he hurried up Charing Cross Road, McColl found himself wondering what Cumming would do if he ever found out. Dismissal might be the best he could hope for.

Caitlin was approaching the Henry Street entrance of the GPO when she heard the sound of explosions a few streets away to the west. Once inside, she learned that shells had been fired at Liberty Hall. As a watcher on the GPO roof reported, the culprit was a Royal Navy gunboat that had advanced up the Liffey under cover of darkness and was now moored just beyond the railway bridge. The shells had missed, he added with some satisfaction.

But the hall's reprieve proved short-lived. Artillery south of the river took up the challenge with greater precision, and by mid-morning its demolition was said to be complete. Caitlin had no way of verifying the sad news — the whole of Sackville Street was now within range of English machine guns, and only the foolish or desperate were still attempting to cross it.

After a long and fruitless wait to interview the fully engaged Connolly, she left by the back door and cautiously walked south. On Liffey Street she ran into a colleague of Maeve's who was carrying a message from de Valera. A battle was raging around the Mount Street Bridge, the woman told Caitlin excitedly, and the British were falling like ninepins.

Caitlin found this hard to believe, but it did seem worth investigating. Intent on avoiding British troops, she took a long loop round St. Stephen's Green and found herself walking through a city at peace, its denizens seemingly deaf to the steadily rising barrage only a few streets away.

How close could she get? When the canal

she was following took a slight right turn, moving figures appeared in the distance, under a cloud of smoke. Simply walking into a battle didn't seem that sensible, and she was wondering what to do next when a neatly dressed young boy popped up right in front of her. Did the lady want to see the fighting?

"Yes," was the simple answer.

"It'll cost you sixpence," the boy told Caitlin, extending an upraised palm.

She crossed it with the appropriate silver.

"This way," he told her, leading her back a few yards, into a narrow alley, through an open side door, and up a gloomy staircase. Even inside the building, which looked like an abandoned works of some kind, the gunfire was almost deafening. When they stepped out onto the roof, it sounded loud enough to wake the dead.

And there were certainly dead to awaken. The first bridge across the canal, some hundred yards away, was littered with bodies. So was that part of the road that approached the bridge from the south. Even as she looked, another soldier flopped to the ground. His body convulsed for several seconds, then suddenly went still.

"Got him!" the boy by her side said quietly.

It was terrible, but she couldn't take her eyes away. Why did the soldiers keep coming? Why not find a way round? There was only one explanation — the man in command had decided otherwise and was driving them into the withering fire with that same indifference to life that his peers were showing in France. It was human sacrifice in all but name — throw enough men onto a fire and their bodies would put it out.

They might be the enemy, but her heart went out to them. Treating men like this was a crime.

And what was worse — on this occasion it seemed certain to work. There actually were enough bodies to extinguish this particular fire, and as the hours went by, the high tide of corpses crept ever closer to de Valera's outposts. Once brought within range, English grenades and machine guns were more than a match for rebel rifles.

Every now and then, as if by unspoken agreement, a lull would occur in the firing and people would run out and tend to the fallen, covering some and carrying others to safety on blood-spattered stretchers. And a few would always be left, their moans and wails soon swallowed by the din of battle resumed.

On and on it went. The boy had long since

disappeared, but Caitlin was not alone — on the roofs all around and at many a window, people were following the battle that fate had provided for their entertainment.

It wouldn't be long now. The rebel-held buildings were shrouded in dust after taking so many hits, and the first flickers of flame could be seen through the shattered windows. As the guns inside fell silent, the English soldiers broke into a horrible victory dirge, and Caitlin caught a whiff of something she knew could only be burning flesh.

What now? The show was over, the spectators leaving their viewing stations. She wanted to run, find somewhere to weep. For the people who cared and those who didn't, for Ireland and England and all the horrors yet to come.

She left the building and began retracing her earlier route through those districts untouched by it all, where people still smiled at one another and at her. She wanted to hit each one. Some men were dying for their independence, others to keep them in the Union, and all not much more than a stone's throw away. But what did they care? They just wanted business as usual.

Walking north, she heard gunfire from several directions. As she scurried over the Ha'penny Bridge, she almost expected a shot in her direction, but this small area was still apparently part of the rapidly shrinking no-man's-land, and much to her relief she reached the Henry Street entrance of the GPO without being fired on. Inside, everyone was talking about the Mount Street battle and the wonderful showing their fellow rebels had put up.

Connolly was resting and couldn't be disturbed, but Caitlin found Maeve and another Cumann na mBan woman in the canteen, both hollow eyed from lack of sleep. According to the latter, all the men in Sackville Street outposts had been withdrawn that afternoon, after the guns on Trinity's simply blew their walls away.

There was something in their eyes worse than tiredness, Caitlin realized. They knew that those guns that had battered Liberty Hall and the outposts would soon be trained in their direction. Tomorrow, perhaps, the next day at the latest. And as if to confirm that fact, an explosion outside seemed to shake the foundations beneath her, and someone yelled that the bastards were shelling the Imperial Hotel, directly across the road.

■ ■ ■ ■

It was getting dark when McColl's train finally reached Stranraer. With the other routes closed down, he half expected the station hotel to be full, but in fact it was almost empty — for the moment at least, the Emerald Isle in springtime had lost its usual appeal. After enjoying the view of Loch Ryan from his window, he lay down on the bed and reread the letters from Caitlin.

There had been four of them at the poste restante, and he'd initially read through them as his train made its way out of London. The first concerned her meeting with his mother, which seemed to have gone well; the second and third described two nights out, one with a woman's patrol, the other in Liverpool, where she'd witnessed a zeppelin raid. The fourth was mostly about Jack Slaney, the American journalist she'd met in Berlin, who had unexpectedly turned up in London. McColl knew that the man had a sweetheart but felt a slight pang of jealousy nevertheless. That letter ended with her saying that she was far too busy to miss him but did so anyway, especially in bed, and that she loved him with all her heart.

And that wherever he was, fighting for his "ridiculous King," she prayed he would come back safe and sound.

"I did," he told the room. And now it was her in danger.

She had not mentioned Ireland in any of the letters, he realized. Was that because it hadn't concerned her lately or because she knew it lay between them?

Next morning the ship left slightly early and docked in Larne less than two hours later. There was no apparent check on arrivals, and the little train was waiting to carry him on to Belfast, where he purchased a morning paper. There had been a major battle in Dublin the previous afternoon, in which as many as two hundred British soldiers had been killed.

McColl found that hard to believe until he remembered whom he was dealing with. Why would British generals prove more adept in Ireland than they had on the Western Front? Or anywhere else, come to that.

But their incompetence wouldn't save the rebels, not in the long run. It would just make their men angrier. And more inclined to lash out.

He went to check on the trains to Dublin and found they were running as normal. He was about to buy a ticket when the thought crossed his mind that the stations would be under army control, if only to greet any rebel arrivals. He would have to get off at the penultimate stop. Or, he suddenly realized, hire an automobile here in Belfast and drive himself down. If he left the car in the suburbs, it would offer them both a means of escape.

Outside on the forecourt, McColl asked a cabbie if he knew where one might be hired.

The man did. His brother, who owned the cab company, also rented out automobiles by the day.

"Take me to him," McColl said.

Half an hour later and several pounds lighter, he was on his way out of the city, following signs for Newry. It was a pleasant enough day, dry for Ireland, with occasional glimpses of sun. The four-cylinder Alldays was not a machine he would have chosen, but it seemed in good enough condition, and there was virtually no other traffic to impede his southerly progress. Purring along at a steady twenty-three miles an hour, he hoped to reach Dublin early that afternoon.

One Man's Flag Is Another Man's Shroud

Awakened several times by marching feet and not-so-distant gunfire, Caitlin emerged in the morning to find Mary Street awash with English troops, effectively penning her in. They were part of a wider cordon, she reckoned, one that would be drawn ever tighter around the GPO until a final assault could be mounted.

The previous night she had lain awake wondering where she should be when the moment arrived, inside with the rebels or watching from the sidelines. And now the British had denied her the choice, which was probably all for the better. No matter how tempted she was — and what a scoop she might have! — common sense suggested caution. She could file no reports from beyond the grave.

But despite the growing volume of gunfire, she had no intention of spending the day indoors, and when the officer in charge of the soldiers outside refused to allow her out, she barely kept her temper in check. After finding that the passage at the rear only led back to the street in front, she made another pot of tea with her rapidly shrinking supply of water and settled down to wait. Surely the soldiers wouldn't stay there all day.

They didn't, but it was early afternoon before the western end of the street was clear. She hurried in that direction, conscious of the heavy bombardment taking place behind her. The sky above was clear and blue, but a huge cloud of smoke hung over the city center.

Now that she was out, she had to decide where to go. The Four Courts, which she hadn't yet visited, or the garrisons south of the river, which as far as she knew were still in rebel hands. At the next crossroads, troops were visible to the west, so she turned south toward the Liffey. She heard voices in some of the houses she passed, but there was no one on the street, and the sound of gunfire, though some way off, seemed to be coming from all directions. Caitlin had experienced flashes of fear several times that week, but this was the first time she had felt truly frightened. Each step she took felt like it might be her last.

There were soldiers farther up the Liffey,

but the Ha'penny Bridge seemed invitingly empty. Almost too much so — as she hurried across, holding her skirt up around her knees, she imagined a sniper's finger tightening on the trigger. But no shot rang out, and soon she was darting across Dame Street, the Castle and City Hall to her right, both flying the Union flag. There were a few pedestrians on South Great George's Street, and a small group was conducting a burial in the garden of one big house. A little farther on, she passed a corpse draped in a tarpaulin, two booted feet sticking out from under one end.

There were troops in the area of Jacob's Factory, but no continuous cordon — either the sheer size of the building precluded one or the British were content to just keep an eye on the place while the war was decided on Sackville Street. The intermittent firing, from both inside and out, was mostly on the Bishop Street side. As Caitlin worked her way round to the entrance she'd used two days before, fifteen rebels on bicycles came pouring out of a delivery gate, rather like knights on horseback sallying forth from a castle. They furiously pedaled their way across Aungier Street, drawing some ineffective fire, and disappeared down the road that led toward St. Stephen's Green.

Thinking that all eyes would be on the cyclists, she made for the closing gates and was only a few feet from them when a bullet gouged into the adjoining brick wall. After half stumbling her way past a surprised sentry, she stood there in the yard, shaking her head at her own foolishness.

"Are you all right, miss?" the sentry asked.

"I'm fine," she told him. "Just not used to being shot at."

"Well, this is a fine place to get accustomed," the man told her. "But I assume you've some better reason for paying us a visit."

She showed him Connolly's letter and asked where the cyclists had been going.

"To visit the Third Battalion," he told her. "After yesterday's fighting they're running a bit short of ammo."

It was almost three when McColl reached the outskirts of Dublin; Irish miles, he had long since decided, were longer than anyone else's. Finding his way had certainly proved no problem over the last twenty of them — the smoke smudging the sky to the south was a large and worrying signpost. How had things gotten this much out of hand?

After passing under a suburban railway bridge, he reckoned he wasn't much more than a mile from the city center. A garage on the right seemed a good place to leave the Alldays, and the proprietor proved amenable to storing it out of sight, albeit at a very steep price. McColl didn't argue, just paid for two days and a full tank of petrol and hoped the car would still be there when he returned. The man was polite, outwardly almost friendly, but after six months in India, McColl had grown very adept at recognizing latent hostility. Another occupied country, he thought, starting out on what the garage owner claimed was a fifteen-minute walk.

He could hear the gunfire now, and the cloud of smoke stretched right across the sky, fed by numerous columns. How was he going to find her? Where should he look? Where *could* he look? In the past she'd stayed at the Imperial Hotel, but that was right on Sackville Street, at the center of the storm. If she *had* been staying there, surely she couldn't still be?

He would have to try all the hotels, or all the ones he could actually reach. With the city divided, some would be in rebel-held territory, some in areas held by the army, so visiting them all would involve some trips between the lines. Which was hardly an inviting prospect, but he didn't seem to have much choice.

After walking about half a mile down a strangely normal Dorset Street — a deaf man looking north would have noticed nothing out of the ordinary — he caught sight of the Rotunda Hospital and turned left toward it down Frederick Street. He was fast approaching the battle zone now, with no idea of what to do next. He could hardly walk down Sackville Street.

There were soldiers ahead, and once he'd been spotted, two came rushing over, shouting that he should turn back.

"I'm with Army Intelligence," McColl told them, carefully removing the Service identification card from his inside pocket and silently blessing the last-minute inspiration that had caused him to collect it from his flat.

Both men studied it with interest. "You'd better see our CO," one decided.

The command post was in the Rotunda, Major Leamington up on the roof. As the major examined the card, McColl took in the shocking view. Beneath him Sackville Street stretched away toward the river, and as he looked, another shell exploded among the burning buildings. Several machine guns were firing, presumably at the GPO, whose battered roof was just visible above the houses on the western side.

"What's your business here?" the major was asking. He seemed young for his rank, but at the rate officers were dying in France, that wasn't really surprising.

"I'm afraid I can't give you any details," McColl said. "But I'm looking for someone. Someone who'll probably be staying in one of the better hotels."

The major looked amused. "A tourist?"

"A possible German agent," McColl half whispered, purely for effect.

That wiped the smile away. "I see. Well, I doubt there are any still open in this part of the city, but south of the river . . ."

"How do I get there?"

The major indicated the street running off to the left. "Our cordon extends up there, then down behind those houses to the Custom House by the river. We hold the railway bridge beyond it, and if you show your card to whoever's in charge, I'm sure they'll take you across."

McColl thanked him, walked downstairs through the strangely silent hospital, and started working his way round the cordoned-off area, trying to keep at least a block between himself and the British soldiers. One of the young ones might get nervous.

He eventually found himself outside Amiens Street station and was able to get his bearings. A short walk around the back of the Custom House brought him to the iron railway bridge and another, shorter interrogation. The ascent to the tracks was by ladder, the view from the bridge one of fire and ruin. Staring down at the empty shell of Liberty Hall, he remembered the NEITHER KING NOR KAISER banner. A red rag to a bull, and the bull had finally charged.

At Tara Street station, he came down off the viaduct, showed his card, and was briefed by another young major. South of the Liffey, he told McColl, the rebels still held a bakery, several buildings around St. Stephen's Green, a biscuit factory, and parts of the South Dublin workhouse complex. All were more or less surrounded, but snipers on the roofs made it advisable to give these buildings as wide a berth as possible. Other than that, the streets were as safe as they could be, given the situation.

After thanking him McColl walked on down to Great Brunswick Street, where he visited several hotels. She was not staying at any of them, and neither, it seemed, was anyone else.

As he skirted the eastern edge of College

Green, he was struck by the sudden thought that she might have chosen the Royal, where they'd spent their wonderful week. Approaching it from the west, he found himself passing the open rear gate and stopped to look inside. The drop from the fire escape looked longer than he remembered. It was a miracle the man hadn't died.

The front entrance was shut up tight, and the man who finally answered his ring told him the hotel was closed, gave him a very strange look, and more or less slammed the door in his face. Memories of his last visit, McColl guessed. As he walked off down the street, he realized he'd never paid the bill.

Where else could he try? There were several hotels on Nassau Street, the Hibernian on Dawson, a couple more on the narrow road that ended just behind the Castle.

The Castle, he thought. Would Dunwood's lot know where she was?

Once inside the candlelit factory — there'd been no power since the day of its capture — Caitlin made for the makeshift canteen, where Cumann na mBan was providing the cooks. There were several groups of young men around the tables, sipping black tea and nibbling biscuits from the factory stores. A couple in uniform — his ICA, hers

Cumann na mBan — were sitting in one corner, and Caitlin suddenly realized that the man was Michael Killen. He recognized her at the same instant, looked surprised for a moment, then offered a slight nod in acknowledgment as the woman beside him carried on talking.

In the kitchen Caitlin found a Cumann na mBan woman she knew, a pretty young blonde friend of Maeve's named Maire. There were two saucepans of potatoes cooking on the stove — "one spud per man," the woman told her — and no other food in sight. Maire hadn't seen Maeve for a couple of days and had little idea what was happening elsewhere. "Thomas MacDonagh's in charge here, and he keeps dispatches to himself," she added, with only a slight trace of bitterness.

The canteen was filling up, and once the potatoes were cooked, Caitlin helped Maire pass them out, one for each hungry man, solemnly placed on the table before him. There were surprisingly few complaints, Caitlin thought; considering the rebels' situation, she had expected more anger by now.

Admittedly, some were still living in dreams. If the talk she overheard was any guide, MacDonagh's clampdown on news from outside had merely encouraged the spread of wild rumors. One voice claimed that the Germans had landed at Wexford, another that the city of Cork was on fire. It was all so stupid and painfully sad.

Out in the street, a sudden spate of gunfire heralded the return of the cyclists. They had turned back after clashing with English troops in Merrion Square and still had the boxes of ammo. MacDonagh was among them, and so was Finian Mulryan, who came over to say hello. "Mr. Connolly told me you were back in Dublin," he said. "And here to tell the world our story."

"That's right."

"A story of sacrifice."

"Yes." She had no desire to discuss anything with Mulryan. Why did she like him so little when she admired his boss so much?

"Well, I hope I live to read it," Mulryan said in parting.

As the canteen slowly emptied, the noise of the guns outside grew louder. Soon it would be dark, and things might quiet down enough for her to leave. Not that the prospect of heading back over the river held much appeal. A thought occurred to her. "The factory towers," she asked Maire, "can you climb up inside them?"

The answer was yes, but only safely in darkness — on the very first day, two lookouts had been shot by army snipers.

An hour or so later, Caitlin was climbing the staircase inside a tower, behind the serious young man whom Maire had found to escort her. Billy was about eighteen and firmly of the opinion that once the news of the Rising spread, the whole country would explode and the English would have to withdraw. She listened but didn't reply. Why, she wondered, did a biscuit factory have towers?

The view from the upper chamber was breathtaking, almost literally so, given the amount of smoke in the air. And though darkness had fallen, the city was lit by flames. To east and west, myriad fires were raging; to the north what seemed like one huge conflagration was consuming the blocks between Sackville Street and the ruins of Liberty Hall. Dublin was burning.

She was appalled, Billy entranced. "We have done this," he said softly. "We have summoned the devil."

Dunwood was in his office at the Castle. He looked tired but must have had a busy week. "She fooled you," was the first thing he said on seeing McColl, albeit with a generous lack of rancor.

"Didn't she just," McColl conceded. "And

569

she's why I'm here."

"To get an explanation?"

"To arrest her," McColl said. It had seemed the most feasible explanation.

Dunwood grunted. "You can safely leave that to us. Assuming she doesn't get herself killed in the next few days."

McColl took care to keep his voice steady. "What's she done here?"

Dunwood rummaged around in a drawer and brought out a sheaf of photographs. He sifted through them, then passed one across. And there was Caitlin, entering a building. She looked happy, McColl thought. Had she really joined the rebels?

He looked up inquiringly.

"She's entering the College of Surgeons, where the Citizen Army had their headquarters after occupying St. Stephen's Green. And one of our undercover people saw her hand their commander a message from the big cheeses in the GPO."

McColl's heart sank. He could hear himself telling the Indian in Balasore that a man who carried messages for a terrorist was as guilty as they were.

"And the politicians are not feeling very forgiving," Dunwood went on. "I don't suppose she'll be shot like her brother, but she's looking at a long time in prison. Like I said, you can leave her to us."

McColl improvised. "It's not as simple as that," he told the Irishman. "We're interested in the German angle, and we know that she met with Casement in Berlin. We badly need to question her, and we can't do that if she's hit by a stray shell or bullet over the next few days. Do you know where she's staying?"

"Yes, with Maeve McCarron."

"In Mary Street," McColl remembered. "The house with the green door, but I can't remember the number."

Dunwood worked his way through a box of filing cards on the shelf behind his desk and eventually plucked one out. "Forty-three," he said, walking across to the city map that covered most of wall. "About here," he said, pushing out a nicotine-stained finger. "And there's the GPO," he added with another forceful prod. "The house is well inside the army cordon."

"Can you get me through it?"

"I suppose so. But you'd be on your own after that."

"Understood."

Dunwood was still not convinced. "You already look dead on your feet."

"I haven't eaten for a while," McColl admitted. Not since the boat, he thought, and only a sandwich then.

"Well, at least we can feed you," Dunwood said.

The Castle canteen was in the basement, and for the first time in hours McColl couldn't hear gunfire. He devoured a plate of beef stew, marveling at how good it tasted, while Dunwood sipped at a large mug of tea. The other patrons were all in uniform, most of them army, a few police.

"Are you sure I can't dissuade you?" Dunwood asked when McColl had finished eating. "It'll all be over in a couple of days, and unless she's inside one of the strongholds, the chances of her being hit by a stray bullet are pretty remote."

"What if she *is* in one of the strongholds?"

"That would be dangerous. The rebels made the mistake of thinking the army would storm their castles and give them a chance to go down fighting, but after Mount Street someone had a better idea. Why try and take a building when you can simply knock it down?"

The cynicism was obvious, but there was also a hint of bitterness in Dunwood's tone. And if an Irishman who worked for British intelligence felt that way, then how would most of his compatriots feel? "We need her alive," McColl said simply.

Outside, the gunfire seemed more intense, the evening air suffused with an acrid odor. The roofs of the buildings lining the river were silhouetted against an orange glow, with occasional tongues of yellow flame rearing toward the smoke-shrouded heavens.

The captain commanding the unit just south of the Ha'penny Bridge reluctantly agreed to let McColl through his cordon and promised he would caution his men against simply opening fire on a couple coming toward them. He also advised McColl to "run like hell" across the bridge.

This was probably unnecessary — a sniper would have been lucky to hit a stationary target in the prevailing gloom — but after wishing Dunwood farewell, McColl did as the captain suggested, catching glimpses of fire in either direction as his feet pounded over the bridge. On the far side of the river, Liffey Street stretched dark and empty into the distance. He started up it, walking slowly, scanning rooftops and windows and the road ahead for any sign of movement, wondering what he would say to Caitlin.

After what Dunwood had told him, he knew he had to get her out of Ireland. And out of British jurisdiction. How was he going to manage that? And if he could, what would that mean for their future?

At the third crossroads, Mary Lane ran left, Mary Street to the right. The latter's junction with Sackville Street was wreathed in flames, like someone's idea of an entrance to hell. Maeve McCarron's house was only fifty yards away, just beyond a silent church.

There was a faint, flickering light around the edge of the drawn curtains in the downstairs window — a candle, McColl assumed. Perhaps Caitlin was writing her report of the day.

He knocked softly on the door, which opened almost immediately. The figure in silhouette was male.

"Is Caitlin here?" McColl asked.

"Sure she is," the man said after only the slightest hesitation. "Come in," he added, stepping aside.

As the door closed behind him, McColl felt the barrel of a gun ram sharply into his back.

"Keep walking," the man said, "through that door."

There were three more men in the back parlor, all of them younger than McColl. At first they seemed surprised to see him, and then they looked really pleased, like children with an unexpected gift.

One face was vaguely familiar, and it took

574

McColl only a few seconds to realize why — the man bore a close resemblance to the two Breslin brothers he'd met, one the would-be bomber who'd been executed the previous year, the other the boy who'd fallen from the Royal's fire escape.

And there was more. On the parlor mantelpiece, another one of Colm's comrades stared out of a framed photograph. The last time McColl had seen that face, it was on a Guildford hospital slab.

Searched and relieved of his Webley, he was pushed toward the corner farthest from the door and ordered into a seat between table and wall. He knew only too well what he'd walked himself into — he only hoped that he hadn't walked Caitlin into it, too.

The oldest of the four gave him a good long stare, then told the youngest to hold McColl at rifle point while he and the others talked in the room beyond. Though he strained to hear what they were saying, McColl could only make out the occasional word.

A minute or so later, the oldest man came back alone. He was about thirty, McColl guessed, thin and bespectacled. His once-smart suit jacket was stained and torn at the cuff, and there was a weariness in the way he moved that suggested several sleepless nights. He took a seat on the opposite wall and lit a half-smoked cigarette that he'd pulled from his breast pocket. Staring at McColl through the smoke, he murmured, " 'Come into my parlor,' said the spider to the fly."

"And who are you?" McColl asked.

"My name is Finian Mulryan, but that needn't concern you. What does is that I speak for the Provisional Government of the Irish Republic, whose jurisdiction you are now within."

McColl almost laughed. "Your republic won't last the week," he said.

Mulryan smiled. "Then we'd best be getting on with things."

"What do you have in mind?"

"Justice, Mr. McColl, that's what we have in mind. You're a spy, and spies are shot. You spied on us in America, you spied on us in Dublin. And here you are again. As they say in Boston, three strikes and you're out."

"And that's your idea of justice?" McColl asked coldly. He could feel a rising sense of panic but was determined not to show it.

"No, Mr. McColl, it's my idea of an indictment. You think that here, now, with your masters laying waste to our city, we have time for a trial? Or that if we did, you'd deserve one? A thousand years of servitude, a million left to die in the Famine. The verdict is already in."

"I haven't been here for a thousand years," McColl said quietly. "And I wasn't here for the Famine."

"Maybe not. But you signed up to serve the same government. You gave it your seal of approval."

"I serve my country."

Mulryan smiled at that. "Have you not heard the old saying? 'One's man flag is another man's shroud.' " He stretched out his arms and yawned. "But you have at least a few hours to live. You're not a Catholic, I presume."

"No."

"Then you won't be needing a priest." He closed his eyes for a moment, resting the hand that held the Webley on his thigh, then slowly got to his feet. "Keep your wits about you, Tom," he warned the young man holding the rifle. Unnecessarily, McColl thought. Neither eyes nor rifle had shown the faintest sign of wavering through his and Mulryan's exchange of pleasantries.

Why the delay? McColl wondered after Mulryan had wandered out. The bombardment of nearby Sackville Street seemed to be growing less intense — maybe the gunners' arms were tired, or maybe shells were running short. A few were still being fired, and the yellow light writhing on the rooftops outside suggested they were mostly incendiaries.

Was this how he was going to spend his last hours on earth — guessing what shells were being fired? What else could he do? The young man's attention showed no sign of faltering, and McColl doubted he'd even be out of his seat before the bullet took him. After his successful escape from the Royal, it seemed unlikely they'd prove so careless again.

There was certainly no chance of an official rescue. He'd not arranged to see Dunwood again, and Cumming didn't even know he'd crossed the Irish Sea. He'd put himself out on a very long limb, which someone would soon be coming to saw off. Loving Caitlin, he'd had no choice.

The minutes ticked slowly by. He told himself there was so much to think of, so much joy to remember, but every time he tried, his mind slid into blankness. Even Caitlin's face, which was always so easy to summon and hold, kept slipping out of his mental grip.

A heavy rap on the front door caused Mulryan to rise and leave the room. Waiting to find out who had arrived, McColl felt a sudden shaft of fear. Was this his executioner? Was this the moment?

A strange squeaking sound heralded the approach of a wheelchair, and there he was, staring at McColl, eyes brimming with hatred. He shook his head, as if in dismissal. "So what are we waiting for?" he asked.

"The American girl," Mulryan told him. He looked at his watch. "We'll give her till one."

Caitlin was awakened by a hand roughly shaking her shoulder, and it took her a few moments to remember where she was, in a makeshift dorm at Jacob's Factory. Had the British assault begun? "What is it?" she asked the man standing over her.

"We've captured the English spy McColl," the young man said.

The shock was intense, coursing through her body like so many rivers of ice. She swung her legs off the mattress and struggled to her feet, thankful the darkness was blurring her face.

"Mulryan says if you want to see justice done, to come with me."

"Where?" she asked, reaching for her shoes. "Where is he?"

"Mary Street. Maeve McCarron's house."

"What?"

"He was coming to arrest you. Our man at the Castle gave us the tip, and we were waiting for him."

"Is Maeve there?"

"No. Look, Mulryan told me to warn you that it may be a dangerous outing, and you don't have to come. The British army are everywhere now."

"You got here," she said, pulling on her coat.

"I did."

"Then let's go."

Most of the factory's defenders seemed asleep at their posts, and it seemed that the British were, too. The area around the factory felt generally quiet, as if everyone were taking a well-earned rest before resuming the battle next day.

"What's your name?" she asked her escort as they hurried down Bishop Street.

"Liam Coleman," he told her.

He led the way west, passing St. Patrick's Cathedral and not turning north until they reached Francis Street. There were troops on Bridge Street, but none on St. Augustine, and Usher's Quay was empty. He held them there for several minutes, watching the Whitworth Bridge, and finally decided it was safe to cross. Lights were burning in the Four Courts, which Liam confirmed were still in rebel hands. "We're all right now," he told her. "All these streets are ours."

And for the moment they were. They walked past the silent fish-and-vegetable market and turned right down Mary Lane. Maeve's house was only a minute away, and Caitlin had no idea what to do. Mulryan and his friends were going to kill McColl, and she didn't see how she could stop them.

Liam rapped on the familiar door, and the Breslin brother that she'd seen in the Royal's backyard came to let them in. It was worse than she'd thought — even if she pleaded for mercy, it didn't seem likely that he would agree, not with one brother dead and another in a wheelchair. And the latter was there in the parlor, mouth self-righteously pursed, eyes crying out for revenge.

"Well, here he is," Mulryan said, gesturing toward the love of her life. The condemned man, she thought, but he looked more anxious than frightened. Was it possible that he doubted her?

McColl met her gaze. He saw hardness in her eyes, but was that fear behind them? He couldn't tell, which was good. If *he* couldn't, then neither could they, and perhaps she would find a way out.

"I was told I would see justice done," Caitlin said. "I assumed that meant a trial."

"He's already been sentenced," Mulryan told her. "Is there anything you'd like to say before we carry it out?"

She looked at the faces around her. Could she plead with them? Plead what? That Colm wouldn't have wanted it this way? He would. Twelve months ago a part of her would have, too. What was the point of telling these men that the world was a lot more complicated than they thought it was? That killing was always the easy answer? She'd known men like this her whole life. They'd wink at each other and put it all down to her being a woman.

Every one of them was looking at her, and suddenly she knew what she had to do. She shook her head. "No, I've nothing to say." She was right, McColl thought as they ushered him into the yard. These men had their hearts set on his death, and no plea from her would change that. Some sign that she loved him was all that he asked.

The only light spilled out from the parlor, and it reminded him of the one in Glasgow. He almost expected to see his father.

It was small for a firing squad, but not for a single bullet.

"Against the wall," Mulryan said. He was still holding McColl's Webley.

McColl backed himself up against the brick. Looking at Caitlin, he saw only coldness in her eyes. Behind her, Tom and Liam were trying and failing to get the wheelchair through the door. "I can see well enough from here," the crippled Breslin said eventually.

His brother, Liam, and Tom were lined up to one side, Liam with his rifle in front of him, stock resting in the dirt. The other rifles had been left inside.

"I want to pull the trigger," Caitlin told Mulryan.

He turned and gave her a searching look.

"He killed my brother."

Mulryan handed her the gun and took a step back, as if offering her the stage.

She moved a couple of steps toward McColl, saw the hope and the doubt in his eyes, and spun on her heel to point the Webley straight at Mulryan. "I can't let you do this," she said.

The rebels looked stunned.

"Liam, let the rifle drop," she added, shifting her aim toward him. Much to her relief, he did as he was told.

"I'll get it," McColl said. He crouched down and reached for the end of the barrel, careful not to block her line of fire.

Caitlin was holding the gun so tightly that her hand was beginning to shake. How should they leave? The wheelchair was blocking the doorway into the house, and its occupant looked ready to grab any enemy who came within reach, gun or no gun. And she knew she couldn't just shoot him.

It had to be the back way out. With any luck the men wouldn't know the passage led round to the street in front.

"We can go that way," she told McColl, nodding toward the gate.

"After you," he offered, covering his captors with Liam's rifle.

"You've betrayed your country for a kiss and a cuddle," was Mulryan's parting shot.

She shook her head. "I'm an American," she said, as much to herself as him, and walked out into the passage.

McColl was right behind her, closing the gate and throwing the rifle over the wall beyond. He felt much more at home with the Webley when it came to deterring the likely pursuit.

"This leads back onto Mary Street," Caitlin was saying as she hurried along, "so we may not be free of them yet."

But when she stuck her head out, there

was no one in sight. She handed McColl the gun and leaned her head forward to rest it on his shoulder. "I don't know how I did that," she said.

"I'm very pleased you did."

A shout from behind them turned both their heads. Outside Maeve's house a figure was silhouetted against the distant flames. He was raising a rifle.

McColl let off a shot, causing him to duck back inside. "Run," he told Caitlin. "Take the first turn right."

"What about —"

"I'll be right after you."

She ran, hoping to hear him behind her, but all she heard was the crack of the Webley. She was almost at the crossroads when he fired for the third time; reaching it, she turned to see McColl sprinting toward her, the Sackville Street inferno rising above and behind him like some monster dragon erupting out of the earth. He was twenty yards short when the rebel reappeared, only ten when the bullet sang past them both and pinged off something metal farther down Mary Lane.

Reaching the crossroads he grabbed her hand and hustled her up the street running north. Both were breathing heavily by the time they reached the next crossroads, but the road behind them was empty. Two more turns and McColl felt confident that they'd put enough distance between themselves and his would-be executioners. The Breslins would want to hunt him through this and a thousand other nights, but Mulryan was obviously in charge, and he didn't have the same motivation. Shooting a spy who fell into his lap was one thing, but the needs of the rebellion would trump any private vendetta. With Dublin burning, he would surely have bigger fish to fry.

There were things McColl needed to tell her. Spotting a deeply shadowed doorway, he tugged her toward it. "Let's stop a moment."

And then they were in each other's arms, pulling each other close, letting the fear drain away.

After a while he loosened his grip and looked her in the eyes. "Thank you," he said.

"You're welcome."

"I know what it cost you."

She shook her head. "I'll want more than a kiss and cuddle."

Away in the distance, a machine gun rattled, then fell silent again.

"How do we get out of here?" she asked.

He smiled. "As it happens, I have a car waiting. On the other side of the army lines, unfortunately. But if I can talk our way through them, we can just drive off."

"To where? I can't leave Dublin until this is over. I've got a story to write. I owe it to . . . to so many people here. Those men back there — they're not typical. The men and women who joined this Rising — they're the best of Ireland."

"I believe you. But you have to leave with me."

"Why?" she asked, pulling away. "They told me you came to arrest me."

"I came to warn you. A man at the Castle, a man I know and trust, he showed me a photograph of you arriving at the Citizen Army HQ at St. Stephen's Green. And he told me they have proof that you came with a message from James Connolly. Is that true?"

"I did take a message. It was the only way I could get into that HQ and interview the rebels."

"Well, they'll arrest you the moment it's over."

"They?"

"Of course 'they.' Given that you just rescued me, you may find this hard to believe, but I came here to rescue you."

"We do make it hard for each other."

"And then there's always the rebels. They

may be the best men in Ireland, but how will they feel about you when Mulryan tells his story?"

She sighed. "So what can I do?"

"Well, you could stay put and try to brazen it out, but I wouldn't recommend it. London wants to make an example, so I think you'd be looking at prison. Your only real hope is a quick escape, and your best bet of that is the US embassy in London. They won't want to hand you over to us, and given how much we'd like America to join the war, we probably won't kick up much of a fuss if they insist on sending you home."

"Home," she said, as if testing out the idea.

"You remember — New York City."

"Yes. You know, I've been wanting to go home."

"First we need to get you out of Dublin."

"Do you know the way?"

"Oh, yes. I lived here for a month in 1914, remember. My lodgings were only a few streets from here. This one would take us to Broadstone station, but if we turn right halfway up, we'll be on the road to Drumcondra, which is where I left the automobile."

After checking to make sure the street was

empty, they started walking north. It was almost two o'clock, and the battles had all died down, leaving only a smoke-filled sky fed by tongues of flame. On Dominick Street the soldiers guarding the church crossroads were gathered round a fire of their own, which someone had lit in a dustbin. If their boisterous laughter was anything to go by, they were in a good mood, and McColl decided to risk a direct approach, simply walking across the street as if he hadn't a care in the world.

"This is Lady Macmillan," he told the NCO in charge. "Her husband works at the Castle, and when this whole thing blew up, she was in a house on Sackville Street, organizing a charity event for the boys in France. She was trapped there until this evening, when I managed to get her away."

"And you are?"

McColl presented his Service card, hoping the man would forget the name.

The NCO handed it back. "And where are you going now?"

"They have a country house just outside the city. I have a car waiting just up the road."

The NCO nodded. "Well, good night, madam. I'm sorry — your ladyship."

"Good night," Caitlin said, in what she

hoped was an English accent. "And thank you."

They carried on up Dorset Street, past shuttered shops and silent houses, only linking arms when the soldiers behind them were far out of sight. Ten minutes later McColl was hammering on the garage owner's door, hoping he wouldn't have to threaten the man with his gun. He didn't, but it took another ten pounds to coax him down with the keys.

The Alldays started the first time, and the city was soon behind them. McColl drove steadily north on the Belfast Road, only pulling over when the first hint of sunlight paled the eastern sky.

"I've been thinking," Caitlin said after a while. "Won't they be watching the boats?"

"I'd guess not yet, but if they are, I'll say you're under arrest and I'm taking you back to London."

"Okay, let's get the boat. But," she said, putting a hand on his shoulder, "is there any reason we should hurry back to London? If I'm going home, I want to spend some time with you before I have to leave."

WINDERMERE

There was no check at Larne and none at Stranraer. Caitlin had always wanted to visit the Lake District — "Wordsworth was a revolutionary, you know" — so they took the local train from Carlisle and changed to another for Windermere. Many of the hotels were closed, either for the season or for the war, but they finally found a rambling stone-built guesthouse with a beautiful view across the lake.

It was Friday evening when they arrived, and the next two mornings brought news of the Dublin GPO's destruction and the surrender of the rebel forces. Having spent most of Saturday in bed, Caitlin insisted on doing some work on the Sunday morning. With the bulk of her interview notes abandoned in Maeve's house on Mary Street, she was anxious to put her memories on paper.

The more she remembered and wrote, the

more uncertain she grew as to what she wanted to say. Out for a walk by the lake that afternoon, she asked McColl how he felt about it all.

"They never had a chance," was his simple answer.

"No. But the leaders knew that. Or at least they did once they knew that there'd be no German help."

"But they went ahead anyway."

"They felt they had to. That if they didn't, nothing would ever change. Maybe you have to be Irish — or Irish-American — to understand that, to feel that weight on your shoulders, that duty, almost, to keep showing the English that you value independence so much that you're willing to die just to keep that dream alive."

"You said the leaders knew," McColl said. "Did they tell their followers it was doomed from the start?"

"A lot of them knew, I think." She fell silent for a moment as they both watched a V of geese fly over the water. "What surprised me — if I'm honest — is how few supported them and how hated they were by some people. You should have seen the working-class women around Jacob's Factory. The people with the most to gain from a socialist republic, and they were its bitterest enemies. You know, the more I think about it, the more I fear it was all for nothing."

McColl considered. "You know more about politics than I do," he said eventually, "but I think you're wrong about that. I'll tell you something I shouldn't — London knew about the Rising a month ago."

"Then why didn't . . . ?"

"They wanted to flush the republicans into the open and give them enough rope to hang themselves. Literally, I expect. They're eager to make an example."

"But that's terrible!"

"It's also very stupid. If the government locks the leaders up for a couple of years, they'll look like one more bunch of failures. If it executes them, they'll end up looking like heroes."

News of the first executions — Patrick Pearse, Thomas Clarke, and Thomas MacDonagh — reached the lakeside guesthouse on Wednesday evening. Meanwhile the other war went on. The besieged forces in Dublin had not been the only ones to surrender on that Saturday — the British garrison in Kut had also raised the white flag after several failed attempts to relieve it.

On the main fronts, it seemed to be business as usual, a tale of minor losses and gains, often at inordinate cost. In France the German-instigated battles around Verdun were entering a third month with no sign of a breakthrough; the level of casualties was considered "concerning." The Anglo-German sector was relatively quiet, but no doubt the dolts on the British General Staff were planning another "big push."

Despite all that, McColl couldn't, like Caitlin, simply oppose the war. "I know the arguments," he told her. They were sitting in a rowboat, happily drifting across the still lake, beneath another perfect blue sky. "How can we be fighting for democracy when the Russians are our allies? How can we demonize the Germans when they have much better social welfare than we do? How can we bang on and on about Belgium when we're occupying India and Egypt and God knows how many other places?"

"Well, how?" she asked calmly.

He sighed. "I guess in the end it has to be personal."

"Jed?"

"Jed and Mac. What if —" He was about to say, *What if your brother were at the front?* but managed to stop himself.

She said it for him. "What if Colm were

out there? Yes, I suppose I'd feel the way you do, but that wouldn't make me *right*."

"Maybe not. But if I refused to do my bit, I know I would feel I was letting him down."

She gave him a wry smile. "So I don't suppose you'd consider resigning — or whatever you call it — and coming back with me?"

"Is that a serious question?"

"No. Yes. I know you won't. And I won't hold it against you."

"The moment it ends, I'll be on my way to New York."

"Well, I might be there. If some socialist paradise springs into existence, I might be visiting."

"Some hope."

"Don't be so pessimistic. And we can write to each other," she added. "Or at least you can write to me — I never know where you are. You can tell me you love me every so often."

"I can. I do."

They spent a week in Windermere, rarely more than an outstretched arm away from each other. Neither could remember a happier time, but both knew it had to end. If McColl didn't show on the following Monday, Cumming would fear the worst, start a search, and uncover the trip to Dublin. Knowing that Caitlin had to be the lure, Cumming would contact Dunwood and find out that she was wanted. The Service chief would then have no choice but to track down the pair of them. Dismissal for him and much worse for her.

There was always the fear that Dunwood had already blown the whistle, but with any luck he was too busy picking up the pieces in Dublin. Still, McColl took them off the train at Watford Junction rather than risk any waiting police at Euston. A cab brought them to Rickmansworth, the Metropolitan to Baker Street and a small hotel that McColl knew from years before.

They made love that night and again in the morning, but both were aware of a growing distance — voices inside them were already rehearsing good-byes. It wasn't a long walk to the American embassy, and the lone policeman outside the entrance gave them a welcoming smile. One last clinging embrace, one last loving kiss, and the door swung shut between them.

McColl stood out on the pavement for several minutes looking up at the windows, as if she might throw one open and blow him a final kiss. Then he walked to Oxford

Street and took an omnibus down past Oxford Circus, staring blankly out the window at the early-morning shoppers. When would he see her again?

There was no one watching his flat and no sign that Cumming had ordered a search — the only changes from ten days ago were an added layer of dust and a letter from Jed on the mat. There were no blacked-out passages for once, and the news was good — his and Mac's division was moving to a quieter stretch of the front, down along the Somme.

He bathed and changed before setting out again, this time for Whitehall. A stop for coffee and cake put off the evil moment and gave him time to work on his story. Not that time was likely to improve it, and in the end he settled for the truth, which at least had the virtue of simplicity. He would appeal to Cumming's romantic streak, if indeed his chief had one.

He didn't really think that Cumming would fire him. A talking-to, no doubt, but the Service wasn't exactly overburdened with multilinguists who could track down Bengali terrorists and blow up Belgian bridges. As he'd thought from the start, he was made for this job, and Cumming was smart enough to appreciate that fact. Now, with Caitlin safely across the Atlantic, there'd be no one to further distract him.

He pictured her in his mind, sitting in the boat on Windermere, lying in their guest-house bed with her glorious hair spread across the pillow. Maybe the war would be over that year, and they could be together. This parting was painful, but nothing like the one before, when he thought she'd never forgive him. He might have lost her again, but this time out of choice, and hopefully not for long.

In the American embassy, officials whom Caitlin knew and trusted told her not to worry — they were sure the British would let her go home. The British reprisals in Ireland — another four had been shot, with more to follow — were enraging a sizable portion of the American public, and the government in London would not want to make matters worse by arresting a well-known American journalist. An agreement would be reached, and the embassy would give her an escort to Liverpool. She had, it seemed, even chosen a good time to sail — under intense pressure from Washington, the Germans had recently agreed not to sink any more civilian ships without a prior warning.

On the morning of the following Thursday, she was told she'd be leaving early the next day, and as if on cue, an hour or so later, a letter arrived from McColl. He was leaving as well, and though he couldn't say where he was going, the Newcastle postmark might be a clue. Perhaps the Allies were planning a northern Gallipoli, with reindeer rather than donkeys.

And of course he said he loved her.

And I you, she thought. The last thing she needed was a man, but by God she wanted this one.

What had Kollontai said? You drank from the cup of love's joy, and then you went back to work.

It rained all the way to Liverpool, and England looked green as an Irish flag. There were no zeppelins above the city, and her ship, though depressingly small, had a good supply of recent American newspapers. The women's Liberty Bell, which von Schön had mentioned in Berlin, was now touring the forty-eight states, ringing up support for suffrage, and a woman named Jeanette Rankin, whom Caitlin had met before the war, looked set to be the first of her gender to win a seat in Congress. Behind the mask of the war, the world was actually changing.

Admittedly, her government seemed

poised to invade the Dominican Republic, but then nothing was ever perfect. Except perhaps those days in Windermere. They'd come pretty close.

ABOUT THE AUTHOR

David Downing grew up in suburban London. He is the author of the first Jack McColl novel, Jack of Spies; the thriller The Red Eagles; and six books in the John Russell espionage series, set in WWII Berlin: Zoo Station, Silesian Station, Stettin Station, Potsdam Station, Lehrter Station, and Masaryk Station. He lives with his wife, an American acupuncturist, in Guildford, England.

The employees of Thorndike Press hope you have enjoyed this Large Print book. All our Thorndike, Wheeler, and Kennebec Large Print titles are designed for easy reading, and all our books are made to last. Other Thorndike Press Large Print books are available at your library, through selected bookstores, or directly from us.

For information about titles, please call:
  (800) 223-1244

or visit our Web site at:
  http://gale.cengage.com/thorndike

To share your comments, please write:
Publisher
Thorndike Press
10 Water St., Suite 310
Waterville, ME 04901